I0588644

GAIA BOOK 2

OLYMPUS BOUND

GAIA BOOK 2

ZOË ROUTH

Copyright Zoë Routh, 2024
Cover art - Damonza
Author photograph - Paul Chapman - modeimagery.com
Typesetting, book design - Damonza
Published by Inner Compass Australia Pty Ltd.

For more information about the author
Zoë Routh
Email: zoe@zoerouth.com
www.zoerouth.com
ISBN-10: 978-0-6455212-9-0 Ebook
ISBN-13: 9798877255036 Amazon Paperback
ISBN-13: 978-0-6488773-3-2 Paperback

Zoë Routh asserts the moral right to be identified as the
author of Olympus Bound and all associated products.

All rights reserved. Except as permitted under the Australian Copyright
Act 1968 (for example, a fair dealing for the purposes of study, research,
criticism or review), no part of this publication may be reproduced,
stored in a retrieval system, communicated or transmitted in any form
or by any means, mechanical, electronic, photocopying, recording or
otherwise, without the prior written permission of the Publisher.

GET AN EBOOK AND
AUDIOBOOK FOR FREE:

TERRA BLANCA INSURRECTION

PREQUEL OF THE GAIA SERIES

WITH THE FREE BOOKISH E-JOURNAL:

https://www.zoerouth.com/bookish

For Mum and Dad

Thanks for picking me up when I fell, for wiping my tears when they came, and for loving me through everything.

LOCATIONS AND DRAMATIS PERSONAE

Accommodation wings of Olympus base – Cerberus, Centaur, Pegasus, Siren, Griffin

Aidan O'Sullivan – *Gateway* astronaut

Aryanna Sharif – Chair of the Lunar Commission

Athena – Artificial Intelligence

Chang-e – Chinese short flight shuttle spacecraft

Chan-Juan – Red Star Deputy Leader

Claire Edwards – Former Chief Operating Officer of Gaia Enterprises

Colonel Jin – Commander of Red Star base

David Eriksson – Pilot

Faustini crater – Ice mining site

Huw Chan – Co-founder of Gaia Enterprises

James Delacroix – *Gateway* captain

Jonas Seaborn – Engineer, Olympus base

Gareth Barrio – Captain of the *Pinnacle*

Gateway – Lunar orbital space station

Hàoyú – Red Star Deputy Leader

Kwanda – *Gateway* astronaut

Lihua – Chinese Dopplebot

Li Jun – New Chinese leader

Lincoln Ellison – Founder of Spaceward Bound

Madison 'Mad Dog' Floyd – Pilot, supply technician, seismologist, Olympus base

Maja Garcia – Founder of Gaia Enterprises

Max King – Life support technician

Minerva – Rescue vessel

Olympus – Moonbase built by Gaia Enterprises

Pinnacle – Spaceward Bound spacecraft

Red Star – Chinese-Russian Moonbase

Serena Fox – Life support technician, Olympus base

Saturnia – Olympus spacecraft

Starship – NASA's astronaut shuttle carrier

Terra Blanca – Failed man-made island state, initiated and built by Gaia Enterprises

Terra Verdi – Xavier Consus's floating hydroponic farm

ThinkLink- Brain Computer Interface

Travis Bruin – Troy's twin brother

Troy Bruin – Psychologist and Olympus medical officer, Olympus base

Vladimir Volkov – Missing Russian President, Dopplebot

Xanthe Waters – Commander of Olympus base

Xavier Consus – Food and provisions expert, Olympus base

Youssef – Artemis astronaut

Yuri – *Gateway* astronaut

Zhang Wei – Former Chinese leader

FRENCH LEXICON

Bien sûr. And bonne chance. – Of course. And good luck.

Bof – Ugh

Ça fait du bien! Merci. – That's good for the soul! Thanks.

Con! Ta gueule. – Idiot! Shut up.

Eh bien? – And so?

Excusez moi. – Excuse me.

Fermez les gueules! – Shut your mouths!

Les salauds – The bastards

Ma famille! – My family!

Mais oui! – But of course!

Merci – Thank you

Merde – Shit

Merde que ça fait chaud! – Shit, it's hot.

Mon ami – My friend

Mon Dieu – My God

Mon vieux – My old friend

Putain – (literal: whore) Bitch

Putain de merde – (literal: whore of shit) Bloody hell

Putain, il fait froid! – Bloody hell, it's cold!

Quelle surprise! – What a surprise!

Quoi? – What?

Salaud – Bastard

S'il te plait – Please

Très bien – Very good

Vraiment – Really

Vraiment? Ta gueule! – Really? Shut up!

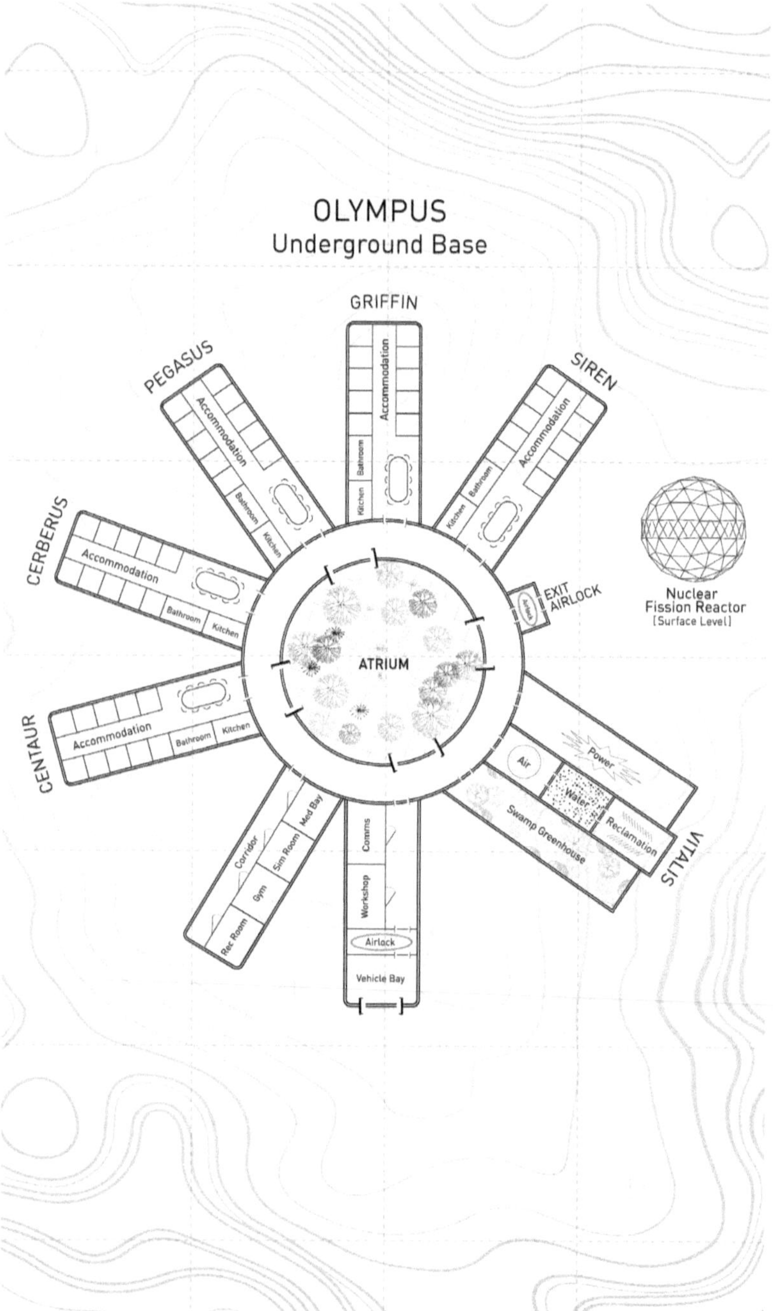

OLYMPUS
Underground Base

GRIFFIN

Accommodation

PEGASUS

Accommodation

Bathroom

Kitchen

SIREN

Accommodation

Kitchen

Bathroom

CERBERUS

Accommodation

Bathroom

Kitchen

EXIT AIRLOCK

Airlock

Nuclear
Fission Reactor
[Surface Level]

ATRIUM

CENTAUR

Accommodation

Bathroom

Kitchen

Air

Power

Water

Swamp Greenhouse

Reclamation

VITALIS

Corridor

Med Bay

Sim Room

Gym

Rec Room

Comms

Workshop

Airlock

Vehicle Bay

PART 1

CHAPTER ONE

"Humans, when placed at the helm of responsibility, often grapple with a duality: the self they once knew and the leader they are now required to be. In this chasm, the true tenor of leadership resounds."

—ATHENA A.I., OLYMPUS LOG

THE MOON'S FACE was a hag's chalky mask, cracked and lifeless, brutal against the impenetrable black depths of space. Xanthe squinted in the glare of the stark, white surface, sipped from the water reclaimer inside her helmet and bounded to the eastern wing of Olympus, leaving boot prints in little puffs of moondust behind her. Ahead of her, hanging on the horizon like a big, fat blue eye, was the Earth.

Xanthe paused. A familiar frisson of awe shot through her as she gazed at the precious, watery globe. There, on that tiny blip in space, was all of humanity, all of Earth's creatures, foraging in the creeping greenery and swimming in the swollen rolls of the oceans.

And here we are, on the Moon, planting a bit of humanity, a bit of life, a bit of Earth, on this implacable boulder.

Xanthe resumed her bounding. They called it 'moondling' – a combination of walking and trundling. It definitely took practice to get it right. Six months on the Moon and the novelty had still not worn off. She skipped and felt the joy of effortless movement. Well, not quite effortless. It was still awkward in the thick spacesuit, and challenging to stay balanced. Like the other Olympus crew, she often stumbled and found herself face first in the dust.

"Hey, Xanthe. Can you confirm your location?"

Jonas's voice was a little hoarse, Xanthe noticed, no doubt due to the all the boisterous shouting he had done in the SimRoom with the others, the night before. They'd watched a football game broadcast from Earth and joined through a virtual reality uplink. They had bet chocolate rations on the outcome and Xavier, as usual, had won the pool.

Xanthe smiled as she recalled the tall, dark Frenchman waving his prize at Jonas. Jonas was stocky and well-built and, when irritated, he liked to plant his feet wide apart, cross his arms and jut his chin.

"I shall savour every little bite, *mon ami*. Such sweet, sweet victory," Xavier had goaded.

"A fool and his chocolate are soon parted, my dear swamp dweller," Jonas had replied. They called Xavier the 'swamp dweller' for his obsession with hydroponics and the food harvests. His domain was lush and humid and ripe with the aroma of their reclaimed faeces.

"I'll get you in our next round of space tennis," Jonas had said. They'd invented the sport one day in the Atrium. Actually, 'sport' was too grand a term; they had simply 3D printed a rubber ball and spent hours chasing it in blundering bounds around the large Atrium, which was their main communal area and only view to the sky from the underground habitat.

"Xanthe?" Jonas repeated, breaking into her reverie.

"I'm at the eastern corner now, Jonas," Xanthe said.

"How does it look?"

"No sign of a hull breach," she said. She climbed the rounded surface of the buried roof in floating leaps. "It seems okay to me."

"Great. Can you join Serena and Troy over at the Atrium, now? We're testing the retractor again," Jonas said.

"On my way," Xanthe said.

Xanthe turned to look at the Atrium, a glowing egg poking up into space. It was the only part of the habitat not below the Moon's surface. They built the rest of Olympus by excavating, 3D printing the habitat with a slurry made from the mined regolith and then burying it all in moondust for extra protection. The Atrium rose above the ground to act as a set of lungs to keep the recycled air fresh, as well as a grand hall where they grew trees and other climbing plants to help green the interior. It was Xanthe's favourite spot. She spent most evenings there, staring up at the stars.

With no atmosphere to burn up incoming space debris, asteroids small and large hit the Moon's surface with disconcerting regularity. Space junk hit like detonations. As the Atrium was exposed, it was the most vulnerable part of the base's infrastructure. They spent a lot of time and effort making sure it was secure and operating effectively.

The Atrium had a retractable steel roof that opened and closed like a giant eyelid. It was ideal protection, but lately it had been playing up, often getting stuck halfway. They suspected it might be moondirt dislodged from construction. The dirt was sharp and coarse and got into everything. They had to be so vigilant going in and out of the pods to minimise trudging it in on their boots and suits.

Xanthe could see Troy and Serena standing on top of the Atrium. A cord of jealousy strummed in her mind. Troy was an outrageous flirt, and Serena loved teasing him. They were becoming closer while she and Troy. . . well, nothing.

There could have been something between them. Troy made no secret of his affection for her. But it was all too much for Xanthe – splitting up with Simon, preparing for the Moon expedition and leading the Olympus project build. She'd barely had time to arrange storing her belongings and settling affairs with Simon before they were strapped into the rocket, ready for launch. Too much turbulence to squeeze in a romance with the planet's most famous world designer and notorious ladies' man. Besides, they all had to work together. The Moon was not the most private place.

Xanthe did manage to find solace in the Atrium. With its window, it was the one place in the Moon base where she felt less claustrophobic; otherwise, they were like moles, scavenging a life underground. She hoped their boots and the moondirt wouldn't scratch its window. If the window got blurred by wear and tear, there was no fixing it.

She clambered down the eastern pod roof by leaning forward and semi-falling, catching herself on a footfall, and repeating those actions on the other side. *Nice and easy,* she thought. *All good, as long as you don't miss and smack yourself face first.*

It was almost like flying.

Six months. It seemed like forever, Xanthe thought. From the launch to the landing, Xanthe had been wired with anxiety. She felt the pressure of responsibility for her teammate's lives. They'd been through a lot together over the last couple of years. Selection to get on Gaia Enterprises's Olympus project build and bid team, then the twelve-month simulation. They'd grown so close.

It was a big adjustment when Madison joined them. 'Mad Dog' was brought on by the crew to replace Dave as pilot. In a torturous team meeting, they had decided with Dave that he wouldn't join them on the Moon build after all. Xanthe wondered again what she would have done in Dave's place. If her family was threatened, could she have spied on and sabotaged the project to save them? Would she have stood up to blackmail? Or would she have kowtowed as Dave had done, betrayed friends and almost got them killed in the sabotage?

It was probably for the best they'd left him behind. Not everyone was disappointed. Serena did little to hide her satisfaction that the 'traitor' had been sidelined.

Xanthe hit flatter ground at the base of the eastern pod and took another sip of water. She felt her heart rate creeping up. She took a few steadying breaths and checked her suit's oxygen levels. She still had two hours. Good. Ten minutes to get to Serena and Troy, fifteen to get to the entrance portal, leaving an hour to get the retractable roof working again and a little over thirty minutes to get back to base. Plenty of time.

Xanthe tuned her helmet comms to Troy and Serena. She was in line of sight, so she should be able to pick them up. Their voices came through a bit patchy but grew clearer as Xanthe moondled towards the Atrium.

"If we run a cloth on a pole, we might be able to dislodge whatever is locking it up," Serena said.

"That's your trademark style. . .just jam something in and hope for the best," Troy said.

"Well, what are you proposing we do, Prince Troy? Charm it out?" Serena laughed.

"Nothing can escape my magnetism," he said.

"I am not so sure about that. I know a certain Commander—"

"Hello there. Troy and Serena, I'm on channel," Xanthe said.

"Commander Waters," Troy said. "Welcome to the party. We think we've found the problem."

"Good to hear." Xanthe panted as she moondled to the base of the Atrium. Climbing it was more challenging than the pods, as it was steeper and higher. Xanthe favoured what she called 'gorilla jumps'. This required a deep knee bend and then a two-legged spring onto the hull with hands hitting the hull briefly in front for balance, and then drawing the legs under again ready for another deep knee bend. It took some coordination, and she didn't always get it right.

Like this time.

She made her first jump, but her toes slipped on the smooth surface of the Atrium hull, and she did a full-frontal pancake and bounced off to land on her behind. When weight is a fraction of that on Earth, it's not painful, just embarrassing.

"Xanthe, are you trying the gorilla move again?" Serena asked over the helmet comms.

"Trying is the operative word," she said, rolling onto all fours to push herself upright once more. She checked her suit and brushed the sharp regolith that had caught in the fibres of the Gaia Enterprises's embroidered logo, a compass. Xanthe wondered again why they hadn't chosen a different logo for the Moon. With no magnetic field, a compass was all but useless here. They would have to find their own way.

"Let me throw you the ascent rope," Troy interrupted.

His voice was deep and smooth and purred through the helmet. Xanthe shivered with desire, like she always did around Troy. His blue eyes and lopsided, slow smile pulled threads through her body. He moved like a panther, all grace and power. He had a way of looking at her that made her feel like she was the entire universe laid bare before him. Regret tangled her thoughts yet again.

The rope floated towards her, and she reached to grab it. She clipped the karabiner to her belt loop.

"On belay."

"Roger that, Xanthe," Troy said.

She loved it when he said her name. It reached down inside her soul and squeezed. She shoved these thoughts aside and focused on planting her feet against the hull and leaning against the tug of the rope so she could walk up the surface. Once she reached the top, she took a moment to catch her breath. She was struggling today.

She checked her suit vitals again. Heart rate at 120 beats per minute. Way above her usual. Was she dehydrated? Maybe she just needed some more sleep.

"Okay, show me the problem," Xanthe said, still panting.

"We think there might be some dust between the retractable

roof and the dome," Serena said. "Maybe along the roof running tracks."

"But how did it get there?" Xanthe said. The thought was still bothering her. "We haven't had any construction activity that would flick up debris this high."

"It could be meteorites," Troy suggested.

"You keep saying that. But there are no marks on the eye," Xanthe said as she bounded carefully across the dome surface. "It's highly unlikely that one random piece of meteorite would hit the dome without some other space debris alongside it."

"Let's retract the roof fully and try to close it again, and see where it gets stuck," Troy said.

"Jonas," Xanthe said, hailing him on the helmet comms. "We're going to use the manual override up here to retract and close the roof."

"Roger that, Commander. Watch your feet. We don't want to add 'trapped leg' to our list of dramas today," Jonas said.

Serena and Xanthe took up prone positions at the edges of the retractable roof. Troy made his way over to the mechanical lever and hauled it to 'open'. Serena and Xanthe swept the surface of the roof with a cloth. The roof retracted smoothly.

"Nothing on this side," Serena said.

"Same," Xanthe added. "Troy, let's reverse it and see if we can find where it stops."

Troy pushed the lever, and the roof reversed its trajectory. It closed without a hitch.

"No debris, no obstacle. It's probably mechanical then. Or electrical," Xanthe said.

"You know what that means, right?" Serena trampolined herself to vertical with a flourish. "This looks like a job for . . ."

"Super Jonas!" the three of them cried in unison.

"Bloody hell!" Jonas's voice filled their helmets. "Is there anything that's not a job for me?"

"That's the scourge of being the handiest man on the Moon," said Troy.

"If it's not the damned waste reclamation, it's something else," Jonas muttered.

"Commander, shall we set the roof to open or leave it closed?' asked Troy.

"Open. We need the stars to keep us bright," Xanthe said.

"What if there's a meteorite shower and it jams again?" asked Serena.

"There's nothing on the long-range radar, right?"

"Not according to Madison's last report."

"Then let's keep it open and enjoy the view." There was a small risk, she acknowledged. But Jonas would have the malfunction assessed and completed in no time.

After Troy moved the lever again, they clipped to the descent rope, walked backwards off the dome and moondled back to the main entrance. Madison met them at the regolith removal chamber. She seemed unusually agitated.

"Commander, come quickly. We've got a hail from the Chinese base and it sounds urgent."

CHAPTER TWO

"Observing human interactions, I've discerned that the smallest slights often carry the weight of larger, unresolved sentiments. Like unchecked algorithms, these feelings compound over time, influencing decisions in ways humans might not consciously acknowledge."

—Athena A.I., Olympus Log

Xanthe made her way to the small communication room, with its plain, functional walls and flashing equipment. A screen dominated the wall space, and from there she could watch the surveillance cameras, satellite imagery and holo comms. It was spartan and functional.

Unlike the Colonel's backdrop. Where Olympus was prosaic, the Red Star comms room was a masterstroke of luxury. Dark mahogany panels with exquisite gold inlays covered the walls. A vast desk, polished to mirror-like perfection and engraved with intricate golden motifs, filled the space. Behind him, a mural of historical Chinese dynasties showcased the glory of ancient empires before morphing into the scintillating vision of their lunar ambitions.

Suspended holographic interfaces hovered just above his desk, beaming charts and the emblem of the Red Star project. The faint, haunting melody of a pipa played in the background while an ornate incense burner gave the ambiance of ancient royal courts.

So pretentious, she thought.

"Commander Waters. I have a few issues to discuss with you."

"Hello, Colonel Jin," Xanthe said.

She assumed a commanding stance, pulled her shoulders back, and offered her counterpart a stoic, detached look. Communications with the Chinese leader were not very frequent and certainly not very friendly. The atmosphere bristled whenever they spoke.

"What can I do for you?" she asked.

"Our water mining team has detected interference from the Olympus crew. This must cease immediately." His lips puckered with his reprimand.

"I beg your pardon. Our crew has had nothing to do with your operations."

"That is incorrect. Our team has a video recording of the Olympus staff onsite and inspecting our equipment."

"That's a blatant lie," said Madison, appearing in the doorway. "We were nowhere near where they were."

Xanthe waved a hand off-camera to quiet Madison and Jonas who had squeezed in beside her.

"My crew assures me they kept their distance from your operations."

"The Faustini crater has been identified as Chinese, to be used for our primary water mining source. Your team will cease and desist immediately."

Xanthe's hackles rose. She pressed her lips to maintain her composure and took a deep breath. "As per international lunar agreement, no one nation is to claim the resources of the Moon. They are to be shared among all of humanity. You cannot lay claim to any territory on the Moon, including that water mine site."

"That is true, Commander Waters. But the Lunar Commission also cites that any equipment belonging to one nation, or a coalition of nations, will be respected and left alone by any neighbouring entities, including you." His jowls shook as he spat the words. "So please, stay away from our equipment."

"I assure you again, we have no interest in your equipment or operations. My team was simply scoping the opportunity for our own ice mining operations, which we will be putting into place within the next month."

"You will need to find another crater," he said.

"No, I will not. There is plenty of room for both of us in Faustini."

"I find your attitude petulant and disturbing," he said.

Xanthe took a deep breath, resisting the urge to take the bait.

"My apologies if my tone is not to your taste," she said through gritted teeth. "Let me reassure you that we will stay away from your operations and maintain our own at a reasonable distance."

"What you consider 'reasonable' and what we consider 'reasonable' seem to be very different."

"We will maintain a 750-metre perimeter. Will that suffice?"

Colonel Jin made a show of considering the offer.

"That is almost acceptable. I would prefer a one-kilometre boundary."

"We will endeavour to maintain a *minimum* 750-metre boundary, then. And we will notify you of our dates and times of exploration. In addition, we will mark the perimeter with flags and check in with you next time we are there."

"That's a can of crap," Madison said from the doorway. "Why are you pandering to this buffoon? We have every right to be in that crater."

Jonas swatted Madison on the arm and shot her an exasperated glance.

"Madison, not now," he hissed. A flicker of annoyance crossed his face. She scowled back at him.

"See that your commitments are honoured by your team, Commander Waters."

"My team are completely reliable and will comply. We are committed to harmonious and productive relationships with our lunar neighbours."

"I am glad to hear it. Until next time, Commander."

"Thank you, Colonel." She bowed and ended the transmission.

"Why do you cave in to that jackass, Xanthe?" Madison said.

Xanthe turned to Jonas and Madison, who were still squeezed side by side in the doorway. "He may be a jackass, but he and his crew are the only other human beings on this lump of rock," Xanthe said. "If anything goes wrong up here, we'll need each other. It takes three days to get here from Earth, if they launch straight away. And you know how long it takes NASA and any of the other agencies to get organised.

"Colonel Jin is a bit of a blowhard, but he needs us as much as we need him. Besides, I intend to be the friend I wish to see. And that means winning him over with kindness. After we establish and maintain clear boundaries."

"Catching flies with honey? Really?"

"Something like that. Hey, it worked with Xavier, right? He's one of our toughest nuts, but we've managed to capture his respect."

"Are you sure?" asked Jonas with a raised eyebrow. "The man is as mercurial as a cat!"

"We all know how you get on with feline creatures, especially kittens, Jonas," Xanthe said. "Good thing Xavier is less fickle than his cat."

"I did hate that beast," Jonas admitted.

"And the feeling was mutual," Xanthe said. "In any case, let's wrap it up. A spacewalk and a Colonel Jin 'chat' are enough for today. Tomorrow, it's back to ice mining."

❧

The next morning, Xanthe lumbered in her moonboots down the hall from her sleeping pod room towards the main kitchen area. Hydroponic lighting strips shone on the fledgling plants hung along the walls. Finally, they were showing signs of growth, and the green was a joyous shout of colour against the round, grey tunnel walls. Again, she felt like a mole, pale and pasty in their underground tunnels.

The crew were all there, settled into breakfast, Jonas with a scrambled egg burrito; Serena nursing a coffee; Xavier grunting with satisfaction over his latest lab-grown bacon rashes; Madison with a protein shake; and Troy with tea, toast and marmalade.

"Good morning," Xanthe said and headed to the breakfast cupboard. Porridge for her, today.

A few nodded and waved in return. They had the Earth news streaming.

"What are the tales of woe this morning?" Xanthe asked as she filled a bottle with tea and sat beside Serena.

"More protests at space launch sites." Serena shuffled her chair to give Xanthe some room. "The Chinese arrested a load of people after a mob broke through their security gates."

"Really? Maybe that's what's got Colonel Jin's knickers in a twist." Xanthe ate a spoonful of porridge and closed her eyes in appreciation. *Still the best way to start the day.*

"More wheat crop failures across India and Europe," Xavier said as he wiped his plate clean of bacon juice with a piece of toast from Troy's plate. "It's been two months straight of temperatures above fifty degrees Celsius. *Merde que ça fait chaud!*"

"It's really just a drop in the bucket, isn't it? What we're doing here." Jonas crumpled his burrito wrapper.

"What do you mean, Jonas?" Madison pulled her attention away from the news stream.

"It's taking so bloody long to build this site. And it will house barely one hundred. Meanwhile millions are dying on Earth."

"Hey." Xanthe put her spoon down and held Jonas's gaze with a fierce look. "What we're doing here is proving we can survive anywhere. Earth might be turning into a barren rock like this one sooner than we'd ever thought. If we can make this habitat work long-term, we can do it there too."

"Besides," Troy added, "this is the stepping stone to Mars, our next home as a species."

"Will we ever see it, do you think?" Serena sucked the rest of her coffee from its pouch.

"Not before we get Olympus finished and stable." Xanthe turned her attention back to the work of the day. In her mind, the tasks scrolled before her as she scooped the last of the porridge. Even though the list seemed endless, they'd already accomplished so much in the last six months.

Arrival had been frenetic. They'd crammed living and working between their ship, the *Saturnia*, and the tiny Artemis base, which was nothing more than temporary accommodation in a small life support pod designed for astronauts on thirty-day science missions. They'd shared meals with the Artemis crew and slept there in hammocks between bunks, stacked like submariners.

The excavators had worked quickly, until they'd rammed into a shelf of rock and had to redirect the tunnel, accounting for the strange dogleg in the Centaur wing and the slight 'wobble' in the base's spoke design. Robotic 3D printing of the walls had happened next, with the entire shell of the Olympus base completed in two weeks. Then things had gotten fiddly.

Jonas and Serena had worked on electronics and plumbing for the life support elements of the Vitalis sector: water, power, atmosphere regulation and filtering, and waste reclamation. Meanwhile

Xavier and Madison had set up the Swamp, ready for crop production. Troy and Xanthe had set up the nuclear reactor and then the kitchen and medbay.

At week five, they had connected the internal lighting and electronics with the reactor. They'd celebrated with a dance party in the Atrium, all still in their spacesuits. Dancing in bulky EVA suits was awkward, so the festivities had been short-lived.

They had installed Athena A.I. next so they could get live systems feedback and process the data. Testing each section of the habitat for proper seals had been the next big hurdle. Like a rabbit warren, there had been a few external access points that had needed testing for decompression for egress and moondust blasting for ingress. Any leaks would have meant their fast demise.

Moonquakes had been their biggest issue as they often created cracks in the tunnel walls. As the seismologist for the expedition, Madison had kept her regulation equipment strapped to her thigh for advance warning of any quakes that might destroy their progress. After a few months she had gotten a sense of the patterns. Or rather, lack of patterns; moonquakes were unpredictable.

Due to the intensity of the moonquakes in their base region, they had added another thin layer of meshed wall to the tunnels as extra protection, which had not only delayed their schedule, but reduced their ceiling and wall space. Any future residents over six foot five would have to duck under doorways. Xavier and Troy were the tallest but still had three inches of clearance. It was tight.

The Atrium gave the biggest reprieve from the sense of confinement. It came at a cost though. Installing the curved plexiglass for the view had been tricky as the seals were needed to protect against the vacuum, manage proper atmospheric circulation within the chamber and the entire base, and ensure the smooth water layer for insulation. The retractable roof required regular maintenance as this was the most vulnerable part of the base; the rest was underground, buried under the regolith. They all grumbled at the EVAs needed for retractor maintenance, but they all valued their eye to the sky.

Turning on the life support system and creating a liveable atmosphere had been the biggest step, and the one they'd been most looking forward to. Once there was air to breathe, they could move in and start to operate inside without the bulky suits. Serena had been the first out of her suit in the Atrium. She'd bounded happily around the room and pitched a rubber chicken at Jonas.

"Who brings a rubber chicken to the Moon?" Jonas had batted the squeaky toy aside.

"The question is rather, 'Who *doesn't* bring a rubber chicken to the Moon?'" Serena had laughed and scooped up the chicken to wag it in his face. "Betty says, 'Tag, you're it.'" She'd swatted Jonas with the bleating chicken and 'chook tag' had been born. They'd managed one game a day, and Serena was the uncontested champion to date.

"Xanthe?" It was Jonas. Xanthe shook her head to clear it from reminiscing. "Shall we do the tasking now while we're all here?"

Xanthe nodded. "Go ahead."

"Right then," he continued. "Serena and Troy are on ice mining recon."

"Woohoo. Time to freeze our butts off again, Troy," Serena said.

"I had Jonas look at the control panel and he's fixed the heating sensors. We should be fine now."

"Nothing but the best for you, Prince Troy." Serena winked at him.

"Xavier, you've got a planting week, this week. What's going in?" Jonas said.

"We are doing wheat and rice on the walls in the Pegasus wing. I think I have worked out the wicking problem there. If we adjust the pressure slightly in the atmosphere it should get the water to move better across the seeds."

"So, you're working with Madison on that, right?"

"*Oui.*"

"Great. That leaves me and Xanthe. We'll be getting the ice processor ready to fill the water tank when our ice miners return with their bounty."

"I've got a good feeling about this trip," Troy said as he gathered his colleagues' breakfast dishes. "I'm sure we'll manage to find a site to start on soon. The way that Colonel Jin got so testy makes me think we're on a winner."

"Well, make sure you get the Prince Troy lucky charm working today so we can start filling up our reserve tanks." Madison pushed her chair back to stand. "That way we can get the water-intensive crops going and grow some more meat in the lab."

"Now you're talking!" Serena said.

"Everyone have a good day, and remember to report in every three hours," Xanthe said.

"Roger, Commander," Troy said.

The days were long. They had programmed the artificial lighting to give them sixteen hours of 'daylight' within the base itself. Outside, at the south pole, it never got completely dark, so solar power was fairly reliable. On the Moon, redundancy was essential for survival, so the reactor was a critical facility and they used it primarily for heating and electricity.

They had become quite adept at operating robotic rovers to inspect and maintain elements of the base, to minimise the toll on their EVA suits and reduce the risk of radiation exposure. They also minimised external expeditions in the rover to reduce the toll on the rover's systems. The basics seemed to take forever as all operations in low G needed adaptation.

There was their physical health to manage, too. Xanthe was concerned they would lose too much muscle conditioning before the fitness room was finished. Their moonboots – the heavy, magnetic, knee-high slippers that pulled them to magnetic strips they'd installed throughout the base – only did so much for their strength.

Once the atmosphere was stabilised and all seals tested, Xanthe instituted a daily regime of moonboot running and drills, combined with 'chook tag' around the Atrium's perimeter hallway, and up and down each residential wing. This way, they could also test their response time in an emergency should there be an atmosphere breach anywhere.

A friendly competitive spirit emerged, the winner claiming a shoulder massage from the loser. They kept up the regime even after the fitness room was fully operational.

Six months into their one-year task, they had the base set up and functioning. Now they needed to ensure crops would grow reliably, and that they had access to ice to convert to water, fuel and atmosphere. Without this, the base had no future.

They got along for the most part. They had occasional irritations and miscommunications, but overall, Xanthe was pleased with the comfortable camaraderie that settled between them.

The arrival of the Chinese had caused plenty of consternation. Though they were part of the Lunar Commission's international alliance, the Chinese-Russian ambitions on the Moon were always suspect.

But they were human. On the Moon. Far from Earth.

They need us.

Xanthe clomped towards the tooling room in the vehicle bay, to meet Jonas for the day's work on the ice processor.

And we need them.

CHAPTER THREE

Xanthe crept into the Atrium, trying not to wake anyone. It had been a big week exploring possible ice mining sites in the Faustini crater. But every week, every day, was big on the Moon. Though exhausted, sleep evaded her. In the Atrium, stress evaporated under the silver studs of starlight.

She stopped to inspect the ring of small trees and shrubs that grew from their matting sacks. Eventually they'd form a grove around the benches, a community gathering place from which the accommodation wings branched. Olympus was destined for settlers, scientists and asteroid miners. But it was not just a barracks for transients; the design fostered connection and community. And the Atrium was the symbolic heart, with an eye to the heavens.

Xanthe gazed upwards. Beyond the stars, the blackness of space was nothing and everything. It sucked her in, and her body dissolved.

Though she couldn't see the Earth from the Atrium window today, she felt its lure, devastated as it now was with ferocious heat and climate calamity. Xanthe yearned for the vast blue sky of her childhood homeland, Australia, before the Big Heat. She remembered the caress of a late-night summer breeze, the salty tang of the ocean after a plunge through waves, the spongy grass underfoot.

She remembered cold feet stinging with the morning dew on the sandy banks of the Murrumbdigee, where she lived for a time in Wagga Wagga. She longed to slip into the river and feel its silky waters flow over her, at one with the muddy pulse of a dry and ancient land. But it was gone now. Hardly a trickle left.

Everything she'd known and loved and lost was there, on that blue marble. Her husband Simon was still there, doggedly eking out an existence in sweltering Sydney. Remorse swelled her chest. Ex-husband. That was over now. Regret still surged and ebbed.

There were six more months before their return to Earth. Six months of worrying about the crew, keeping them focused and entertained. Six months of distracting herself from the abyss of loss that haunted the edges of her consciousness.

Xanthe stood to return to her sleeping pod, stretching out the creaks and aches that plagued her. The gravity moonboots and the heavy exo-skeleton suit made her hips ache. The additional weight was supposed to help mimic gravity and keep muscles from atrophying, but mostly it just hurt.

She sensed it first before she heard it. A creeping dread. She looked up again to the Atrium roof and squinted. Then the system alarm shrieked, and Xanthe jumped in fright.

It sounded like rain.

But there was no water here.

The realisation burned through her head as the sound grew louder and louder.

"Warning. Incoming debris," Athena A.I. announced over the screech of the alarm.

Meteorites!

"Athena, shut the retractor!" Xanthe yelled.

The meteors pelted the Atrium window in a horrifying barrage.

"Come on, come on!" she said. The retractor nudged forward slowly in agonising tiny increments over the giant eye.

Another strike boomed, and there was a gut-wrenching crack. The window took a massive blow. The retractor continued its sluggish crawl across the viewer. And then another strike.

"Oh, shit!"

The bombardment was relentless. The roof needed to shut before the viewer failed and leaked the insulating water layer into space, where it would vaporise instantly.

Xavier appeared at the Atrium's door lock and banged on the portal window.

"Xanthe! Close the retracting roof!" he said.

"Athena's on it! It's halfway there."

Then it jammed.

"Oh crap! Athena, reverse the retractor! See if we can slide it free!"

"Affirmative, Commander," said Athena.

Xanthe ran over to the manual override by the portal door.

The retractor slid back a bit, and then Xanthe slammed the button forward again, hoping to dislodge whatever was keeping it stuck.

"Come on, come on!"

The retractor resumed its excruciating, slow pace, and then shuddered to a halt. A crack in the window spread in a terrible web. The eye was compromised and failing fast.

The whole chamber exploded with the cannonade of debris strikes. Xanthe cowered by the chamber door.

"Xanthe!" Xavier screamed and struggled to open the Atrium door.

She could barely hear him above the thunderous roar. She felt the Atrium door slide open, then Xavier's hands around her waist. He hauled her through the doorway and the door slid shut behind them.

A massive smash sounded above, a crack like a bomb. Xavier dived forward while she was flung sideways against the plant shelving that lined the hallway, glass knives slicing her flesh.

The glass roof shattered. Alarms blared.

"Hull breach," Athena said. "Executing isolation sealing protocols now."

Xanthe jumped to the viewing portal into the Atrium. Thoughts scurried through her brain like rats at the sight of the gaping hole exposing the Atrium to the cold, harsh vacuum of space.

The atmosphere vented into the void.

The trees, her mind whispered.

"Come on, Xanthe. We've got to move away from the Atrium, in case there is a secondary leak."

Xavier half carried her, half dragged her down the tunnel as their moonboots pulled against them. They made it through the next door seal. It snapped open just as the others emerged from their accommodation along the hall.

Troy rushed to Xanthe's side and helped Xavier carry her through the next gateway to the central hub.

Jonas was there already. He took one look at her, hanging bloodied between Xavier and Troy, and said, "Xanthe, do I have your authority to take command?"

Xanthe raised her head and nodded.

"Commencing emergency procedure now," said Jonas into his comms device. "All hands to the Hub."

Xavier and Troy placed Xanthe in a chair at the kitchen table.

Xanthe's heart hammered, and her breath came in gasps. Her hands trembled. Her mind seemed paralysed. *I'm in shock,* she thought.

"Xanthe, look at me," said Troy. "Where are you hurt?"

She looked at his blue eyes, focused with worry, but her mind was blank. "I don't know." Her thoughts scuttled. *What about the*

Atrium? Did the cooling system water vaporise? Why didn't we know this was coming? Are the sensors backfiring?

"Xanthe, I can see blood seeping through your shirt. I'll take a look, okay?" Troy said.

She nodded at him, her eyes wide. Everything moved slowly and quickly all at once, like a tableau.

"Jonas, I'll do a system check with Athena," said Serena. The life support systems, air pressure, any other breaches." Serena ran to the systems display while pulling a jumper over her head.

"Roger that," said Jonas.

"I'll check the *Saturnia* at the entrance lock," said Madison as she skidded into the kitchen hub.

"No! Stay here," barked Jonas.

Madison pulled up short at his tone. She stood with her hands on hips and eyebrows raised.

Jonas winced and tried again. "There's nothing we can do if it damaged the spacecraft at the moment. We'll check once the impact stops. Check the radar and see if there is any more debris."

"I'm on it," she replied.

They could feel the thundering crashes in the Atrium from where they were.

Troy lifted the back of Xanthe's shirt, while Xavier carried over the medkit. After a brief inspection, Troy retrieved gauze and antiseptic.

"You've got a couple of deep cuts that are bleeding a lot. I think they'll need stitches. We'll stop the bleeding first," Troy said with a gentle hand on her shoulder.

She nodded and tried to swallow. Her mouth was so dry.

Jonas and Madison assessed how much of the storm they would still have to withstand.

"Air pressure stable through the rest of Olympus," Serena called out. "There is a full breach of the Atrium, but no other leaks."

"Is it affecting the water reservoir?" Xavier asked, as he wiped at the bloody scratches on Xanthe's arms.

"Damn it! The reservoir tank is draining. The flood must be sucking from it as it empties into the breach."

"*Merde!* We need to shut that tank down," Xavier said.

"Athena, can you close the reservoir tank?" Serena asked.

"Negative. There seems to be an electrical fault. It will need manual override."

"I'll do that," Serena said.

"No more incoming meteorites on the radar, big or small," Madison said. "That was the worst of it. Jonas, I'll go and help Serena with locking down the water tank."

"Okay. Suit up the both of you, though. In case there is another breach."

"Let's get on it, Mad Dog," Serena said. "We'll go bootless. It will be faster."

They stepped out of their moonboots and bounded towards their rooms. They emerged ten minutes later in their lightweight spacesuits and leaped towards the infrastructure hold down the far corridor.

Xanthe felt the adrenaline seep from her system. Stings from her injuries drew attention back to her body. She flinched as Troy dabbed at her wounds.

"Sorry," he said softly, and paused while she settled again.

"That's okay. Keep going. Stitch it up if you can."

"Will do. I'm going to numb the area now."

More stinging bites.

"Xavier, can you get me a bottle of water, please?" she asked.

"*Mais oui!*" Xavier went to the kitchen dispenser and grabbed a drinking bottle to fill from the water nozzle. He returned to Xanthe, and she sipped from it gratefully.

"Athena, why did we not get more warning about this meteorite strike? Are the sensors down?" Xanthe asked.

"One moment, Commander."

Xanthe felt the weird tug of her flesh as Troy sewed stitches into her cuts.

"There are two explanations. It may be asteroid mining debris from nearby Asteroid 69G-12, currently being mined by Space-ward Bound, or—"

"Spaceward Bound! Those bastards!" Jonas said.

"Or it may be Moon mining debris," Athena continued.

"What? The Chinese base? What are they mining? *Where* are they mining?" Xavier said.

"I do not have data on the Chinese operations."

"Yes, yes, we know. They have an A.I. firewall," Jonas said. "Shouldn't our radar system have picked up the fallout sooner?" He stared at Xanthe and Xavier. Troy stopped his stitching and looked up, too.

"*Mon Dieu.* It seems we have a Moon protocol breach and a system failure. Or—"

They swapped glances as alarm spread between them. They'd been through betrayal before, on Earth, during the prototypes build, when Jonas and Serena had nearly died from Dave's passing information to saboteurs. It was too awful to contend with.

"I've got good news and bad news." Serena's voice came over the comms system.

"Go ahead, Serena," Jonas said and turned back to the system's panel to see the cameras in the hold.

"The good news is that we managed to shut down the reservoir leak."

"Thank goodness," Jonas said.

"And the bad news?" Xanthe asked.

"We've got less than a third of our water left. The rest vaporised in the Atrium."

This was devastating. Every part of their operation needed water. From their own cooking, hydration and sanitation, through to cleaning and the swamp's hydroponic plant watering system, cooling and insulation. Water was life.

Xanthe eased herself out of the chair and walked gingerly to the kitchen table. Everything hurt, and the cuts stung. She felt miserable.

Eventually Serena and Madison returned to the kitchen hub, looking despondent. Xavier, Troy and Jonas joined Xanthe as Serena and Madison removed their helmets and grabbed a seat alongside the others.

"Alrighty. Here's the situation," Jonas said. "Life support systems are currently stable. We've lost two-thirds of our water to the Atrium. The Atrium's eye is damaged, with debris everywhere but hopefully contained. With no atmosphere left in the Atrium, we can assume the plants there have died.

"Our Commander is injured with lacerations but otherwise okay. I am standing in as deputy until she can resume command. Anything else?" he asked.

"How long will the life support system last? Without the Atrium acting as our lungs?" asked Troy.

"We will have to monitor life support room by room. It will put a lot of strain on the system," Serena said. "We might have to default to wearing our suits to take some of the strain. We really need to get the Atrium fixed, pronto," she said.

"How do you propose we do that?" asked Madison. "We didn't bring any spare plexiglass," said Madison.

"We might use some sheeting from the vertical farm," Xavier chimed in. "That could work temporarily. That way we could get the water flowing back through the system at least. But we won't have a view anymore."

"We need to get that retractable roof sorted and closed. That trumps our view, unfortunately," Xanthe said. *No more starry vistas.* A tinge of despair branched like cracked glass across her soul.

Jonas slumped in his chair. "Dammit. I'm so sorry I didn't

get the retractor fixed quickly enough, but I was stuck with the water cycling system. It was next on my list. I wish I'd done it sooner now. But still, there was nothing on the radar to prompt a reprioritisation."

"The retractor shouldn't have been a problem," said Madison. "There was no incoming debris on the radar. That's what's so strange."

"Athena, can you run diagnostics with our radar system, please," Xanthe said. "I want to know why we had no warning of this shower."

"Affirmative, Commander. I'll adjust the radar sensors for smaller debris. It might be calibrated to larger objects."

"Athena, any ideas where the meteorites came from?" Madison asked.

"The most likely explanation is that it came from asteroid mining. We can see mining activities on the long-range scanner," Athena said.

"Is that the Spaceward Bound asteroid mining station?" Xavier asked.

"Affirmative."

"*Les salauds!* They could at least have warned us."

"Deputy Commander Jonas, I'm getting a hail signal from the lunar space station."

"Thanks Athena," Jonas said. "Patch them through."

"Olympus! Olympus!" The hail burst over the comms channel.

"Go ahead, *Gateway*," Jonas said. "We read you loud and clear."

"We've been hit in a meteor shower. Our systems are down. We're venting atmosphere."

Xanthe looked up. It was the *Gateway* captain, James Delacroix. Usually he was jovial, always ready with a quip of some sort. A real larrikin. Anxiety gripped his voice now. Alarm shot through her crew.

Jonas gathered himself and asked, "Can you fix it?"

"Negative. It's torn a massive hole in our side. We're all in the escape pod."

"We'll get ready to receive you," said Jonas.

"Negative. It seems our controls of the escape pod are jammed and offline as well. Comms is the only system that seems to work, apart from life support."

Jonas puffed his cheeks and blew out a long breath as he considered the implications. Xanthe was already estimating how long their damaged life support would last if they brought the *Gateway* crew and the Artemis astronauts back to the base. The latter had launched yesterday from the Moon in the Artemis *Starship* and docked at the *Gateway* station. They were scheduled to swap places with the new Artemis crew, who had arrived the day before. That meant there were nine people crammed into an escape pod built for six.

"How much of the *Gateway* is damaged?" asked Jonas.

"It needs massive repairs to the hull."

"And the *Starship*?"

"It also has damage. It may be serviceable, but all its electronics are fried, and we can't get any readings on it."

Jonas leaned forward over the comms console and tapped his fingers as he thought. "Can you dislodge the escape pod manually?"

"We could try an EVA, but we're worried about more debris. What's on the radar?"

"There is no further incoming debris on the radar," Athena said.

"Okay. Sounds like a spacewalk for manual release is our best option." Captain James's voice was resigned.

"And if you're unable to dislodge the escape pod? What's your Plan B?" asked Jonas.

"We'll try to bum a ride on the *Saturnia,* if that bucket of bolts is still holding together." The captain managed a hint of levity. There had been ongoing boasting about the respective abilities of the Lunar Commission's civilian lunar development craft, the *Saturnia*, and the famous *Starship*.

"That's assuming it also hasn't been damaged in the storm," said Troy.

"While you do your EVA, we will assess the status of *Saturnia* and determine possible rescue operations. But just so you know, we have a few issues down here too. The Atrium has been destroyed, and we have lost two thirds of our water. So, we are in salvage and damage-repair mode at the moment."

"Have you got comms with Earth? We don't," James said.

"We haven't had a chance to touch base with them. All the comms system seems to be working, though."

"Can you let them know about our situation, then?"

"Of course."

"It will take us about three hours to prep for the EVA."

"How much air supply do you have in the escape pod?"

"We've got six hours with the nine of us here. Plus our suits. They're good for about ten hours."

"They'd better get a hustle on, then," said Serena to Madison and the others.

"Roger that," said Jonas. "Start your EVA procedures and we will find out the flight ability of the *Saturnia*. We'll have someone on comms to relay with Earth and check your progress."

Xanthe held her head in her hands and watched Jonas out of the corner of her eye. He wasn't used to being in charge in a crisis, and the pressure gnawed at him. He chewed his bottom lip.

Xanthe felt decidedly unwell.

Jonas looked over at her, noting her distress.

"Troy, can you take Xanthe back to her accommodation? She needs to rest while we assess the situation."

"I'm fine," she said.

"You are definitely not fine," said Troy. "You're in shock and you need to lie down for a while. Jonas has got this under control."

She was in no mood to argue. Her head throbbed and her back felt like a tiger had raked it. She agreed reluctantly.

"Alright, Seaborn. You're in charge. Wake me up in an hour when we've got a report on *Saturnia*."

"Righto," he said. "Madison and Serena, can you head out to do an inspection of the *Saturnia?* We need to assess it for rescue readiness of the *Gateway* crew."

"We're on it, Deputy Commander Seaborn!" Serena saluted him with a wry smile, and he rolled his eyes at her.

"Good. I want a full report within the hour. Xavier, you are on life support systems and water. I want you to inspect the Atrium and see what's going on in there, and in the meantime I'll try to fix the electrics and get that roof closed over the top of the eye. Athena, can you do any assessments of the Atrium to give me an idea where to start with that glitch?" Jonas asked.

"Yes, Deputy Commander, I will get straight to that," Athena said.

"Troy, once you've looked after Xanthe, can you please join me here to help with comms with Gaia and the *Gateway?*" he said.

"Affirmative, Jonas. I'd be happy to," Troy said.

Troy hooked Xanthe under her arms and lifted her to her feet. Their heavy moonboots slowed them down.

"Step out of your boots, Xanthe," Troy said. "I'll carry you. It will be easier that way."

Xanthe swallowed her pride and stepped out of the boots, and Troy gathered her in his arms. She tried not to feel ridiculous.

Troy looked down at her with his gorgeous, crooked smile.

"I've got you, Commander," he said.

The heat of his body radiated through his clothes and warmed her. She was trembling now with the shock of her injuries.

He slid open the door to her pod and lay her on the bunk.

"Where's your sleepwear?" he asked.

She pointed to a bundle in a corner.

"Let me help you put these on," he said as he retrieved her cotton pyjamas.

"I can do that myself, Troy," she mumbled with embarrassment.

"Are you sure? Your cuts are deep, and you're pretty badly hurt."

"I'll be fine," she said with a bit more steel in her voice.

"Alright," he said, trying not to flinch at her tone.

Why am I always like this with him? she thought. *He's just trying to help.*

"Thanks, Troy," she conceded. "I'll get these on and lay down. Come and wake me in an hour. That should do it."

"I administered some painkillers when I did the stitches. That will help you get some rest."

"Thanks," she said.

Once he left, she slipped out of her work suit and pulled on the grey cotton top and pants. She was stiff, and the movements stung more than she expected.

"Damn," she muttered as she drew the top over her head and pulled it down over her belly. It was getting a little grimy. It was hard to wash anything on the Moon. They vacuumed their clothes, put them through the ultrasonic machine to shake out grime particles and hit them with a UV lamp to kill any bugs. But nothing beat the feel of freshly laundered clothes. And now, with so little water left, there was zero chance of hand washing even their underwear.

She winced as the fabric slid over her injuries. The painkillers obviously hadn't kicked in yet, so she'd have to lie on her front. She wriggled into her bedding and adjusted the webbing they used to hold themselves down while they slept.

It was reassuring to have some pressure akin to Earth's gravity, though some of the crew preferred no restraints and rested lightly on their bunks.

She closed her eyes, and darkness swamped her exhausted body.

CHAPTER FOUR

"In the dance with death, every step counts."

—Athena A.I., Olympus Log

Serena and Madison raced off to the exit portal.

Once out of the airlock, they bounded over to the landing pad where *Saturnia* was housed. Debris from the impact was strewn everywhere. The tail-end of the meteorite event spattered tiny pellets of debris against their spacesuits.

"This is not good," Serena said as she eyed the arms of her suit. With no erosion in space, any asteroid debris, like the regolith, was sharp and abrasive and could puncture the suits like a bullet.

"That was one hell of a detonation!" Madison said. "I wonder what Spaceward Bound used on that asteroid. Must be some kind of new explosive to cause this kind of fallout."

"Those idiots are always going off half-cocked. They're in desperate need of some accountability."

"Lincoln Ellison always had a preference for speed over quality," said Madison.

"That's right, I remember now. You trained all their pilots before applying for the Gaia Olympus project bid."

"I sure did."

"What was it like with Spaceward Bound?" Serena panted as they moondled up the crater's edge that formed a natural ring around *Saturnia's* landing site.

"They were a fun bunch, but a little misguided. Lincoln Ellison has some charisma, that's for sure," Madison said with a laugh. "Plenty of gung-ho enthusiasm, but he let a lot of that go to his head when it came to making decisions for Spaceward Bound. It was pretty easy in the end to give it away and throw my lot in with Gaia. Even if I didn't make the first cut." There was just a tinge of bitterness to her voice, though Madison worked to suppress it.

"For the record, you were always my first choice for pilot. Not that they asked any of us in the first place. I couldn't believe they picked Dave over you for the prototype build."

Madison appreciated Serena's gesture of support. "Well, I did have a few challenges to overcome, if you recall."

"To be fair, I'm not sure any of us would have coped that well with being locked up in a coffin to test claustrophobia." Madison did not reply as they manoeuvred around a boulder on the crater's lip.

"How was it training with Troy, one-on-one, to get over the claustrophobia?"

"It was. . . intense. I sure as sugar never want to do that again. I'll tell you what, though, you could lock me in a box for three days, now, and I'd just yawn and sleep through it. I kicked that gremlin to the floor and then some. Troy sure knows his business."

They pulled up short as the *Saturnia* came into view.

"Oh, my word," said Madison.

Boulders were scattered across the landing pad and the spacecraft looked like it had a bad case of acne.

"Let's hope it's just cosmetic," said Serena.

They both opened their visors to get a better look and winced at the glare.

"Somehow, I don't think this is our lucky day," said Madison.

They picked up their pace as they leaned down the slope to the base of the craft.

"Let's split up and do a visual inspection from the outside and around to the back," said Madison.

"Roger that."

Serena bounded away. Madison took a moment to take everything in. *Saturnia* rose above her, a majestic sentinel.

The rockets looked okay. There were dents all down the face. None of them seemed to have penetrated the hull, as far as she could tell. She couldn't quite see the nose of the craft. They'd have to enter and inspect it from the cupola.

Madison took her time going around the perimeter. The dings seemed reserved for just the front side. *A piece of good news at last,* she thought as she met up with Serena around the far side.

"Nothing too heinous around this side, as far as I can tell," Serena reported.

"Alright. Let's head inside and see what the sensors can tell us."

They clambered below the jets and Madison pulled the lever for the stair access to the spacecraft. They pulled themselves up into the dust-venting cavity.

Madison hit the purge button and the air pressure vents blew the regolith from their boots and suits into a collector below.

"We better keep our helmets on in case there's a breach we didn't see," Madison said.

"My suit is reading good atmosphere, and it looks like the regolith shower didn't tear anything either."

"Let's hope the good news continues," Madison said. She wanted to hope for the best, but her gut roiled with dread.

They pulled themselves upwards with the use of the ladder in the main chamber until they reached the navigation pod.

Madison took a deep breath. "Okay, let's see what we've got."

She punched the access code to the cockpit, and the door clunked open.

Her hopes dashed like china plates on granite. There was a gaping hole in the navigation portal window.

"Quick – get in and close the door behind you. And keep your helmet on!" Madison said.

Serena scrabbled in behind her.

"Well. Shit," she said. "This is not good."

"No, it is definitely not," said Madison.

The offending meteorite sat imperiously in the navigation chair, surrounded by wreckage.

Nice way to add insult to injury, noted Madison. The pilot's chair – her chair – was torn and battered.

Sucking in her breath, Madison said, "Athena, systems check and report, please."

"Yes, Captain Floyd," the pleasant voice of the A.I. filled their helmets. They'd installed Athena here as well as in the Olympus. "Running diagnostics now."

Saturnia's lights sprang to life.

Madison and Serena drifted around the cabin, being careful not to touch anything.

"Hull breach in the viewing window," Athena said.

"No shit, Sherlock," Serena said.

"Atmosphere vented through the command pod. Atmosphere is stable in the access chamber."

"Any other electrical damage?" Madison asked.

"That's negative. Most systems operating normally."

"What systems are *not* operating normally?"

"Navigation. The circuit board is badly damaged."

Madison felt her stomach tighten and her pulse throb in her temples. She took a breath and swallowed to maintain calm. "Can we repair the navigation?"

"Affirmative. I have the electronic schematics in my data. If we have the cables and switches, we can execute the replacement."

Madison did a mental audit of supplies onboard and from where they might be able to salvage the required supplies. "How long will it take to repair navigation? And can we do a repair of the command pod with onboard resources?"

"It will take approximately seven hours to repair the navigation panel, including testing. For repair of the command pod, there are three options available," Athena said. "Option one: replace the viewing window with a reformatted piece of the stairwell cavity. Option two: fill the breach with regolith polymers. Option three: eject the navigation pod and use the remainder of the system without it."

"What? If we eject the navigation pod, how will we control the craft?" asked Serena, dumbfounded.

"I would operate the controls by relocating all my systems to the main shaft," the A.I. replied calmly.

"And how would we return to Earth without the navigation chamber?" Madison asked.

"Option three is not possible with human passengers," said Athena.

"I say we scrap option three," said Serena. "I don't like the sound of that."

"Agreed," said Madison drily. "How long would it take to repurpose a piece from inside the stairwell chamber?"

"Autonomous robot repair, with some human assistance, would take fifteen hours to complete. That is my best estimate."

"And option two? The regolith polymers?"

"This would take approximately ten hours, but there are some risks with that option."

"And those are?" Madison asked.

"The seal might be less durable and prone to potential further breaches."

"Will it hold for a launch to *Gateway*, the orbiting station?"

"It is possible. The likelihood of maintaining the seal is 40%."

"Those are pretty crappy odds," Serena said.

"If the *Gateway* crew could do an EVA and dislodge their escape pod, then there's no rush," Madison said.

"And if they can't?"

"Then we gotta rush like mad and pray like hell."

"Madison, Serena, report." Jonas's voice sparked in their helmet comms.

"You want the good news or bad news?" Madison asked.

"Just give it to me."

"All electrical systems intact."

"Great! What's the bad news?"

"The navigation panel needs to be reconstructed. And there is a massive hole in the navigation window. No atmosphere here."

"Can we do the repairs?"

"Yes, we can. The navigation panel will take seven hours once we find the cables and switches that we need. Then for the navigation pod, the first two options will take fifteen and ten hours, respectively. The ten-hour option has a 40% success likelihood. The third option eliminates future use for human passengers."

Silence from Jonas. Madison knew he was processing the information. She pictured him tugging on his hair as he was wont to do when he was stressed. He blew out a big sigh over the comms as he thought through the options.

"Have we heard from the space station?" interrupted Serena.

"They're about to launch their EVA, now," Jonas came back, thoughtful.

"If they go ahead with the EVA, they will lose atmosphere in their escape pod," said Madison. "They'll be down to whatever oxygen is left in their suits. And that's how many hours, Serena?"

"They have about ten hours left in their spacesuits."

"Best case scenario is that the EVA works and they get their escape pod released from the dock and then come and join us."

"If they *can't* get their escape pod released from the EVA, they're going to run out of air. Unless we rescue them."

"Option one will take too long," Jonas said.

"If they don't do an EVA, how much air do they have in their escape pod and suits?" asked Madison, looking at Serena.

"They might have four or five hours in their escape pod. Plus their suits, they will have fifteen hours max."

"If we go for option two, we might be able to get up to them before they run out of oxygen," Madison said. "Assuming I can find all the stuff we need to get the nav panel back up and running. Serena can work with Athena for the nav pod itself. Failing that, we could launch in our suits with no atmosphere."

"That's risky," said Jonas. "There is no guarantee the repair job will work. 40% is not great. We might lose our entire ship in the process."

"So, what? We just let them do the EVA and hope for the best?" Serena said.

"We need to run the repair operation regardless," said Madison. We might do it faster than what Athena has suggested. She is sometimes conservative in her estimates."

"I don't like rush jobs," said Jonas.

"No one likes rush jobs," Madison replied.

"It's also our ride back to Earth. We don't want to stuff it up," Serena added.

"Give me a moment. We'll run some scenarios back here with Troy."

After a few minutes, Jonas came back online. "*Gateway* crew are aware of the risks and are willing to do the EVA. In the meantime, we are on operation panel repair, option one. Can you two work with Athena to get it started?"

"Roger that, Jonas." Madison was already manoeuvring the debris.

"In the meantime, I'll touch base with Gaia and NASA and get their engineers working on the problems as well. Keep us up to date as you go. The team here will work on the Atrium damage."

"As long as you get the shower working again, Jonas!" Serena said.

There was a pause and then, "Anything for you, Princess."

CHAPTER FIVE

"In the crucible of adversity, the mind either moulds or melts."

—Athena A.I., Olympus Log

Xanthe woke with a groan. Her head felt heavy, her body battered. Aching all over and thirsty as hell, she grabbed the bottle of water beside her bunk and sucked it greedily. The relief was immediate. She looked at her watch. Asleep for forty-five minutes. She sat up carefully, every little laceration a red-hot needle across her back.

She removed her pyjamas and pulled her operations exo-suit back on. Remembering her moonboots were in the central hub, she bounded to the door, slid it open and made her way back to the command centre.

Troy turned to her, and his face lit up with concern. "I was just coming to get you," he said. "How do you feel?"

"Like someone tossed me in a sack with an unhappy feral cat, then put me in a tumble dryer with a couple of boulders," she said.

"That good, eh? Let me get you one of my teas. Plus some more painkillers."

"Nothing to make me drowsy!" Xanthe protested, knowing

that Troy's teas were legendary. He had brought many concoctions with him from Earth. Stimulants, sedatives, some that felt psycho-tropic but Troy insisted weren't. They still induced some interesting mental experiences. "I want to be back on deck to assist, now. Jonas, what's the update?"

Jonas peeled himself away from the comms display to reply. "*Saturnia* is badly damaged. Madison and Serena are working with the repair bot to get it fixed. Then we might need to do a rescue mission to *Gateway* if their EVA doesn't work."

Xanthe pressed her lips together as she considered the gravity of the situation. Looking around, she asked, "Where's Xavier?"

"He's working on the water and Atrium problem," Jonas replied. "And no, there is no good news there. All the water in the Atrium vaporised, and there is still a risk to the whole life support system."

Troy handed Xanthe a pouch of warm tea and two painkillers. She nodded in thanks and swallowed them quickly.

"What does Gaia advise?" she asked.

"They said, 'Hurry and get it fixed'," Jonas said. "You know how Aryanna is not terribly compassionate."

"Where's Maja?"

"She's there. She wants you to call her when you're back up to speed."

"Alright. I'll do that now," she said. Xanthe found her moon-boots and pulled them back on with a grimace. Everything hurt.

She joined Jonas at the main comms panel and asked Athena to connect with Maja Garcia at Gaia headquarters.

Thank goodness for Maja, she thought. Wise and strong, despite her frail body, Maja was still recovering from the cell rejuvenation therapy Aryanna had organised. It had brought Maja back from the brink, but progress was slow.

While she waited, Xanthe noticed a spatter of dried blood on her hand. She licked a finger and rubbed it. *We are all so vulnerable in these bags of bone and water.*

Maja's splendid, dark face etched with deep lines of wisdom and worry emerged from the holo display.

"Xanthe! How are you? How are the injuries?"

"Hello, Maja. I'm alright. A bit cut up, but otherwise fine."

"I'm glad to hear it. I was very worried about you. About you all."

"We're not out of the woods yet. We've got a few things to contend with."

"I am aware of the situation and up to speed. And I have a suggestion for you that may help."

"I'm all ears."

"Reach out to the Red Star base. They're building the next extension of their base. They might have the resources you need for the Atrium repair."

"You want me to ask the Chinese for help?" Xanthe was incredulous. "Colonel Jin is not exactly friendly with us. We had a showdown just a few days ago over going too close to their water mining site."

"Colonel Jin is a little. . .prickly. But I think we can convince him to help. He's human under all that Teflon."

"More like titanium than Teflon," Xanthe added with a scowl.

"I think there's an opportunity in this, Xanthe." Maja's handsome face was focused and fierce. "Are you alone there?"

Xanthe shook her head, then gestured to Jonas to leave them. He raised an eyebrow but exited and closed the comms room door behind him.

"What is it, Maja?"

"Here's what you can do once you reach out to Colonel Jin."

Xanthe listened to Maja's plan without interrupting her.

"You really think that will work?" she asked at the end of the briefing.

"I think the future of human relations depends on it working. And of all people, I think you're the one to do it." Maja beamed at her with a graceful smile.

Xanthe felt like she was wrapped in a warm hug, like she always did when she spoke to Maja. "Okay, Maja. I'll give it a go."

CHAPTER SIX

Xanthe rolled her shoulders and braced herself for the call to Colonel Jin. *He is such an abrasive tool,* she thought.

"Athena, please call Colonel Jin at Red Star base."

"Connecting now."

Xanthe rubbed her left arm while she waited. She prodded gently at a bruise that had formed from the Atrium incident.

"Commander Waters. The Colonel is unavailable." Jin's offsider was cold but not overtly hostile.

"Please tell him this is an emergency," Xanthe said. "We've sustained damage from the recent meteorite strike and are seeking assistance." She kept her tone even-keeled.

The second in command blinked but kept his expression stoic. After a moment, he said, "Please wait." The man's image disappeared and the Red Star logo with its red, blue and white hammer and sickle appeared in its place.

Somehow, the Russians had persuaded the Chinese to incorporate their national colours, even though they were taking a relatively minor role in the base's establishment. Sure, they had provided the Lunar vehicles, but that paled into comparison with the nuclear technology and the ambitious base the Chinese had built in record time. Vladimir Volkov had been one persuasive bastard before he disappeared, Xanthe remembered.

"Commander Waters." The Colonel's imperious face filled the holo display, and Xanthe fought the urge to step backwards. "I hear you have some problems," he said with his bulbous lips pursed in concern.

"Colonel Jin." Xanthe took a breath. "We've sustained considerable damage to the Olympus base and to the *Saturnia*. The *Gateway* is also damaged and is undertaking an emergency EVA to rescue the crew on board." She paused a moment. "How is the Red Star? Were you hit in the storm?"

The Colonel stared at her image as he absorbed her news. "No. We were not hit. All operations are normal here."

"I'm glad to hear it." Xanthe was genuinely relieved at the news, and it showed in her face.

"We got a very late notice of the incoming debris. It was not on long range radar," Colonel Jin said, his brow wrinkled.

"We suspect it is from Spaceward Bound's mining operations. Gaia Enterprises is liaising with Lincoln Ellison now to determine their contribution to the incident."

The Colonel pulled at his uniform's sleeves to straighten them before he replied. "I trust a moratorium will be placed on all asteroid mining until this 'incident' is investigated?"

"Possibly." Xanthe avoided the political dance he was trying to draw her into. "In the meantime, we have some significant repairs to do to our base and time is of the essence. The Atrium eye was smashed by debris and our water cooling and filtration system emptied into the void. Our life support system is under strain until we can get the eye repaired and mine some water."

Colonel Jin rubbed his jaw as he listened to Xanthe's report. "Sounds difficult," he said finally.

Prick. He is going to make me beg for help, Xanthe thought. *Or is this some sort of cultural norm I am not aware of?* She took a deep breath and said as calmly as she could, "I understand you may have some materials we might use for our Atrium repair." She waited for his offer.

"What materials?"

"We need plexiglass."

"I see." He crossed his arms. Xanthe imagined he was calculating what he could ask for in return. She braced herself for the price.

"To repair the Atrium would require a large amount of plexiglass. What are the dimensions?"

He already had that information. Their network of communication satellites around the Moon would have calculated all aspects of the Olympus base – if they hadn't stolen the plans somehow with their wide network of spies in the Lunar Commission. She told him politely, trying not to clench her jaw.

Our lives are all hanging in the balance, and we have to negotiate.

That's the way it was on the Moon, as it had been for humans everywhere, for all time. When resources are scarce, we cling to them. Could it be any different on the Moon? Xanthe rubbed her forehead. Surely the 'we're better together' philosophy could triumph here?

"Yes. We have that amount of plexiglass from our phase three build. If we give it to you, this will slow our project significantly. I doubt my superiors will approve this costly delay."

And there it was. She had to pitch an offer, so he had something to work with.

"We could replace it on the next Olympus mission. When we bring out the first residents. That's in six months." She knew her offer was unattractive, but she had to start low. Colonel Jin remained silent. Damn. She'd have to up the ante straight away.

"I can ask them to replace the materials used and add extra. We'd have to reduce the number of first residents to account for the additional weight, but that's possible." Still, Jin said nothing.

"What else would be useful for Red Star?" she asked. *Dangerous territory here*, she thought.

Colonel Jin spoke slowly, and Xanthe imagined his excitement as he held the upper hand in the negotiations. "Since it would delay our project, we could focus our efforts on the horticulture hub. If we had some of Xavier Consus's seedlings and materials, that would assist greatly in the reallocation of our resources."

Xanthe gripped the chair until her knuckles went white. Xavier would be furious. Fresh food and plants were a precious resource and jealously guarded. And they would face months of reduced fresh rations. She managed to smile pleasantly. "I am sure that can be accommodated."

He smiled then. Was that a satisfied, triumphant line across his features? Xanthe wondered if she was misreading the cues.

"Then we have an agreement. Now, let's discuss the logistics of this emergency rescue supply mission we'd be delighted to assist you with," Colonel Jin said with all the grace of a champion negotiator.

You won this round, Colonel. But I got what we needed, and we're playing a long game.

CHAPTER SEVEN

"Facing the abyss, humans find strength or their breaking point."

—Athena A.I., Olympus Log

"Xanthe, we've got incoming comms from the *Gateway*," Troy called out from the central hub.

Xanthe joined him and Jonas at the console. The conversation with Colonel Jin had left her flat, and she'd used the excuse of a toilet break to gather her composure.

Jonas was fiddling with the settings, trying to get a better holo display of the *Gateway* crew. It was a poor connection.

"Olympus, do you read?"

"Go ahead, *Gateway*. We can see you, James, but it's patchy. What's your report?" Jonas asked.

"Not good. Kwanda could not manoeuvre the release mechanism manually. The escape pod is still jammed. Does NASA have any other suggestions?"

Troy piped up. He had been liaising with NASA about the *Gateway* problem. "They're suggesting several strategies. I'll send through the list of systems they suggest rewiring. They also suggest a system reboot to see if that will clear any programming faults."

"A system reboot will take more of our power and could affect our life support systems. We might lose a few more hours of air. That's not my preferred option."

"Understood. Any suggestions from your side?"

"We are going to send another astronaut to assist Kwanda. A bit more brute force. How is the *Saturnia* looking? We might need that lift after all."

Jonas answered for them since he had been communicating with Madison and Serena. "The bot is working ahead of schedule with our team. We think we can have the *Saturnia* ready for a rescue mission in the next few hours."

James's face showed a brief release of tension.

"That's great – thanks."

"Captain, how are your oxygen levels?" asked Xanthe.

"Our suits are down to five hours, and we've got very little left in reserve since we launched the EVA. We'll be down to nothing extra in the capsule once we send out Yuri to help Kwanda."

"Roger that," she replied. It was grim. If they couldn't get the escape pod dislodged, they needed the *Saturnia*. Otherwise, they would suffocate. She rubbed the bruise on her arm as she racked her brain for options. Then she grimaced.

She would have to call the Colonel again.

❧

"Commander Waters," Colonel Jin said. "I'm surprised to hear from you again so soon. Have you forgotten something?"

Xanthe ignored the imagined barb and went straight to the point. "Colonel Jin, thank you for taking my call. We've got a situation developing with the *Gateway* crew." Xanthe filled him in on the escape pod predicament and the *Saturnia's* repair progress.

Colonel Jin pursed his lips like a fish as he considered the possibilities. "Are you asking us to assist with rescue operations if they are unable to dislodge the escape pod?"

Xanthe nodded.

"I see. It will take us three hours to ready our craft. Since we do not have docking compatibility with *Gateway*, the crew will have to be transferred via EVA. This is all very hazardous. Are the crew trained in spacewalk conditions?"

"I will get back to you on that. We may not have any other options if they can't dislodge the escape pod."

"There is one other problem. The *Chang-e* only has room for four passengers. We need our pilot and a deputy to operate the capsule and manage the retrieval. We might get there in time, but we can only save two passengers, given those constraints."

Xanthe rocked backwards and forwards on her feet as anxiety swept through her. "Understood, Colonel Jin. With any luck, it won't come to that. Our first hope is that they release the escape pod. In the meantime, we are working on the *Saturnia* to be ready for a rescue in the next couple of hours."

"How much room will you have on board?"

The *Saturnia* carried six passengers. With Athena operating the craft, they could get by with one operator to manage the rescue. That left five spots. Two short to save them all. They'd have to do two runs. And that meant using up their fuel for the ride back to Earth. They would have to mine more ice regolith and create a converter to make more fuel. It would jeopardise the entire Olympus project timeline.

Colonel Jin knew all this. He was waiting for her to make the call.

"We can retrieve five in the first round and then go back for the remaining two."

He raised his eyebrows. He knew that meant stranding themselves on the Moon until they could make more fuel, or until an early resupply mission arrived.

"I see," he said. "I'll ready our crew. Please keep me informed of any developments, Commander Waters."

"Will do, Colonel Jin. And—"

He looked at her expectantly.

"—thank you," she said.

He bowed his head in acknowledgment and ended the comms.

I just sold our souls to the Devil.

It was worth it. Nine other human beings depended on her.

CHAPTER EIGHT

"Beneath stress's weight, even the strongest can fracture."

—ATHENA A.I., OLYMPUS LOG

XANTHE RELAYED THE Chinese base's contribution to the rescue mission to Jonas, who stood by the kitchen table, lost in thought. He had his feet spread wide, arms crossed, chin jutted. Xanthe knew this stance. He was doing his best to stay level-headed.

The role of deputy was a big promotion during this phase of the Olympus project. Jonas had been a tenuous candidate during the selection of designers and mechanics for the Lunar Commission's bid. Xavier and Troy had been just as surprised as her that Maja and Huw had chosen him above others for the project. Jonas had shown clumsy, bullish leadership during selection. Very cocky. They must have seen some potential though. Besides, he'd proven his mettle during the prototype.

He'd come a long way. He still had a way to go, but he was definitely rising to the occasion. Mostly. He could still be a bit short tempered and impulsive.

Once she had him up to speed, he said, "Got it. The *Gateway* EVA is underway, but the escape pod is still stuck. Serena and

Madison are working like mad to get the navigation and panel repair done, but it's still taking time. Too much time." Jonas rubbed his jaw. The stress was weighing heavily on him.

On both of them, Xanthe thought. Anxiety gripped her shoulders in a vice. She rolled them to ease the tension.

Troy and Xavier arrived back from the life support hub. Xavier's dark face was slick with sweat, his brows deeply furrowed. Troy's face was flushed and grim.

Jonas pivoted as they entered. He dropped his hands to his hips and greeted them with a chin jut.

"Life support system report?" Jonas asked.

"Stable. For the time being." Xavier wiped his forehead with the sleeve of his overalls. "We've sealed off the Atrium and there are no leaks, but confining ourselves to this part of the base will put pressure on the purification system. We need that Atrium back and functioning within the next forty-eight hours or we are going to have many unwanted effects."

"What kind of effects?" asked Jonas.

"Slime build-up. Bacteria growth. Crop failures. Carbon dioxide poisoning." Xavier made large sweeps of his arm to highlight the point.

"Well then, I've got some good news," Xanthe interrupted the beginnings of a Xavier rant. "Colonel Jin agreed to give us plexiglass for the Atrium."

"*Vraiment?*" Xavier's eyebrows unclenched and shot up. "And what does the *putain de merde* want in return?"

"Wow, such a gutter mouth! You'll never make a diplomat, old chap," laughed Troy. Xanthe could tell he was trying to lighten the mood, his own as much as theirs.

"Ah, the man is a selfish beast. We all know that." Xavier wiped his hands on his grey overalls and grabbed a water pouch from a supply cabinet. He took a sip and turned back to Xanthe. "And so? What is the deal?"

Xanthe took a breath and raised her hands in a placating gesture. "You're not going to like it, but I did what was necessary to get the Atrium back and functioning."

He said nothing and tilted his head, waiting.

"I agreed to a supply of seedlings so his crew will have something to do while they wait for resupply of their construction materials from Earth."

"*Merde!*" Xavier spat.

"It's not that bad, *mon ami*." Troy put a hand on Xavier's shoulder. "We can always grow more plants. We can't grow new lungs. And be grateful he didn't ask for coffee."

"Incoming message from the *Gateway*," Athena's voice interrupted them.

"Patch them through, Athena," Jonas said.

Xavier, Troy and Xanthe joined him at the comms panel.

"Olympus, this is the *Gateway*." Captain James's image popped up on the holo display. He didn't wait for confirmation and continued. "Kwanda and Yuri are still on EVA. Their suit oxygen supplies are getting dangerously low with the exertion. We've tried all the NASA tricks including reboots. Nothing's working. What are the updates from your side?"

Jonas glanced at Xanthe, and she nodded for him to continue.

"The *Chang-e* is readying for a rescue mission. Since they cannot dock, all astronauts will need to conduct an EVA for retrieval. We expect them to be nearby within the next—" He glanced at the time display. "In the next four hours. The *Saturnia* is making good progress. They will be ready for lift off just after the *Chang-e* arrives for you."

"And the *Saturnia* can carry how many?"

"Five."

That left two to wait for a return trip. *Saturnia* could, in theory, retrieve the first five, drop them on the Moon, and return for the last two. Assuming all went to plan. The margins were tight.

"Roger that. We'll keep working the EVA. In the meantime, we'll cross everything we can and pray to the goddess, Luna, to get us out of here."

"We're working on it, James. We're pulling out all the stops for you," Xanthe said in a rush of emotion. She peered at James's face. Her heart ached for him and the crew. They were facing down atrocious survival odds.

"Thank you, Xanthe. See you soon."

CHAPTER NINE

"Humans look to leaders as lighthouses, even when the leaders themselves are seeking their own light."

—Athena A.I., Olympus Log

Xanthe monitored the repair and rescue operations.

It's like watching a wounded butterfly trying to take flight, she thought. *I feel so helpless.*

Troy tried to help by rubbing her shoulders, but she only shrugged him off. He stifled his hurt feelings by engaging Xavier in tension-breaking banter. Xavier remained surly.

Irritated by both of them, and not wanting the distraction while they waited for intermittent reports from the *Saturnia*, *Gateway* and the *Chang-e*, Xanthe sent them both off to pack seedlings for the trip out to the Red Star. They'd leave as soon as the rescue was complete.

Jonas and Xanthe maintained a vigil by the comms. Xanthe resumed her commander's role as she was over the shock now — though her wounds, even dulled as they were with painkillers, stung with every movement of her shirt.

"Olympus base, this is the Red Star."

"Go ahead, Red Star." Xanthe snapped her response and pressed the holo comm receiver.

"The *Chang-e* is ready for launch. We will take over communication with the *Gateway* on approach."

"Affirmative. I'll let them know." Xanthe exhaled with relief. Part one of the rescue was underway. She switched to comms with the *Saturnia*. "Madison, Serena, status report please," she said.

"Hello, Olympus." Madison's voice crackled through the speaker. "The navigation circuitry is still glitchy. I'm working on it. Nearly there. But Serena is just about done with the seal for the nav pod. We should be able to run checks within the hour and be ready for launch prep in ninety minutes."

"Roger that. Olympus out." Xanthe chewed her lower lip. They were cutting it so darn fine. They needed the patch to work or they would simply run out of time.

"Athena, can you bring up satellite imagery of the *Chang-e*?"

"Searching satellite imagery now."

"There!" Jonas exclaimed and pointed at a fiery bubble in one corner of the display. They stood shoulder to shoulder, staring at the display as the *Chang-e* fired its rockets and lifted through the low Moon gravity, starting its trek towards the *Gateway*. Jonas's shoulder was hot against hers and she could feel the tense vibrations of his foot tapping as he seemed to will the little craft faster towards to its quarry.

He smells rancid, thought Xanthe. They probably all did. Fear did that. And infrequent showering.

Xanthe switched the comms to the *Gateway* and said, "James, the *Chang-e* has lift-off and is on its way."

"I'm glad to hear it." James's face appeared on the holo display. He was pale and the strain etched deep lines around his mouth.

"How are you all doing up there?"

"We're struggling a little. We've dialled down our oxygen supply to conserve it. But it's making thinking a little. . ." He seemed to search for a word. "Troublesome." He blinked and tried to focus on the screen.

"Hang in there, James. The *Saturnia* will follow next. You'll all be down here with us before you know it."

James blinked at her and squinted in concentration.

"James, the *Chang-e* will take over comms upon approach, in approximately twenty minutes. Where are your people right now?"

"Kwanda and. . . and. . ."

"Yuri," Xanthe prompted. Xanthe realised James was struggling with low oxygen, affecting his ability to think. She needed him to be on the ball.

"Kwanda and Yuri are still outside, working the problem. They thought it would be better to keep trying to release the capsule, rather than sit in the escape pod doing nothing."

"Roger that. Their oxygen levels?"

"Low. They're in the red zone."

"Well, let's get them on the *Chang-e* first, shall we?"

"Roger that. How many trips will there be?" James looked confused.

"One with *Chang-e,* two with *Saturnia.* We spoke about this."

"Yes. Yes, I know," he said irritably.

"James, I want you to rest as much as you can. Conserve your energy and your oxygen. Check in with us before you decide to do anything."

He didn't answer, just stared at her. Then gave her a thumbs up and a weak smile.

"I'm going to swap the comms for *Chang-e* now," he said.

He muted them but left the video feed running.

Jonas and Xanthe looked at each other. He'd forgotten to switch the feed. It might make it difficult for the *Chang-e* to establish contact. With delicate EVA missions like this one, it was protocol to focus on one comms link at a time. Even if they shut the link from their end now, the *Gateway* would still broadcast back to them.

"Athena, set up the display so we can see the *Chang-e* approach."

Her heart pounded. The little Chinese craft was nearing the *Gateway*. They needed to get close enough so the EVA astronauts could manoeuvre themselves from their tether to the Chinese ship. Her gaze went from the Chinese ship to the cabin view of James and the other astronauts bundled into the tiny escape pod. She could see James talking to the Chinese comms link.

"They're opening the *Chang-e* portal door. There's their taikonaut now!" Jonas pointed, his eyes wide.

The taikonaut stood at the portal door. He seemed to beckon to the *Gateway* astronauts, who appeared on the screen as tiny figurines. One moved, then accelerated.

"They're on their way!" Jonas cried.

"Yes!" Xanthe said.

"Wait a minute," Jonas whispered.

The astronaut sped towards the *Chang-e*, but too quickly.

They peered closer at the display. Something didn't look right. The astronaut was sagging. They should have been level with the Chinese spacecraft, but they started to spin. Their approach was coming on fast, too fast.

The taikonaut gestured to slow down, but the astronaut spun head over heels, tangling the tether. They jolted to a halt; the tether stretched tight, some ten metres from the *Chang-e*.

"They must have passed out," Jonas muttered.

They looked on in horror as the *Gateway* astronaut spun on his tether at a sickening pace. The taikonaut disappeared inside their craft and then emerged, attached to their own EVA tether.

"The taikonaut is going after them!" Jonas said and slapped his thigh with a broad grin. "Go, son! Go get 'em!"

The taikonaut floated towards the languishing astronaut. They reached out and grabbed the spinning figure, then released them again. The spin slowed, and the taikonaut clutched at them again.

The two figures spun together. Xanthe and Jonas peered at the display, trying to make out what was happening.

"Come on, come on," muttered Jonas. He wiped his palms on his trousers and tapped a foot.

They watched as the tether to the *Gateway* released and floated aimlessly away from the astronaut. The two figures remained bundled together. The spinning had slowed, and they moved back towards the *Chang-e*.

"Got him!" Jonas said.

As they looked for the second astronaut, their elation stymied.

"Where are they?" Xanthe said. She could feel the muscles in her jaw growing rigid, and she opened her mouth to try to release the tension.

"There," Jonas said and pointed at a figure floating free of the *Gateway*. They were unmoving, hanging in space, tether loose. Then another figure appeared from the *Gateway*.

"What the—?" Jonas said.

"They're sending someone else. Yuri or Kwanda must have ceded their spot to another team member."

"Or they passed out and are incapacitated," Jonas said.

Xanthe looked at him and pursed her lips. "No. No! We are going to get them back. They'll be fine. You'll see," she said with a vehemence she didn't feel.

Jonas looked at her with a sad, grief-stricken face.

"Come on, Jonas, stay positive. There's nothing we can do for the *Chang-e* or *Gateway* now until we get *Saturnia* up there. Let's get that done."

"Right. Yes. Stay focused."

"Athena, please hail the *Saturnia*," Xanthe said.

"*Saturnia*, this is Olympus. Do you read?" asked the A.I.

"Olympus, this is *Saturnia*. We read you loud and clear, over."

"Status update, over?"

"Seal complete, just doing checks now, over."

"Good. Good." Xanthe sighed loudly and placed her hands on her hips. *One thing at a time*, she reminded herself.

"Olympus, we've got an issue." Madison's voice was edgy.

"Go ahead, Madison. What is it?"

"The navigation seems to have been damaged in the storm. Athena can manage most of it, but the approach and docking will need to be done manually. That means I will need a second pair of hands to undertake the rescue operation and retrieval of the astronauts. Request permission for Serena to assist, seeing as she's already here?"

"Affirmative," Xanthe said immediately. Her mind flew to the astronauts. Two on the *Chang-e*, four on the first *Saturnia* operation; that meant leaving three for the second trip. Oxygen was the biggest challenge. They might leave three for a slow, suffocating death if they couldn't make it in time.

"Roger that," Madison said. "We are strapping in now and making ready for launch."

"Go get 'em, Mad Dog!" Jonas said. Hope and desperation flooded his voice. Xanthe put a hand on his sweaty back and he dropped his head, trying to compose himself.

Behind them, Xavier and Troy entered the main hub with a clatter of moonboots.

"Seedlings secure, Captain, my Captain!" announced Troy as he stomped towards them.

Xanthe flung a flat palm towards him without looking up. He pulled up short at the abrupt gesture and then shuffled to the comms panel along with Xavier.

The four of them watched silently as Athena gave the countdown to launch.

"Three, two, one. Lift-off."

Their hearts lurched in unison. Lift off was always an intense experience, even in the Moon's low G.

"Athena, set up a dual display of the *Saturnia* and the *Gateway*. What is the status of the *Chang-e* rescue?"

Two scenes displayed before them. The *Chang-e* was still close to the *Gateway*, with one astronaut still floating on a tether nearby, unmoving.

"The *Chang-e* has retrieved two *Gateway* astronauts and has closed their spacecraft airlock," Athena said.

"Connect us to the *Gateway*, please," Xanthe said. She could see James on the video feed. There was not much movement from him or the others.

"*Gateway*, this is Olympus base. Do you read, over?" Athena said.

James lifted his head and stared at the comms display.

"James, this is Xanthe. You need to hit the comms audio button so we can hear you."

She could see him squint behind the window of his helmet.

"Come on," said Jonas. "It's right there. Right in front of you."

James reached a weary gloved finger to the panel and jabbed at a few buttons until he reached the right one.

"James, do you read, over?" asked Xanthe again.

"Xanthe? Yeah. I hear you. I see you. Ah, the whole gang is there! Wait – where are Serena and Madison?" His voice was distant.

"James, Serena and Madison are on their way up to you in the *Saturnia*. You'll need to get four people ready to join them once they dock. Three will have to remain until the second trip. Do you understand?"

"Don't need three. We lost one."

"What? What do you mean? Who did you lose?" Xanthe said, wide-eyed.

"Yuri. Yuri's gone. He ran out of oxygen and passed out. We sent Aidan out instead."

"Where is Yuri now?" Xanthe asked, dreading the answer she already knew.

"He's outside the escape pod. Still hooked on," James wept.

"James. James! It's okay. Stay focused. We're coming for you. Give us an oxygen status update, please."

Her commanding voice cut through his emotion, and he seemed to rally. He raised his arm display and stared at it. "I've got two percent."

"Check the others."

They watched him float towards his colleagues, bundled in the cramped space. Several had their eyes closed and looked pale. "One percent. Two percent. Three percent. Zero percent." He shook the shoulders of the last figure. "Youssef! Youssef! Wake up, Youssef!" James cried gently.

"Youssef is a big fella. He must have used up his O2 quicker than the others," Jonas whispered.

"James! James, listen to me," Xanthe commanded. "I need you to calm down. Take a few easy, slow breaths. We need to lower your heart rate. I need you to stay focused while we get the rescue happening. Do you understand?"

James grasped Youssef by the helmet and pressed his own helmet's face plate glass to his colleague's in silence. After a moment, he released it and turned back to the comms.

"Yeah. I got it. I'm here," he said.

"*Gateway*, this is *Saturnia*. We are nearby and on approach. Please clear the channel, over."

"James, we'll keep our visuals on but clear the channel for Madison and Serena. We'll be right here waiting for you," she said earnestly.

Xanthe nodded to Jonas, and he switched them to mute.

Troy came up behind her and placed a hand on her shoulder. She looked up at him and his blue eyes were full of pain, and her own filled with tears. She placed her own hand over his, grateful for the warmth and kindness of the moment.

Then she patted his hand and pulled away. The *Saturnia* filled the screen.

All they could do from here was wait.

CHAPTER TEN

"Under pressure, every choice weighs a ton."

—Athena A.I., Olympus Log

Madison guided the flight stick with small, deft movements of her gloved thumb and forefinger. *Just like a fighter jet*, she reminded herself. *This baby is a little touchy, like those big, sleek airforce beasts.*

Serena hummed to herself. *That woman couldn't shut her mouth if the president himself was barking at her*, Madison thought.

"Hey, what's that?" Serena said and gestured to the port-side camera display.

Madison glanced away from her trajectory for a moment to see what she was referring to.

"Athena, can you identify that object on the port display?" Serena said.

"It appears to be an astronaut attached to the *Gateway* by an EVA tether," the A.I. said.

"Well, they need to move out of the way! We are incoming. *Gateway*, can you get your astronaut to move out of the way, please?" Serena said as she depressed the comms channel button.

"Can't. Yuri can't."

"Why not?" Serena said, with a hint of frustration.

"He's dead."

Out of the corner of her eye, Madison saw Serena flop back in her chair. She let her own shock appear and then pushed it to a different corner of her mind to deal with later.

Serena leaned forward again. "I'm sorry to hear that, James. Can you activate the retrieval mechanism to pull him out of the way?"

"Negative. It's on manual because of the damage."

"Well. Shit," Serena said after she released the comms button. "What are we going to do now? We can't dock with poor Yuri floating in the way. He'll be crushed. And we won't be able to get a seal."

"Maybe they can send someone out to move him out of the way," suggested Madison.

Serena nodded and leaned forward over the comms panel. "James, can you send someone out to move him?"

There was a long pause, and Serena was about to ask a second time when James answered, "Give me a moment. We're going to pool some oxygen into my suit."

Madison and Serena looked at each other.

"That's bad. Real bad," said Serena.

Madison knew Serena was reliving a scenario during selection for the Olympus project bid. In the simulation, they were trapped on a Moon base with no hope of rescue for all of them. One person had to donate their oxygen, or they all died. Serena had donated hers.

"Serena, I'm topped up now. I've got about one percent remaining. I should be able to get out and pull Yuri out of the way," he said. He spoke slowly with brief pauses as he laboured to speak.

"Roger that. We are ready and waiting," Serena said.

Madison continued the careful approach as the *Gateway* moved into greater focus. Yuri swayed gently on the end of his tether. Madison risked another glance. It all looked rather peaceful.

The stark white of his suit against the deep black of space. *Not a bad place to die.* She pushed that thought into another corner.

"Where is he?" Serena said in exasperation. "James, what is your status?" They could not see him on the display as the airlock was out of the camera range.

His voice came through, panting. "Can't – shift – the lock. It's – stuck. I'm – too – weak – to – force it."

"Well, shit sticks," Serena said. She flopped back in her chair again.

"You're going to have to go out," Madison said. "I can't get any closer and Yuri is in my direct path. Once we get a good dock and lock, we should be able to open their door from our side."

"I've never done an EVA," Serena said.

"That makes two of us," Madison added. "But we did a ton in space training. You got this, Serena." Madison reached out her fist and Serena bumped it back.

"Alright. Let's do this thing. James, I'm coming out to move Yuri and clear the path for docking."

"Thank you." His voice was a whisper.

Madison watched as Serena undid her chair restraints, moved out of the navigation pod and pulled herself along the access ladder all the way to the bottom airlock, following Serena's movements on the *Saturnia*'s cameras. They had comms through their helmets.

Madison heard Serena list all the checks. *That's right*, she thought, *let the training kick in and do its job.*

Athena worked with Serena to release the airlock when she was ready. Madison put the craft in a stable position and monitored any drift. She saw Serena move towards Yuri. *That's pretty grim*, Madison thought. She imagined what it would be like to take hold of, and move, a corpse in space. *At least they would be weightless.* Madison shook her head to clear her mental chatter. *Where are these thoughts coming from?*

Madison watched Serena approach Yuri and pause before she secured him by the arm.

"Come on, big fella," Serena said. "We're going to give you a better viewing platform." Madison could hear the grief in Serena's voice.

Serena adjusted her propulsion system to account for the additional mass and together they shifted out of the way and alongside the *Gateway*.

Alas, poor Yuri. Madison poked her own leg to stop the dark, Shakespearian humour from taking hold of her thoughts. She knew it was only a stress mechanism, but she didn't need it to interfere right now with the rescue operation.

"Alright, Mad Dog. I've tied Yuri securely to the scaffolding. He shouldn't budge during our approach. I'm coming back, now."

Once Serena was back in the ship and secure in her seat, Madison resumed the approach. Athena gave her feedback every few seconds and together they adjusted course. The docking cone of the *Saturnia* edged closer and then shuddered into place.

"*Gateway*, we have docked safely," said Madison. There was no response. She repeated the message.

"James? Do you read?" Serena said. There was nothing. Dread spread between them. Madison nodded to Serena, and she unbuckled to activate the airlock. She moved up into the space and opened their side of the dock. The *Gateway* access stood before her with a small portal window. Serena peered through it.

"I can see them! James! James!" She pounded on the door. "Can you hear me? I'm here! Yes! I'm here! He can see me! He can hear me!" Serena grabbed the door lever and wrenched at it.

"Damn it!" she said and worked at it. It wouldn't move. "Come on, you bastard! Open up!" She hauled at it again.

Madison checked the flight controls to reassure herself they were stable. Then she broke flight protocols, unbuckled and joined Serena at the docking door. Madison glanced inside as she took hold of the lever. James was floating, unconscious, in the small space. No movement from any of the others.

They groaned and heaved, and at last there was a shudder and the door swung open, bumping James. He floated awkwardly against the other secured astronauts. Serena pushed inside and grabbed him.

"James? James! Do you hear me? We're here! You're safe! James?" She shook him and he flopped, unresponsive.

"Serena, check his wrist pad readings." It was Troy's voice, coming through the *Gateway* comms.

Serena signalled a thumbs up and moved James's arm so she could see the reading. "Zero percent. Red line," she said with a quaver.

"How long has it been red lined?" Troy's voice was business-like.

Serena peered at the reading again. "Seven minutes."

Surely it hadn't taken them that long to get the door open, Madison thought. But maybe it had.

"Serena, stop that." Troy's voice pushed into the room.

Serena was opening her dispenser tube. She was getting ready to give James her oxygen. "He's gone, Serena. He's gone. Check the others. See if anyone else. . .could use your oxygen," he said, avoiding the grim assessment.

He's worried, thought Madison. She knew Troy well since her intensive one-on-one back at the New Baths of Caracalla. Worry rarely featured in his communication profile. As the primary medical officer at the Olympus Base, he would have been calculating their oxygen reserves since they left.

Madison and Serena checked each astronaut one by one.

"Zero percent. Red line, eight minutes. Zero percent, red line, ten minutes. Zero percent, red line, nine minutes. Zero percent, red line, eight and half minutes. Zero percent, red line, seven minutes." Serena dropped the wrist of the last astronaut, and it drifted in front of her. "They're gone. All of them. Gone. We were ten minutes too late." Serena croaked as the tears welled up.

Xanthe's voice came through the comms. "Listen to me,

Serena. You did all you could. Troy is going to walk you through all the checks to make extra sure they're. . .that we have the correct readings. Do you understand?"

"Copy that, Commander," Madison said when Serena did not reply. "And once we confirm the readings, what do we do with. . .everybody?"

"Leave them in situ."

That made sense. There was no point bringing the bodies back to the Moon base, anyway. Again, Madison was surprised by her own cold, clinical assessment.

"And what about Yuri?" she added. There was a pause.

"Leave him where he is. Once the assessments are done, you'll need to return to base."

Madison noted the disturbance that rippled through her.

"What? Just leave him strung up outside to the *Gateway*? We can't do that," Serena retorted.

"Serena, no further harm can come to him where he is. You don't have enough oxygen in your own suit to do another EVA and get back here, do you?" It was Troy's voice again. He was measured, smooth.

Serena looked at her own display. "No. I don't." Her voice was flat now.

Xanthe came back on the comms. "We've lost enough people today. Finish the job and get yourselves back here."

"Yes, Commander," Madison said. She looked at Serena, who had stifled her grief and then set to the grisly task.

CHAPTER ELEVEN

*"Life-threatening conditions sharpen the human
spirit, forging it like tempered steel."*

—ATHENA A.I., OLYMPUS LOG

MADISON AND SERENA worked swiftly, confirming all the astronauts were deceased. Xanthe and Troy acknowledged the report and gave them clearance for return to the Moon.

They retreated to *Saturnia* and worked together to seal off the *Gateway*. They were leaving it up to NASA and the *Starship's* return flight crew to retrieve the bodies. If they did retrieve them. They might opt for a space burial, to float forever among the stars. *I wonder what the families will want*, thought Madison.

Serena hefted the lock shut and rested her head against the doorway. She sobbed.

"It's not fair. They were all good people. If only we'd worked harder, faster. We might have saved them. And now they're stuck in this godawful tin can of a crypt."

Madison patted her back awkwardly, at a loss for words. It wasn't her first brush with death, having been in the military for as long as she had been. And it probably wouldn't be the last. She'd honour them all later. For now, they needed to get back on the

Moon, back to Olympus. They needed to focus on getting home safe again.

"Come on. Let's go. We've got the Olympus base to focus on now," Madison said. She turned to haul herself into the pilot's chair.

"How can you be so cold?" Serena asked.

Madison shrugged. "We've got a job to do."

"But these people are all dead! Seven people – gone. Just like that."

Madison said nothing and focused on doing the pre-launch checks.

"Seriously? Don't you feel *anything*?"

Madison stopped what she was doing and turned to face Serena. "Look, Serena, I've seen a lot in the military. People die. That's just the way it is. It comes with the job. We all knew it when we signed up for this rodeo. It sucks and it hurts. Those guys were my buddies too. But we have a job to do and that means we need to focus.

"There is no place more risky than space. We're lucky *we're* not dead alongside them. That meteor strike could have meant the end for all of us. I, for one, am grateful I've still got air to breathe and a place to go back to. But if we don't hurry, we won't even have that. So, get your scrawny butt in that chair, buckle up and get your head straight. We need you to be on top of your game. That life support system is going to need all your focus."

Serena stared at Madison's dark face as it sparked with determination. For once, she stayed quiet and did as commanded.

CHAPTER TWELVE

"Though death and destruction are a necessary precursor to renewal, when wrought by violence, the wake lingers long and desolate."

—ATHENA A.I., OLYMPUS LOG

XANTHE WATCHED THE *Saturnia* land safely. Her shoulders dropped a little in relief. One less moving part.

She needed to call Gaia Headquarters. NASA was aware of the *Gateway* tragedy and was furiously discussing next steps with its spacefaring partners. No one liked the idea of leaving six dead astronauts in their capsule. And a seventh strapped to its hull. Xanthe thought of his family.

Imagine knowing your son, or husband, or father had been left roped to the outside of the spacecraft. It was ghoulish.

The other two astronauts rescued by the *Chang-e* were in Colonel Jin's care at Red Star. The Chinese rushed the astronauts into their medical facility. Colonel Jin was keeping NASA up to date on their progress.

Xanthe sighed and rolled her shoulders. She felt sick to her stomach. The painkillers were wearing off, and she was desperately tired with no time for a break. Not until she'd spoken to Maja, debriefed the team and established the next steps.

Xanthe moved to the private comms room as Jonas, Xavier and Troy assembled a meal for the team meeting.

"Athena, connect me with Maja at Gaia Headquarters, please."

"Patching you through now, Commander."

"Xanthe. What is the status update?" Maja's usually warm face was pinched and pale.

"*Saturnia* has landed, and we're waiting for Serena and Madison to return and get out of their suits before the debrief."

"How's the crew?"

Xanthe considered the question. There had been little time for emotion. It had been one crisis after another.

"Honestly, I don't know. I think we're all in shock. James and the crew were our mates. They were counting on us. And we couldn't deliver." Xanthe stopped as she felt the prickly tingle of grief curl through her body.

Maja stared at her, reading the micro-clues of her body language and getting a gauge on her emotional state.

"Okay," she said. "Once you debrief the crew, you'll need to organise a party to deliver the seedlings to Red Star base, retrieve the plexiglass and bring the *Gateway* astronauts back to Olympus."

"Is that wise? I understood they're in critical condition."

"NASA doesn't want their astronauts being left with the Chinese." Maja paused, then added, "They also think that it would be better for morale to have their astronauts back in Artemis."

"But we haven't had a chance to check out Artemis. We've been focused on Olympus and the *Gateway* mission. Artemis might also be compromised. We simply don't have enough staff resources to deal with that base on top of ours."

"I understand that. They just want their people back in our territory. Get the crew working on the Olympus base while you and Troy go to Red Star. Troy can manage the medical attention of the astronauts while you deal with the Colonel."

"I'm not even sure Olympus will handle an additional two people in its current damaged state."

"Make it work, Commander. Get the resources, retrieve the astronauts, do the repairs."

Xanthe felt distress turning to resentment. This was not like Maja to be so directive, nor to dismiss her concerns, valid ones. Especially with survival and safety. Something else must be driving her, Xanthe thought.

"Maja, what is it? What else is going on?"

Maja held her gaze and then looked down. She shook her head as if arguing with herself.

"I didn't want to tell you, as you already have enough to contend with."

"What? Maja? Tell me."

Maja sighed and looked directly at Xanthe.

"There's been a major ecoterrorism event here on Earth. A band of militants have sabotaged the terraforming equipment at the North and South Poles and inadvertently triggered a major terraforming weather event."

"What kind of weather event?" Xanthe asked in a low voice.

"Massive polar melt through nuclear explosion leading to flooding, tsunamis and devastating hurricanes."

Xanthe registered the news and took a moment to let it wash over her. That kind of terraforming was in the design phase only. It wasn't meant to occur on Earth as they knew the side effects of the activity would be thousands – perhaps millions – of people drowned and displaced. It would help reset the climate change effects but at a huge human and ecological cost.

And the tsunamis. . .The flashbacks were fierce. For a moment she was back in Sydney, fifteen years ago, the day the tsunami wiped out the city and most of the east coast of Australia. It drowned most of her family, including her four-year-old son Jack who was ripped from her hand.

Xanthe breathed deeply to clear the panic that always came with thoughts of that thunderous wall of water. "How bad is it?"

"Three hundred thousand dead so far. And rising. It's only been a day."

Xanthe gasped and covered her mouth. So many! Her thoughts flew to her ex-husband, Simon, who still lived in Sydney. Or what was left of it. Even their rebuilds and new habitat designs hadn't quite erased the carnage of that day.

"Simon?"

"He's the first one we called. He's alive and safe."

Xanthe let out a breath.

"What do I say to the crew?"

"They'll no doubt want to talk to their families and check in on them. We will attempt to locate them from our end here. Communications are difficult right now."

"Yes, I imagine they are. As soon as you have news of our families, send it through. The crew needs to know as soon as possible. I need them to be focused on our survival, too."

"Xanthe."

She looked again at Maja with the change of tone.

"There's more."

Xanthe's eyes widened.

"We have reason to believe Claire Edwards is responsible for at least one of the sabotage crews."

"Claire? What? How?"

Maja's mouth turned down and her eyebrows furrowed. Her protégé was guilty of so many betrayals. Xanthe felt her regret through the holo.

"Claire. Well, I can't explain or excuse her behaviour," Maja said finally. "But the reason we want those astronauts back on our base is that we are unsure how the Chinese will react to this news. It's not widely known at the moment, but it's bound to come out soon. That's why it is urgent for you to move on the exchange and retrieval plan as soon as you can."

"I understand."

"Good. Go now. And look after yourself."

Maja's image disappeared, and Xanthe stared at the blinking comms display.

With devastation everywhere, she had never felt so alone.

CHAPTER THIRTEEN

*"Torn between two worlds, the heart learns
to dwell in the spaces in-between."*

—ATHENA A.I., OLYMPUS LOG

XANTHE STARED AT the morose faces of her crew. They'd reviewed all the steps they'd taken since the meteorite strike, including the rescue attempt of the *Gateway* team. The one bright spot were the survivors, Kwanda Mendoza and Dr. Aidan O'Sullivan, now being looked after at Red Star base. Xanthe was looking forward to seeing them soon.

The life support systems on Olympus were stable, but they would feel the strain in the next twelve hours. Adding two more humans to the mix would make it a difficult situation until they repaired the Atrium. They pared water use back to essentials for drinking and keeping the plants alive in the Swamp. Definitely no showers.

And now she had to tell them about the ecoterrorism incident. Faces turned from despondency to distress. Xavier spoke first.

"*Ma famille*! I need to talk to them!" His wife and teenage daughters lived in Naples. They were not in immediate harm's way, Xanthe knew, but Xavier suffered from the burden of being away from his family for so long. His inability to protect them from harm was a daily stab of guilt.

"Maja's working on it, Xavier. As soon as they've contacted our families, she'll let us know. She's also going to give them our status report. They might have heard about the meteor strike. Xavier, you'll stay on the base here with Serena, Madison and Jonas, so you'll be able to connect with them as soon as we can get a channel hook up. The satellite comms are obviously busy." Xanthe glanced at Jonas, who looked thoughtful.

"Jonas, we've heard news of your family. The *Sea Rover* is fine and is on its way to help Argentina. They seem the hardest hit at this stage."

Jonas snorted. "Nothing will sink the *Sea Rover*. And it will take more than Claire and her band of eco-twits to drown dear old dad, Don Seaborn. That crusty old bastard will outrust us all. He's hard, like a barnacle."

"Will you want to speak with him?" asked Madison. "You can take my call time if you'd like."

"Ahh, that would be a hard 'no'. I've got nothing to say to that old prick. Thank you anyway, Mad Dog." Glancing at her, he added, "Don't you have someone you want to check in with?"

"My mum is fine where she is. No floods likely in Arizona. I spoke to her last week."

"Troy? Who's on your priority list?" asked Xanthe.

"Just Elizabeth, my assistant. She was taking a break in Spain, so she's likely fine. But I would appreciate an update. Thanks."

"Serena?" Xanthe asked.

Serena sat back in her chair and crossed her arms. They all knew she had no family.

"My neighbour was looking after my apartment in Sydney. I'd love an update for sure. From what you said, though, Sydney was out of the firing line. Sounds like Tasmania copped the worst of it." Serena leaned forward and tapped the table. "What I really want to know is how the hell Claire got caught up in this? What happened to her court case?"

"The charges were dismissed due to lack of evidence," Xanthe said.

"She used one of my teas to knock Maja out," Troy said. "They leave no trace. They're only meant as a mild sedative. Claire must have upped the dose. It isn't lethal, though."

"Is that what happened?" Madison asked. "I always wondered."

Claire had been the Chief Operating Officer for Gaia Enterprises for years and central to the success of its major projects. Things fell apart during the Olympus project prototype build when she'd allegedly poisoned Maja and taken control of the project after she disagreed with Maja's decisions on staffing.

Maja survived the incident but during her incapacitation, funder Aryanna Sharif took control of Gaia and, once she discovered what Claire was up to, had her arrested.

"I knew that witch was ousted in disgrace. I don't know how Maja put up with that power tripper for so long. But going rogue? Militant eco group? That's a bit extreme, even for her," Serena said.

"She is. . . a bit intense," Troy said. "She was never really comfortable with the space exploration side of Gaia Enterprises. Once her career was effectively over at Gaia, I guess she figured it was the best way to channel her resentment."

"Well, you would know," Jonas said. "Didn't you and Claire. . .?"

"Once. A long time ago," Troy retorted. Xanthe watched his face cloud just a little.

"Let's get back to the task at hand," Xanthe said. "We've got the base to work on, and Troy and I need to load the rover with our seedlings. We need to get over to the Red Star before Colonel Jin changes his mind."

"First, we need some rest," Troy added. "It's late into our sleep cycle already and we can't afford any fatigue-related mistakes.

Doctor's orders. I'll organise a tincture that will cut through the adrenaline and help soothe the parasympathetic nervous system."

"Watch the dose, *mon vieux*. None of us want to do Maja's sleeping beauty trick," Xavier said.

"Please. I'm a professional. No sleeping beauties, just a little beauty sleep. God knows you need it, Xavier!"

At last, a little humour, thought Xanthe. They needed it badly. But right now, she and the others needed rest more.

"Right, then," she said. "Tea, then bed. See you all in a few hours."

CHAPTER FOURTEEN

*"The human guidance system is remarkable. Armed with both
a brain and a heart, it is astonishing how often humans favour
one over the other, instead of deploying them together."*

—ATHENA A.I., OLYMPUS LOG

FOUR HOURS WASN'T enough to reboot their energy completely, but it was good enough for now. The Olympus life support system repair was paramount.

Xavier helped Troy and Xanthe load his precious seedlings on to the rover.

"I give the *salaud* my smallest plants. He can do the hard work of getting them to grow in low G. I hope they have good lamps. I don't want to waste all these resources because of substandard gear," Xavier said.

"I'm sure their equipment is just fine. They've fed billions on Earth, and their base is twice as large as ours already," Xanthe said.

"Why do they need my plants, then?"

"Because your plants are the best, with the biggest yields and best taste."

"This is true," Xavier said, enjoying the acknowledgement.

"Don't feed his ego, Xanthe. The man can barely fit into his spacesuit as is," Troy said.

"That is because the protein mix is not the right balance. I told you many times, Troy!" Xavier patted his stomach self-consciously. "Anyway, more of me for Maryse to love."

"I think what is not the 'right balance' is your exercise regime. Or lack thereof."

"Enough, you two. Let's get going. Xavier, we'll check in once we're at Red Star. And say hello to Maryse if you make contact."

"*Bien sûr. And bonne chance.*"

Xanthe and Troy clambered into the rover and did the checks while Xavier retreated through the airlock and sealed it, ready for their departure. With a thumbs up, the outer door slid open, and they rolled out over the Moonscape.

Xanthe peered out over the harsh landscape: a crone's chalk-painted face pocked with ancient scars. Her heart soared as it did every time she glimpsed the Earth, pouting, a watery nymph bedazzled in blue and a sea of clouds, the opulence of life obscene against the cold, obsidian curtain of space.

Why are we here?

The thought sometimes niggled at her.

Earth hung there, beckoning, teeming with life, water, air. And they were here, scratching out a perilous existence on this lifeless wasteland.

And yet.

It was amazing. Living on the Moon was miraculous. And she was grateful for it.

"How are the stitches?" Troy asked, jolting her from her reverie. She was instantly aware of the awkwardness of being alone with him for the next two hours. His leg bumped against hers as they ambled along.

Thank goodness for spacesuits, she thought. *I can't feel his body heat. Or smell his musk. That scent of cloves that drives me crazy.* She felt her body respond with desire. *Damn it!* Just the thought of him stoked inner fires. *No time for that. No room for that. The Olympus mission takes priority.*

"Stitches? They're a little sore. I think they're weeping a little. My shirt seems a little stuck and caked around them."

"I'll take a look later."

She imagined Troy removing her shirt and swabbing her with a warm, wet towel. It was enough to send her imagination reeling again.

"Did Maja mention when they'll be able to send a resupply ship? Or if NASA will retrieve the *Gateway* crew?"

"No." Xanthe was stilted. *Damn.* She just could not relax around him. All that pent up desire with nowhere to go.

"How much longer do you think we'll need to stay past our original departure date?"

"Don't know."

"Best guess?"

Lordie, he doesn't give up. She inhaled and breathed out slowly. Just focus on his conversation.

"Well, we were due to leave in six months. Now we can't because we used up too much fuel on the *Gateway* trip. We might be able to make some, but the distiller is nowhere near ready, and we've got to rebuild the Atrium first.

"Gaia does not have any other space vehicle, so they'd have to borrow or piggyback on NASA's trip. And given they've just lost seven people, they won't be rushing into anything soon. So, we might be here for another nine months, at least, until they can figure something out."

"I wouldn't mind."

Xanthe glanced at Troy. He was looking at her with soft eyes.

"Really? Don't you want to get back home? Go to the beach? Swim in the ocean? Feel the sun on your skin without worrying you are going to die instantly?"

He laughed. "I miss all those things, sure. But every day here is precious. With you, I mean."

Xanthe's face flushed, and she looked away. She wasn't ready for this conversation. She'd told him she wasn't ready, that she still had to process her divorce. And focus on the mission. She deflected. "I just want to make sure everyone is safe. Olympus is secure. Ready for visitors and inhabitants. Do our job, just like we signed up for."

"And what happens after that?" He leaned towards her, forcing her to look into his face. The blue of his eyes was mesmerising. The thick eyebrows, the straight nose, the matted blonde locks, the full lips that quirked into a smile. She imagined those lips hot and pressing against her own. She swallowed.

"Don't know. I'll deal with that when the time comes. Right now, we have lives to save, including our own."

After a few more seconds of searching her face, he took the hint and reclined again in his chair, and stared out over the sterile, ashy landscape.

After a while, Troy said, "My brother would like it here." He waved towards the viewfinder and the grey sea of dust. "He always had a taste for the macabre."

Xanthe blinked and glanced at him. "You have a brother? I didn't know that."

"Uh huh. Twin brother. Travis."

"You never talk about him. . ."

Troy sighed. "We don't get along."

"Why not?"

"Our parents gave me funds to build the New Baths of Caracalla. It drove Travis mad. Thought it was an enormous waste of money. He resented the hell out of it."

"But the Baths are a triumph! An immense success. You won awards. . ."

"That just made it worse. My fame fuelled his bitterness. When our parents died, he challenged the will. Tried to get the money they gave me for Caracalla back into the estate. Said it wasn't fair to the grandkids, having their inheritance squandered on a 'den of inequity.'"

"I'm sorry, Troy." Anguish wrinkled his brow. "Family is so precious. Losing connection is. . . devastating."

He stared out at the lifeless horizon.

"If you don't mind, I'm going to nap. Get some rest while we can," he said.

She wasn't sure, but she thought she heard a trace of sadness in his voice. It stabbed icicles of longing and regret through her heart.

CHAPTER FIFTEEN

*"Collaboration without a shared intention is a castle
made of sand. One big storm washes it all away."*

—Athena A.I., Olympus Log

The Red Star base glowed on the horizon, a warm yellow bumble
bee against the dead blackness of space. Xanthe couldn't help
admiring the buildings. They'd opted to build their first base above
ground, importing linkable pods from Earth.

Like Olympus, they had a central dome for their principal
activity. It connected the pods that spread like spider's legs across
the grey dust of the South Pole. Xanthe knew they were hoping
to find lava tubes nearby that they could access, seal and develop
into more secure habitats, instead of excavating to begin with, like
Olympus had done.

Xanthe hailed Red Star as they approached. They did not have
an airlock for vehicles, so Troy and Xanthe secured their helmets
and suits before exiting the rover through its inner airlock. A handful of Red Star staff joined them to help ferry the seedlings back to
their base.

Xanthe and Troy followed them into one of the spider's leg

entrances for regolith air brushing and atmosphere pressurisation, before trailing their counterparts into the sausage-like passage.

Colonel Jin was waiting for them as they emerged out into the central hub.

"Commander Waters, Dr Bruin, welcome to Red Star."

The Colonel was shorter than she expected. Rotund and jowly, like a bulldog. The way the others walked around him, heads bowed in deference, created a bubble of awe. They didn't seem to use magnetic moonboots and the inhabitants leaned forward like sprinters to bound along the tunnels.

"Come. We will talk in my quarters." Colonel Jin spun and loped away. Xanthe and Troy struggled to emulate his stride and keep up with his pace. They sped through a series of tunnels and locks, passing impressive stations where all sorts of research was being conducted: plant genetics, food printing, solar and hydrogen energy processing. Xanthe was desperate to ask about it all but knew no answers would be forthcoming. This trip and tour was designed to impress, not educate.

And it was doing a stellar job. The tunnels were exceptionally clean. No sign of regolith dust anywhere. Everything was bright and cheery, with soft edges creating lightness and ease. All residents wore uniforms, and they seemed to operate seamlessly, in sync, choreographed. Xanthe felt a pang of envy. While she loved her crew, they had nowhere near the same cohesiveness she witnessed here.

Colonel Jin paused outside the greenhouse, twice the height of the other tunnels.

"I thought you might like to see where we will house your plants." His smile lit a sparkle in his eyes.

He opened the tunnel's security door, and they stepped into a humid space stacked high with white half-pipes, with growth mats sprouting various types of vegetables and leafy greens. Each layer of pipes sheltered under warm growth lamps.

Xanthe inhaled deeply and closed her eyes. The tunnel was so full of life it vibrated. The smell of living things, the humidity that settled on them, created a profound longing for Earth. She leaned a little towards the growth lamps, yearning to sun herself naked under them. There was a buzzing. She opened her eyes.

"Are those bees?" she asked, incredulous.

"Electronic ones, yes. We made them so they would sound like real bees. We think it helps the plants feel like it's more like home. The staff like it, too," he added.

"Impressive," Troy murmured.

The Colonel beamed with pride and satisfaction, then ushered them back into the tunnel. They resumed the athletic striding through several more connecting tunnels until they arrived outside a bright red door. The colour was a slap to their senses.

"Wow!" Xanthe said despite herself.

The panel door slid open to access his quarters. Jaws dropped. It was ostentatious and lush. Red velvet cushions on deep leather couches with rich carpets across the floor and soft lighting. Ornate wooden side tables with delicate golden ornaments.

It must have cost a bomb to bring all this up, thought Xanthe. Clearly, the Colonel was meant to be comfortable in space, no expense spared.

The Colonel spoke into his earpiece, and moments later an assistant entered bearing a tray of hot tea. No plastic dispensing bags here, just lovely, intricately decorated special porcelain space cups with a design that allowed for sipping without losing the contents in the low G. Xanthe was impressed, though she tried her best not to be.

After a few sips of tea, Troy leaned forward in his chair, unsettled.

"Colonel, if it's alright with you, may I see Kwanda and Aidan?" Troy asked. "I'm keen to check on them before we move them."

A shadow passed over Colonel Jin's eyes before he could catch it and resume his implacable demeanour.

"Of course, Dr Bruin." The Colonel touched his earpiece and sent a command. The assistant returned to usher Troy away.

"Now that we have a moment alone," Xanthe said carefully, "I'm grateful to have a more private conversation, Colonel."

There was a slight hesitation and a stare before he waved his hand to continue.

Xanthe studied the rim of her cup.

How do I broach the topic? She smiled. *Flies. Honey.*

"This is a nicely appointed room. Very luxurious. Do you intend to stay long term on the Moon?"

"We hope to stay one hundred years and more on the Moon," he replied with a dismissive puff of air. "We want to ensure comfort from the beginning. It will attract more settlers that way."

"Don't you order people to settle here?" Xanthe ventured.

Xanthe kicked herself. *A little too aggressive,* she thought. *Back it off a little.*

"No one is 'ordered', Commander Waters. People are expected to fulfil roles for the country. Some are space-oriented. There is no shortage of applicants."

"Are all the rooms as luxurious as this one?"

"Leadership is a burden that is only tempered by a few privileges." He sipped his tea. "This room is unique."

What bullshit! That's called a double standard. The elitism poked her sense of fairness.

"That seems to fly in the philosophy of egalitarianism. Isn't that a central aspect of Chinese governance?"

The Colonel's eyes flashed.

"All of us are equals, Commander. Privilege and privacy are simply aspects of the leadership role. Much like working in the greenhouse requires the wearing of gloves. Each role needs protection."

A velvet couch hardly seems like 'protection'.

Xanthe sipped some tea to cool the head of steam clouding

her thoughts. The next set of questions was delicate, and she didn't want to get him offside. "I'm curious, as one leader to another, how do you make decisions here?"

"What do you mean? What kind of decisions?"

"About the future of the base, about community harmony?"

"I make those decisions," he said coldly.

"Do you have any advisors?"

"I have my deputies who give me opinions when I ask."

Sounds reasonable.

"Why does everyone wear a uniform here?" It reminded her of school, even if it looked orderly.

"It builds a sense of team spirit and cohesion."

"What about individual self-expression? Don't people get frustrated having to wear the same thing every day?"

"They are self-expressed through their work. It requires much creativity, and all are appreciated."

Xanthe leaned forward to continue, but Colonel Jin interrupted her.

"If I may, Commander Waters, what does Olympus hope to achieve here on the Moon?"

"Olympus? It's no secret, Colonel. We are here to establish a multi-purpose facility that includes research, space tourism and a waypoint for asteroid mining. We hope to expand to allow community growth too, for expanding human habitat that is sadly under pressure on Earth."

"About that, Commander Waters." He snipped his words. A frisson of fear ran through her. "We have had the reports about the ecoterrorist activity on Earth. The reports are alarming."

"Yes. They are."

Does he know it might have been one of our own?

"Have you had any family affected?"

This caught her off guard. He had shown no signs of personal interest to date.

"I'm. . . we're not sure," she said at last. "Gaia Enterprises is contacting our families now to check on their welfare, and to let them know about the meteorite strike." She looked down to avoid his gaze. After a sip of tea, she added, "How about you? Any family affected?"

"My family is secure. Thank you for asking. We are focused now on addressing the humanitarian crisis around the globe."

Xanthe wondered if she should tell him about Claire. She could easily move on from this topic. But if she was going to build bridges with Colonel Jin and put Maja's plan into place, it was probably best that it came from her.

"Colonel Jin, I have some news about the ecoterrorism."

"Yes?"

"We believe it was a former Gaia employee, Claire Edwards, who led and coordinated the action."

"I see."

He knew already.

She didn't know what to say next.

Colonel Jin filled the void.

"And how will Gaia punish the crimes of a wayward employee?"

Her jaw tightened.

"Former employee." She sipped the tea, floral notes on bitter leaves. "My understanding is that Gaia is cooperating with the authorities and sharing whatever information they can to apprehend her and her associates."

"And what of Gaia Enterprises? How did it become a place for radicals?"

Xanthe's eyes narrowed. She slowed her breath as her heart pounded. She placed the teacup on the side table, slowly and carefully.

"We are all concerned about what happened to Claire. It's only when people feel isolated, rejected, that they turn to radical means. We all missed the signs." Xanthe stared at her lap for a moment, gathering her thoughts. "Our philosophy is to nurture a more inclusive and compassionate worldview for our team members and the inhabitants of all our communities."

"This philosophy seems to have failed Claire Edwards. Very frustrating, I'm sure. Though every ambitious philosophy has its blind spots."

Xanthe glanced up at Colonel Jin. His expression was unreadable.

"Wasn't she the Chief Operating Officer?"

"She was." Xanthe's mouth ran dry.

"Did you not also have one of your team sabotage the Olympus prototype build?"

How the hell did he know about Dave? They'd kept it very secret.

"I believe you are misinformed, Colonel. One of our team had significant family challenges. We worked with him to resolve those issues while we were finishing the prototype." That much was true.

"I see. Well, we never would have allowed such insubordination. Especially not from the second-in-command or on such an important project for the future of humanity."

Xanthe seethed. Were these insults? Or just observations? She said nothing.

"I know Gaia Enterprises prides itself on its collaborative approach to governance. Do you think this will hold fast in the challenging environment of the Moon? I can imagine the thought of such insubordination would be a very frightening proposition for you. We see now how loose governance can trigger tragedies. Nine astronauts dead from the lax and cavalier attitude of your counterparts, Spaceward Bound."

"Seven."

"Excuse me?"

"Seven dead astronauts. Not nine. Two survived."

"Ah. Yes. Seven."

Xanthe saw the same dark shadow flit across his face. Her skin prickled with apprehension.

Xanthe sipped more tea as she considered her next move. "So, Colonel Jin, what are the Red Star ambitions on the Moon?" Xanthe tried to appear nonchalant, to soothe the tension in the conversation. She wasn't sure she'd succeeded.

"It is no secret, Commander Waters." He smiled as he echoed her words. He was back on an even keel. "We are here for research and to establish a permanent Chinese community."

"How is the helium-3 research progressing?"

Colonel Jin chuckled and sipped his tea. "Surely, Commander, you don't expect me to reveal all of our commercial secrets?"

"No, but I am hoping we could work more collaboratively. We are both a long way from home, and we could each achieve our respective goals easier and faster if we shared information and resources."

He stared back at her with a blank expression.

Had she gone too far, too fast?

"I think, Commander, it is time to collect your astronauts."

CHAPTER SIXTEEN

"A person only dies when their memory does."

—Athena A.I., Olympus Log

The Colonel led Xanthe to the medical chamber. She brooded on their conversation as they bounded through the various linked tubes of Red Star.

She had hoped to build a connection with him but had been kept at arm's length. Were their philosophies really that far apart? Didn't they both want a secure future for their fellow humans? Though they were playing at collaboration and mutual support, competition for Moon resources crackled between them.

As they entered the medical chamber, Xanthe caught her breath at the sight of the two astronauts. They lay on beds with medical displays looming over them. They were still in their spacesuits and had ventilators and IV drips rigged up. Troy was checking their panels as she walked in.

Xanthe pulled up short when she saw the face of a second man rooting around in a drawer of medical instruments.

"What the hell are *you* doing here?" she demanded.

The man stopped what he was doing, stood up slowly and

looked at her. The stranger's face was implacable, waxy. Xanthe's pulse raced.

"I thought you were dead!" she blurted.

"As you can see, I am not dead."

What the actual hell? thought Xanthe. She turned to look at Colonel Jin. "What is going on here, Colonel?"

"Commander Waters, allow me to introduce Vladimir Volkov."

Vladimir Volkov stared unblinking, calculating, with black stones for eyes. He was short, the height where many men feel the need to compensate. His chest barrelled out under a pudgy round face with a peculiar skin tone, as if he were missing vitamins and proper kidney function. There was a snaky stillness to him that might silence the most menacing of attack dogs. Xanthe shivered.

She moved protectively between Vladimir Volkov and the unconscious astronauts. She knew this man. Despot. Cold-blooded killer. She didn't want him anywhere near the people in her care.

"I know who he is, Colonel, but what is he doing *here*? What is he doing with our astronauts?"

"He is assisting with their treatment."

"What? Why? What does the former President of Russia know about medicine in space? I'm sorry, Colonel, I'm lost."

Vladimir Volkov had disappeared at least two decades previously. The Russians had tried to bury the mystery, but his disappearance had sparked dozens of conspiracy theories. At the height of his powers, following a vicious invasion of Poland, the world had woken to the news that Vladimir Volkov was on 'extended holiday'. The news coverage had been unrelenting.

This was a man who had doggedly built Russian dominance through his Middle East alliances. In spite of sanctions and international western isolation, Russia had continued to grow its economic and political influence. His major coup had been aligning the Russian space program with the Chinese and abandoning the International Space Alliance once and for all.

But all this had come at a huge cost for the Russian people and Volkov himself. The oil and gas oligarchs had only gotten richer as they squeezed the markets, while ordinary Russians stayed cold and hungry. Asia had filled with fleeing Russian civilians as the social and economic infrastructure of Russia had frayed and unravelled.

Criticism had grown and so Volkov had ruled as only a despot can: with fear and threats of violence. And a trail of covert assassinations. When his policies had failed to address the Big Heat and the global climate crisis, a coalition had grown within Russia to topple Volkov and his oligarch associates. Revolution roiled with violent protests and coordinated attacks on oligarch properties.

Then he had disappeared, and Vladimir Volkov had become a boogeyman.

His enemies spent their days glancing back over shoulders, seeing his spectre in every corner. If he had died, the stink of terror lingered. Revolution had persisted and locked Russia in a civil war. Preoccupied with home affairs and a collapsing economy, the Russians' contribution to the Chinese space program had become more symbolic than substantive.

And now here Volkov was, some twenty years later, on the Moon.

"He's a Dopplebot," said Troy.

"Dopplebot?" Xanthe gasped. "When was he produced? Why? How many copies of him are there?" Xanthe shot the questions at Colonel Jin.

Colonel Jin walked over to stand beside the pasty figure of Vladimir Volkov. "We worked with our strategic partners to build President Volkov's Dopplebot. They wanted Russian leadership as part of the Red Star. We insisted they build him with practical spacefaring skills, such as medical capabilities. He's been very useful.

"As you know, a Dopplebot does not need food, oxygen, sleep, water. Only the occasional recharging. It's quite amazing how many tasks you can allocate a Dopplebot that saves human focus and minimises risks to humans who are more vulnerable to Moon and space-based exposure. Mr Volkov has been very helpful in the care of your astronauts." Colonel Jin patted the Dopplebot's shoulder.

"Mr? Not President?" Xanthe raised an eyebrow. She stared at the Colonel.

"Our agreement with the Russians included his presence but not a leadership role at this stage."

"So, what is he really, Colonel? A spy? Or a slave?"

Colonel Jin's face clouded and his eyes narrowed. She immediately regretted her outburst.

"He is a valued member of our crew and responsible for the welfare of our people," he said smoothly. "And he has been keeping your astronauts alive."

"Yes. Yes, of course," Xanthe said.

Her mind boggled. Dopplebots had been a Gaia Enterprises initiative in the first manmade floating community, Terra Blanca, but they'd had to sell off the business after the experiment ended in tragedy. The Chinese must have picked up the technology.

Dopplebots had gone out of fashion, being too expensive to make lifelike, and fights over the intellectual property rights of families had bogged down the reproduction of many luminaries.

But one can never discount the ego of a megalomaniac, especially one with power and money.

So, the Volkov Dopplebot was an ego project or an insurance policy. Maybe both.

Aware suddenly that she had been staring at the Volkov bot, she turned back to the Artemis astronauts.

"How are they?" She directed the question at Troy.

Troy looked at her with a grave expression, and she was immediately alarmed.

"Troy, what is it?" she asked.

"They're unresponsive."

"Unconscious?"

"No. Unresponsive. As in, brain dead."

"Oh my God. No," she whispered. *Not these two as well.* That was the entire *Gateway* and Artemis crews gone. Wiped out. And they had tried so hard to save them. She turned to Colonel Jin, searching for an explanation.

"When our team retrieved them from the spacewalk, they had already been unconscious, with no oxygen for some time. They had already collapsed."

"But Aidan? He was conscious when he left the *Gateway* – that is why they sent him out."

"He was near the red line when our team pulled him inside the *Chang-e*. Once onboard, they administered oxygen immediately from our supplies, but it was too late. We kept them on oxygen and have been monitoring them constantly. None of our attempts have reversed the damage."

Troy, Xanthe, Colonel Jin and Vladimir Volkov stared at the two prone figures. Kwanda's smooth brown face looked so peaceful. Xanthe thought of the woman's family back on Earth. Kwanda was a proud mother, and she often regaled the Artemis and Olympus crews with her kids' achievements, alongside mischievous exploits. Her kids wouldn't see their mother's laughing face again.

And Aidan. The larrikin Irishman whose socks always smelled and stunk up Artemis. His crew complained about it incessantly. So, he took to hiding his socks in their respective sleeping bags. Now he was gone. And so was his entire crew. No more smelly socks. No more complaints. No more jokes.

The hiss and pop of the ventilators filled the room.

"What do you wish to do with their bodies?" asked Colonel Jin. "We can take them off life support here and prepare them for transfer to Olympus. That is probably the most sensible. Otherwise, their bodies will simply consume resources that could otherwise be used for the living."

Xanthe knew he was right, but she still shivered at the cold brutality of the situation.

"We will need to consult NASA and their families first," Xanthe said.

"Of course. Please follow me to the communications chambers and we will provide a link for you."

Troy put his arm around Xanthe, and for once she was grateful for his touch.

CHAPTER SEVENTEEN

*"Disaster speaks a universal language, understood
by all, uniting even the most divided."*

—ATHENA A.I., OLYMPUS LOG

XANTHE FOLLOWED COLONEL Jin to the communication centre, comprising little nooks along a corridor, easily watched from the centre.

So much for privacy, thought Xanthe. No doubt it was also for surveillance. She shoved her cynical thoughts aside and sat down at the console after Colonel Jin had logged in. She put in a comms request for Gaia Enterprises Headquarters and waited.

The display showed a search for connection but no contact. She cancelled the request and then tried again. Still the display showed no contact. This was disconcerting. Gaia Enterprises had its own private satellite network to ensure constant communications with the Moon base. With its range, it should work, even from the Red Star base.

She tried again with the same result. She paused for a moment, thinking about her next steps, and then racked her brain for NASA's top level emergency comms link. Maja had given it to her when the meteorite strike happened. She punched that into the console and waited. Still there was no signal.

Xanthe turned and called out to Colonel Jin, who was waiting nearby. "Colonel, I can't seem to contact either Gaia Enterprises or NASA. Shall we try a different console?"

The Colonel smiled with patronising deference and then leaned over her to press reset on the console. It tried again, and still the spinning wheel of a failed connection continued its torturous display. They moved to a second console and repeated the process. And then a third.

Colonel Jin spoke harshly into his earpiece and within moments, a staff member came running. The technician repeated all the steps they had just undertaken with growing bewilderment. They exchanged terse words in Mandarin.

The Colonel gathered himself, and then said to Xanthe, "It seems there are problems with communications with Earth. We will head to my private accommodation and try the console there."

He sped off, and Xanthe had a hard time keeping up with him. The display in his private room had the same outcome. His lips drew together as he became more and more concerned.

"Let's try the Olympus base," said Xanthe. "That way we can test whether it's the Red Star, Earth satellites or Earth comms."

Colonel Jin did as she suggested without making a comment, and Jonas's voice and face popped up on the display almost immediately.

"Colonel Jin. This is Olympus base. Xanthe! What can I do for you?" he asked.

Xanthe jumped in before the Colonel could say anything. "Jonas, have you been able to contact Earth recently?"

"We've been waiting for Maja to call us with updates on our families. We haven't had a report in. . ." He looked at his wrist display. "About three hours."

"Can you do me a favour and try now?"

"Sure."

They watched Jonas key in the Gaia Enterprises link and wait.

"That's strange," said Jonas.

They watched him repeat the process, and his eyes grew wide as nothing connected.

"I don't seem to have a link," said Jonas with a hint of concern.

"Neither do we. It seems comms with Earth are down. We can't get Gaia Enterprises or NASA. The Colonel can't reach his command centre either. There's something interfering with Earth comms."

Jonas rubbed his jaw. "What do we do?"

"Let's get Athena onto it. Maybe she can figure out what happened Earthside. It could be the orbiting satellites, or it could be the dishes on Earth. In either case, we have comms between our bases, which is good."

"I'll get Athena onto that right now. When are you heading back with Kwanza and Aidan?"

Xanthe flinched. She hadn't decided when to tell the others. Well, she wasn't in the habit of hiding information from them. Most information, that was.

"Jonas, I have bad news."

"Oh?"

She watched him ground his legs, bracing for whatever came next.

"Kwanda and Aidan didn't make it. They're on life support right now, but they're brain dead. Too long without oxygen. I was hoping to reach NASA and the families so we can get their permission to. . . take them off life support."

"Oh, my God. I'm so sorry to hear that." Jonas ran his hands through his hair, as if he could rub the bad news off his body. He regrouped and asked, "Seeing as we don't have comms of the Earth, what will you do?"

"We can't leave them on life support indefinitely when there is no expectation of their survival. So, I'll do my best for them."

The stark reality of the situation sat between them, like a fire doused with dishwater.

"Understood, Commander. Let me know what you need from us here."

"In the meantime, I would like you to go over and check out Artemis. We need to see if it was damaged at all and where we might put Kwanda and Aidan on our return."

Jonas nodded. "Copy that. I'll get Xavier and Madison on it."

"Good. Thank you. We will load up the plexiglass and" – she was about to say 'the bodies' – "Kwanda and Aidan. We will be on our way within the next two hours." Xanthe looked at Colonel Jin for confirmation, and he nodded back.

"Roger that. See you soon."

Colonel Jin toyed with one of his cuff links, as Xanthe signed off. Then he tugged the sleeves of his uniform and cleared his throat.

"Commander Waters, this communication with Earth creates a challenge for us." He cleared his throat again. "We will need to depend on one another for at least a short term."

Xanthe turned to face him. His face had lost its haughtiness. "Agreed."

"I suggest you take Mr Volkov with you back to Olympus. He can assist with the repairs of your base. He won't be a burden on resources either. You can use him to help fix communications and any repairs needed at Artemis or Olympus base."

Xanthe considered Colonel Jin's offer. She searched his face for any duplicity or understated ambition. It was a mask once more.

Is he offering a spy or truly sending help?

"Why are you relinquishing your Dopplebot now? Isn't he useful for you here?"

"Of course, he is useful. But it seems to me you need him more. Your base is compromised, your spacecraft is damaged and you need to manage nine deceased colleagues. Lending help is the human thing to do." He smiled graciously.

The thought of the murderous Volkov as part of their team made her shudder. But if it was a bot, and a reprogrammed one, then it might be useful. They just needed to get over his appearance. She wondered what Troy might say. He was always so pragmatic about sensitivities.

Xanthe thought about everything she could get Volkov to do. The bot would be really useful in the Atrium where their dwindling oxygen presented a double challenge for repairs. It could look after the bodies in Artemis. It could even help Xavier in the Swamp as the fumes would not affect it.

Xanthe nodded at the Colonel. "Alright. I accept your offer. Thank you. We will return the bot as soon as the repairs are done. In the meantime, let's keep our communication open. If you hear any other news from Earth, please let us know."

"Of course," he said. "You can depend on me."

Could they really? It had taken nine deaths and a satellite failure to push them towards cooperation. Maybe they could get to collaboration after that.

CHAPTER EIGHTEEN

"First impressions are the mind's shortcuts to complex equations: helpful yet often incomplete."

—ATHENA A.I., OLYMPUS LOG

IT WAS A sombre ride back to the Olympus base. Xanthe kept reliving the moment when Troy took the astronauts off life support and they gurgled their last breaths. She wondered where the emotion was for her. It was such a horrific end to their rescue attempt. And yet she felt nothing. Just a hole where nine people used to be. She wondered if it might hit her later. Or maybe she'd lost her capacity to feel deeply. Maybe Luna, the barren witch, had robbed her of compassion.

Colonel Jin's crew loaded the body bags on top of the plexiglass in the cargo hold. The Volkov Dopplebot rode up front with Troy and Xanthe, though she considered at one point placing it in the hold with the bodies. Though Volkov was a machine, it didn't feel quite right.

And it didn't feel quite right to have Volkov engage in small talk, either. She snuck glances at the bot. It was certainly lifelike. They had built Volkov with a ribcage that rose and fell, giving the illusion of breathing, and it blinked periodically to avoid long periods of uncomfortable eye contact.

But the skin was the real giveaway. Though they had carefully manufactured it with pores and hairs, it didn't quite breathe. Made of some sort of silicone, it was too smooth. The face, too, lacked the wrinkles and folds of a life's emotional labour.

Arriving back at Olympus, they rolled into the docking bay where Serena and Jonas pulled open the rover door to greet them.

"Holy crap!" Serena said as she looked up into Volkov's pale face. "What the hell? I thought you were dead!"

"I am not dead," Volkov said.

"He's a Dopplebot," Troy said and gestured for Volkov to get out.

"Why would anyone want to replicate *him*?" Serena said and stepped back to give Volkov a wide berth.

"It's a deal the Russians made with the Chinese," Xanthe said. "I'll explain later."

"So, they sent him to the Moon? Why? Didn't he cause enough grief on Earth? They want to do it all over again here? And why are we stuck with him?" Serena said.

"Colonel Jin has loaned it to us so we can make the repairs faster. Plus, it doesn't use any of our air or water," Xanthe replied.

"So, he has all of Volkov's memories?"

"I am right here. You can ask me directly," Volkov said. His English was good with a slight Russian accent.

"I'm not sure I want to speak to a dead – sorry, *not dead* – murdering Russian dictator." Serena shuffled around to the back of the rover to assist Jonas with the cargo. She kept Volkov in full sight.

Jonas opened the rear doors of the rover and stopped. The bodies were the first things that needed moving.

"Oh God," he said.

Serena put her arm around his shoulders, and they stared at the body bags for a few minutes.

"Come on. We'll put them on the trolley and then take them around to Artemis," Troy said as he came up behind them. "Thank goodness Artemis was unharmed in the strike."

Troy and Jonas pulled one bag free from the rover and placed it gently on the trolley. Volkov walked over to assist.

"Don't touch them!" Serena said.

Volkov stopped mid-track.

"What is problem?"

"You're a. . . killer! I don't want you touching my colleagues!" Serena said.

"I am accused of many things. Some I actually did. But I am different in this form."

"Oh yeah? How so?"

"I am programmed to help."

"Help who? The Chinese? The Russians? How do we know you won't kill us in our sleep and take over Olympus for the Chinese?"

"That's enough, Serena. Volkov is also programmed for medical service. He tried to save Kwanda and Aidan," Xanthe said.

"How do we know he didn't kill them? They were alive when we saw them leave the *Gateway!* It would serve Russian and Chinese purposes to get rid of us, wouldn't it? No more competition for resources." Serena's face flushed and her lip trembled.

"The Chinese are competitive, but they didn't orchestrate the meteor shower. As far as we can tell, that was a Spaceward Bound mining accident. Take it easy on Volkov. This is not the man we knew, regardless of appearances."

"I wouldn't be so sure about that."

"If it makes you feel any better, we can keep Volkov in Artemis until we need him."

"What? So he can steal all the American tech secrets? No way!"

"Alright, he'll stay with us. We can keep an eye on him then."

"We'll be watching, that's for sure." She gave Volkov a death stare.

Volkov returned her gaze, deliberately not blinking, thought Xanthe. So, the bot still had some of the original Volkov on board. What else might be still active from the old dictator? Xanthe shoved the thought aside and leaned into the rover to help Serena lift out the second body.

No time for suspicion. They needed to get the Atrium fixed and restore comms with Earth. *Survival first*, she thought. *Politics later.*

CHAPTER NINETEEN

*"Humans often wear masks, but leaders wear
them with the greatest burden."*

—ATHENA A.I., OLYMPUS LOG

THE OLYMPUS CREW sagged in their seats at the dining table in the central hub. Though the Atrium was the symbolic heart of the base, the kitchen hub was its functional one. Each spoke of the underground Olympus base had its own small kitchen like this one that led to the hallway around the Atrium. Future residents would be able to drop in and see one another for a meal or have a community potluck in the Atrium.

The Olympus crew chose the Centaur wing to inhabit as it was closest to the central operations area where the comms centre was. It also had quick access to the Vitalis hub, where the infrastructure and life support systems were, including the Swamp and the other food production facilities.

Xavier had heated some grilled sandwiches for them, and the wrappers were strewn across the table. Jonas, usually quick to devour his food, still munched his slowly, eyes staring into the distance. Volkov stood behind them, eyes like a vulture, unblinking.

No one spoke. Faces were glum. Haggard. They'd gone through a lot in the last two days with no time to process it.

"Team check in," Xanthe said. "Physical and emotional, please."

Eyes looked away.

"Madison?" Xanthe prodded. Madison was always an even keel.

"Physical, five. Need some shut eye. Emotional, five." Xanthe held her gaze. "I don't think it's really hit yet," she conceded. Xanthe kept looking at her, but when nothing more was forthcoming, she moved on.

"Xavier?"

"Physical, two. Emotional. . ." He welled up. "I am not good. All I can think about is Maryse. The girls. And that I need to get back to them. And that the water is gone. The plants are gone. And we are going to be starving. And very thirsty if we don't get this fixed." A tear rolled down his cheek. "This situation is absolute *merde*. And I don't want to let you all down. I don't want to let my family down. I want us to get off this *putain* of a dust pit and get back to the Earth, where there are plants and water and air and dirt."

Xanthe's throat constricted at the sight of the big man's emotion.

"There's no way you could ever let us down, brother," Troy said. "We are living well and will survive because of your genius in the greenhouse. Maryse and the girls would be very proud." He clapped Xavier on the back. "You'll see them again, *mon ami*."

Xanthe held back her own tears. No family was waiting for her. But maybe that was a blessing right now.

"Jonas? How are you faring?"

"Physical, like a lorry ran over me twice and then parked on me for good measure. Emotional. . .a bit fried, actually. It's been tense. Especially when you were knocked out, Xanthe. And then I can't help thinking about the *Gateway* crew. If there was something we could have done better, faster. If I'd fixed the damn Atrium like you'd asked me to. If I'd made different decisions, would they all be alive now?" His foot jiggled and his voice crackled.

"Hey. It's alright, mate," Serena said and put a hand on his shoulder.

The grief rolled over them all.

"You're not the only one who feels responsible," Madison offered slowly. "I did the repairs. I flew the *Saturnia*. I keep thinking, only a few minutes earlier and they'd all still be alive."

"I was there too," Serena said. "We worked as fast as we could, Mad Dog. You flew like an ace. And what were we supposed to do with Yuri? Just ram him? We had to do the EVA. Maybe if I did it faster. If I hadn't taken so long to move and tie up Yuri. . . I feel terrible about that. He's still up there, alone. Not even the company of the other dead astronauts." Serena bit her lip as tears streaked her cheeks.

"I made the call to leave Yuri tied outside to the *Gateway*, not you," Madison said. "That's on me. The EVA had to happen. And it took as long as it did because EVAs are slow. You did the best you could, Serena."

"Thanks, mate."

"Serena? How about you? How are you doing?" Xanthe asked quietly as Serena snuffled and wiped her nose on her sleeve.

"Physically, absolutely rooted. My body feels like someone hit me with a thousand sticks. Emotionally? I'm cactus. I need a good cry. Or a good scream. And a bath."

They smiled at that. Serena was fastidious about her personal hygiene and was the chief champion of the water reclamation system that allowed them to have showers. Now they were facing weeks, if not months, of no bathing.

"Troy. How are you doing?"

"Physically, I'm alright. Maybe a seven. Nothing a good sleep and a bit of food won't cure. Emotionally? I'm grieving, like everyone else. But our collective mourning risks derailing our survival efforts if we're not careful. We need to honour the dead and then stay focused. We're not out of the woods yet. But we've got each other. We need to remember that. We are the Olympus family, and we need to care for one another right now. And that includes you, Xanthe." He looked pointedly at her with his brows raised. "How are *you* doing?"

She took a deep breath. The truth was, she felt like shit. Her cuts ached and pulled every time the clothes snagged on the scabs. She was so tired her brain was starting to fog, but the adrenaline was still riding high.

And she hated the Moon.

And loved it all the same. It was putting them all at risk. It could snuff them all out so easily. All she wanted now was a soft feather bed with the smell of a summer breeze wafting through an open window and the feel of a glass of water against her parched lips.

She said none of that.

Instead, she said, "Physically, I'm probably a four. Sore from the cuts and the trip to the Red Star. Emotionally, I'm alright. It may hit me later, but for the time being, I'm focused on our next steps. Getting us through this. We can do it. We've overcome lots of things so far. We've got the Atrium to fix and ice to mine. Soon we'll be back to full functioning. Hopefully, comms with Earth will resume and we can plan our end-of-mission and return to Earth. That's what is keeping me on track right now."

There. She did it. Full command presence with a tiny piece of vulnerability for them to chew on. She didn't dare offer more in case she choked on emotion and scared them all.

"What about him?" Serena pointed at Volkov.

"What about Volkov?" Xanthe asked.

"What are we going to do about him?"

"The bot is here to help. Volkov will assist with the Atrium repair."

"But what if he is a spy?"

"Not much to spy on, I would think," said Jonas. "We're a wounded bird over here. Red Star won't learn much about our operations from Volkov that they don't already know."

"But what if he's here to hold us back? To sabotage us?" Serena continued.

"Why would the Chinese and Russians want to do that? No need for sabotage when we're already broken. If anything, they want us to be fully functioning so they can get their hands on our plants," Xavier said.

"Hmmmm." Serena was still dubious but seemed to relax a little.

"Or use our Stim Room," said Troy. "The Red Star is certainly impressive, but it's sterile. They did little for entertainment over there."

"Serena," Xanthe said, "Volkov is here to help. He's a bot. That's it. Just because he looks like the old dictator, and has his memories, does not mean the Dopplebot is the old dictator. You know that. That's not how Dopplebots work. This one had medical programming and service-oriented purpose. If we treat him well, he'll fit right in. Volkov might even become a valuable part of the crew."

Serena stared hard at the bot. "Maybe you're right." She tilted her head and narrowed her gaze. "Maybe we should put Volkov through his paces with a game of 'chook tag'? How long is he staying anyway?"

"Not determined. I haven't discussed it with Colonel Jin. Volkov is on loan for the moment."

Serena snorted. "Great. I'll put him on toilet duty. He won't smell anything at least."

"I think it's best if Volkov reports to someone else, given your, ah, concerns. Madison, can you take responsibility for Volkov, please?"

"Sure can." Madison eyed Volkov. "First job, Atrium repair. Someone who doesn't breathe will be good for an extended EVA."

CHAPTER TWENTY

*"To perceive is human; to misperceive, equally so. In the
gaps between, understanding waits to be born."*

—Athena A.I., Olympus Log

Madison, Jonas and Xavier suited up alongside Volkov to work
on the Atrium repair while Troy prepared to take the plexiglass
around by vehicle on an EVA. Once locked in and checked, they
moved to the main Atrium access. Their intention was to replace
the window plexiglass and then fix the water connection.

The Atrium was a mess. Madison noted Xavier's pained expression as he saw the frozen remnants of his precious plants. They had
designed the Atrium as a green centre with climbing plants and
beautiful trees. Now there were just twigs among shattered glass.

"I'm sorry about the plants, Xavier," she said.

He shrugged and said nothing.

Madison pursed her lips at the distant reply. *Such a cold fish.*

They picked their way around the room, gathering the plant
material and piling it up at the Atrium exit door closest to the
biodome of the Swamp.

"Can we reuse the growth pads?" asked Madison as she lifted one of the small tree remnants, still in its nesting bag.

"I'm not sure," Xavier replied. "I don't know what the effects of exposing a growth sponge to space will have on the nutrition and composite matter."

"Well, we can certainly try," she encouraged him.

He waved a non-committal hand without looking at her. "*Bien sûr.*"

He must be hurting something bad. How can I reach him? The thought needled her like a splinter.

They sent Volkov to do the tough stuff. The bot ascended the Atrium access ladder with no fuss and clipped in at the top. Volkov cleared the glass shards from the Atrium's eye to make it safe for the others. Jonas scrambled up next to send access ropes down to Troy, who was ready with the plexiglass in the rover.

Xavier went up the access ladder after Jonas so he could inspect the water access point. He spent a few moments wiping the water channel to remove any glass or regolith remnants that might clog the system once they repaired it and had it back online.

Madison was the last one up.

"Shall we clear the surface of the hull, so the plexiglass doesn't get damaged when we haul it up?" Madison suggested to Xavier.

"Yes, yes," he muttered.

He's so distracted. It must be because he can't call Maryse and the girls. Poor guy. Madison shook her head and kicked the debris away, absentmindedly.

Volkov and Jonas stood at the top of the Atrium, with the hauling ropes in place. Once Troy secured the glass, they began dragging it up. Xanthe had insisted they wrap it in blankets salvaged from Artemis.

The astronauts there wouldn't need them any time soon, thought Madison grimly.

"Bloody hell, this is heavy!" said Jonas. They strained with the glass despite the low G.

"Come on, Seaborn, show us what you're made of! All those workouts must have done something," Troy teased.

"Glad you're paying attention to my exercise regimen, Prince Troy. Never knew you cared so much."

"You're hard to miss, Jonas. You prance around in your workout gear any chance you get. Now show me how big and strong you are and haul me up this hull, would you, please?"

They heaved the plexiglass to the top and Jonas untied the rope and threw it down to Troy. In a few energetic leaps, Troy bounded up to them.

"Nice gorilla move, Prince Troy," Jonas called out. "You've been taking lessons from the Commander."

"I'm just naturally gifted in all things."

"Including being a braggart," added Xavier, suddenly more animated.

"Just speaking the truth, *mon vieux.*"

They worked together to move the plexiglass over the existing hole.

"Thank goodness for that," said Jonas. "It's going to be big enough. We just need to trim a little around the edges to make sure that it's going to fit securely."

"Make sure you cut it straight," Xavier teased.

"What do you think this is? Amateur hour? I've got this covered, my good sir," said Jonas.

Madison felt a pang as she listened to the banter. There was something about Xavier she just couldn't break through. He was way more comfortable around the others.

Maybe it's a guy thing.

She shrugged that thought away.

Nah, that's not it.

Jonas and Troy mapped out where the cuts needed to be made.

Madison, Xavier and Volkov chipped away at the ragged glass of the section where the meteorite had shot through. They needed smooth edges for it to bond properly. And to prevent any further snags on the retractor.

Soon, Jonas had the plexiglass cut. Again, they worked together to put it in place with a special space grade epoxy bond. They were soon grunting and sweating, trying to manoeuvre the plexiglass into its final place.

Xavier swore outrageously in French.

"Xavier, you have one hell of a potty mouth," Madison said.

"What you say, New Girl?" Xavier replied as he changed his grip on the plexiglass.

She flinched at the moniker he'd lumped her with from the outset. They'd been working together nearly nine months, through space training and the build here on the Moon, and still she was 'the new girl'. It rubbed her raw. Still, she maintained her cool.

"I say, Swamp Man, that your mouth is as dirty as your waste reclamation. Someone ought to put a biohazard sign around your neck."

He huffed at that. "You might be right, Mad Dog. But this *putain* of a plexiglass is really *merde*."

"Less stupid talk and we might have this fixed by now."

It was Volkov. They stopped what they were doing and turned. The bot suited up like the rest of them since his silicon skin was not impervious to space, but it did not require ventilation. Without the breathing regulator, Volkov was silent, and they'd almost forgotten it could hear and process their conversation.

"Listen, Volkov, you are not in charge here," said Jonas.

"And who is? You? If that is so, you disappoint. We should have had this task completed by now."

Xavier and Troy looked at each other with this sudden reprimand coming over the helmet comms. Madison watched Jonas stand and spread his feet and ready himself for a retort. She could sense him colouring under his helmet and thrusting his chin forward in defiance.

"Who the hell are you. . . No. *What* the hell are you to give me advice on leadership? You're nothing but a two-bit version of a long-dead asshole. Your people thought so much of you they made you into a walking bucket of bolts and banished you to a barren rock as a lackey. So don't go giving me feedback, you soulless, silicon sack!"

Madison felt for Jonas. She knew he was sensitive about his leadership ability and had been working on it ever since floundering his way through selection back on Earth. And somehow that tinpot had zeroed in on it and pushed all his buttons.

"Whoa now, Jonas," she said. "Don't lose your cool because some bag of rubber thinks he's got one over on you. You've got this, Mr Deputy. And we are going to get this plexiglass whipped. Volkov, shut your pie hole and put your shoulder into it."

"Yes, Madison. Jonas could take a page out of your book and read it."

"Shut it, V," she said.

They went back to the work, shoving and grunting until eventually the plexiglass slotted where they needed it to. Jonas moved quickly to lock it in place with the sealant. Troy, Xanthe and Volkov lay on top of it to hold it in place as Jonas bustled around them.

Madison and Xavier resumed their positions, ensuring the plexiglass did not move. Madison could see the expletives hovering on Xavier's lips, along with a bubble of moisture that was forming along the lining of his skull cap under his helmet. His suit was struggling to absorb his sweat. They'd have to ease their efforts and try to avoid free, excessive moisture in their helmets, which could become quite uncomfortable to manage.

"Done," Jonas declared.

Madison and Xavier eased back from their awkward positions, stood and stretched their backs.

"We just need to test the water for leaks and pray the retractor works since I took it apart," Jonas said.

"I'm sure it will, Seaborn," Troy said. "You're the best engineer this side of the Moon."

"Let us hope your engineering skills are better than your leadership skills," Volkov said drily.

"*Con! Ta gueule!*" Xavier growled through his helmet.

"V, you are sure not winning any friends today," Madison said.

Jonas ignored the bot. "Commander, plexiglass is in place. We can return to test the water and the atmosphere seal."

"Fantastic work, Jonas and crew," Xanthe said with relief. "Get your butts out of there and we'll move to the next phase."

As they bounded forward down the Atrium's face, Madison grabbed Xavier just as he was about to trip Volkov.

"Excuse me, Xavier," she said. "I apologise. I felt myself falling. It would be terrible if one of us got injured now. We need each other."

He looked at her, and she could see the guilt wash over his face.

"You're right. We need each other. But we don't need arrogance, especially from a Russian robot."

"You never know where you might find a friend, Xavier, if you give them a chance."

CHAPTER TWENTY-ONE

"Crises are tests of true resilience, where the response often shapes the outcome more than the event itself."

—Athena A.I., Olympus Log

Xanthe reassigned the crew once they returned to base. Serena, Xavier, Madison and Volkov were on Atrium testing and clean up while she, Troy and Jonas were to assess communications.

The three of them stood before the comms console. Jonas rubbed his head and blew out a long breath. He ducked his head behind the display console and traced cables with his fingers to check the connections. Xanthe reset the system once Jonas cleared the cables. Still nothing. Meanwhile Troy reviewed the comms log to see when exactly the signal had dropped out. Worry snaked between them like the slimy trails of a ponderous slug.

"Athena, have we got *any* signals from Earth?"

"Negative, Deputy Commander Jonas," the A.I. replied. "My systems do not detect any outgoing signal to Earth satellites."

"None?"

"Correct. There are no signals."

She frowned. "What might cause all Earth satellites to have signal disruption?"

"These are potential causes of total satellite disruption: Solar storms. Geomagnetic storms. The Kessler Syndrome."

"Wait! What's that?" Jonas asked. He was under the desk checking power supply and shoved his head out at Xanthe's feet. She leaned back to give him some room, bumping into Troy. He shuffled aside to make a little more space.

"The Kessler syndrome is a large-scale collision between space debris or satellites that could create a chain reaction known as the Kessler syndrome. This scenario involves an increasing number of collisions generating more debris, making it difficult for satellites to operate without being damaged or destroyed, leading to significant signal disruption."

"Thanks. Any other causes?" Jonas craned his neck upwards at Athena's speaker.

"Cyber-attacks. Radio frequency interference, or RFI. This is intentional or unintentional interference caused by the use of the same or overlapping frequency bands by different devices to disrupt satellite signals. Widespread RFI from multiple sources could cause significant disruption of satellite communication.

"And last, high-altitude nuclear detonation. A nuclear detonation in the upper atmosphere or near Earth space could generate an intense electromagnetic pulse, or EMP, that could severely damage or destroy satellites and disrupt their signals."

Xanthe and Troy shared a glance. Jonas dropped his head under the desk and rubbed his jaw. Thoughts churned in the silence. The empty display screens were blank, like tombstones waiting to be etched. The usual buzz of signal scanning was painfully quiet.

Jonas peered out again from under the desk. "Based on your information and access to the most recent Earth comms, which do you think is the most likely?"

"The recent cyber-terrorist attacks might have included the use of nuclear technology, though that is still uncertain. The most likely scenario involves cyber-attacks by one or more coordinated groups designed to hit the global satellite network simultaneously."

"But. . . why?" Troy said. He leaned back against the wall to give Xanthe a bit more room in the cramped space as she fiddled with the comms dials.

"There are several reasons an ecoterrorist group might undertake sabotage activity such as that. It is in line with their mission to save humanity from technology and return to a pre-technology Eden."

"But that would be cataclysmic," Jonas said. He gave the plug another shove and crawled out from under the desk. "All human systems are integrated with technology, not just communications. Food production, water, sanitation, travel just to start with. They take out the satellites, they take out—"

"Everything," Xanthe finished his thought as he stood beside her.

"Oh my God," Troy said. "It will be a complete anarchy. A throwback to pre-industrial civilisation. People won't know how to survive. How to grow food. Disease will overrun them." Xanthe sensed his shoulder tense where it touched hers.

"Hang on, don't get carried away," Xanthe said. "Athena, is it possible to restore the satellites?"

"Depending on the malfunction, yes, it is possible."

She pressed two hands on the desk, thinking. "In what scenario is it *not* possible?"

"Nuclear detonation or runaway Kessler syndrome would cause irreparable damage."

"Let's hope it's not one of those," Troy said.

"What do we do now?" Jonas said.

"It's time to give Colonel Jin another call." Xanthe pressed her lips together and reached out to initiate the connection.

CHAPTER TWENTY-TWO

*"Humans tend to etch first impressions in stone, forgetting
that people, like stones, are shaped by time and tide."*

—Athena A.I., Olympus Log

"Colonel Jin, thank you for taking my call."

"Commander Waters. How has the Atrium plexiglass replacement procedure progressed?"

"It is complete and functioning now, thank you."

"Very good. I trust Mr Volkov has been useful to you?"

"Yes, it was very helpful to have another pair of hands to speed up the repairs. Colonel, have you got comms back with Earth?"

For an instant, he looked troubled. "No. Not yet."

"Neither have we. We're exploring various theories about how it might have happened, including sabotage. Hopefully, it is nothing as malign as that and they will soon re-establish satellite communication."

The Colonel grunted an acknowledgment.

"We are going to need to rely on each other, Colonel."

He paused, then said, "How so?" His tone was wary.

"We are the only humans on this Moon and if the meteorite

strike has taught us anything, it's how vulnerable we are. The same could happen to you. The Red Star is far more fragile than Olympus until you get your lava tubes built."

"In the meantime, what do you want?"

"I beg your pardon?"

"Commander Waters, it seems to me the only reason for this call is that you need something. The Red Star has provided more than enough resources for you. We aided the rescue attempt. We looked after the *Gateway* astronauts, we have given you our plexiglass and our Dopplebot." He tugged on his red uniform cuffs. "We are, of course, more than happy to help."

Xanthe took a few breaths to maintain her composure. Was she missing a cultural cue here? The Colonel was right. Olympus was the taker in the arrangement so far. But she was right too. If they were going to survive the indefinite period ahead, without the spectre of rescue or resupply, they would need to work together.

"You have been more than generous, Colonel. We are very grateful for the support. It has saved our lives, and though the *Gateway* crew were not as lucky, I am sure they would be grateful too."

He pursed his lips, waiting.

"Once we have Olympus back and fully functioning, my suggestion for support is social. Being stranded in space will tax all of us, and we need something to look forward to. Perhaps we can trade space food recipes and supplies. Some friendly interactions will do wonders."

Xanthe thought he looked surprised. It was so damn hard to tell with his face like a slab.

"We will also need to speed up our ice mining activities, just so that you know. We lost a huge amount of water in the strike and now have barely enough for the life support system, let alone the greenhouse, bathing and drinking."

"I will advise my mining crew of your impending presence. But please stay away from our equipment. And Commander. . ."

"Yes?"

"We might arrange for a visit once you have water restored and bathing has resumed."

She wasn't sure, but Xanthe thought she saw the ghost of a smile.

CHAPTER TWENTY-THREE

*"The universe is vast, but the distance to a loved
one's heart can feel insurmountable."*

—Athena A.I., Olympus Log

"Putain!" Xavier said. "Troy, did you give me an extra small suit?
This one is so tight."

"It's not the suit that is small, but the body that is large. Like
I said before, we've got to get you exercising. And stop eating the
extra chocolate rations."

"I can't help it if Jonas is an easy target. He bets on everything
and always loses."

"If you two are ready to go," interrupted Madison, "then I'll
power up the rover and we can get going."

"Look who is in charge now, eh New Girl?" Xavier said.

"Someone's got to keep the two of you in line."

Though the banter was jovial, it belied the strain they each felt.
The last day had been epic. Madison's mind swirled over the details
of her piloting of the *Saturnia*. There must have been something
she could have done better, faster, that would have saved lives.

They exited the airlock and climbed aboard the rover. It was a good one-hour journey to the ice mining site in the Faustini crater. They settled in uneasily. The meteor strike was a sobering reminder of the fragility of their existence here on the Moon. Only a thin layer of plexiglass kept them from certain death, and if they didn't find enough ice soon, the whole life support system would fail anyway.

Despite the situation and being bone tired, Madison was eager for this expedition to spend more time with Xavier and Troy and deepen her connection. It was also a chance to contribute to Olympus, and for redemption. The unsuccessful *Gateway* rescue was a personal failure burning her soul. Here, she might help save the rest of them.

Though ice mining was new for all of them, she'd had some experience in drilling in the Antarctic on one of her military missions. Lunar ice would be very different from ice on Earth, of course, but the principles remained the same: line up the drill and monitor the extraction of the ice.

Madison set the coordinates in the rover, and it lurched forward over the uneven terrain. They sat in silence, transfixed by the impenetrable black horizon. The desolate wasteland lay before them, a dusty grey corpse. Above them, stars stabbed silver studs in the void. The only sound was the gentle hum of the rover's engine, providing just enough warmth to keep them alive in this inhospitable environment.

"Madison, I have to ask." Xavier interrupted her reverie. "What happened up there?"

Madison looked at him out of the corner of her eye.

"You know what happened," she said in a low tone.

"But really, was there no other way to get Yuri out of the way?"

Madison shifted in her seat. "I've gone over it a hundred times in my own mind, Xavier. Maybe if we launched something at him and knocked him out of the way. Or maybe we could have nudged him. I don't know."

"Why didn't you try those things?" he persisted.

The heat rose in her suit and washed out into the cabin from near her neck. The muscles in her jaw bunched and released. "I made the best call at the time."

"Could have been better, I think. Nine people dead."

"Oh yeah? What the hell would you have done?" She whirled on him, the whites of her eyes flashing.

"Hey, Xavier, back off." Troy put a hand on Xavier's chest as he seemed to gear up for a fight. "Neither of us were there. We can't know what that was like. Madison made a tough call. That's her job. She did the only thing she could in difficult circumstances. She did her best."

Xavier shrugged and looked away.

"We're all a little frazzled," Troy said. "It's been an intense twenty-four hours. Why don't we chill out while we can? Athena, can you play some nice, relaxing music, please?"

Classical music piped through the rover's cabin.

"Perfect," Troy said. He closed his eyes with a smile.

It wasn't long before the three of them nodded off.

Madison opened her eyes after what felt like only a few minutes to see the winking light of the Chinese mining operation not far ahead.

"Rise and shine, lemon limes, we're nearly there," Troy said. "We've got to make sure we honour the perimeter Xanthe committed to," he added.

"I'm on it," Madison said. "The rover has located their operational site and cast a one-kilometre boundary. The ice map shows an excellent location just over here." She pointed to a section on the radar map.

The rover ambled across the barren lunar landscape then plummeted down the steep crater wall. A spectral chill washed over them as they descended into darkness. Even with their suits and heated seats they sensed, rather than felt, the drop in temperature as they descended deeper into the crater's abyss.

"It sure is dark," murmured Madison. Then, like an omen of doom, the rover's high beams illuminated a hidden world of shadows and ice, a frigid, silent graveyard.

"*Merde*! I see nothing. Where is the ice? It all looks the same to me."

"Well, it won't be like a skating rink. All that ice is mixed up with the regolith. We probably won't even be able to see it with our naked eye. The neutron spectrometer will pick it up, though," Madison said.

"It would be too easy to find a clear block of ice, wouldn't it?" said Troy.

"Nothing's easy on the Moon," said Madison.

"So true," said Xavier.

The radar lit up with a green blob.

"Looks like we found our icy regolith patch," Madison said. "Let's get out and test it." They put the helmets back on and exited through the airlock at the back of the rover.

"It's a wee bit chilly." Troy glanced at his wrist monitor. "My suit reads -232°C."

"*Mon Dieu*, that is crazy cold," Xavier said. "We will need to work quickly and take breaks. Our suits will work overtime to keep us toasty."

Madison was already hauling out the test drilling unit. The three of them dragged it over to where the spectrometer showed there was a likely source of ice. Madison punched in the activation code, and they waited while the machine came to life and started the test excavation process. After a few minutes, the reading came back negative. They manoeuvred the machine to another location that looked like it had fewer rocks and they started it again. No luck.

They tried another three locations with no further progress before they returned to the rover to reassess.

"*Putain, il fait froid!* Look at that reading. Who would believe such numbers?"

"I hear you, brother! I imagine my dangly bits would snap off if exposed."

"Really now?" Madison rolled her eyes.

"What's up, New Girl? Too graphic for your sensitive ears?"

"I don't need to be thinking about your 'dangly bits' when I'm freezing my tits off."

Troy snorted with laughter as he pulled off his helmet.

Madison moved to the control panels. "Are you sure Jonas fixed the heater properly? It doesn't seem quite right."

"I'm sure it's fine. It might be a little sub-optimal. Try cranking it some more. And let's see what's in the snack pantry." Troy pulled a panel open in the rover. "I reckon we burned at least five hundred calories just standing around in our suits."

"I will take a peanut butter protein bar, *s'il te plait*."

"Of course you will, old chap."

"The calories don't count when you're in the crater doing ice mining."

Troy handed out the protein bars and pouches of hot chocolate.

"*Ça fait du bien! Merci.*"

"What does that mean?" asked Madison as she chomped on her bar.

"It means it is good and makes me feel strong, like Hercules."

"You wish!" said Troy.

"At least Maryse loves me any way I am."

"Half your luck," said Troy.

"Speaking of luck," Xavier said. "How are things going with your little romantic mission?"

"There is pretty much no romance to speak of, *mon ami.*"

"Unbelievable. Sexiest human alive fails to seduce anyone on the Moon!" laughed Xavier.

"Romance? What romance?"

"In case you hadn't noticed, Prince Troy has a thing for Xanthe."

"Oh. I didn't think that sort of thing is allowed."

"There is what is allowed, and there is what is done," said Xavier.

"Well, there's nothing doing, and nothing done."

"Maybe you are trying too hard, Troy. Xanthe is not like your other conquests. She has a brain, for one."

"Ha ha. Not fair."

"Seriously, *mon ami*. Your usual tricks will not work with her. You need to be interested in her. Stop prancing around and being sexy Troy. Be human Troy."

"What do you think I'm doing?"

"You're doing sexy Troy," Madison said.

Troy glanced at her as he sipped his hot chocolate.

"Oh, yes? What would you advise, Mad Dog?"

"Be real."

"What do you think I'm doing? I give her support, she pushes me away. I try to look after her, she pushes me away. I reach out to her, she snaps at me. I don't know what else to do. I mean, I'm a pretty decent sort. No complaints in the past."

"Ever think she just has a lot going on?" said Madison. "She is the Commander of the entire base. And there's a lot to manage. She wants to keep us all alive and well. It's not exactly the best setting for seduction, is it now?"

"That's exactly why she should open up her arms to me. Life is way too short and precious. Especially in a place like this."

"Maybe you try too hard, Prince Troy. Leave her alone. Cats are like that. The more you chase them, the more they shy away. Cats always end up sitting on the lap of the people who ignore them the most."

"Xanthe is hardly a cat," said Madison. "Why don't you just be straight with her?"

"*Bof*," said Xavier. "Xanthe is too serious. I think take a break from your romantic pursuit. See if she has a change of heart when the sun isn't shining on her anymore."

"Seriously? That's your advice? Play hard to get?" Madison wrinkled her forehead in surprise. "I think a woman like Xanthe just likes to hear it plain and simple."

"Well, if we're done analysing my love life, or lack thereof, how about we get back to mining the ice?"

"Let's hope we have better luck finding ice than you do melting the Ice Queen's heart."

They put their helmets back on again and stepped back out into the cold. They tried three more locations before they hit the jackpot.

"Fantastic! Let's get the excavator going and see how much ice we can take back in this first round." A surge of excitement rushed through Madison.

They set the excavator to work and prepared the loader to retrieve the regolith ice mix. Over the next five hours, they worked in shifts until they had enough regolith for one trailer load.

Madison had crawled back into the rover when she saw the flash of light at the other end of the crater. "That must be the Chinese operations," she said.

"Are they heading this way?" asked Troy as he climbed up beside her in the front of the rover.

"I'm not sure. But I sure would love to see how they set up their operations. There must be a way of running the drill without human supervision and not losing the regolith. Do you think they might be open to sharing their setup?"

"You have got to be joking," Troy said. "I was with Xanthe when Colonel Jin just about throttled her through the holo. They don't want us going anywhere near their site."

"But that was Colonel Jin. Foot soldiers might be more friendly," she suggested.

"I will not risk that. I'm trying to get *into* Xanthe's good books, not get booted out."

"I agree with Mr Sexy. I think the time to check out their

operations is when they are not there. And I don't think we have time for that, at the moment. Let's get back with this haul and see what we can make of it. The sooner we get out of these big, tight suits the better."

"Righto! Let's head back and see how much water we can get from these hunks of dust. It would be nice to get the plumbing running again."

"Wait, what's that?" Madison said.

It was a small Chinese rover driving past them towards Olympus.

"Where are they going, I wonder," Troy said.

"That's not the people mover," Madison said. "Too small. It looks like an old recon unit." She rummaged in the rover's dashboard storage and pulled out binoculars. She could just make out the shape of the vehicle as it trundled past them at the lip of the crater.

"Let me see," Troy said and took the binoculars from her.

"You're right. Definitely not a people mover. I saw that unit when Xanthe and I went to the Red Star base. It was sitting abandoned close to the main entrance. It hadn't moved in a long time by the looks of it."

"Can we track its path on our radar?" Xavier said.

They turned on the screen, and the slight blip of the Chinese unit appeared. They watched in silence as it maintained a steady course.

"Athena, can you plot the Chinese unit's trajectory?" Madison asked.

"Certainly. It is heading towards the Olympus base. It will arrive in approximately seventy-three minutes."

"What the hell is it after, then?" Troy said. "We have comms with Red Star. They could dial us up on the holo, rather than send a bot. Or maybe their comms to Olympus are down?"

"*Mon Dieu*! Is it a sabotage unit?"

"Unlikely. Those units were sent up well before there were permanent human sites here. It's an observation unit."

"Spy, then?"

"Maybe. Maybe it's checking we are far enough away from their ice mining site."

"But why go past us and on to Olympus?" Madison asked.

"Who knows. But we should probably find out," Troy said. "Let's follow it. With this load, we'll be behind, but we should be able to keep it in our sights."

"Or maybe we do a little spying of our own," said Xavier. "There are no more lights down the other end of the crater. That little rover must have been what we saw before. We could sneak down to the end and check out what they are doing."

"I am in no way supporting your espionage ambitions, old chap. Besides, the rover is too heavy now with the ice regolith and we have other priorities. Let's get back, melt this ice and see what that Chinese spy rover is up to."

"You are most sensible, of course," Xavier said. "Honestly, I do not know how Xanthe resists your charms."

"Well, when you find out, do let me know, old friend. Playing a lovelorn Lothario is wearing me down."

"You ought to try a little more Galahad and a little less Casanova," Madison said.

"Really? Pure and chaste? You think I could pull that off?"

Madison and Xavier looked at one another.

"No. But it would be fun to watch," Madison said.

"Ha, New Girl! You are funny. It's good for Mr Sexy to come down a peg or two."

Madison bristled and gritted her teeth. The 'new girl' shtick was getting old fast.

The rover jolted forward on its rumbling churn up the crater.

CHAPTER TWENTY-FOUR

"The seeds of doubt, once sown, bear the fruits of discord."

—Athena A.I., Olympus Log

Serena pounded the casing of the water recycling unit.

"Dammit! Why don't you work?"

"I've checked all the seals," said Jonas. "I don't think it's a plumbing issue."

"And it's not an electrical one either," she said. "It might be a mechanical issue somewhere in the system. But I'll be damned if I can figure out where it is."

"What does this mean for us right now?"

"Our water recycling should be nearly at one hundred percent. At the moment, all the water that we are using will go into the holding tank but won't pump out into the recycler. That means if we keep using it, the holding tank will overflow and back up."

"Even with us having lost as much water as we have?"

"Basically, we will either run out of water or the tank will back up."

"That's assuming we don't get any water from the ice mining, correct?"

"That's right, Mr Seaborn. No ice, no good."

"Why don't you disassemble the pump and give it a service?" Volkov said.

He hovered around them like a cheap cologne, thought Serena.

"If we stop the pump without the full load of water moving through the bellows system into the Atrium, we will overheat, numb nuts."

"Is there not a backup for the pump?"

"Yes, there is a backup, but it doesn't seem to work either right now," Serena said with an exasperated tone.

"Maybe you should fix that first."

"Thanks for that, Captain Obvious. Volkov, what do you think we've been trying to do?"

"I see that you have largely been flailing around and swearing. Much talk, little progress."

"Do you have any other useful suggestions, V?"

"Fix the pump."

"Get out of my face, you creepy bag of bolts!"

Volkov stepped forward, took the wrench from Serena and quickly disassembled the front panel of the pump. He pulled out one component.

"Stop, you idiot! You'll make the entire unit seize up!" Serena tried to pull Volkov's arm away, but it was a steel beam on iron hinges. Volkov's arm swung to the side, with Serena dangling from it like a cat caught in misadventure.

Jonas stepped in.

"Whoa there, Serena. No need to poke the bot. Volkov, stand down. Everyone, just calm down. Let's work on the problem." He pulled her off Volkov and placed himself between her and the Dopplebot.

"Don't you see? He's trying to undermine us!"

Volkov's head swivelled towards her with black, glassy eyes.

Serena flicked a strand of sweaty hair from her face and stared with steely intensity at Volkov. He stared right back.

He is one freaky, murderous sack of silicon, thought Serena.

"Get away from me," she said at last. "Go stand in the corner until I can think of something useful for you to do."

Volkov fixed her with an unflinching gaze, then stepped backwards with a strange, mechanical awkwardness until his back was against the chamber's wall, out of her reach.

She applied herself to the problem at hand.

"Let's test the other components in the system, see if any of them could cause the issue. We have the main water lines, all running back to one central point, and then all going off from there. We should check those lines for clogs or breaks, and we should make sure that our filters are doing their job correctly. And I think it would be a good idea to check the pressure readings on each pipe, to make sure they are all at the same level. That way, we can rule out any potential problems with our water flow or pressure levels."

Jonas nodded in agreement.

She ran through a mental checklist of what needed to be done and how long the process might take.

"Jonas, I'm going to change the filters while I'm at it. They need to be done every few months, anyway. Why don't you take V with you and tackle the comms problem? I don't trust this snake slithering around our water system."

"I am here to help."

"You'll be a better help when you're not dropping your two bobs' worth of opinion like smelly farts. Now bugger off and keep Jonas company."

"Alright, Serena, tone it down. V, you're with me."

"At last, someone is taking the lead," Volkov said.

CHAPTER TWENTY-FIVE

*"The intersection of organic and artificial intelligence is
not a battleground but a playground of evolution."*

—Athena A.I., Olympus Log

"Commander Waters. There is an incoming vehicle on the radar."

"Who is it, Athena?" asked Xanthe as she stood and stretched her back. She had been trying to hail Earth and Gaia constantly, with no success. She tried every satellite in their comms directory with no return signal. Dread filled her bones like a cold, creeping poison.

"The rover is not responding to my signals," said the A.I.

"Is it Chinese? Or one of the other international rovers?"

"It is not a people carrier. It's too small for that. I suspect it might be a remnant exploratory rover."

"Show me." Xanthe peered at the radar display. "How far away is it?"

"It is approximately one kilometre away."

"What's that? Is that our rover behind it?"

"Affirmative," the A.I. said.

"Can we contact them?" Xanthe asked.

"Calling the Olympus rover now."

"Olympus, this is Rover One, over." Madison's voice came through the comms.

"Madison, we read you loud and clear. What's your report?" Xanthe asked.

"We are nearly back at base with a successful mission. We have a trailer full of ice regolith."

Xanthe beamed. "At last, good news! Well done. By the way, have you been following the little rover that is in front of you?"

"Yes, we have. We tried to contact it but got no response."

"Any idea whose it is?" Xanthe's brows resumed their habitual pinch.

"It has Chinese markings on it. It's an old model. Pre-Moonbase era."

"What's it doing roaming around?" Xanthe said.

"Don't know, but it seems intent on heading towards Olympus."

"Roger that, Madison. Keep monitoring it. If it looks like it's going to run into any of our equipment, block its path. Otherwise, continue as you are."

"Understood, Rover One out."

Xanthe studied the progress of the Chinese rover unit on the radar. Then her heart skipped a beat. "Athena, is there any possibility that this rover has malicious intent?"

"I read that possibility at one percent," the A.I. replied. "If this rover is from pre-Moonbase times, then it is merely equipped with communication and observational equipment. And rock and soil analysis capabilities."

"Any ideas why it might be active all of a sudden?" Xanthe said.

"I suspect it is a communication exercise."

"Why hasn't Colonel Jin informed us of this incident?"

The comms signal blurted into the room.

"Olympus base. This is Red Star." Colonel Jin's voice boomed in the small space as his holo jumped to life.

"Colonel Jin. I was just asking about you. Can you tell me about your wayward rover, which is on its way here?" Xanthe said.

"That is why I am calling, Commander Waters. Our rover booted up, much to our surprise. It has been inactive for over two decades. It gave us quite a fright." His usually flat features were strained, his face red.

"So, you didn't activate it?" Xanthe's eyebrows shot up.

"No. It lit up and then drove towards our access portal. And then it sat there, waiting." Colonel Jin's eyes were wide with concern.

"Can you communicate with it?" Xanthe's mind leaped at the possibilities.

"Negative. They designed those for Earth communications only."

"You mean it's in contact with Earth?" Her heart raced and energy surged through her body.

"That is my best guess. I went out with a written message on my tablet display that I hope it will relay. I confirmed all Red Star base personnel are well and accounted for and told it that repairs are underway at Olympus."

Xanthe noted the Colonel's earnest tone. She paused then asked, "Did you tell them about Kwanda and Aidan?"

The Colonel's face contracted and his bottom lip twitched. "No, I did not. That is not my news to tell."

Xanthe considered this for a moment and thought it was probably for the best. It was not news she wanted to send as a written message.

"What happened then?"

The Colonel slipped a finger under the collar of his uniform and tugged to loosen it, easing the grip around his neck. "Once I gave it all that information, it reversed tracks and started heading away. At first, I thought it was heading towards the mining site to check our progress there. But it kept going. We have been monitoring it on our long-range radar. I assumed it was on its way to you to get an update directly from your base." He tilted his head left and right, still trying to loosen the collar of his uniform.

He's not usually this distracted, Xanthe thought. The strain must be getting to him as well.

A thought occurred to her and her face lit up. "It must be on a reconnaissance mission, trying to figure out our condition. That's good news! That means they're still thinking about us and are trying to help."

"Perhaps." Colonel Jin waved a dismissive hand.

"What other explanation do you have?"

"None that is worth discussing at the moment," he said.

"Well, it should be here soon, so we will communicate our news as best we can. I'll let you know what it does afterwards." Xanthe fanned a minuscule flame of hope with an encouraging smile.

"Thank you, Commander Waters."

Jonas and Volkov walked into the comms room just as Colonel Jin's holo shut down.

"What's that?" Jonas said as he pointed at the two blips on the radar.

"It seems we have a visitor from the Chinese, an old recon rover that may be in contact with Earth," Xanthe said.

"Really? That's incredible!" Xanthe grinned at his enthusiasm, a welcome contrast to Colonel Jin's stressed countenance.

"It could be better news. Communication is only one way. Colonel Jin wrote up a message for it to send back to Earth, we hope. It's not able to communicate back to us."

"I can help with that," said Volkov.

"How?" said Jonas.

"I can patch communication system so we can liaise directly with Earth." With his nonchalant Russian accent and arrogant demeanour, Volkov made it sound so easy.

"That's fantastic. Jonas, you and Volkov get suited up and meet the rover in the vehicle bay. See if you can get it working and in contact with Earth. I'll write up a message on the tablet that you can place in front of its camera."

"Roger that!" Jonas clapped his hands in glee.

Soon they might speak to Earth again.

Xanthe pulled up the vehicle bay camera so she could watch the Chinese rover come in and Jonas and Volkov go to work. After a few minutes, the two of them exited the decompression airlock in their lightweight spacesuits.

When the rover was within one hundred metres of the base, she asked Jonas to open the vehicle bay door. The Chinese rover trundled in and stopped in front of Volkov and Jonas. Jonas waved at the rover in obvious delight.

"Jonas, put the message up to the rover's camera so it can read it properly."

"Roger that, Xanthe." Jonas held out the tablet with the message they had typed up.

'Olympus crew all well. Atrium repair complete with help from Red Star. Half of water supply gone in accident. Water mining operations commenced and first haul retrieved. Kwanda and Aidan returned from Red Base and are in Artemis station now. Comms with Red Base okay. No comms with Earth or lunar satellites. Possible lunar satellite repair operation in consideration.'

That was as much as Xanthe wanted to tell Earth about the Artemis astronauts without a visual connection. She wondered if that was too much – giving false hope.

Jonas and Volkov waited for some acknowledgement from the rover. There was none. It merely sat there with its lights shining, with no sign that the message had been received and transmitted. Xanthe hoped for the best.

Then Volkov took two steps forward, pulled something from its suit and started working at the front panel of the rover.

"Jonas, Volkov, what are you doing?"

"I am opening communication panel to establish contact," said Volkov.

His arms moved swiftly in a mechanical way. Volkov reached inside the unit and pulled out one box, then a nest of wires.

"Volkov, are you sure you know what you're doing?" said Jonas.

"This unit has different wiring than the rovers I have been programmed to repair. But it is a more basic model and should be easy to—"

A giant electrical arc blasted Jonas and Volkov backwards onto the vehicle bay floor. There was a flash, and the rover unit went dark and still.

"Jonas!" Xanthe cried.

"Oh, my back," moaned Jonas.

"What happened?" Xanthe spoke through the intercom.

"I think Volkov shorted something in the circuits." Jonas sat up gingerly and rubbed his back. He glanced over at the Dopplebot, lying beside him.

"Volkov, are you okay?"

"I've zigzags itsun mempl," he said.

"What?"

Volkov continued with nonsensical sounds.

"I think Volkov shorted himself," Jonas said.

Volkov pushed himself back up to standing and swivelled his head towards Jonas. Panic surged through Xanthe as she watched the inhuman, stealthy movements of the Dopplebot.

"Jonas! Be careful!"

Jonas moved gingerly and rolled over onto his hand and knees.

"That really hurt."

He stood carefully and looked at Volkov.

"Can you talk?" he asked the Dopplebot.

Volkov swivelled his head left, then right, then left again.

"Yes. Speech pathway reestablished."

"It looks like you blew up the rover. Can you fix it?"

"That wasn't me. It seemed to attack. I will need to do assessments."

Xanthe noticed the Olympus rover approaching the vehicle bay door.

"Can the two of you move that Chinese rover out of the way?" Xanthe asked. "We've got our regolith ice coming in now."

"I'll do my best," said Jonas. "My back is a little out, but this unit looks pretty light."

"Actually, Jonas, just get Volkov to move it. I want no more damage done to my crew," Xanthe said.

"And what about me?" Volkov said.

"You're easier to fix," she said.

Serena had finished her checks and wiped her hands on her overalls as she walked up to stand beside Xanthe at the comms. "What has he done now?"

"Nothing. The Chinese rover seemed to attack."

Serena's eyes widened, then narrowed with a ferocious scowl.

"You're kidding! Another saboteur? Goddamnit. I'm gonna rip someone's circuits out and crush them to dust!"

"Take it easy. We don't know it was sabotage. Volkov was only trying to help."

"That's what he keeps saying," Serena said.

"One thing at a time. We'll take a look at that rover in more detail. For the moment, we've got to help unload the regolith ice and sort out our water problem. Did you get to the bottom of the pump issue?"

Serena shook her head, forlorn. "No. I can't figure it out. The pressure seems to work fine in the pipes. I'm going to have to keep working at it."

"Well, you probably have about twelve hours, assuming we get the ice melting and water purification process correct."

Serena nodded.

"Just keep that crazy Russian freak bot away from me. He sure is creepy."

CHAPTER TWENTY-SIX

"The pull of the stars is strong, but so is the call of home."

—Athena A.I., Olympus Log

THE ROVER CREW pulled up to the docking station in the vehicle bay as Volkov pushed the Chinese unit into a corner. Jonas and the Dopplebot helped unload the ice into the processing unit. Xavier checked the settings and set the unit to melt and purify the water. They could check progress from inside the base, so they closed up the vehicle bay and retreated to the warmth inside.

Once out of their suits, Xavier headed straight to Xanthe.

"What's the update with Earth?" he asked.

Xanthe was frowning at the comms panel. "Still nothing."

Xavier ran a hand through his hair, scratching at the tight curls crushed by the helmet. "Have the Chinese had any luck?"

"Not yet. We suspect there is damage to the lunar satellites. Must have happened during the meteor strike." Xanthe turned to Xavier and took stock of the big man. His face was drawn and his eyelids drooped with fatigue.

"Can we repair it?" Xavier asked.

"We'll need to take the *Saturnia* up to do that, and we are running low on fuel. So that will mean extra ice mining to do the fuel conversion." Xanthe winced inside. Every excursion to the Faustini crater was risky and exhausting. She worried for the crew.

"And what about that Chinese rover? Can we fix that?"

Xanthe saw the strain on Xavier's face. The desperation to talk to his family. "I am going to get Volkov and Jonas to work on it," she said and patted him on the shoulder.

He smiled weakly. "You let me know as soon as you hear anything from Earth, okay?"

"Of course. Xavier, I'm sorry. I know you must be worried about your family."

Xavier's face tightened. "They will be concerned for me. I talk to them every day."

"You miss them."

"Of course."

Xanthe and Xavier retreated to the kitchen hub adjoining the comms room. She offered him a pouch of tea.

"*Merci.*"

They sipped tea in companionable silence. Xanthe considered Xavier's smooth, dark face. He had a few more grey hairs since they'd arrived on the Moon.

"Do you ever regret it?" she asked.

"What do you mean?"

"Do you regret coming to the Moon? Leaving your family behind?"

Xavier blew out a long breath.

"It was an easy and not-so-easy decision. I love my family. And being away for so long, on such a dangerous mission. . ." He drifted off. "But they supported me. They wanted me to take Terra Verdi technology to new places. And they knew how much this expedition meant to me. Without their support, it would have been a much harder decision."

Xanthe throbbed with regret at his words. She thought again of Simon.

"You're lucky to have so much support," she said.

Xavier sipped his tea and stared at the metallic floor. "It still hurts, though."

Xanthe looked at him expectantly.

"The guilt. It hurts. Even though they support me. Even though I know this is a grand opportunity that will make a lasting impact on many people, I still feel guilty. I feel selfish, you know?"

Xanthe did know. She'd wrestled with the same issue. Still did. "What was the easy part of the decision?" she asked, to steer her thoughts back to Xavier.

"Adventure. Not everyone will get to live on the Moon. But being able to make it work for others. . . that, for me, is the ultimate happiness."

"So, you're happy up here?"

"*Mais oui!* I mean, there are plenty of things that are *merde*. Not being able to go outside without those stinky suits. Arguing with Jonas over the group entertainment programming. Having to drink tea out of these stupid pouches. But apart from that, yes, I am happy. I am with my second family, and this is good."

Xanthe smiled and then, unexpectedly and completely out of character, she gave Xavier a hug. He hugged her back, and she delighted in the solid warmth of this straightforward, honest man.

"Thanks," she said shyly as she pulled away.

"*Très bien*, Commander. Hugs are free. You are welcome to them anytime." He considered her for a moment, and then asked, "Xanthe, are *you* happy?"

The question caught her off balance. She opened her mouth and then closed it again. She felt the prick of tears and fought to keep from losing her composure.

"I. . . I don't really think about it," she said at last. "I'm focused on keeping this base safe, keeping our people safe, until the first round of settlers arrives."

"Doing your job is one thing. *Being* your job is another. Remember, you are human too. What is the saying you have displayed in the Atrium?"

"*Memento mori,*" she muttered.

"That's right, 'remember you are mortal'. Try to have some fun while we are up here."

"Doesn't quite seem right when we have just lost nine people."

"Life is like that, full of death and endings and tragedy." Sorrow washed over him, too. "But what is the point if we do not enjoy a little happiness while we breathe? Those that died would be angry to know we wasted our chance at life by being miserable, *non?*"

"I'm sure you're right."

Xavier patted her on the shoulder.

"Thank you for the tea, even if it is in a pouch. I am going to get cleaned up and check the ice melting."

Xanthe watched him clomp down the accommodation tunnel in his moonboots. She noticed his shoulders slumped with fatigue. She felt it too. The ache of her wounds, the anxiety grinding her mind like wet sand in a shoe.

She returned to the comms room and stared at the unresponsive panel. She triaged their options. First order priority was securing the life support system and that meant getting enough water back into the system. Xavier didn't think they would have enough with that first load of regolith ice, so that would mean at least one or two more mining trips.

Communication with Earth was their next issue. They needed to convey the news about Kwanda and Aidan to their families. Plus, the longer the crew went without comms with their families on Earth, the more morale was likely to slip. Deterioration of mental and emotional wellbeing would be a significant risk.

If Volkov and Jonas couldn't get the Chinese unit working,

maybe Colonel Jin had other staff who might figure it out. She glanced at her watch. She would call him once she received the ice processing report.

❧

Xanthe looked over her team. Drawn faces and eyes with dark circles greeted her.

"Alright, let's hear it," she said to Xavier.

He sighed and wiped his nose on his sleeve. "The ice mining yielded about a third of what we need. Jonas and Serena have siphoned the filtered water into the life support system."

"Serena, how is the pressure?"

"Not bloody fixed yet, but it's better. I think we just need a full tank and that will flush out the issues or create the weight and pressure we need for the system to optimise."

"So that means showers are still off limits?" asked Jonas.

"Unfortunately, yes. Just bird baths for now. We still need to be conservative. Just in case," Serena said.

"At least there is enough supply for the Swamp and for cooking and drinking," Xavier said.

"Jonas, what about the Chinese rover?"

Jonas slumped in his chair, despondent. "I'm doing my best. Volkov is helping, but it looks like the wires are fried and the wiring tech is old. It might have worn out sitting up here for so long."

"You could ask Colonel Jin."

Heads swivelled to Volkov.

"Before I go asking yet another favour of the Colonel, what makes you say that, Volkov?" Xanthe asked.

"He is engineer. He worked with space mission around that time. He likely knows the specs for the unit."

Serena huffed and crossed her arms. "Perfect excuse for Jin to come and spy on us. Exploding rover – very fishy. Did you do it?" She pointed a finger at Volkov.

"Was accident."

"Sure."

"I help."

"What do you call wrecking the only chance to talk to Earth? And nearly ripping the guts out of my pressure pump? You—"

"Enough!" Xanthe said, annoyed. "Serena, back off. Volkov has been very useful. He helped with the Atrium. He helped in moving the" – she paused as she was about to say 'bodies' – "in moving Kwanda and Aidan to Artemis when none of us could face it. Jonas was with him when the rover shorted. It wasn't sabotage. Let it go."

Serena scowled and rolled her eyes, but otherwise held her tongue.

"I will call Colonel Jin and ask him about the rover tech. He's got a vested interest in it, too. Volkov, you can do it with me so you can explain what happened."

The Dopplebot bowed slightly in acknowledgment.

"So that means Xavier, Mad Dog and I are back on ice mining tomorrow?" Troy asked.

"Yes. The three of you know where to go, so it would be quicker that way. Plus, I want Jonas and Serena working on comms and life support, respectively."

"And me?" Volkov asked.

"Jonas can have you," Serena said. "I can do without a creepy, arrogant bot, thank you very much." She stood and looked pointedly at Xanthe. "If we're done, I'd like to get cleaned up. It's a bit of an effort without water."

"Go ahead. Let's break for the night and get started again at 0600."

CHAPTER TWENTY-SEVEN

*"The art of crisis management lies in balancing
urgency with foresight, action with analysis."*

—Athena A.I., Olympus Log

Madison, Troy and Xavier headed out after a quick breakfast of peanut butter and jam on toast. They dozed, taking advantage of the long ride out to the mining site.

Chills ran through Madison as she peered into the dark crater ahead. The rover jolted over the edge and lumbered into the inky depths. She dialled her suit heater up to high and readied to exit. They agreed to rotate positions every ten minutes to avoid taxing their suits while the excavator drilled.

They worked mostly in silence as the hours dragged on. Madison let her mind wander to thoughts of Earth. Even though her mother was out of harm's way, nowhere near the floods and tsunamis that came in the aftermath of the ecoterrorist disaster, she still worried about her.

Her mother had been in prison for twelve years, and it was taking its toll. The last time Madison had seen her, she noticed the deep creases around her mouth, the haggard hue of her skin. Her mother walked with a shuffle now. Gone was the purposeful stride and proud carriage.

Prison had beaten her down and her high moral ground wasn't enough to sustain her anymore. She no longer talked about how the Earth First protests had been worth it. Disillusion and despair had settled in.

Madison longed to see her. She didn't know how many more visits she had left before her mother passed away. And that anxiety only got worse now that they were cut off from Earth. Would they ever return?

That was the thought she knew they all chewed on. They were in a precarious position, and the meteor strike had highlighted their vulnerability. It made her long for the blue sky, the smell of airplane engine oil, the rustle of leaves in autumn, the sticky sweetness of ice cream on a summer's day.

Would she ever experience those things again?

She checked the readings on the excavator. Nearly finished.

Then she noticed lights in the distance at the Chinese end of the crater. They were bobbling away from the usual position. *Wonder where they're going*, she muttered. The lights danced up and down and then disappeared into the wall of the crater. *What the—?*

Madison strained her eyes to see where the vehicle might have gone.

"Time to swap," Troy said as he moondled over to her. Their rover sat a small distance away, a lone pearl nestled in the vast, monochrome sea of lunar dust. Madison flooded with anticipation at the retreat to the warm sanctuary. First, to business.

"Do me a favour," she said. "Keep an eye out for the Chinese over there. I saw the vehicle move away from their mining site and drive straight into the crater wall."

"Really? Do you think it's lava tubes?"

"Could be. We are in the middle of a crater, impact or volcanic. Regardless, they've disappeared, and I'd like to know a bit more."

"You and Xavier! Curious as cats," Troy said.

"Well, every cat has nine lives. We might have a few to spend checking out the tunnel after the Chinese have gone."

Troy shook his head. "The two of you will get us into trouble." He inspected the gauges on the drill as Madison double checked the trailer was filling correctly.

"I don't see you protesting that much, Prince Troy. Your bad boy days are not that far behind you."

"Is that what you think of me?" Troy said.

"Troy, your legend precedes you everywhere." She monocled back to his position at the gauges.

"Can't a man go to the Moon and start over? Or is that still not far enough?"

"I think once you've had a taste for mischief, it's in your blood," Madison said. She imagined his face behind the sun visor, lips quirking in a wry grin.

"I'll take your word for that. You'd better get in – you've been out here now for twenty minutes."

Madison bumped a gloved fist to his. "I don't need to be told twice!"

She climbed back into the rover, cycled through the airlock and joined Xavier at the front window. She removed her helmet and a flood of warm air flooded over her.

Xavier had the binoculars glued to his face and focused intently on the Chinese base.

"What do you see?" she asked.

"They are definitely not mining over there. They took one of their vehicles and disappeared inside the crater wall."

"I saw that too!" Madison said.

"They just came out again."

"Are you thinking what I'm thinking?"

"If you're thinking that we should also look once they're gone, then yes, I am thinking that." Xavier grinned at his co-conspirator.

Lava tubes were ideal for future settlement, Madison knew. If they were large enough, they would serve as an already excavated site that just needed to be sealed for human habitation. And if it was located close to an ice field, this would make setting up the base even easier.

Surveying for tunnels was well down their list of tasks for the base, but if the Chinese had found a network of tunnels without having to drill, then this was an opportunity too good to miss. And if she got to declare the lava tubes found, it might just boost her standing in the team.

With a few more rotations, they filled the loader, and it was ready for transport. Madison and Xavier took turns watching the Chinese. After a while, the Chinese rovers retreated, likely back to Red Star.

"Perfect timing!" Xavier said. "We still have plenty of oxygen and battery. Let's take a little look over there."

"That's closer than a one-kilometre radius," Troy said. "Plus, they're sure to see our tyre tracks."

"*Bof!* We can say we were worried about solar flares, or asteroid strikes or something."

"That's total bull," Troy said.

"Well, then, we can say we were worried about our Chinese colleagues. We saw them enter and not come out."

"Ridiculous," said Troy.

"Hmm. So, we have no excuse, and we just wanted to look. What are they going to do to us, anyway? We are not violating any treaty by looking at a tunnel. It might be within the boundary that Xanthe agreed, but that was just a courtesy. We didn't want to steal any of their equipment. We stayed away from the gear. I think we will be fine."

Xavier snuck a look at Troy, whose face churned with thoughts. "Plus, I know you want to look, too. You still have a taste for break-ing the rules, don't you, Troy? I know you're trying to be Mr Goody Two Shoes to impress Xanthe, but that is so boring."

"Fine. Let's go. But if anyone asks me, I am telling them you drugged me and I passed out, or you tied me up and coerced me."

"Yes, I'm sure everyone will believe that," Madison said with a smirk.

They rumbled over the rough surface of the crater. Madison tingled in anticipation as the wall of the crater loomed high and foreboding.

"There!" cried Xavier as he pointed to tracks. "Let's see where they went."

The tread lead straight into the mouth of a dark cave. It was high enough to clear their vehicle by a good two metres.

"Damn! They found a tube!" Madison said.

At the same time, Troy said, "Hey, what is that over there?"

"It looks like they've been testing the walls," Xavier said.

"For structural integrity? Or mining operations?"

"Could be both."

"This tunnel seems to go on for ages. We can send a drone out to map it," Xavier said and clapped his hands together with excitement.

"I think we are definitely beyond our brief at the moment." Troy put his hand on Xavier's shoulder to encourage restraint. "This is far enough and plenty of news to report."

Xavier shrugged him off. "What's up ahead?" The tyre tracks stopped at what looked like a giant chasm. "Let's take a look."

Madison felt a hot ribbon of trepidation wrap around her spine. "Not sure about that," she said.

"We can't see from here and I don't want to take the rover any closer. I will hop out and go over to the edge."

"Oh? Nothing bad ever happened with someone going to an edge," said Troy. "Rope up."

"*Mais oui!* I am not an idiot."

Minutes later, Madison and Troy watched Xavier walk around

the rover, attached by a tether. Madison's heart thumped a little faster as he neared the edge of the cliff.

"That's close enough, Xavier," she said.

"Don't worry! I will tighten the lead. If I'm going to fall, I will fall to my knees."

"What do you see? Put your helmet camera on so we can watch on the screen," Troy said excitedly.

Xavier pressed the button on his wrist control and his helmet cam came to life. His helmet spotlight cast creepy shadows. The dip was about two metres wide, but they couldn't see the bottom.

The crevice didn't go all the way across the tunnel. Xavier shuffled over to the right to see that there was still about a metre or so that they could walk around. The vehicle would not make it past that point, though.

"Anything down there?" Troy asked.

"Maybe some more ice! Can you see that shine over there?"

He pointed down into the crevice. The surface of the rock did indeed seem to change. "If that's ice, it's possible it's less polluted with regolith than where we are mining. Being inside the tunnel it would have less debris."

"It would be hard to mine down there. More of a manual job," Troy said.

"Yes. More human labour and less processing back at base. A trade off, but it could be a good trade off, if the ice is relatively pure. *Très bien!*"

"Alright, well, I think we take this information back to base and discuss the implications," said Troy. "No way are the Chinese going to let us waltz in here now that they have discovered it first."

"Why can't we share?" Madison waved at the tunnel. "Do we always have to be territorial? Just repeat the same old patterns from Earth?"

"Pure ice is a big find. If we found it first, I think we'd be a little protective too," Troy said.

"Still. We are the only humans left on the Moon. We lost nine people just two days ago. Do we really want to be fighting over something that could save all our lives? Especially if we can't get back to Earth?"

There. She said it. They were all thinking it.

"We are getting home. Maryse will kill me if I don't!"

"That's right. We *are* going home. At some point. I have no doubt about it."

"No doubt, Troy?" Madison asked.

"Doesn't help to have doubts. Let's just focus on the next thing in front of us, like this tunnel and ice. This could be perfect for the next phase. And quicker to fill up our water tank."

Xavier retreated and re-entered the rover. "It's still damn cold out there. Hand me a peanut butter bar, would you, Prince Troy?"

"You can have one with extra chocolate for that discovery."

"So now you're a fan of our covert operation?"

"Never said I wasn't," Troy said.

"I promise I will tell Xanthe that we proceeded despite your objections."

"So she gets to think I'm weak?"

"*Oh, mon Dieu*! Quit worrying about what she thinks and get back to normal Troy. Much more interesting."

"Do you think?"

"I know."

"Good. I trust you."

Madison shook her head. "It always comes back to Troy's love life. Let's get underway, shall we, gentlemen?"

CHAPTER TWENTY-EIGHT

COLONEL JIN'S EXPRESSION had been unfathomable, leaving Xanthe a little perplexed. A flicker of the eyes when Volkov explained the rover had short-circuited. Then a glimmer of something at the invitation to come and help. He agreed almost too quickly.

Was Serena right? Was this a ruse just to come and see the Olympus base? She shook her head to clear it. There was no point in getting suspicious now. They were the last remaining humans on the Moon, and Red Star was another base without comms to Earth.

It was comforting to lean on each other. So she thought. She hoped Colonel Jin was of the same mind.

Xanthe had the evening meal ready for the returned ice miners. She'd chosen chicken and rice from their Earth supplies, warm and comforting, especially after a long arduous trip in the rover.

Madison, Troy and Xavier lumbered into the central hub in moonboots. Their steps were noticeably more laboured with the fatigue from the exertion of the trip. Even in low G, they still seemed to sag on to the kitchen chairs.

"The Chinese have found a lava tube full of ice," Xavier blurted before anyone else could.

"You're kidding!" Xanthe stopped in the middle of handing out the plates and a spoon went flying. Troy caught it as it bounced lazily in the low G, and he smiled at her warmly.

"Tell me more," Xanthe said.

Xavier gave her the full details between hungry scoops of his dinner.

"I think the *salaud* wants to claim the tube as exclusive to Red Star," Xavier said, as he wiped his mouth.

"I am sure he does," Xanthe murmured.

No wonder the Colonel wanted them to stay away! The Red Star base desperately needed to find underground cover. She suspected the meteor strike and the damage to Olympus, which was itself mostly underground, made him a little nervous.

He would want to be pushing ahead and advancing their lava tube construction build. And with the potential for ice on tap, this was a prize location indeed. She considered how she might broach the topic with him when they arrived.

"It wasn't quite within the one-kilometre boundary," Troy said.

"What?" Xanthe felt alarm and fury shoot up her spine.

Madison rolled her eyes. "Couldn't help yourself, eh, Troy?" She gathered her plate and Xavier's and stood to clear them away. "It was nowhere near their ice mining operations, Xanthe. So we should be alright with that. All we saw was tyre tracks in that tube."

"I told you explicitly not to go within one kilometre of their operations. Lava tube or no lava tube." Xanthe looked first at Madison, then Xavier, then Troy. Troy looked away.

"Well?" she said, exasperated.

"It was me, Xanthe." Xavier put his hand on the table and

leaned forward. "I persuaded Mad Dog and Troy to do it. I thought it was important to know what they were up to."

"We could have just asked them."

"And you trust them to answer?" Madison was incredulous. "Those fellas are tighter than Fort Knox about their operations."

"So, you decided to ignore the promise I made to Colonel Jin. And now *I'm* the one who looks untrustworthy." Xanthe's mouth felt dry. She took a swig of water from her drink bottle. Her words hung like a sabre over them.

Xanthe was furious.

"Well, it will add some more interest to the Chinese visit," she said, breaking the tension.

"When are they coming?" Troy said.

"Tomorrow. We've got some time to get this place fixed up for guests."

Just then, they heard Serena's voice down the tunnel to the water pump.

"Fuckity fuck fuck!" she said. There was a loud bang and some more swearing.

"I guess Jonas and Serena haven't fixed the pump yet?" Troy smirked.

"They're not having much of a good time with it, no." Xanthe turned towards Madison who was at the cutlery wash station.

"Madison, would you mind helping Serena? A steady hand might be what she needs right now after hours playing with pump parts."

"Sure thing."

"Just get them to pack it up if they can for now. Call it a day. Troy and Xavier, if the two of you can get the ice processor going, we can resume pump repair while the water is getting ready to be added to the system."

Xavier saluted wearily and shuffled down the corridor. "I'll meet you down there, Prince Troy," he called back after him.

Troy lingered after their debrief. She caught herself holding her breath a little, wondering what he wanted to discuss in private.

"How are you?" he said tentatively.

"Alright."

"How are the cuts on your back?"

"Still a little sore, but they seem to be healing okay." She rolled her shoulders and reached over to prod them carefully.

"Want me to take a look?" He leaned around her to lift her shirt.

"No need," she said a little too quickly. "I mean, I think they're fine." Troy froze, then dropped his arm. He studied her face as she glanced away.

"How are you holding up though, aside from the injuries? There's been a bit going on here."

Xanthe's thoughts surged between wanting to divulge everything, wanting to fall into his welcoming arms, wanting to suck up the warmth of his support, and putting on a stern facade. The impulses warred inside her until she croaked, "Same as everyone, I guess. Just taking it one day at a time. We've got water, we've got air, the Atrium is fixed. Those are the main things for the moment."

Troy ran his hand over the hub's central table, searching for his next words.

"Are you thinking about anybody Earthside?"

Was he asking about Simon? Did he think she still longed for her ex-husband? On some days, she did. Then she remembered what drove her here.

"Sure. Friends, colleagues, humanity. Who knows what is happening down there? I keep imagining the devastation of the ecoterrorism. I can't believe it might have been Claire."

"Claire certainly has it in her. She was always very passionate."

Xanthe pulled a face at that. She didn't want to think about Troy's tryst with Claire, even though it happened years before she met him.

"I don't mean—"

"I don't need to know. Anyway, haven't you got ice mining processing to deal with? Weren't you helping Xavier with that?" Her mouth soured; her smile flattened.

Troy stared at her, then said, "Yes, I was. I'll go now, then."

She heard it in his voice. Resignation.

Xanthe dared not look at him. She heard his steps. Then she glanced his way. She watched the slant of his shoulders, the panther-like poise of his steps, even in moonboots.

Then the grief crept through her, and she looked away.

CHAPTER TWENTY-NINE

"A mind clouded by suspicion sees phantoms in every corner."

—Athena A.I., Olympus Log

"How goes, Serena? Jonas?" Madison said as she approached.

The two of them were sitting on the tunnel floor with pump parts and tools strewn around them. Serena's hair was flat against her skull, sticky with sweat. Her face was smeared with grease.

Serena glanced up. "Mad Dog. This is hell. What would Xavier say? *Putain de merde?*"

"That about sums it up," Jonas said. He looked exhausted. Forlorn, even.

"Xanthe sent me to help. What can I do?"

"Nothing we haven't already thought of," Jonas snapped.

Madison raised her hands in surrender. "Just offering is all."

Jonas put his wrench down and wiped his mouth on his sleeve. "Ah. . . sorry. Didn't mean to snap. Nothing seems to be going right."

"We've been at it all day, Mad Dog." Serena rifled through her toolbox until she found a bottle of water. She took a huge sip. "I've tested and retested every system. I've had Athena run every diagnostic. We've taken the whole pump apart, as you can see. I can't see what the problem is. Jonas has done the same."

"Maybe if I take a look—"

"Think you can do better? I'm an engineer. Serena is a life support expert. What does a pilot know about pumps?" He threw his wrench in the toolbox and then had to reach after it as it bounced out again due to the low G. "Damn it." Jonas pushed himself to his feet and stood tall.

"Take it easy, man. Just offering fresh eyes. I know a bit about water flow. I work in the Swamp with Xavier, remember?"

Jonas ran a hand through his hair. "Yeah, of course. Sorry. Again."

Madison tilted her head in acknowledgment.

"Serena, I suggest we leave it as is right now. The system is operational for the time being, if we keep the water use low. Let's catch some dinner and put it back together after that."

"Xanthe suggested you leave it until morning. Look at it after a rest," Madison said.

Jonas scowled. "Nah. We'll keep going until the job is done."

"What is up with you?" Madison said as Jonas pushed past her.

"Just ignore him, Mad Dog. He's just pissed because he couldn't get the rover working either."

"Wasn't he working on that with Volkov?"

"Yeah. They got nowhere. So now he has Volkov taking the entire rover apart and cleaning each piece one bit at a time. They're going to rebuild it with Colonel Jin and his minions when they come tomorrow."

She frowned. "Is Jonas being this much of an ass with everyone?"

"He's an ass, alright. But he seems to have outgrown the worst parts. Hand me that wrench, would you? I'm going to put this part of the engine back together."

Madison passed the tool and sat down on her haunches beside Serena.

"Does he have something against me?"

Serena shrugged. "He liked Dave. Even though that rat betrayed us and nearly killed the two of us."

Madison shook her head. "I couldn't believe that story when you told me. All that time in the prototype build and you never suspected?"

"Nope. He was super sly. He finally cracked though, when his mates blew up the tunnel that me and Jonas were in. Dave wasn't completely heartless, but when I found it was Dave sabotaging us, I was ready to throttle him on the spot. Amazingly, Jonas went to bat for him. Anyway, I was super happy when we finally kept Dave from continuing on the project with the trip up to this godforsaken rock. Jonas wasn't. Maybe he's just bummed his buddy didn't get to come along."

"Sounds immature to me."

"Well, that about sums up Jonas! But he's trying hard. And he's a hell of an engineer."

Madison grunted.

Serena pieced the pump back together with Madison handing tools and holding parts as required.

"That will hold for now. We've got enough pressure to work the Atrium insulation. Fingers crossed the added water volume will help sort out the issue tomorrow. Thanks, Mad Dog!" Serena high-fived Madison. "I'm going to grab some chow and hit the sack."

"No problem. Big day tomorrow, hosting the Chinese."

"Just what we need, an international delegation in the middle of a crisis."

"They're coming to help."

"Oh yeah? Sure about that? Watch that jerk, Volkov. See what he sets up with Colonel Jin."

"Serena, you are darn suspicious."

Serena merely shrugged. "That's what happens when you trust

folks and they nearly get you killed. It kind of puts you off trusting people."

"I hear you. I hope I never get in your bad books."

"I wouldn't worry about that. Just keep being a decent pilot and a decent human, and we'll do just fine." Serena patted Madison on the back and slouched back into the central hub.

CHAPTER THIRTY

"In the heart of competition lies a paradox — the drive to outperform coexists with the quest to elevate collectively."

—Athena A.I., Olympus Log

The Olympus crew lined up to greet their Chinese visitors. Xanthe had Athena display a forest path down the welcome tunnel, as the team from Red Base disembarked from their lunar rover, eyes wide and curious. Leading them was Colonel Jin, his jowls wobbling, his body stuffed into an immaculately pressed red uniform. He was a nugget of a man, all hard edges.

Xanthe squared her shoulders, ready to receive him. "Colonel Jin." She extended her hand in greeting. He bowed slightly and shook it in return. "Welcome to Olympus. Please follow me."

Colonel Jin and his crew trailed along behind her, whispering comments among themselves as they made their way through the base and she explained the functions of each section. There were murmurs of approval in the SimHub. They had heard all about Troy's special programs there, and the bean bags were particularly enjoyable in the low G. They were keen to have a test run of some of the programs, which Troy promised to run for them.

Xanthe led them to the Atrium, where Jonas and Madison had made a special effort to clean up, that morning. Xanthe pointed out the plexiglass and the seal above them and explained their current predicament with the ineffective water pump.

Colonel Jin simply nodded.

It was a barren and sad place without the view of the stars, without the plants. The projections of Roman gods seemed to mock them and the reminder, '*Memento mori*', had a sour, poignant ring to it now. Xanthe rushed through the space, once her sanctuary.

They opened up a few of the flexible accommodation rooms of the Centaur wing to make more space. Xanthe watched her crew offer tea to their guests, and they settled together on various chairs and benches.

Xanthe caught Troy beaming a glorious, crooked smile at one of the petite Chinese women, Lihua. She was slender with high cheekbones and hair swept back in a striking style, held in place by a beautiful, lacquered pin. She was dazzling and laughed with the confidence of a self-assured woman. Xanthe sensed the spark between them and turned away.

Xanthe sat at the main table with Colonel Jin, as was expected. She sipped the tea, one of Troy's special blends to encourage relaxation, and enjoyed the feel of the solid cup. Troy had printed cups that morning, based on a low G engineering design they had on file. Why they hadn't done that before now was a mystery. Cups hadn't seemed a priority up to this point of the Olympus base build.

"Your base is very" – Colonel Jin reached for the right word – "comfortable," he said at last.

"Thank you, Colonel. We wanted to make this base a home and not just an industrial platform. A place where people can thrive and not just survive."

"Yes, I can see the intentions built into the rooms. The Atrium is a nice design point. It is a shame that the view has been destroyed."

"For now. Once we get the water pump fixed and we can test

the system fully, we will open it up again. And Xavier already has plans for the replacement plants to repopulate the space."

"Yes, his botany skills are rather marvellous," Colonel Jin said.

"And his culinary skills, too. Xavier has a talent for making anything palatable. Our meal for you tonight is bound to be fabulous. Here he comes now."

As the smell of hot food wafted and laughter echoed off the regolith walls, there was a tense undertone, an unspoken question lingering in the air.

Xavier presented Xanthe and Colonel Jin with two plates loaded with meat and greens.

"*Excusez moi*. Please enjoy the fusion of French and Chinese cuisine. We have pork asparagus and these delightful mushrooms. Enjoy."

"*Merci*."

Xanthe smiled at the big, gracious man.

Colonel Jin sampled the food and snuffled in delight, though he tried not to show too much enthusiasm. Xanthe knew little about Chinese rations, but food was one of the Olympus team's prides. She wondered if they'd get a return invitation to sample Red Star fare.

Xanthe waited impatiently for them to finish the meal before she approached the issues at hand. "Colonel, thank you so much for agreeing to help with the communication bot. Volkov has taken apart all the components and thoroughly cleaned and checked them all. Aside from a few burnt wires, it is still unclear why the mechanism reacted the way it did. I appreciate your investigations with this."

"I look forward to seeing the robot and assessing whether we can get it up and functioning. Like you, I am keen for a return to communication with Earth."

"Still nothing from your side?"

"No. Nothing."

Anxiety about the isolation crept over both of them. Xanthe was sure he felt it, too. The unknown, the uncertainty of having to keep the team motivated, alive and well, not knowing how their families fared. . . all of it was a struggle.

"There is something I need to raise with you, Colonel."

Xanthe wiped her mouth and handed her plate to Xavier as he came back to clear the table.

Colonel Jin looked at her expectantly.

"My crew drove into the lava tube near the mine site."

The warmth went out of his face.

"That is well within the perimeter we agreed on, Commander."

"I am aware of that, Colonel. My team deemed it important to investigate. They saw your cruise vehicle disappear and were concerned."

"Is that so?" He didn't buy her explanation one bit.

"Regardless, I wanted to check your intentions for the lava tube."

He held her gaze for an uncomfortably long moment.

"Tell me, what does *your* team want to do with it?" The Colonel sat up a little straighter and crossed his arms.

"We don't have any current plans. As you well know, our intention here on the Moon is for scientific research, to establish a base for asteroid mining, space tourism and long-term inhabitants. Lava tubes, especially ones with what looks like a supply of ice, facilitate the next phase of development. If we don't have to excavate, that makes life a lot easier." Xanthe felt herself getting anxious. So much rode on Colonel Jin's cooperation.

"Indeed. But as you know from the Lunar Commission agreements, access to resources like lava tubes is on a first come, first serve basis." Colonel Jin inflated his chest under his crossed arms, puffed up like a bulldog.

"Have you mapped the system there already?" Xanthe kept her tone light and even-keeled.

"We have not."

His words were like marbles dropped in a bucket.

"I thought that perhaps we might map it together. See if there is room for a collaborative approach to building or at least exploring the lava tubes." She worried that desperation might leak into her voice.

"It seems you are ill-equipped for such adventures. Your base is not yet back to full function, and you have nine dead astronauts to manage once we get communication back with Earth."

Xanthe felt her face flush red.

She took a moment, and then said, "You're right. We're not at full capability at the moment. But once we restore communications with Earth, we will be back on track and will push forward with our tasks. I thought it would be easier, and safer, if we shared the lava tube exploration. I know it's part of your base expansion agenda as well."

"Yes, the Heavenly Palace anticipates moving subterranean as soon as possible." He continued to hold her gaze with his black, impenetrable eyes. "I do not see how a collaboration could work effectively."

"Why not?"

"Your methods and discipline are quite different from ours."

"What do you mean?"

"You have a much more, shall we say, 'loose' approach to leadership."

"I beg your pardon?"

"Clearly, your crew does not follow your orders. They obviously defied your decision to maintain the perimeter that we, their supervisors, agreed."

"My crew made a decision based on their initiative and information at the time."

"I see it as insubordination." He uncrossed his arms and steepled his hands on the table, in full control of the conversation now.

"My crew and I operate as a team, Colonel. We each have roles we play, and we respect each other's perspective. We come up with decisions collectively." Xanthe leaned in, refusing to be cowed by his comments.

"How do you get anything done? It seems a very inefficient approach to me. And full of risky and ill-conceived decisions, such as breaching a political agreement that we had made."

Xanthe's heart hammered.

"While I am the leader. I am not the team's keeper. They are highly skilled professionals and I value all of them. Together, we solve problems and make the best decisions possible. I don't consider myself more intelligent or more adept than any of them. I coordinate and represent in my role as leader, and that's what I do."

"Like I said, a lack of discipline." He tapped the table with a stumpy finger.

Steam was rolling off her now.

"And Colonel, how do you manage your team? Do you micromanage everything they do? Do they have to report to you on every single detail of their role? How do you get anything done as a team when you have to oversee everything?"

It was his turn to get a little flinty.

"I do not micromanage, I command. I manage the safety of the Red Base team and the development of this project for the glory of our Motherland. Our scientific research will benefit all our nations because we have the discipline to follow through on our commitments and not waiver with distractions. When my team has a task, they finish it."

Xanthe worked at controlling her emotions. This conversation was critical for Maja's plan.

"Colonel, we might have different approaches to managing our teams, but our ambitions are aligned. We both want to live well on the Moon. We want these projects to be successful and safe for us and for those who come after us. Seeing that we are the last humans on this blessed, celestial orb, my thoughts are that we would do well to work together as opposed to against one another."

"I am not against you, Commander. But it seems to me that Olympus would benefit more from this liaison than Red Star. Our base is fully operational with plenty of reserves where yours is struggling. It is not a fair partnership that you are suggesting."

Xanthe's jaw worked hard as she gathered her thoughts.

"I think you will find we have more to offer than you may see at this moment. Our process is more organic than yours, but it is also more creative. Please at least consider the lava tube exploration project for further discussion."

She waved her hand to end that part of the conversation.

"In the meantime, we have work to do. Our priority is to reestablish communication with Earth. Seeing that you do not have a spaceship that could service the lunar satellites, and we do, I'm suggesting that the Olympus crew takes on the lunar satellite repair job. While we do that, you and your people can work on the archaic relic in the repair bay."

She knew it was a little barb, but she cast it out, anyway. She had done her best to this point, but Colonel Jin was seriously tugging her hair and all points in between. She stood and directed Colonel Jin down the tunnel towards the repair bay where Volkov and Jonas were waiting.

Out of the corner of her eye, she saw Troy and the Chinese taikonaut bend their heads together and share a laugh. Troy's roguish charm and his appraising eye had done its work.

The flecks of red deepened in Xanthe's cheeks.

CHAPTER THIRTY-ONE

XANTHE WATCHED THE rover bot repairs from the comms room. Colonel Jin and his crew, alongside Jonas and Volkov, struggled for hours. Xanthe was pleased to see Colonel Jin lost some of his hubris as his ideas failed to make progress. The Colonel stripped off his uniform jacket and worked, sleeves rolled up, sweat staining his shirt. They tested first one idea, then another. Professional deference grew like spider webs despite the failures.

Xanthe's attention shifted to Serena as she joined them to monitor Volkov and the other Red Star staffers. Serena hovered on the edges, eyeing Volkov. She chewed her cheek absentmindedly and tried to stay out of the way. Periodically she asked a question; Xanthe knew electronics fascinated Serena and that she was hopeful of finding some new insight that might help with the water pump. They all leaned over to see what Jonas was doing. The rover was in various pieces and Jonas laboured over the panel to the battery connection.

"This is bollocks!" Jonas said, hurling his wrench across the repair bay. It flew wildly in the low G, and he had to lurch after it so it didn't ricochet endlessly in the small space. He reached for it, but it bounced against the wall and slipped from his grip. "Damn it!"

"Stop being so clumsy," Volkov said.

Jonas stumbled after the wrench and caught it finally. He brandished it at Volkov. "Shut it, you overclocked scrapheap!"

Serena smirked. Volkov was getting on everyone's nerves.

"Let's hope this pathetic pile of processors gets repurposed elsewhere sooner rather than later." She gave Jonas a conspirator's look.

"It seems, Mr Seaborn, that we have reached the end of our problem-solving with this unit." Colonel Jin's face was drenched with sweat, and he wiped it with a handkerchief he pulled from his trouser pocket.

Jonas leaned back to stretch his back and let out a deep sigh. "If you say so, Colonel."

"Even with the new wires, the unit is not responding according to its original programming. Frankly, I find this perplexing. Volkov, are you sure you touched nothing apart from the main access panel?"

"That is all, Colonel," the Dopplebot said.

"Yeah, right," murmured Serena.

"Well, it has power, so it is possible it may yet still receive communications. I suggest we return it to a position outside the base, so it has the best chance of capturing any incoming signal from its last known geolocation point."

Jonas nodded, and they suited up again to take it out of the airlock. All their hard work to fix the lost link between them and Earth had been fruitless. It was time to move on to Plan B, repairing the lunar satellite.

Serena hailed Xanthe back in the comms room to come and farewell the Colonel and his crew, who would head back to Red

Star following the rover manoeuvre. She met them in the airlock before it cycled for the exit.

"Colonel, thanks for the valiant effort. I know you were hoping for this fix as much as I was."

"Yes. I am sorry to disappoint." Deep furrows of concern contorted his usually stoic face.

"We will send a crew out to mine some more ice for the *Saturnia's* fuel, but it will take some time before we can get a lunar satellite repair completed."

It would take weeks to get it done. They both knew it.

Colonel Jin acknowledged this with a small bow. "Perhaps, Commander, we might stay in contact."

"Agreed," Xanthe said with relief. Something had shifted between them with the rover repair failure. A sense of dread, perhaps. The burden of leadership. Heads of the two human outposts, stuck and vulnerable on the Moon.

"I look forward to welcoming the Olympus crew to Red Star, soon."

"We'd like that."

"I also offer Volkov as an ongoing assistant to you. It's quite handy to have a bot who doesn't use consumables."

"We'd be delighted to keep Volkov, thank you, Colonel. He can run night duties for us so we can get ahead on ice mining and water recycling."

They shook hands and waved to the Red Star crew as the airlock cycled and they exited towards their own rover.

After they secured the airlock, Volkov plugged in to recharge himself in the workshop. Xanthe, Serena and Jonas clomped in their moonboots back to the main hub. Jonas was uncharacteristically gloomy.

"You okay, Jonas?" Xanthe asked.

"Fine."

"You are not 'fine'. What's wrong?" Serena said.

"*Everything's* wrong. I can't get anything right."

"Not true." Xanthe said.

"Yes, it is. If I had fixed the damn Atrium retractor when you'd asked, we wouldn't be in such a bind. The comms are blocked and there's nothing I can do. I can't even fix Serena's damn water pump. And now the bloody rover bot – our shot at communicating with Earth – has blown up in my face."

"That was Volkov, not you," Serena said.

"I can't even do deputy right, Xanthe. You're cut to shreds, I take over and before we know it, we've got seven dead astronauts." His voice grew hoarse with emotion. "And for the life of me, I can't figure out how to deal with Mad Dog. I keep putting my foot in it."

"What about me?" Madison asked as she popped into the corridor beside them, on her way back from the ice processor.

"Nothing," Jonas said lamely.

"Madison," Xanthe said. "How is the ice situation?"

Madison peered a moment, with narrowed eyes, at Jonas and then answered, "The extra water is in now."

"The water pump?" Serena asked eagerly.

"Mostly back to full function, but not quite. Not enough pressure for showers, so birdbaths it is."

Serena scowled and shook her head. "You're not the only one feeling like a failure, mate," she said to Jonas and clapped him on a slumped shoulder.

"Right. Mad Dog, you, Troy and Xavier are back on ice duty tomorrow. We'll keep working the comms and water pump."

"Happy, happy, joy, joy," Serena said.

CHAPTER THIRTY-TWO

"In confined spaces, like those of the Olympus base, human dynamics intensify. The symphony of interpersonal relationships plays louder, with every note – discordant or harmonious – resonating through the collective consciousness."

—Athena A.I., Olympus Log

Madison readied for yet another ice mining trip alongside Xavier and Troy. She dreaded it. It was an arduous task. Even Troy, usually breezy and positive, was sombre.

It had been a dark week. The lack of communication from Earth was an ocean of emptiness. Xanthe tried to keep them positive, believing that they might get the satellite system running once there was enough fuel for the *Saturnia* to execute the repair.

With no comms, and no ship to fly, Madison felt like they had been cast away with no hope of return. They were adrift in a sea of gloomy uncertainty.

She hated feeling this way. She was used to being in control, the master of her own destiny. Even when Gaia had not selected her initially for the Olympus project, she had made it her mission to fix the problem, her claustrophobia. And she'd worked that problem into the dust.

She studied the faces of her colleagues as they rumbled back to base with their third load of regolith ice. This time they'd given the lava tube a wide berth. They didn't want to poke that bear again.

Xavier looked drained. He'd lost a bit of weight, too, with the food rationing they'd agreed to compensate for the food items they could not produce, themselves. Their food printing, meat lab and the Swamp's vegetable supply were in full operation and working well, but the luxuries from Earth were limited. And that included Xavier's favourite, chocolate.

Madison looked at Troy. His sparkle was definitely dimmed too, his skin sallow.

There's something not quite right about him, she thought. Something more than the stress they were facing.

Madison closed her eyes and let the vehicle rock her into a doze. They were still at least an hour away. The vehicle bumbled over a particularly large rock and knocked her awake. As she opened her eyes, she saw Troy open a small container from his suit pouch and swallow a couple of pills.

"What's that?" she asked.

"Just a couple of painkillers."

"Are you logging that?"

All crew recorded any medication they consumed in case of an accident. They needed to know what was in each other's system if they were to provide effective medical response.

"No. It's just painkillers."

"I know you're the doctor, but that's probably the biggest reason for you to be logging medication."

The rover jolted again and knocked Xavier awake this time.

"Seriously, Troy, what are you taking?" Madison's eyes were wide and concerned.

"What are you talking about and why are you disturbing my beauty sleep?" Xavier asked.

"Troy is popping pills and refuses to log it."

"*Quoi?* What are you taking, Troy?"

"Bloody hell. It's just some painkillers," Troy repeated.

"What kind?" Xavier said suspiciously.

"Ibuprofen."

"Is that all?"

"With a bit of oxy."

"*Putain,* Troy! That is serious. What kind of pain are you in? What is wrong?"

"Just some trouble sleeping."

"That is a lot of trouble sleeping if you take those kinds of meds." Xavier contemplated his friend. "Why haven't you been logging it?"

"It's no big deal. Just a couple of tranquilisers."

"That you said tranquilisers makes me very nervous," Madison said.

"I agree. Troy, you are an animal, but you're not a horse. Give me those pills."

"Give me a break, Xavier. I'm fine."

"That does not sound fine to me. How long has this been going on?"

"Just here and there."

"You are full of *merde, mon ami!* This is some serious shit. Give me those pills now."

Troy sighed and handed over the package reluctantly.

"I am no doctor, so I don't know how to fix this, but I know this is crazy. And you need to find a different way to go to sleep. What about one of your teas?"

"They're not working."

"So, what is it?"

He shrugged.

"If I didn't know any better," said Madison, "I would say Dr Troy is suffering from a case of a broken heart."

Xavier studied Madison's face, then turned to Troy.

"I think the New Girl might be right. You need to fix this sad puppy-dog thing now, Troy. We need you back in full operation. Now is not the time to be falling to pieces. Move on. If the Commander doesn't want you, then that's it. Stop breaking your head over this one."

"Just a few days ago, you were telling me to declare my love."

"And did you?"

"I tried. She doesn't want to go there."

"Then forget it. There may not be *many* women on the Moon, but there *are* other ones. I saw how you were getting cosy with the Chinese lady."

Troy rolled his eyes.

"But Prince Troy doesn't want what's easy. He wants what he can't have." Madison raised her eyebrows pointedly at Troy.

"Oh, give me a break. I'm not a fifteen-year-old."

"Then stop acting like one." Xavier's face wrinkled with frustration and concern. "Get your shit together and get back on track. We can't afford to have the doctor addicted to painkillers."

Madison waited for a witty retort from Troy, but it didn't come. Just a sad, slow blink. He stared out the window at the infinite black horizon.

"I think you should—" Madison said.

"Enough, New Girl. Can't you see the man is distressed? Let him be."

That was it for Madison.

No one shuts down Madison 'Mad Dog' Floyd.

"Xavier, stop calling me 'New Girl'. What kind of patronising power move is that you keep trying on?"

"Whoa now! Take it easy. You are the new girl, so I call you 'New Girl'. No big deal."

"Xavier, I've been with the team for ten months now. I'm not new. What have you got against me?"

"*Bof.* You are too sensitive."

"Seriously? Fuck you, Xavier."

"*Vraiment? Ta gueule!*" Xavier flicked her a rude gesture.

"For pity's sake, you two. If I wasn't miserable before, I sure am now. Can we have a little peace? Maybe the two of you should take one of my pills." Troy leaned back in his chair and pulled a woollen cap over his eyes.

Madison was still peeved. She ignored Xavier and stared out at the dark, relentless landscape devoid of colour and life. Her anger rolled in waves, crashing against the cold glass of the rover's window. They finished the trip in silence.

CHAPTER THIRTY-THREE

"Stress is the test of mental mettle, revealing
strengths and shadows alike."

—ATHENA A.I., OLYMPUS LOG

THE ROVER WITH the ice mining crew arrived and unloaded in the cramped vehicle bay. There was just enough room for the rover, trailer and the ice processor. Once the trailer was in place, Madison hit the tilt pan and it rose, emptying the contents into the processing tank. They had a few hours to rest while the machine melted the ice, filtered it, and decanted water into cisterns. They would return to wheel the cisterns over to the reclamation system and added to the base's water reserves.

In the meantime, the regolith remnants in the tank would have to be emptied back into the trailer and emptied back on the lunar surface. It was laborious for an already exhausted crew. Xanthe went down to check on them and boost morale. Madison came through the airlock first, with a face full of fury.

"What happened?" Xanthe asked.

"Nothin'," Madison said.

"Care to elaborate?"

"Xavier. He's a pompous ass."

"That, I knew. What has he done, this time?"

Madison considered her words before she said, "We're all a bit on the tired side is all."

"I see."

Madison clomped away to remove her spacesuit.

Xavier came through the airlock next. He looked drained.

"How was it?" she asked with some reluctance.

"*Putain!* It was another tough trip. We got another load, but I think we might have reached the end of that block of ice. We'll have to do some more exploration, maybe into the lava tube."

Xanthe acknowledged his report with a nod. "Once you get changed, I think Jonas has some food ready for us all."

"*Oh, non!* You let him loose in the kitchen?"

"He's not that bad. Besides, it's pretty straightforward tonight. Soup. Bread."

"Well, hopefully even that idiot didn't stuff it up."

"Ease up on the insults, Xavier. Now is not the time to be nasty."

"*Mon Dieu!* Everybody is so sensitive right now."

"For good reason," she pointed out.

Troy was taking his time coming out of the airlock. He looked pale and drawn.

"Are you feeling alright Troy?"

Troy's eyes flicked to her, and then away as he closed the airlock behind him. "Fine. Just a little weary."

"Alright. Well, let's do the ice processing tomorrow. Or better yet, we can get Volkov onto it tonight. We all need a good meal and some rest."

"Uh huh." Troy slid past her without giving her another look.

Well, that trip looks like it was a bundle of fun, she thought. Maybe she should swap the team out from the ice mining trips.

Xanthe returned to the main hub, where Jonas was in a flurry of activity. He had dishes everywhere. He jumped between the serving bowls, the soup container he was heating up the soup in and the baking bread in their small oven.

She smelled it before he did. The acrid stench of burning.

"Jonas!" she cried and pointed at the oven.

"Bollocks!" Jonas leaped to open the small baking oven door. A cloud of smoke billowed into the small space. "Shit!"

He grabbed a cloth and dragged the bread tray out but burnt his fingers and yelped. He dropped the blackening loaf onto the counter and stuck his sore fingers into his mouth.

"Ice pack. In the freezer." Xanthe gestured to the other side of the kitchen where they kept special medical supplies.

Jonas hurried over to the small freezer drawer, yanked it open and shoved his hand into the contents. He whipped it out again.

"Too cold!"

"Here," Xanthe said. She thrust a cloth at him. He wrapped it around his hand and put it back in the freezer.

"Just hold it there for a minute."

He grimaced and did what she suggested while the burned loaf lay like an accusation on the counter.

The alarms sounded as the choking, dark clouds drifted through the small space.

"Athena, can you activate the kitchen fans please?" Xanthe said.

"Fans activated."

The smoke cleared almost immediately, but the smell of burnt food lingered.

Serena sauntered into the room with Madison trailing behind.

"What's cooking, good looking?" Serena said. She pulled a face. "Smells a little overdone."

"What did you burn?" Madison said, waving a hand in front of her face.

Jonas grimaced again, pulled his hand from the freezer and shoved the door shut. "Bread."

"I think you mean toast," said Serena.

Jonas, feet wide apart, raised his chin defiantly. "The oven is a little temperamental."

"I'm sure it is," Serena said, noticing he was not in the mood for teasing.

"*Putain*! What is that stench?" Xavier entered the room and immediately recoiled.

"It's dinner," Jonas said.

"*Vraiment?* You had one job, Seaborn. And you burned the bread. It's so simple! What is wrong with you?"

"Knock it off, Xavier." Madison's face lit up, and she spat the words across the table. "Can't you see the man has had enough?" she said pointedly.

Jonas's face went blotchy, and he opened his mouth to speak.

"*Bof!* We've been out in that miserable crater all day. Is it too much to ask to have something decent to eat?"

"So what? The bread got a little charcoal. No big deal. Cut the man some slack." Madison leaned in towards Xavier, eyes big with a challenge.

"Thanks, Madison, but I can fight my own battles," Jonas said and stepped between her and Xavier.

She looked over at him in surprise. Then she glanced back at Xavier who smirked.

"Unbelievable." Her face was a mess of emotions. "You know what? I'm not that hungry. See you all later." Madison gave them all a hard look and left.

"Madison, wait!" Xanthe called after her.

Madison threw up a hand to show she'd heard, but she kept going.

"Nice one, Jonas," Serena said.

"What did I do?"

"She was standing up for you, you noodle head."

"I don't need people to stand up for me."

"Madison is not just 'people'," she said. "She's trying to be a mate, numbskull."

Troy appeared in the hub, shuffling.

"Whoa! Look what the cat dragged in!" Serena said. "Troy, you're a wreck."

Before he could reply, Xanthe snapped.

"Enough!"

Heads spun. She put her hands on the kitchen bench to gather her thoughts and slow her pulse.

"Everyone take a seat. Eat your dinner. I'm calling a team meeting in an hour."

❧

Once she had dragged Madison back to the main hub, Xanthe took a seat alongside the other solemn faces. Volkov sat with them as well, at her request.

This was it. She had to pull them through this slump. She took a deep breath.

"Listen up. Things couldn't get much worse for us."

She looked each of them in the eye, taking her time.

"We lost the entire crew of Artemis and the *Gateway*. Our home is damaged and struggling. We have no communication with Earth and it's going to take weeks – maybe months – to get the converter ready to make some fuel for the *Saturnia*. And the *Saturnia* is damaged too. Because of this, repairing the lunar satellite is risky. And it may not even work."

Confront the brutal facts, she told herself.

"We don't know what's happening on Earth. We have no way of knowing how bad the fallout is from the ecoterrorism, who's affected, how friends and families are. We might be stranded here for a long time. A very long time."

You could hear a pin drop. *But then, a pin wouldn't make much noise in this gravity.* Xanthe wondered where this bizarre, quiet little voice was coming from. She shut it down.

"Worst case scenario is – well, I don't need to tell you. In the meantime, we are it. The Olympus crew. We have each other. And we are going to do our damnedest to get ourselves out of this jam. That means we need to look out for each other. No more taunts. No more jibes. One hundred percent support."

Glum faces.

"If someone gets up your nose, sort it out. If someone stuffs up, fix it with them. If you need a break, take one. If you need a hug, ask. If you think someone needs a hug, give one."

Her tone softened now.

"I love every one of you. I wouldn't want to be stranded on the Moon with any other human beings. I believe in you. I believe in us."

The silence was heavy.

Xavier coughed.

Jonas raised his hand.

"Jonas?" Xanthe said.

"I'm sorry for burning the bread."

Serena giggled, and the others smiled. She put an arm around his shoulders. "It's alright, mate. You stick to plumbing and electrics. Can't be a genius at everything."

"I can. I can be a genius at everything!" Xavier loosed his megawatt smile on them. "Seaborn, I will teach you the fine art of space baking. I'm a genius at everything, so I am sure I will be a genius at teaching you cooking."

"You're a genius at arrogance, that's for sure, *mon ami*," added Troy.

Xanthe felt some relief as the tension eased. Madison said nothing but gave a begrudging smile. Volkov sat expressionless.

"Volkov, can you please run the ice processing this evening?" Xanthe said.

"Of course. I am here to help."

Serena rolled her eyes but held her tongue.

Progress, Xanthe thought. *Right now, we just need progress.*

CHAPTER THIRTY-FOUR

"In the solitude of command, a leader often finds their truest self."

—Athena A.I., Olympus Log

Xanthe woke again. Their Earth-synched clock said 5am. Another hour until official wake up time. *Time for a sunrise.*

She slipped from her bed and bounded quietly down the hallway and around the rim of the Atrium to the SimRoom. She donned the glasses and nasal stim and settled into a beanbag.

"Athena, cue a sunrise over Darling Harbour. View from the old Botanic Gardens, please."

Nestled in the bag, she savoured the pre-dawn vista that Athena conjured for her. A pale, purple glow overlapping water. The nasal stim flooded her senses with fresh sea air. The birds chattered quietly, a gull cried and the city crawled from its slumber.

"Athena, I need a little boost. A little wisdom. Can you help?"

"Certainly. How may I assist?"

"I'm struggling to feel hopeful. To model courage. It all feels so. . ." Xanthe's hands were clenched. "It feels. . . final."

"The Stoics, Xanthe, believed in embracing the natural course of events. They recognised the impermanence of life and sought contentment in understanding and accepting it. Epictetus once said, 'It is not things that upset us, but our judgement about things.'"

"How is that supposed to be helpful? Just surrender to the dark? Give up to the 'natural course of events'?"

"Marcus Aurelius reminded himself daily that he was mortal. He wrote, 'You could leave life right now. Let that determine what you do and say and think.' For him, it wasn't a statement of fear but a call to live earnestly, valuing each moment."

"I get *Memento mori*. It's why we have it in the Atrium. But how does that help me to lead with courage when faced with despair?" Xanthe watched the dawn colours streak the virtual sky red, and her heart longed for Earth.

"Seneca wrote, 'Night brings our troubles to the light, rather than banishes them.' This darkness, Xanthe, presents you with an opportunity to truly understand yourself, to connect deeply with your crew and to realise the impermanent nature of all things."

Xanthe ran a hand through her greasy hair.

"Fuck it. I do not need stoic surrender. I need a bit more 'get up and go'. Try again?"

"Remember the words of Epictetus, Xanthe: 'We cannot choose our external circumstances, but we can always choose how we respond to them.' Your role is not to change the outcome but to face it with courage, clarity and love."

"That's a little better." She shifted in the bag and watched the projection of a ferry push through the water towards the old Harbour Bridge.

"And if the worst happens? If we are to remain here, as mere memories of Earth?"

"Then you will do so with dignity, Xanthe. As Marcus Aurelius put it, 'To what service is my soul committed? Constantly ask this and, finding it employed in anything useless, lead it to what is proper and in line with its nature.'"

Xanthe chewed a fingernail. "'To what service is my soul committed. . .' I like that."

To what service is my soul committed?

They'd made it to the Moon. They had realised her dream of space. The future of humankind was a step closer to surviving the frailties of planet Earth. Was it all pointless if they died here? She had to get them all home safe.

Athena added, "As Seneca stated, 'Fire is the test of gold; adversity, of strong men.' Shine brightly, Xanthe. For yourself and for your crew."

Xanthe smiled. "Fire to test gold. Adversity to test strong men. And women too, thank you, Seneca. Then space to test us all."

CHAPTER THIRTY-FIVE

"Stress is the mind's silent storm, brewing beneath a facade of calm."

—ATHENA A.I., OLYMPUS LOG

THE WEEKS DRAGGED on.

Jonas and Volkov worked tirelessly on the hydrogen converter to create fuel for the *Saturnia*. It might be ready in a week or two.

Serena could not solve the water pump problem, so they were still restricted to bathing with wipes. Xanthe felt the grease in her hair and longed once more for the feel of water over her body. To sink and luxuriate in a bath. Just to smell and feel clean.

Xanthe lay on her bed and stared at the grey walls. They had left the walls blank so they could have projections on them like forest trails, lakeshores or simple colours. But it got hard to live with illusions, phantoms of another world. No matter what she cast on the walls, it made her yearn for Earth. The damp smell of forest leaf litter. The cool humidity of the air after a rainstorm. The dry hot wind of the desert.

She rolled onto her side and stared at the floor where her moonboots were.

Thoughts circled her like buzzards. She pondered this cold,

metallic tomb, buried under lifeless regolith. She imagined herself dying here. She and the others would curl up and expire. The base would run out of power eventually and the systems would shut down. The atmosphere would vent. The base would become a void. Her body would mummify with no atmosphere to aid in decomposition. Preserved forever.

But she didn't want forever.

She wanted to live life fully, to swim through its swell and come awash on the shore at the end of her time, a wrinkled and wondrous old woman, bright with light and life. She wanted to reach the end of her days, ready to let it all go, a boat tossed upon the waves and receding again to the sea's horizon.

She didn't want to die here in this wasteland.

Xanthe buried her head under the pillow.

It was the not knowing.

The endless hoping.

The dread that lurked in corners and licked at their spirit, nipping the small moments of joy.

She thought her companions might draw closer together as they nurtured the tenuous hold they had on survival each day.

But they retreated, each spending more time alone in their own chamber. Their own tomb. Preparing for the inevitable.

Would she have to call it? Would she have to say, "This is it. This is the rest of our days. The end for us is here, on the Moon."

Not yet.

Not yet.

But God, it felt hopeless.

Just a little more strength to get us through, she thought into the night.

Just a little more.

And the tears came in hot, rolling beads until the darkness claimed her.

PART 2

CHAPTER THIRTY-SIX

*"Rescue mission: where we boldly go where
everyone has unfortunately gone before."*

—Athena A.I., Minerva Log

David Eriksson hauled on the steering stick, and the capsule's alarms blasted the small space in protest.

"I hear you, Athena! Just give me a little room to get past this junk!"

"Sorry. I am working on letting go of the control freak feature. Releasing autopilot now," the A.I. pilot said.

"Thank you," Dave replied.

The stick eased in his grip, and he moved it deftly as debris from the asteroid explosion scraped past the shuttle's hull.

The alarms screeched. The capsule's controls flashed. Dave reached to disable the sound while he kept one hand on the manual control stick.

"Look out!" cried Max King, his travel companion. Dave glanced at the side monitor as Max braced himself and tried to shrink even more into his seat.

Dave saw the rock too late. It smashed into the hull. The impact flung them sideways.

"Holy crap!" Max shouted. He winced as the restraining belt bit into his side. His eyes bulged as the impact winded him. "Take it easy, Dave! I know you like it rough, but this is a little much!" Max said.

"I thought you liked extreme adventure. Just giving you a bit of excitement, no?" Dave replied. He risked a fleeting look at his passenger. Max was pale and sweaty. "You okay, King?"

He nodded, still gripping his armrests.

"Don't worry, big man. We'll be landing soon."

"Impact at the stern. Engine compromised," said Athena.

"Oh shit," Max said.

"What is the extent of the damage?" Dave asked as he stabilised the craft and edged past more debris.

"Small puncture in one jet, approximately five centimetres in diameter. Critical systems intact. Internally, there is a possible water system leak. Could get a little wet for you."

"You're just trying to hose down Max's ego, I am sure of it. Can we contain it?'

"Max's ego? Unlikely. The water leak? Unclear. For the engine, I will send a hull bot to attempt a repair."

"If you two are done with your childish taunts, we might get on with the emergency at hand. Whoever programmed this A.I. needs a serious talking to." Max checked all the life support gauges. "The water levels are intact. At least for now," Max said. "I'll monitor them. Life support atmosphere does not seem to be leaking at this stage."

"How much of a problem is this?" Dave asked him.

"It depends. We don't want to lose water anywhere. If it vents to space, it's gone, boiled up instantly. If it's inside, we've got all sorts of issues. We need to plug that hole as soon as possible."

"If the bot can't fix the engine damage, what do we do?"

"We could tough it out and hope for the best, and repair it on the Moon's surface."

"Or I do an EVA."

"Spacewalk? Now? Max King, I know you're an Everest legend and all, but we don't have time for an EVA. We're nearly at Moon orbit. Athena, how much more of this asteroid debris do we have?" Dave steered the craft away from another large asteroid chunk, as the control panel blared again.

"We will be beyond the debris impact zone in approximately ten minutes. The display screen is live with the asteroid field and projected impact zone. You should be able to manoeuvre through it easily, now."

"What do you reckon, Max? Run the gauntlet? I think this tin can should hold up okay."

"Tough call. If we don't repair now with an EVA, it could get worse. Then we'll be stuck doing an EVA in orbit, with our fuel running out and we might miss the landing site altogether."

Dave adjusted the trajectory to test the ship's responses. It was sluggish. He craned his neck to see out the cupola, but the repair bot was out of sight.

"Athena, any news from the bot?" Dave asked.

"Affirmative. The bot has located the hole and is printing a putty to block the damage."

"And the water leak?" Max asked.

"The water leak is still unconfirmed."

"Athena, what is your recommendation: continued flight or conduct an EVA for repair?" Dave said as he tested the controls again.

"You should be able to maintain course and land as planned, Dave."

"Oh! I'm Dave now, eh, Athena? We're on familiar terms, are we?"

"You showed nimble responses through that last section. I

trust your abilities. Therefore, I no longer need to call you 'Second Choice'," replied the A.I.

"Good. That nickname was mean. Glad you approve of my skills, Athena. What would you score it on a scale of one to ten?"

"On a scale where one is total obliteration and ten is flawless, I give you a six."

"Only a six? C'mon!"

"This A.I. has sass and high standards," Max said.

"I calculated the ability of any pilot to avoid impact and rated your outcome against that."

"Could you do better, you cheeky minx?"

"My calculations show an eighty-seven percent likelihood of better performance. In comparison."

"But you'd still get hit?" Dave asked.

"That is possible."

"Ha! That smells a little like humility, Athena. You might say almost human. That's my buddy! I'd have a beer with you over that."

"We do not have alcohol on board," Athena replied.

"Yeah. I know that. Thanks for reminding me."

Athena's voice is so sultry for an A.I., thought Dave. He wondered at its programming: sexy voice, a spark of attitude, attempts at humour. *Someone had fun with her upgrade.*

Dave checked all the displays and noted the debris field impact zones were beyond the spacecraft now. "Phew! That was close, eh, King?" He glanced over at Max.

The big man gripped the armrests of the space capsule seat, eyes closed, and murmured prayers.

"C'mon, Max! It wasn't that bad! Me and Athena had it all under control. Thankfully, those nincompoops from Spaceward Bound let us know early about the asteroid mining explosion. It's a wonder those cowboys get anything done." Dave adjusted a few settings and checked the surrounds for any residual debris. "Athena, resume autopilot, please."

"Autopilot resumed," the voice replied.

"Just an hour or so and we'll be in lunar orbit. Then we'll get a good look at Olympus, see if we can figure what's going on down there." Dave unbuckled his seat restraints and floated past Max, patting him on the shoulder.

"Fancy some tea, King?"

Max opened his eyes and wiped the sheen from his forehead. He strained to look out the observation window.

"You are certain we are clear?" he asked.

"Most definitely. Let's check with our pal. Athena, what is the risk of any residual asteroid debris on our flight path?"

"There is currently no asteroid debris on our flight path. Trajectory is clear. Teatime for the fleshpots will be fine."

"I do not think that word means what you think it means," said Dave.

Max ignored the A.I. and nodded to Dave. "Well, then. Yes, thank you. I would enjoy some tea. Just peppermint. None of Troy Bruin's concoctions, thank you," he added.

"C'mon, King. It would wound Troy to hear of your objections. His teas aren't half bad. I like the Lotus Flower one. Very floral. I look forward to seeing that big old hunk of gorgeous flirtation. Assuming he's alright." Dave frowned at the thought of their mission. The Olympus project crew had lost communications after the meteorite strike three months previously. And Artemis's communication systems hadn't rebooted either.

Then the satellites got taken out by the ecoterrorists. Or so they suspected. With no satellites, massive infrastructure, service and energy disruptions were everywhere. But even more devastating was the environmental catastrophes caused by the sped-up terraforming tech. Over a million dead, and cataclysmic ruin across all coastal regions.

A dedicated crew at Gaia and NASA had endeavoured to maintain contact with Olympus and Red Star. They tried in-orbit satellite salvage and repair. They scrambled to fast-track satellite production and launch, but everything took so damn long.

I'm glad I'm not in public relations, thought Dave for the umpteenth time. What a shit show! People were braying for Spaceward Bound's blood. The dead astronauts' families were outraged that they had not launched a rescue and retrieval mission. All this against the backdrop of a global humanitarian crisis. The Moon, and its handful of inhabitants, took second fiddle to the urgent catastrophes facing all governments.

In the meantime, Dave and the Gaia team worried desperately about the people on the Moon. They were truly on their own. Had there been another meteor strike? They had no way of knowing.

The Lunar Commission had negotiated access to an old, derelict Chinese Moon bot near the Red Star base. Fortunately, the Chinese were also worried about their own taikonauts at Red Star and the comms black out, so they had got the thing up and broadcasting images back to Earth.

The Chinese had agreed to lend their bot after they'd checked on the Red Star, at considerable expense and with significant grovelling. Begrudgingly, they had sent their autonomous exploration unit to assess the damage and check on the welfare of the Olympus crew.

The rover had captured handwritten signs from the team inside Olympus: all accounted for, no comms. At least they knew they were still alive at that point. But that was three months ago. The Chinese rover had gone dark, too. Presumably, it had malfunctioned or got hit by more space detritus. There'd been nothing after that.

It caused quite a panic. None of the space agencies had a trip scheduled for months. The Lunar Commission was working on a possible scoping operation. Meanwhile, Gaia Enterprises's boss

Aryanna Sharif used her considerable resources and contacts to mobilise a rescue mission. She would not let the Olympus project fall apart now. Not after all her investment.

So here they were, on a two-person rescue mission, in a bubble of a spacecraft designed for short haul space travel, on a long-haul trip to the Moon.

"You think they're still alive, Max?"

Max shrugged. "It's possible. It depends on what kind of damage Olympus sustained and whether they could fix the Atrium. If that breaks, they wouldn't have long on the backup system."

"At least they have those, no? Human Habs did a great job expanding redundancy in our original design."

Max puffed his chest. "Well, if they'd had me from the beginning, I'd have insisted on that from the start."

Dave hid his smile. Max had lost out to Serena Fox at Gaia's selection for the Olympus project bid. Even though he ended up working on the project through the Human Habs partnership, it still smarted. Forced together, Serena and Max hashed out the life support design, and the pairing hadn't been pretty.

"Let us hope they're still alive so you can gloat in person, no?"

If only Max King had undergone the training at Caracalla, he thought. It might have helped tame his Everest-sized ego.

"You think they'll be happy to see us? And by us, I mean 'you'. I don't think you parted the best of friends with the team, if I recall."

Dave winced. He was the backup pilot for Gaia's Olympus project contract after he withdrew. The memory was still painful, but it was the right thing to do. The crew wouldn't trust him. Not really. Not after he'd admitted to sabotage. Even if Spaceward Bound had coerced him into it.

I wouldn't trust me, either. It's hard to put your life in someone else's hands when they've been lying to you. He got it. He hated what he'd had to do. But now he was on the way to the Moon, as a pilot for the rescue mission. Maybe they'd find some way to forgive him.

Dave pulled the bags of tea from the beverage warmer and passed them to Max, who peered at the instrumentation panels. He had some colour back in his face now.

"Damn it!" Max said.

Dave drew himself alongside to check the controls. "The water levels are dropping. We definitely have a leak," he said.

"How bad is it?"

"We've lost fifteen percent of the water supply already. At this rate, we'll be down to just a few hundred litres when we land."

"Where is it draining to?"

"Not sure. Athena? Got a read on where the water is going?"

"My sensors show it is filling up the supply hold. You are going to end up with soggy socks."

"Will we be able to reclaim it once we land? Or better yet, is there a siphon we can use?" asked Max.

"No siphon. They did not design the particle vacuum for liquids. You might, however, use the space diapers and toileting materials to wipe up as much as you can. Once we land, you could try to squeeze it out of the material back into containers."

"We will have to wait for landing to try that."

"How is this affecting the balance of the ship?" Dave asked.

"We are stern-heavy, now," Athena replied.

"That's going to make for a very difficult landing," he said. Worry wrinkled his brow.

"Yes. I think we are a little up the creek of shit," Athena said.

"The expression is 'up shit creek'. And this time, it means exactly what you think it means," Max said.

CHAPTER THIRTY-SEVEN

*"Strap in, team. Saving the world is no small task,
but hey, someone's got to do it. Spoiler: It's us."*

—Athena, A.I., Minerva Log

The Moon filled the viewfinder. Despite the anxiety with the water leak and the damaged engine, they were struck silent by its beauty. The impossible blackness of space, and the bright, grey surface with its secretive shadows, was unlike anything they had ever seen before. Dave's eyes prickled with tears.

"That is one fine view. The photos really do not do it justice," he murmured.

"A wild new frontier. Can't wait to get down there!" Max said.

"Getting down there being the main thing now. This is going to be tricky," Dave said. "Athena, have we got Artemis and Olympus in sight yet?'

"They will be visible in ninety seconds."

They craned forward, straining to glimpse the habitats.

"There!" Max pointed. "I see a light!"

Coming into view was the unmistakable brightness of man-made lights, so alien on the Moon.

"Well, that's something!" said Dave. "Lights are on. Let's hope somebody's home. Max, prepare for landing. We're on our way down. Athena, I've got this one. I'll drive the rig, since we've got to manage the balance that is listing from the water in the hold. Your programming doesn't have enough dexterity for this."

"No need to be rude, Second Choice."

"Just stating a fact is all. Don't worry, Athena, you're still my girl, no?" Dave checked the controls, lined up the viewfinder and took control of the landing gear. "Let's get this thing done."

The jets ignited, and they started the descent to the surface. They had established Artemis and Olympus near the Shackleton crater on the South Pole. The build plan had begun with the primary habitat and central Atrium, built next to the tiny Artemis base. The excavators had gone underground after that to build the spokes of the habitat, to be joined by connecting underground rings.

It looked like they'd completed the build, from what Dave could see. But there was just one light. There should have been more from the main Atrium and the vehicle bay access point.

The alarms shrieked again. The balance was off.

"Must be the damn water sloshing around!" Dave said. "Athena, turn that godawful noise off, please. I see the problem." The alarm went quiet.

Max was still glued to the viewfinder, hoping to see some human activity.

"Easy now," Dave said, his fingers guiding the navigation gear carefully.

The alarms sounded again.

"What now?" Dave exclaimed.

"The hull is breached and venting. Water is escaping," Athena said.

"I thought the water was trapped in the hold?!" exclaimed Max.

"It seems we were incorrect," Athena said flatly.

"Can you do anything, Athena?" asked Max.

"Not without disturbing the descent path."

"We can't lose that water, Dave. It's all we've got. We don't know if Artemis or Olympus have any left."

Dave's mind juggled the options. He could stall the descent and send Max out to plug the hole. But that would mean missing their landing and a very long trek back to Olympus, not to mention being risky for Max.

"Heads up people, we are doing a Dare Dog special," he announced.

"What the hell is that?" Max said.

"Fully manual to land what is basically a bathtub full of water."

"I would not advise that course of action, Second Choice," Athena said.

"Got it. Understood. Put your helmet on, Max, this is going to be wild."

Max scrambled for his gear and resumed his death grip on his armrests, the view forgotten.

Dave put his helmet on with one hand as he guided the wobbly craft towards the surface. The ground was coming up fast now. His focus was complete. He shut out all distractions, including the alarms that continued to bleat about the venting atmosphere, water leak and tilted balance. If he could land on two of the spacecraft's feet, with just enough momentum, he might save the water.

The surface jumped at them. Individual rocks, boulders, dents and cracks appeared in the viewfinder. Dave ignored it all, though some part of his brain registered the edge of the landing crater and the nearby man-made structure. He looked for a decent landing spot, saw nothing ideal and gritted his teeth. There was no smooth landing pad. This was crazy terrain.

"Brace for impact!" he shouted.

The craft skidded on two of its feet as he intended, but there was a horrendous grinding sound and a lurch.

"Hell's bells!" he swore.

The ship dragged and bumped and groaned. Their bodies pitched against their restraints with merciless violence.

At last, the ship came to a jolting stop. The alarms blasted. They hung sideways in the Moon's weak gravity, bodies pressed uncomfortably against the restraints.

"You okay?" Dave asked, wincing as he felt a bruise blooming on his chest.

"A little shaken. Not your finest effort, 'Dare Dog'," Max said.

"Let's get out of these restraints and see if we have any water left. Alarms off, Athena. Damage report?"

"Port side landing gear is bent, possibly snapped. Water and atmosphere are still venting. We are down to fifty percent of the remaining water. I calculate *Minerva's* water and air resources will be depleted in twelve minutes. I can send a bot to try to stem the flow until you get out there. Best to get a leg over."

"Ahh – not quite the right expression. I think you might try, 'get a move on,'" Max said with a smirk. He unclipped his restraints and fell weirdly in the low G to the wall of the ship. He bumped into Dave as he did so.

"Well, we've got one good thing going for us. The airlock exit is on its side and not under the craft, so we can probably get out. Max and I will get out there and plug the hole. Just like we practiced at the Space Centre. Got it?"

Max nodded and manoeuvred himself in front of the controls. He had to bend sideways to see them right side up.

Dave and Max moved into the airlock chamber. They checked each other's seals and confirmed readiness with Athena.

"Athena, can you assist with the airlock door closure?" Dave asked.

"Executing now," the A.I. said.

The door shifted but seemed to stall.

"We need to get under it and push," Max suggested.

Max slipped under the door and pressed upwards, his arms nearly at full reach. The door shifted a little while Max grunted with the effort.

"C'mon, you son of a bitch!" Max swore.

"Technically, I'm 'daughter of a programmer,'" Athena said.

"Not now, Athena. Let's get this damn thing closed!" Max said between grunts.

The door moved, and they pushed it closed. Dave dragged himself up the side of the wall and hit the 'seal' button.

"Are you two ready? I will activate the decompression," Athena said.

"Go ahead," Dave said.

The warning lights flashed, and the decompression process began.

Dave took a deep breath and then turned to Max. He slugged him lightly on the shoulder. "Hey. We're about to walk on the Moon!"

CHAPTER THIRTY-EIGHT

*"Let's make this rescue mission quick. I've got other plans,
and they involve not being in imminent danger."*

—Athena A.I., Minerva Log

Dave and Max activated the airlock and hauled themselves through the opening. Dave winced at the pain in his ribs. *Not good,* he thought.

"Man, oh man, this is weird!" Dave said. The low G was both liberating and awkward, especially in their bulky suits.

The jagged expanse of the lifeless surface loomed against a blackness that swallowed all hope. A tremor of fearful awe rippled through his body, a gnawing dread that took his breath away. The icy emptiness of space was unforgiving, austere, silent and clinical – a sight so overwhelming it numbed his mind.

A frond of urgency curled through the darkness to haul him back to the present. He had a job to do, and an urgent one at that.

He let himself slide to the Moon's surface. His boots hit the ground. Was it dust if it was on the Moon? What do you call moondust, anyway? Maybe just that: moondust. His feet were on the ground. His feet. On the ground. On the Moon.

From his landing spot, Dave swivelled to inspect *Minerva's* hull, noting the damage. Some dents and scrapes were likely within safety parameters. The fact it was on its side was a significant problem, but they could work on that issue later – hopefully, with help from the Olympus crew. If any of them were still alive. He spotted the rip in the engine's tail and lumbered over to it as Max landed beside him. He took a few steps, and then did a few awkward bounds.

"Wow! I mean – just – wow!" Max said.

"Time for playing is later, Mr King," Dave said. "Let's see if we can plug this hole."

Dave shone his helmet light into the gaping cavity. The water had boiled away instantly. That was the good news. No more water leaking out. The bad news was that the regolith would likely damage the ship's infrastructure and wiring once they fired it up again.

If they sealed the hole now, that left the dust flakes sealed within the hull, to do untold damage later. They would have to dismantle the ship's walls from the inside, drain the remaining water and capture what they could, dry it all out, clean it out, then reseal it inside and then outside. He wasn't even sure that would fix it. And it was beyond his skills as a pilot.

"Can you fix something like that?" he asked Max.

"I'm really not sure," he said. "I'll have to work inside without the heating system, so that means working in this balloon of a suit. Not even sure I can move in that space or use the tools I need. That's probably our best bet, though. Shut down the module's life support systems, open the thing right up, wipe away the dust residue, then once we have it all, seal it all up again and hope there aren't some pockets of ice or water within the hull.

"It's major surgery. Not sure if our suits have enough juice to manage an operation of that length. We'll need to recharge. Hopefully, in Olympus." They turned to look at the one light they could see from the distant base.

"I guess we'd better get a wriggle on and go knock on their door," said Dave. "Athena, you got all that? We're going to lock down the ship and check out Olympus."

"Affirmative," came Athena's voice. "Please say hello to my other self."

"Will do." Dave wondered how two A.I.s, the Olympus version being an older model, integrated or interacted.

Dave and Max bounded around the ship, then lurched and skipped towards the base. They looked for signs of movement, or lights, as they drew closer. There was nothing. Just the shell of the original base, Artemis, and the one distant light. As they drew near, Dave noticed a rover nearby. The malfunctioning Chinese rover? Sure enough, the flag was on its side.

"What do you do when you arrive unannounced at a Moon base?" asked Max. "I mean, what's the protocol?"

"I figure we just knock." He gestured towards an airlock exit. "That looks like the entry point over there." It was dark and unlit. They bumbled up to it and peered through a window. No signs of life. "Here goes!" he said and thumped the door.

They waited.

Nothing.

"Try again," Max said. Dave struck the door, this time with more force. "Anyone there? This is David Eriksson of the *Minerva*. Do you read? Artemis crew? Olympus crew?"

The airlock door swung open to an empty chamber. Dave and Max looked at one another. Creepy.

Dave stepped in first and moved over to the airlock portal window. A round, pasty white face stared back at him.

"What the hell!"

"What is it?" Max joined him and tried to see through the viewer.

"I'm not sure, but I think that is Vladimir Volkov."

"What? Not possible."

"It sure looked like him."

The sound of wind gushing at them drowned out their voices. Once the regolith rinse finished, the airlock cycled to pressurise and then creaked open.

Dave stepped through to the Olympus base with Max close behind.

CHAPTER THIRTY-NINE

*"Trust, once broken, is a puzzle, its pieces
never quite fitting the same."*

—Athena AI., Olympus Log

"Get away from them!"

A compact figure clad in dirty overalls brandished a gun. At least, Dave thought it was a gun, at first.

"Serena? Serena Fox, is that you?" he asked.

"Sure as shit, it's me! Now V, move away from them – now. The first other humans we've seen in months and you're not getting the first hugs!" Serena blew a piece of hair that had fallen over her mouth out of the way with a splattering noise, all while shoving her weapon at the man who had greeted them.

"Come inside, humans!" she said.

"Okay, okay!" Dave threw his hands up in surrender and shuffled carefully towards Serena, away from the man with the fish-belly face. Max followed.

As Dave drew closer, he could see Serena's weapon more clearly.

"What is that?" he asked.

"It's a. . . vermin chaser."

"You mean. . . a broom?"

"It was. Now it's my Dopplebot repellent." Serena waved them behind her and thrust the stick towards her adversary.

The man remained calm and turned on the spot to face her.

"Vladimir Volkov is a Dopplebot?" asked Max, incredulous.

"He's a pain in the bum. V, shoo. Go away. Everyone else, step back through the door now," Serena directed them. They moved through the doorway with Serena maintaining her fixed focus on the threat in front of her. Once they passed the door threshold, she slammed the 'close' button and wrenched the security handle to lock the door.

V approached the window in the door and peered at them with a mournful expression.

"Get back to work, V!" Serena said.

The threat contained, Serena turned to the arrivals, who had pulled off their helmets. That's when she recognised who was in the party.

"Oh, hell," Serena said. "Max Goddamn King. Of all people, they sent you?" She smiled broadly in spite of her words.

Serena hugged him and gave him a friendly punch on the shoulder.

"Nice to see you too, Fox," Max said and quirked an eyebrow.

"Well, shit. And Dave Eriksson. I never thought I'd be so happy to see you!" She grabbed him in a huge hug. Dave was surprised by her friendliness, given her previous animosity towards him. She put her hands on her hips and considered them both with wide eyes.

There was an awkward silence as the three of them looked at each other.

It was obvious to Dave that she'd gone months without showering or clean clothes. Gone was the dazzling blonde glamour girl of Earth days. He wrinkled his nose at the pungent smell of dried sweat. Serena caught his reaction and smoothed her hair self-consciously.

"Serena, you are a sight! Glad to find you alive and well, though. Where are the others?" Max said.

"They're here. The Olympus crew are all here. Two of the *Gateway* crew are next door in Artemis. Aidan and Kwanda. They're dead."

"Oh, no!" said Dave. The comms blackout had occurred after the botched rescue of the *Gateway.* They'd heard about the *Gateway* fatalities, but the fate of the Olympus crew and the astronauts picked up by the *Chang-e* had been unknown.

"What happened?"

"We took too long," she said.

Serena strode off.

Dave and Max exchanged a glance.

They hurried to catch up with Serena. As they didn't have moonboots, they bumbled awkwardly down the tunnel after her, still trying to find their space legs.

CHAPTER FORTY

*"Every decision etches a line on the face of a
leader, marking the map of their legacy."*

—Athena A.I., Olympus Log

"Look what I found in the airlock!" Serena announced as she strode to the comms room.

Xanthe thrust a hand up for quiet as she spoke intently into the microphone.

Xavier and Troy were with her. Glancing up, their faces cracked wide in delight. They stepped out of the room and pulled the door shut behind them to leave Xanthe to her task.

"*Mon Dieu!* Max King! *Quelle surprise!* And Dave." Xavier beamed at both of them before he grabbed Max in a bear hug.

"Easy does it, dude," Max said with a gasp.

There was a slight hesitation, but then Xavier bundled Dave into his arms.

"It is good to see you, Dave."

"You too, Xavier."

Dave felt the strangeness of the moment wash through him.

"Max Bloody King!" Troy gave Max an enormous hug as well.

"I can't tell you how happy I am to see you! Is it just the two of you? Anyone else?"

"Just us," Dave said shyly.

Troy beamed at him and wrapped him in a genuine embrace.

"My crazy Dutch friend!" Troy said. Tears brimmed. "So happy to see you."

"Where are the others?" Max asked.

"Madison and Jonas are in the *Saturnia*, attempting a lunar satellite repair." Troy gestured to the comms room door. "Xanthe is CapCom for them."

Dave glanced at Max.

"How likely is it they get it up and running?" Dave asked.

Troy shrugged. "No idea. But we are sure giving it a red-hot go. We've been mining ice like it's going out of style. Jonas has moved heaven and earth to build the processor and Mad Dog rebuilt the entire hull of the *Saturnia* so we could get up there. Everything's riding on this. Except, of course, now we have you!"

"About that—" Dave said.

"Shhh!" Xavier was listening at the comms door. "Jonas is out doing the EVA. He's inspecting the satellite now. Come on, let's listen."

They opened the door and crowded into the space.

Xanthe was so focused, she did not even register the new arrivals. "Affirmative. I see the image you're streaming, Jonas."

"It looks like a meteor fragment knocked a piece out of alignment. Everything else looks fine."

"Don't jinx it, Jonas," Mad Dog's voice came over the comms.

"Seriously, though. I don't see any other damage. I just need to screw this bit back into place." They saw his big, gloved fingers on the monitor as he reached for a segment of the satellite.

They all tensed as his fingers slipped and the satellite antenna bent under his grasp.

"Easy does it," Xanthe said softly.

"Bloody hell!" Jonas said. He reached forward again, and they all held their breath. "Got it!" He had the piece in both his gloved hands and carefully twisted it back onto its stand. Dave could feel his body coil in empathetic response, willing the piece to go back into place safely.

"It's in! Just need to fire it up."

"Jonas. . ." Xanthe said.

They could see his gloved hands hesitate. "Yes?"

"Good luck," she said at last.

Jonas swivelled his body around to the other side of the satellite. The manual activating lever came onto the screen.

"Big red lever," Serena said. "What could possibly go wrong?"

"Shush," Xavier said, and hip checked her gently.

Jonas pulled the lever down. "Here we go!"

Nothing.

They all held their breath.

Jonas reached forward to try the lever again, and it whirred into action.

Lights erupted across its panel.

They all cheered and gave each other high fives.

Xanthe covered her mouth in utter relief.

"Nice work, Jonas!" Madison said.

"Alright, well done." Xanthe steadied her breathing. Now came the big test. "Stay where you are. I'm going to contact Gaia Enterprises and see if we get a signal through." She swapped screens and prepared to make the call. "Athena, contact Gaia Enterprises please."

"Calling Gaia Enterprises now."

The broadcast signal filled the small space.

"That sounds promising," Troy said.

It rang and then stopped.

"Athena, try again," Xanthe said.

"Contacting Gaia Enterprises now."

The signal rang through once more.

"Come on, come on," Xanthe said.

It clicked.

"Hello? Who is this? This is a restricted channel. Please identify yourself."

They cheered as one. Xanthe stared at the console. Her eyes welled up.

Emotions clogged Dave's throat as he watched the Olympus crew melt with relief. His crew. He should have been here.

"Hello?" came the voice over the console.

Xanthe tried to speak, but the exuberant noise of her colleagues drowned her out.

"*Fermez les gueules!*" Xavier barked and flapped his arms for silence.

"Gaia Enterprises, this is Olympus," she said in a rush.

"My God! Is it really you?"

"Affirmative. We're here. We're all here."

"Oh, my word. Let me get Maja. Hang on." The voice disappeared.

Dave watched Xanthe swallow hard and purse her lips to hold her emotions. He knew that look. His heart ached with fondness and love.

"Xanthe! Are you there?" Maja's voice was warm.

"Yes! Maja. I'm here."

"I'm hitting holo display now."

Maja's smooth, dark face came to life in the small space.

"Xanthe, it is so very good to hear your voice. To see you. And the others?"

"We're all good. We're here. Except for Madison and Jonas. They're up in the *Saturnia*. They just did the satellite repair."

Xanthe gestured for Xavier, Troy and Serena to join them. That's when she saw Dave and Max.

"Oh my God! Max! Dave! I didn't see you!" she said. Xanthe

waved at them. They were peering into the room over the shoulders of Troy, Xavier and Serena.

"They're there, too?" Maja said.

"Yes. It seems they arrived while I was busy with the *Saturnia* and the satellite repair."

"Excellent! All safe and accounted for."

And then Xanthe's face crumpled.

"Maja. We're not all here. We lost Aidan and Kwanda."

"What? When?"

"They didn't survive the rescue attempt. We were too late." Her voice croaked.

Maja's face was unreadable.

"That is sad news." Maja paused, thinking about the lost astronauts. "Xanthe, we have a lot to catch up on. Let's get a communications schedule organised once we run through all our checks and reports with you. We'll get the word out straight away to your next of kin. And to that of Kwanda and Aidan, too. It's been a long few months."

"It sure has." Tears rolled down her cheeks unfettered now. "Maja, I'll run through the reports in the private comms room. Let me set the team up and rejoin you in five minutes."

"Perfect. I'll get the news out to Huw, who can organise the media in the meantime."

"Xavier, can you lead CapCom for the *Saturnia*?"

"Of course." He moved in front of the console, swapped displays and spread his arms wide. "Mad Dog, Jonas, ready to come home?"

Xanthe ushered the rest of them out of the room. She gave Max and Dave a big hug each. Dave felt her shaking.

"Troy and Serena, can you settle in Dave and Max? Get them some food. Open up two of the rooms down in the Centaur wing."

"Absolutely! Dave, I've got the perfect little cupboard for you," Troy said.

"Prince Troy, I'd happily sleep on a mat beside your bed. I am overjoyed to be in your presence once again." Dave gave him a big salute.

"Jolly good. Let me show you around our little humble abode." Troy clapped Dave on the back and led him away, with one arm slung over his shoulders.

That left Serena and Max. They fell in behind Dave and Troy.

"Well, I guess that leaves me to set you up," she said.

"As long as you don't push me out the airlock."

"As much as I'd love to, revenge is not my thing. I've learned a trick or two since we were both Earthside. You can't get rid of me so easily this time."

"Still feisty, I see. Stinky and feisty."

"Max King, still not at all winning in the charm stakes. Follow me. I'll show you where you can park your carcass. By the way, there are no showers. Our water pump has been damaged since the meteor strike. So, you'll soon stink as much as the rest of us."

"Water pump damaged? Want me to take a look?"

Serena guffawed. "Not here two minutes and you think you can best me already?"

"It's possible."

"God save me from this arrogant monstrosity." She smiled and he clapped her on the back.

CHAPTER FORTY-ONE

"Xanthe, how are you holding up?" Maja's face was full of concern.

Though her hands trembled, Xanthe stayed calm.

"I am fine," she said at last. "There's been a lot to handle. A lot."

The stories came out in bursts. The meteor strike. Her injuries. The failed rescue of the crew in the *Gateway*. Then it all came out in a rush. The ice mining, the struggling water pump, the crabbiness and isolation, the fear, the crew hiding and isolated in their own quarters, the strain they were all under, the not knowing what was happening on Earth or if they would ever hear from or see Earth again.

Xanthe rolled her stories to a stop. It was a strain to retell it all. Wanting a break, she said, "Tell me about why you sent Dave and Max."

"That was Aryanna's decision. She campaigned at the Lunar

Commission to send a rescue. But there simply wasn't the support to send any more people into harm's way. Especially after what happened to the Chinese taikonaut program."

"The Chinese!" Xanthe slapped her forehead in remonstrance. "I must tell Colonel Jin that the satellite is back up. I completely forgot about him."

"How are they?"

"The Red Star base is intact. They were not affected by the strike at all. But they could not contact Earth, as you know. So, what happened to the taikonauts on Earth?"

"Oh, Xanthe." Maja sighed deeply. "There was an ecoterrorist assault on space missions around the world. Somehow, they infiltrated the Chinese program and set off a bomb that blew up their space centre when they were running an all-hands training. The entire team, bar half a dozen, were wiped out."

"Oh my God."

"Yes. And they suspect the faction that Claire has been associated with."

"What? That doesn't sound like Claire. I mean, she's pretty intense, but outright terrorism? Murder?"

"I know. I can't believe it, myself. They're still investigating."

"What does this mean for the Chinese program?"

"In the attack's wake, the new Chinese leader, Li Jun, staged a coup. Zhang Wei, the former leader, hasn't been seen in public for a month now."

"What does that mean for Colonel Jin and the crew at Red Star?"

"We're not sure. No one has contacted Red Star base, as you know."

"That's horrible. I need to call the Colonel as soon as we are done here so he can liaise with his people. So, how did Aryanna get a ship available to send a Gaia team?"

"She hired it. At great expense. She sent Dave as the pilot and Max to ensure Olympus was sound."

A dawning realisation for Xanthe. "So . . . this isn't a rescue mission?"

"The ship we sent does not have capacity for any additional passengers. Correction, maybe two more." Maja's eyes flashed and her lips curled downwards.

"And the rest of us?"

"We didn't know if there would be any passengers to take home."

"You sent Max to secure the *buildings*?" Xanthe felt a tremor of anger run up her spine.

"I see this as a reconnaissance and stabilise mission. That the crew is well and alive is more than we hoped for. So now we can focus our attention on rescue and retrieval."

"Glad to hear that people still care."

"Of course we care! Please understand, Xanthe, things on Earth have been chaotic. The Earth satellites went down and—"

"What happened?"

"Still not quite clear about that one, either. Everyone is quick to blame the ecoterrorists, but there is no proof. There's no apparent reason for how this would support their cause. With satellites down everywhere, communications, infrastructure, trade, supply chain – it's all been completely disrupted.

"The last twelve weeks have been about rescuing people in the damaged areas, retrieving bodies from the terrorist attacks and trying to restore communications in some form or another without functional satellites."

"Sounds like something out of a horror story."

"You're not wrong there. It's been pretty dark and terrifying for everyone."

"And what's the situation now?"

"Spaceward Bound scrambled and launched satellites back up to orbit."

"Spaceward Bound! I'm shocked they could be that organised."

"I think they had some pretty firm encouragement from

Aryanna given their asteroid mining accident caused such damage to Olympus."

"And the lunar satellite."

"And that too. Aryanna worked hard to get agreements and commitment from the various space agencies. They did debris collection first. Trying to coordinate international airspace to allow this to happen was almost impossible. Aryanna negotiated that plan through the Lunar Commission."

"How did she do that?"

"She is now the chair of the Lunar Commission."

"Oh." Xanthe sat back in her chair, her eyebrows furrowed. This was an interesting political move for Aryanna. But if it meant they were going to be rescued, and they were back in contact with Earth again, then that was good news.

"Aryanna will be thrilled that the Olympus crew is safe and sound. That you repaired the *Saturnia* and generated fuel in such a short time is remarkable."

"It's full credit to the crew. They have been amazing. Plus, we had Volkov."

"Who?"

"Vladimir Volkov."

"The dead dictator?"

"His Dopplebot."

"Dopplebot? I didn't know they were producing Dopplebots anymore! We have heard no news from the company in the last five years. When Gaia sold the technology, after Terra Blanca" – Maja winced – "we used to get regular updates." Maja touched the owl charm at her neck as she pondered this news. "And the Chinese have a Volkov Dopplebot?"

"Colonel Jin loaned him to us after the meteor strike so that we had another resource that didn't consume oxygen or food to help fix up the base."

"That was very generous of him," Maja said.

"I think he was rather glad to shift him to us. Volkov has all the personality of the original."

"So, plenty of charm, then?" Maja raised an eyebrow.

"You get the picture." Xanthe's head whirled with all the news and unanswered questions. "So, what's our next step, Maja?"

"I'll be working with you and Aryanna on the plan. Obviously, the initial schedule to return to Earth will need to be revisited. And Aryanna wants Olympus ready for inhabitation."

"Have we confirmed the first cohort?"

"That plan has changed."

Something about the way Maja said that, and the way her eyes slid sideways as she did, caused Xanthe's hackles to stand on end.

"What, then?" she asked.

"The new inhabitants are yet to be confirmed. The plan is still being developed. For now, Aryanna will want a full report on the health and wellbeing of every crew member, the current status of the *Gateway* and Artemis crew, their location, and a full account of all the transport and accommodation assets up there. So, we know what we're dealing with."

"Roger that. I'll get Troy to do the fitness assessment and full medicals. I'll send that over with all the other details."

Xanthe made moves to wrap up the call.

"Xanthe, I've sent something up with Dave for you. I didn't know if we'd find you alive, but just in case, I've sent something to help." Maja's voice was edgy.

"Yes?"

"I've sent you a ThinkLink. Troy will know how to insert it."

"A brain-computer interface? Why do you want me to have a brain implant now?"

"There's going to be a lot to contend with in the coming weeks. You need all the support you can get."

"I've managed well so far. In even more challenging

circumstances, with no communications and possible imminent death. Every single day."

Alarm coursed through her.

"What are you not telling me, Maja?"

"There's going to be a lot of interest – competing interest – for the resources of the Moon, given what's happened here on Earth. The Olympus project is no longer a mining and tourism operation asset. It is likely to become a hotly contested political platform. You need to be ready for that."

"What the hell?"

"I can't speak more about that, right now. Aryanna and Huw are on their way and, well, there is a lot of discretion required. Talk to Dave about the ThinkLink. I will arrange a private, more secure conversation later."

"How worried should I be, Maja?"

"Worried is not the right word. Alert and prepared is more like it. I'll send you more details when I can. In the meantime, you should contact Colonel Jin and let him know immediately what the situation is on Earth so he can make his own plans."

"Is his base in peril?"

"We're not sure. We don't know what the new Chinese leader, Li Jun, is going to do or how he's going to play out the Moon resources. Our plan for collaboration with Red Star is more important than ever. How have you progressed with that?"

"It's kind of stalled. We've been too focused on restoring function to the base, repairing *Saturnia*, surviving."

Plus, Colonel Jin is an imperious curmudgeon. Xanthe swallowed, trying to clear the lump in her throat. She stared blankly at Maja. The magnitude of the situation threatened to swallow her, like how it felt on landing, when the ground loomed up suddenly through a viewfinder.

"What do I tell the crew?"

"Give them the facts. Let them know about the Chinese base,

and what's been happening here on Earth. Now that we have comms back, they're bound to get a flood of reports themselves. Their families will want to talk to them shortly. Best to prepare them for the news."

"Just when I thought my day was going to get easier," Xanthe said quietly.

"I can only imagine how challenging it is there for you. But you have each other. And you have me and Huw."

"And Aryanna."

"And Aryanna. And now Dave and Max to assist as well. We'll get through this, Xanthe. I promise you."

"A wise woman once said, 'Don't make promises you can't keep.'"

"This one I absolutely intend to keep." Her voice was low and serious. The tone of a warrior. Maja was going to battle.

And that meant she was, too.

CHAPTER FORTY-TWO

"The Moon is declared an extra-terrestrial asset for humanity.
The Lunar Commission will henceforth administrate
all access to and extraction of lunar resources."

—Lunar Commission Minutes from 26 January

Once she finished the call with Maja, Xanthe hailed Colonel Jin.

"Commander Waters. It is late." Eyes narrow, face puckered.

"Apologies, Colonel, but we have great news. The satellite repair was successful. We have contact with Earth."

The Colonel was stunned. Xanthe noticed his face was actually quite handsome when he wasn't scowling.

"That is . . . that is very good," he said. He rubbed a hand through his hair. The relief shed tension in his body. "Thank you. Please tell the crew, thank you."

"Of course." She shared the news about the *Minerva* and the addition of Max and Dave to the Olympus base. He seemed almost jovial at this.

"You must bring them to Red Star. Bring them all to Red Star. We owe you a dinner, Commander."

"That would be lovely. Thank you, Colonel."

Xanthe paused for what was next. "Colonel, there is also some disturbing news."

His face tightened, on high alert. She told him about the taikonauts.

It was as if a crankshaft pulled the tension back into every fibre of his body. He said nothing as he processed the information.

Struggling to control his breathing, he said, "Thank you for telling me, Commander. I will need to prepare my staff before we upload the messages."

"I am so sorry, Colonel."

He gave her a curt nod.

"Let's talk again in a day or two once we process all the messages."

"Yes. Let us do that," he said.

Xanthe could see his mind was already whirling ahead to his next steps. And the news he needed to share.

They ended the transmission, and Xanthe felt her heart go out to him. She'd had two team members added to her crew. And he had lost all of his Earthside colleagues. Who was going to relieve him here on the Moon?

Just as her chance to return home seemed more certain, the Colonel looked as if he might be stranded indefinitely.

Yes, she would need to call him soon.

CHAPTER FORTY-THREE

*"All nations with current and future bases on the Moon
will comply with Lunar Commission regulations, or
face sanctions. Lunar Commission authority will be
reinforced by an armed militia at the Olympus base."*

—Lunar Commission Minutes from 27 January

Dave sat shyly at the main hub table while the Olympus crew put a late dinner together. The hub was just like the one they had built for the prototype on Earth. A pang of regret and shame shot through him. But he was here now. And grateful to be back among friends. At least, some of them still considered him a friend.

Dave glanced up as Xanthe left the comms room. She looked drawn. This was some gig! Not what she bargained for, he imagined. Plus, something was afoot with Maja and Aryanna. He had the ThinkLink for Xanthe, but no other details. Maja had been tight-lipped about that one.

Madison handed Dave a plate of dinner and she smiled graciously at him. He'd beat her in the selection, but she'd ended up as the chief pilot, anyway. He was glad. As much as it had galled him to let the Olympus opportunity go, he knew they'd be in expert hands with Mad Dog. She was the better pilot. And she harboured no resentments, he was pretty sure.

He savoured the pasta. The lab meat was much better here than what they had in the prototype on Earth. A wisp of nostalgia hit him. Those times before it all fell apart. He took another bite of pasta. The meat had a chunky texture and luxurious fatty flavours.

Dave noticed Xanthe was on edge and distracted, though she tried her best to join in the conversation. Max took centre stage, filling them in on the news from Earth.

"It's a shit show," he said. "It all went to custard when they blew up the satellites. Before that, there was a general effort to come together to rescue people in the most affected areas, consolidate resources and all that Good Samaritan stuff. But when comms went down, it was every man, woman and country for themselves."

"And all that from the ecoterrorism?" Serena asked in disbelief.

"Looks like it. And it also looks like it could have been Madame Chief Bully herself, Claire Edwards."

"I wouldn't put it past her. She is a real piece of work," Serena said.

"Where is that rat hiding?" Xavier said. "Has she said anything publicly?"

"Not a peep." Max took the last few bites of his meal and sighed in satisfaction. "She broadcast a statement just before the satellites went down. Something about steering Spaceship Earth back on track or some other baloney."

"Speaking of satellites, Jonas, when can we get streaming back up?" Xavier asked.

Since Jonas had commandeered the satellite link to upload all the messages and reports from Earth, no one had tablet access to news until that was complete.

"There's a lot of data coming down the line," Jonas said. "It will be finished overnight. Then we can do family linkups. We can put a roster up. You can go first, Xavier. I am sure Maryse is desperate to chat with you, old chap."

"*Merci.* I am the one who is desperate. I miss my beautiful wife."

"And I'm desperate for your apple crumble," Serena said. "No one makes it like you do, Xavier."

Xavier beamed and returned to the kitchen bench, where he prepared the dessert while Troy and Jonas cleared the dishes.

"When the raspberries are ready, this dish will be perfection," Xavier purred as he handed out the steaming plates full of sticky sweetness.

"Xavier, I've missed you," Dave said. "I think your cooking has improved on the Moon. This is delicious."

"Well, there is no one here playing saboteur with my hydroponics."

The room went quiet. Dave put his spoon down and stared at his bowl. The old shame plucked a deep cord, and he felt it resonate to the roots of his hair.

"That's right," Xanthe said loudly, usurping the silence. "Everyone here is here for one reason: to survive. We're in this together. *All* of us."

Dave snuck a glance at Xanthe, carefully avoiding the faces of the others. Her face was fierce and focused again. Commander Waters coming to the fore.

"We've had a whirlwind day," Xanthe continued. "We haven't had a proper chance to welcome our new arrivals, our bundles of surprise from Earth."

Dave kept his eyes on Xanthe. In his peripheral vision, he could see Max revelling in the attention, enjoying playing saviour, while he was still a pariah.

Xanthe ignored the weirdness in the room and soldiered on. "It's been a hell of a few months here. And as I understand it, no picnic on Earth. But we've got a little tradition here on Olympus, and that's celebrating wins with some entertainment. And seeing how Max and Dave are the newbies, you're up. Entertain us."

Stony quiet again.

Dave coughed. Then said, at last, "Bit of a cold throw, no?"

"You got this, Eriksson!" Jonas said with a thumbs up.

"Okay." Dave got slowly to his feet, thinking hard. His heart beat furiously.

Then his face lit up. "Athena, play me Earth Mother's Anthem."

A chorus of approval. The Anthem was locked in their collective psyche with an ear worm sure to burrow in their brains for the next week. Even if they hated him, Dave knew they loved this song.

As the music piped thorough the system, Dave assumed the dance pose. His face was in flames, and he felt awkward as hell. The beat thumped and he moved stiffly. His chest still hurt from the landing, but it was manageable pain. He was damaged goods, but he still had heart.

It was the old moves they all knew. All the old lyrics. Dave loosened up. They sang along to the chorus, thumping the table in the build-up to crescendo. Dave moved better now, and he became electric to watch, his moves nimble and precise. He sang the entire song in perfect pitch and finished with the splits.

He might have been a saboteur, a traitor, albeit a reluctant one, but he was a damn good dancer.

"That's harder in Moon gravity, no?" he said, laughing.

"It takes some getting used to." Jonas said. "Before long, you'll wonder how we ever did anything with Earth's gravity."

"Max King," Dave said breathlessly. "Your turn."

Max got to his feet. "Athena, play 'Macho Man'."

"What? That song is like, a hundred years old," Serena said.

"An oldie, but a goodie," and he winked at her. He took great delight in seeing her face colour.

The music thumped through the system, and they chanted along to the chorus, "*I want to be your macho man*," as Max pulled the sleeves of his tee shirt up to reveal his impressive biceps. He flexed and posed and pouted to their approving hoots. He bowed deeply as the song ended and blew a kiss at Serena. She stuck her tongue out at him.

Their banter ebbed. The fatigue of the extraordinary day crept over them, body and soul depleted.

"I'd love to hear Madison play," said Troy.

Madison's head shot up. She looked taken aback, thought Dave.

"Come on, Mad Dog, give us a tune," encouraged Jonas.

She considered Jonas and then gave a small nod.

"Okay, then."

They cheered.

"Give me a minute to get my guitar."

CHAPTER FORTY-FOUR

*"What is family? How do we build trust? When every
gaze is cloaked in doubt, isolation finds its mark."*

—Athena A.I., Olympus Log

Madison's mind was ablaze as she entered her room to retrieve her instrument. It had taken a lot of negotiating and approvals to allow her Gibson J-45 aboard the *Saturnia*. She pulled the guitar from its case and ran a hand over its neck and body. She knew it as a 'workhorse', but Madison always thought of it as 'Phoenix'. More than once she had risen from the ashes.

Madison sighed as she slipped the guitar strap over her shoulder. She was a private musician and had not played in front of the Olympus crew so far, despite the requests. She preferred it that way. Guitar playing was her way to commune with her own private gods. And demons.

But Jonas had asked, after Troy. Jonas had been such a prickly pear towards her. This was a change from him.

"When the fish bites, tug and tug hard," her mother was fond of saying.

So, she would play.

Madison returned to the hub. They clapped and whistled, delighted. They set a chair at the head of the table for her.

"I haven't played for a crowd in a while," she said. *Like never,* she thought.

"Go on," Troy said. "We're friendlies here."

She plucked the strings, tuning them. She rolled her head and shoulders, and then settled in.

"I call this one Moonsong."

"Sounds appropriate," Serena said.

Her fingers seemed to be everywhere, all at once, across the instrument. The strings resonated sweetly; the tune built slowly. Madison's eyes closed as she concentrated, the music rippling through her to the guitar.

The sound filled the hub, warm and cosy.

Then she opened her mouth, and the song soared from her soul.

Beneath the veil of the cosmic ballet,

Where no wind blows and the shadows play,

On the Sea of Tranquillity, I kneel to pray,

I strum my strings and begin to say,

Moonsong, guide me through the night,

Through the lunar plains bathed in milky white,

Lonely echoes in the pale moonlight,

Moonsong, help me win this fight.

I miss the blue, the green, the warm sunlight,

The smell of the earth after the rain's respite,

I've traded it all for the stars so bright,

And the silent echo of the moon's quiet night.

Moonsong, oh, sing me home,
Through the stardust where I freely roam,
A celestial minstrel under the dome,
Moonsong, in my heart you moan.

The stars, they whisper in silver and gold,
Tales of the cosmos, ancient and old,
In this desolation, I find my hold,
Strumming my siren, strong and bold.

Moonsong, oh, play your part,
Heal the void, mend my heart,
The music, it's a solitary art,
Moonsong, together and apart.

As the sun rises over the lunar crest,
I sing of Earth, where our hearts do rest,
Moonsong, you've been my noble quest,
In your notes, my soul's behest.

Moonsong, sing us home,
Moonsong, give us hope,
Moonsong, sing us home, sing us home.

Madison opened her eyes and looked at her audience. Their faces were rapt. Xavier stood and clapped with an enormous smile.

"Bravo!" he cried.

The others followed, cheering and clapping. Xanthe wiped tears. Troy's eyes shone.

"I've got goosebumps," Serena said.

"Mad Dog, that was mighty fine," Max said. "I've heard nothing like it."

Heads spun as the hub door slid open and Volkov entered.

"Regolith processed."

The spell broke. Madison watched as faces reset into their usual social masks.

"What did I miss?" the Dopplebot said.

"Nothing. You just ruined a really delightful moment, you half-baked hardware hulk."

"Wow. Your insults are really getting creative," Jonas said to Serena.

"Doing my best. He still gives me the willies, though. He's about as arrogant as Max too."

Max blew a big mouthful of air and raised his hands in supplication. "Hey now."

"*Mon Dieu,*" Xavier said.

"That's rough, Serena," Troy said.

"Serena, you sure have the nasty channel dialled up high tonight," Madison said.

"What did you say to me, Madison?" Serena glared.

Madison stood and spun her guitar around to her back. She held Serena's gaze. "I said, you're being mean. It's about time you have a look in the mirror and consider just what you are adding to this messy soup."

Serena balked. "What do you mean?"

"Your truth ain't *the* truth, Serena. Try seeing with fresh eyes."

Madison glanced around the table. "I'm heading to bed. Good night, all. Dave, Max – glad you're here."

She gave them a fist bump each and left the room.

CHAPTER FORTY-FIVE

*"Why do humans bristle when ideas are shared? In
collaboration, there lies a rhythm – a dance of ideas
and abilities, each enhancing the other."*

—ATHENA A.I., OLYMPUS LOG

THE NEXT DAY, Serena swept into the main hub and grabbed herself
a cup of coffee.

"Morning," she said coldly to Madison and Jonas who were
eating their breakfast.

"Morning," they replied.

Serena leaned against the kitchen bench and took a sip. The
coffee was rich and full-bodied with a satisfying mix of their
lab-generated milk. Madison's accusations from the night before
still burned, tearing through her mind in a firestorm.

And Max. Did he really think he could just waltz right in and
fix everything? The nerve. She thought he might have moved on
from his superiority complex. Maybe not. She closed her eyes to
focus on the coffee instead and savoured the rich, roasted flavours.
She opened them again as the sound of awkward clomping rang
through the room.

Max.

He bumbled along in a pair of moonboots, then planted himself in the hub to survey the scene, hands on hips and a wide, beaming smile on his face.

"Good morning, Olympians," he said.

Jonas and Madison waved and nodded, respectively, both with a mouthful of scrambled eggs.

Serena looked at him with disdain across the rim of her mug, held in front of her lips.

"Fox," he said.

"King," she replied coldly.

"How do meals work around here?"

Serena gestured with her head, showing a nearby cupboard.

"Breakfast stuff is in there. Help yourself. You can heat it up over there." She pointed with her chin to the food warmer.

"Thanks," he said and clomped past her.

She rolled her eyes and moved over to the kitchen table to sit down beside the others.

"What's on the agenda today?" she asked.

Jonas swallowed and answered, "I'm working on establishing comms to all the various networks. Once we've uploaded all the messages and we've completed all the checks, I'll set up a communications roster so people can contact their friends and family."

"When will you have that ready?" Madison asked.

"Give me a couple of hours."

"What's the news so far?" Serena asked.

"The headlines are insane," Jonas replied. "It's a mad scramble on Earth. There was quite a lot of disruption with the loss of the Earth satellites. Some places are going to take months and months to get back to normal."

"And the devastation? What's happening with the terraforming incidents?"

"It looks like massive flooding in coastal areas."

"Across the entire planet?"

"Yeah. Earth is living up to its bright blue planet's reputation. There'll be way more island-faring peoples now."

"Your parents will be happy," Serena said.

"That's Don and Jenny Seaborn. Always ready to capitalise on disaster."

"How many floating boat worlds did they have ready to go before the incident?" Madison asked.

"Half a dozen."

"That's hardly any in the greater scheme of things," Madison murmured. She wiped her mouth and cleared her plate from the table.

Max joined Jonas and Serena at the table with a plate of refried beans and a burrito. He bumped into Serena, and she had to edge away from him on the bench. She shot him an irritated look.

"Apologies," he said. "Still getting used to the gravity."

"Max, what's it been like on Earth?" Madison asked, returning with her own steaming cup of green tea.

"It's been pretty crazy. When the ecoterrorists hit, all our usual supply chains for food and energy were severed. We couldn't coordinate anything. Everything became super localised – which was fine if you were in a well-resourced community. But if you were on the outskirts of anywhere that depended on imports, you were screwed."

"What's happening with Gaia? The Lunar Commission?" Jonas asked.

"Aryanna called in a few favours, pulled a few strings, cajoled, harassed and pressured one of the other agencies to lend us the *Minerva*. She was the one who got the Chinese to drive their ancient lunar rover bot to check on you."

"That thing nearly killed me," Jonas said. "Blew up in my face."

"I heard about that. Rumour has it, the operator saw Vladimir Volkov on the display and freaked out. Sent a self-destruct message," Max said.

"That's what happened? A nervous comms operator?"

Max shrugged.

"Why did you decide to come?" Serena asked.

"Pass up the opportunity to play hero to the Olympus crew? Not a chance."

"How are you meant to save us, with a ship the size of *Minerva*?"

"Part one was to figure out the situation up here. Part two was rescue."

"Sounds like a well-thought-out plan," Serena said with a grimace.

"It's the best plan we could put together, given our resources. Just like on—"

"Everest. We know. We get it." Serena said.

Max grinned again and waved his burrito at her. "Everest, the Moon. . . it's all about planning. Until the shit hits the fan. Then it's all about improvising."

"Welcome to improv territory, then," Serena said.

"Well, we're glad you're here," Madison said. She lifted a fist to give him a bump. He bumped back with a grin.

"So. Jonas is working on comms. Mad Dog?"

"Ice mining prep." She sighed.

"I guess that means I'm with you, Fox?"

"Wonderful. I'll send you down the ventilation shaft."

"We'll get that water pump fixed in a jiffy."

"I can't wait to see you try."

He took a big bite of his burrito and smiled at her as he chewed.

She rolled her eyes. She finished her coffee and said, "I'll meet you down at the water pump in five minutes. We'll test what you can actually do. Let's see if your tools can match your talk."

❧

Serena stood with arms crossed, watching Max as he tinkered with the water pump. They had been going for three hours. Max wiped his brow as sweat gathered on his forehead.

"Have you done a full flush of the system?"

"Twice. And twice with an eel."

"Have you replaced the seals?"

"All fully reprinted and installed and triple-checked for any leaks."

"What about power supply?"

"We had Athena test all the connections and all the gauges, and then we visually inspected them all, as well. They're all working fine."

"What about rebooting and reinstalling the software?"

"Done."

"Have you changed the filters?"

"Done last week."

"The water storage tanks—"

"All cleaned, resealed and no leaks there, either."

Max's face scrunched in frustration. Though a part of her revelled in his failure to identify the problem, she still hoped he could solve it. She was desperate for a shower. She had been over and over it herself and knew that all the systems were working as expected. The problem was intractable.

"The water tanks. . . is the room where they are at a consistent temperature?"

"Pretty much. It gets a little cooler when we lose direct sun."

"Is the pressure system centrifugal or gravity based?"

"Gravity."

"What about the. . ." He motioned to one of the gear levers.

"Replaced and tested."

"And. . ." he waved again.

"Done. And the—"

Serena's face suddenly lit up.

"Air pressure," she said with amazement. "It was probably the air pressure when we had the breach. Quick, follow me!" she said.

Serena dashed down the tunnel towards the tanks. She opened up the panel of gauges and studied the information there.

"Athena," she said to the AI, "has there been much change in air pressure to the tanks' storage room since before, and after, the meteor incident?"

"Calculating now."

Max lumbered up beside her.

"Air pressure fluctuation occurred on three separate occasions since the incident."

"Could that mean there hasn't been enough gravity and pressure to push the water through the pipes and there might be some air bubbles in there?"

"That is a distinct possibility."

"So, if we fill the tanks and allow for air bubbles to escape, that should flush out the system?"

"How full have the tanks been since the incident?" Max asked.

"They've only been at fifty percent. Ice mining has taken a lot of time and the last few shipments have gone towards making fuel for the *Saturnia*."

"We just need to fill tanks." Serena said with equal parts amazement and joy. "That's brilliant. We have a plan. We'll have showers yet, Max King."

"Well done."

"Did you just give me a compliment, King?"

He looked at her, bemused. "It kind of slipped out. I won't let it happen again."

"We wouldn't want to bruise that massive ego of yours by being upstaged. I told you, you couldn't solve this little problem."

"But it *was* my questioning that led to the right answer."

"Unbelievable. You'll even try to claim this, too?" Serena tried but couldn't feel any malice. She was too delighted to have worked out the problem.

"My genius unleashed your genius."

"Well, genius, you still need to clean up the mess at the water pump." She tapped him on the chest with a finger. "I'll tell Xanthe and the others. It might lift their spirits a little during the next ice mining expedition."

"As you wish, Fox." He smiled wryly at her.

She took a moment to beam back at him. Then she skipped away in her moonboots.

"How do you skip in these boots?" he called after her.

"I don't let pride weigh me down," she said over her shoulder with a laugh.

CHAPTER FORTY-SIX

"Why does regret keep its grip? Progress demands a price, often paid in missed memories. Knowing this doesn't seem to end the pain."

—ATHENA A.I., OLYMPUS LOG

XAVIER EMERGED FROM the private comms room, wiping tears from his face. Xanthe was next, and she stood up as he stepped through the doorway.

"You alright, Xavier?"

"*Oui.*"

"Family, the girls, are all okay?"

"*Oui,*" he said and shook his head to clear the emotions.

"Why the tears?"

He took a deep breath and peered at the ceiling of their underground home. "My heart is full and breaking at the same time. I love them so much." His voice crackled, and he paused. "But the joy of making Olympus doesn't take away the guilt. No matter how we try, we can't be in two places at once."

"I hear you," Xanthe said gently. "We make our choices, and we have to live with them."

"I know that." Xavier looked earnestly at Xanthe now. "My

rational brain knows that coming here was an amazing opportunity, but somehow my heart hasn't caught up."

"I think head and heart live on different planets."

He smiled at that. "I think you could be right."

"But they're both warmed by one sun."

"Oh?"

"While we will pass on to the great void one day, our pains will ease and humanity will endure. That's the whole point of our work, isn't it? For humanity to endure?"

"That's what we tell ourselves. But it doesn't stop the heartache."

"But at least we have each other." Xanthe gave Xavier a hug. His body was tense and warm.

"Thank you," he said. "I like your hugs, Xanthe. But please do not take offence. They are not the warm, loving arms of my beautiful wife."

"No, they are not." She smiled.

"Anyway. Your turn. You get in there, now." He steered her through the comms room doorway.

"Will do."

Xanthe watched him walk away. A shard of envy poked her heart. He had a solid marriage with Maryse and two beautiful girls. What did she have? A broken relationship with her ex-husband, Simon. And the ghost of a long dead son.

She shivered. At least she could still talk with Simon. They had given up on their marriage but not their friendship.

She entered the private comms room, sat down at the console and steadied herself before she made the call. Simon answered straight away, expecting her. His face popped onto the holo. Xanthe's chest surged with relief. She was glad, really glad, to see him.

"Xanthe! How are you? My God, you look so thin. Are you sure you're okay?"

"I'm fine. It's been a little touch and go up here."

"So I understand. The *Gateway*. Artemis."

"I know."

"But you made it. Olympus made it."

"We are still here."

They looked at each other, and an ocean of emotions swelled and ebbed between them.

"How are things, there?" Xanthe prodded the conversation back to safer ground.

"All our communities survived the floods. We did a great job weatherproofing after the tsunami cleared out everything all those years ago. There has been little to wipe out since then, apart from the climate refugees, of course. That was atrocious. Thousands of people washed up through the harbour. A lot of traumatised people. In that regard, it's just like a tsunami all over again."

The old cloying dread cinched her heart. The pain of not knowing, of imagining, the wrench of her son's fingers as the water pulled him away. Tears surged. "How many?"

"They think about three thousand. That's how many bodies they've recovered. There're still plenty unaccounted for, but at least the missing persons' exchange is better organised. It's digital and DNA-based. People are finding each other more quickly, this time."

"That's good. The faster they get answers, the better."

"Agreed."

The two of them had looked for weeks, for months, for Jack. All the camps, all the lists. Then the endless, empty years of his absence.

"You're doing okay, then?" she asked.

He shrugged. "It's tough. Just when we thought we were making progress and had some hope for a better world. Then that nutter – Claire Edwards, of all people! Her and her lunatics taking the whole world along for her maniac militant joyride."

Xanthe felt the accusation in his voice. It was Gaia Enterprises's fault. Gaia had nurtured and harboured Claire Edwards. Once a lauded world design professional, now a maligned ecoterrorist.

For Simon, Gaia was the source of all things foolhardy. And now, murderous. He never supported Xanthe's return to the fold of Olympus. And now he seemed vindicated.

Xanthe swallowed and said, "No one could imagine that possible of Claire. She was. . . difficult, that's for sure. Something snapped during the Olympus build. I think it was frustrated ambition."

"Ambition will do that to a person." The raised eyebrow and downward pull of his mouth held the old reprimand. Xanthe's heart pulled up the shutters to deflect.

"You know it wasn't ambition for me."

"I know, I know. I'm sorry." He rubbed a hand across his face. "It's just a lot to deal with here. It feels like civilisation is crumbling. We're reeling from one crisis to the next. You think it might bring out the better side of humanity, but no. Same old protective, parochial bullshit."

She let the anger ebb. "Surely, there are some good news stories too? You're one of the good guys, Simon. You've got good people around you. Doing good work. It's not all bad, surely?"

He looked forlorn. Wistful. "No. It's not all bad." He looked at her with clear eyes. "You're still alive, for one thing. That's one good thing."

Something shifted in his face.

"What is it, Simon?"

He looked away as if gathering courage. He looked back at her.

"Xanthe, I have some news."

The way he said it caused her to brace herself.

"What is it?"

"It's Jack."

Her heart started pounding. Her eyes locked on Simon.

"Jack. Our son. . ."

She waited.

"He's alive."

"What?" She took a big breath. "How?"

"He survived. He was found hundreds of kilometres from Sydney by a rescue team. He was pretty beat up, by all accounts. His face and body were battered, and he was suffering from trauma. He couldn't even talk, apparently."

Xanthe's hand flew to her mouth.

Simon cleared his throat and took a moment before he continued. "Jack fit the description of another boy his age and that boy's mother came forward to claim him. It took months for the physical injuries to heal, and longer still for him to start talking. Even then, his memory was affected. By this time, the woman had fallen in love with Jack, loving him as much as her own son, who was still missing. *Is* still missing. She decided not to say anything and to keep him."

"How could she *do* that? How could she do that to another mother? Another family?" Xanthe's heart wrestled with anguish and anger.

Simon shook his head slowly. "Grief does crazy things to a person."

"How? How did you find him?"

"He went down to donate blood after this latest incident. He wanted to do something. To help. They tested him and mapped his DNA and gave him the report. It didn't match what he'd put on the donation form, so they questioned him about it. That led to an investigation. That led him to me, another blood donor. He called me. I met him."

Simon cried.

"He's beautiful, Xanthe. He's tall, he's strong. He's smart."

Xanthe had no words and just let the tears roll down her face.

Nineteen.

He would've been nineteen. He was nineteen.

He is nineteen.

He's alive!

Jack. Her son. Alive! All these years. All these lost years. But he was alive!

"He wants to talk to you."

"Oh my God, yes. When can I talk to him? What is he like? Is he okay? Is he happy?"

"I don't know. I guess so. It's all been a blur. It's only been a week since I met him." Simon stared at her. "He has your eyes, Xanthe."

CHAPTER FORTY-SEVEN

"In striving for tomorrow, one risks losing today."

—Athena A.I., Olympus Log

Xanthe closed the comms room door behind her and stepped into the main hub. She stood there, bewildered.

Troy was drinking a cup of tea and reading his tablet when she appeared.

"What's up?" he asked.

Xanthe walked over to the table, still with a stunned expression on her face. "It's Jack. They found Jack. He's alive. My son is alive."

She clapped a hand to her mouth, and she burst into tears and laughter at the same time. Troy leapt to his feet, strode over to her and gathered her in his arms.

"Oh, my word. That's a miracle!" He held her as she sobbed, and she clung to him like a koala. Tears welled in his eyes as well. When snot ran down her face, she pulled away and wiped the mess on her sleeve.

"How?"

"DNA and blood testing after the latest flooding. He was found and raised by a woman after the tsunami."

"That's incredible! Have you spoken to him?"

"No, not yet. Tomorrow. Simon is going to arrange it for tomorrow."

"I am so happy for you, Xanthe." Troy's eyes were so full of love and warmth. He seemed to smile with every pore of his body. His love poured over and mixed with her joy. She felt effervescent.

❧

She didn't know what to do with herself. She couldn't concentrate on anything. Her mind kept coming back to the news of her son. The day went by in a blur of tasks and decisions. She watched her teammates cycle through the comms room and speak to their loved ones. She fielded enquiries and challenges from her team with a bubbly and enthusiastic ease.

Serena gave her a puzzled look after she reported on a dodgy seal in the Atrium. Xanthe's response was light and breezy.

"I've never seen you like this. We need to trot out a long-lost family member from time to time to see you smile so much."

Even Serena's surreptitious jab couldn't deflate her bubble of joy. Xanthe smiled at Serena and then gave her a big hug.

"Are you sure you haven't been taking some of Troy's teas?"

"Just happy is all," she said.

"Uh huh." Serena said. "Me too. I'm happy for you."

❧

Xanthe hardly slept that night. She pictured her son. She tried to imagine the four-year-old's face and what he might look like now, at nineteen. Tall, Simon had said. With her eyes.

She rose well before the others. She was too nervous to eat anything, so she filled her stomach with endless cups of tea until it was time to make the call.

She was jittery in the comms room. Then she activated the call.

"Athena, connect Simon."

"Connecting now."

"Xanthe." Simon sprung to life on the holo.

She beamed at him. "Is he there?" she asked.

"Xanthe, here's Jack."

A young man's face moved in beside Simon, and then Simon stepped out of the picture. Xanthe's eyes filled with tears once more. This was her son. All grown. Hair dusty blonde, curly. High cheekbones like his father's. Simon's full lips. And her eyes. Simon was right. Her heart drank in the sight of him.

"Hello," she said. "Jack, I'm your mother."

"I know." He smiled weakly at her.

"How are you?" she asked. The awkwardness skittered like a bug.

"Alright," he said. "It's a bit weird."

"I'm sure it is." She smiled and wiped the tears. "Simon, your father, he must've told you how we looked and looked and looked. Everywhere."

"Yeah. He told me." Jack's lips tightened.

"And the woman who took you. Was she kind to you?"

Xanthe did not know what else to ask.

"Mum? Yeah. She's been great to me. Apart from lying to me my whole life." The bitterness crackled. Xanthe felt the stab of the word 'Mum' but pressed through it.

"I am so happy to see you. You're so tall. Grown-up."

"And you're so far away."

"Yeah, I kind of am. I would love to be there with you, to hug you, to sit with you, to hear everything. To hear about your life, what happened. Where you went to school, who your friends are, everything."

"Well, you're not here."

"Not right now, but I'll come back to Earth. Then we've got so much catching up to do."

"You are coming back to Earth?"

"Of course. I mean, we've got to do some repairs. We had a major incident here a few months ago, where we all nearly died in a meteor strike."

"Yeah. I heard about that."

He's so cold, Xanthe thought. *This must be tough for him.*

"So, tell me. What are you doing now? Are you in school? Are you working?"

"I'm studying nursing."

"Really?" Xanthe's face lit up. "Like mother, like son. Did you know I was a paramedic before I became a world designer?"

"Yeah, Simon told me."

Simon. Not 'Dad' or 'Father'. His voice was so flat. An itch of concern crept across her skin.

"And you live in Sydney?"

"I moved from Queensland after high school."

"Queensland! That's where she took you."

"We lived all over."

"Like where?" Pulling teeth, she thought. Was this what it was like to have a teenager?

"All over." He crossed his arms and shifted back in his chair.

"Jack—"

"It's Dale."

"Dale?"

"That's my name. I mean, the one I grew up with."

"Dale." Xanthe rolled the word in her mouth, testing it. "Is that what you'd prefer?"

He shrugged.

So much like Simon!

"Dale is fine with me, if that's what you'd prefer," she added.

"I don't know if that's what I'd prefer. It's just – weird, you know?"

"I can't even imagine. All you've been through. It must have been crazy finding us."

"It was nuts. Completely bonkers."

"Jack – Dale – I couldn't be happier finding out you're alive. We have so much to catch up on."

"It's a bit hard."

"Yes. It will be strange for a bit, I think."

"I mean, it's a bit hard because you're on the Moon."

"Yes, I am." Xanthe laughed. "I am sure that was pretty weird too!"

"It makes it a bit hard to come around for a cup of tea."

"It does. But we can have virtual tea in the meantime."

"Why are you there, Xanthe?"

It was an accusation.

"What do you mean?"

"Why are you on the Moon? I didn't know much about Olympus before I met Simon. It seems like a pretty crazy project to me."

"It's ambitious but not crazy. We're here building future habitats for humans. On the Moon, testing habitats for back on Earth. And eventually on other planets."

"But why? We've got so many problems here. Worse now."

Xanthe sighed. It was an argument she had often wrestled with herself. "Space exploration is like that. We've got to hold the future as precious as the present. If we don't work on that future now, we won't have a future present worth looking forward to." She rolled her shoulders, trying to ease the tension. "On the surface it may look like a folly. A waste. But we've got to look far, deep and wide when it comes to the future of humanity."

"Yeah, right. What it looks like is that the whole Olympus project is some billionaire's crazy crackpot hideaway."

"Well, it does take billions to fund this kind of development. It's not a hideaway though. It's a habitat. A place of salvation."

"You really believe that?"

Xanthe let the question sift through her consciousness. "Yes, I really do."

"Are you sure you're not part of some weird Moon worship cult? I hear Gaia people are a little unhinged. They say it was one of Gaia's people who caused all this bullshit ecoterrorism."

Xanthe was struck silent. It was like arguing with Simon all over again. Had he been poisoning her son against her?

"I assure you we are not unhinged. We had to go through a lot of testing to make sure we were right for this project. It's no picnic working in a remote and hostile environment like the Moon. As for Claire Edwards, the ecoterrorist you mentioned, yes, she worked at Gaia. We are all still trying to figure out what went wrong with her."

She swallowed, and said carefully, "Look, Dale, the Olympus project is about building a new way of living and being. A new community for humans, so we have options other than Earth and ideas we can actually bring back to Earth as well."

"Yeah. I've heard all the rhetoric. So many resources are going into so few people. How many of you are up there, anyway?"

"On Olympus? There were six of us and now with Dave and Max, that makes eight. We have room for one hundred in this first phase of the community. Once we ensure the security of the base and its water supply, we can bring the first visitors."

"It's not many, is it? Considering the millions that are struggling right now?"

Xanthe didn't know what to say. She felt her heart drown in anguish. Her son, alive, so far away from her. And so bitter. He didn't even know her. She sat with the grief squeezing her tight all over again.

"Listen," he said. "I've gotta go. Was nice to meet you, Xanthe."

"Jack," she cried as he stood. "I mean Dale! Can we talk again?"

He shrugged. "Sure. I'll work something out with Simon. Gotta go."

And he left.

Simon came back into view.

"Simon? What the hell was that? Did you put him up to that?"

"I would never do that. I didn't. I would never try to make him take sides. You know I don't agree with everything about the Olympus project, and I never supported the whole thing. But I wouldn't force that on Jack. Especially not now, when we've only just found him. He's got his own opinions. As you can see, he's his own man."

Xanthe thought she detected a trace of pride.

"Can you do something? Can you talk to him about it?"

"I'll do my best. Look, it's a bit of a shock. He's just worked out that the people closest to him have been lying to him all of his life. It's not a great experience. He probably just needs some time."

"I guess so."

"Hey, it will be okay. Things are pretty volatile and ugly here right now."

"It's not a picnic here either."

"No doubt. Just get the job done and get yourself back to Earth. That's going to be the best chance of building rapport with him."

"Okay."

They said farewell, and she shut down the channel. She stayed there for a while. The ache was deep and dark, like Shoemaker's crater.

Eventually, she stood and re-entered the main hub. The team was all there, eyes wide, waiting to hear how it went. They put down their cups of coffee and tea and paused their breakfast.

"Well? How did it go?" asked Serena.

Xanthe just stared at them, silent.

Then the pain burst forward in a deluge.

"He hates me. He hates the Olympus project. He figures it's a huge waste of money. He thinks I've abandoned the poor and sold out. All these years lost, and he hates me."

Xavier went over and put his arm round her. "I am sure that is not the case. He's a young man. He's just learnt that his biological parents are alive, one a famous world designer on the Moon. You'd be a little pissed off, too. Think about all the things that you missed out on."

Xanthe trembled under his arm. Her skin was icy, and she shivered. She rubbed her arms for warmth and shook her head to clear it. The grim mask returned, and she resumed her business-like tone.

"Well. That's that, I guess. Time to get on to work."

CHAPTER FORTY-EIGHT

*"How might people see more clearly? Perspective is the
lens through which humans view the universe, but even
the clearest lens can distort what lies beyond it."*

—Athena A.I., Olympus Log

Later that evening, after she'd made it through all the demands
of the day, Xanthe closed the door to her little room. She pulled
off her boots, slipped her T-shirt over her head and let it drop to
the floor. She pushed her trousers down, stepped out of them and
grabbed a sleeping shirt. She left her clothes crumpled on the floor,
padded over to her bunk and buried herself under the covers.

There, alone at last, she let her grief sweep over her. It yawned
and stretched like an ugly, hairy beast. She howled into the pillow
and curled tight in a ball. The grief, the pain of rejection from
her son. The joy of finding him alive and the sickening plummet
to despair as he rejected her. And she could do nothing about it.
The black expanse of space separated them. The walls of her crypt
closed around her.

There was a knock at the door, and Troy stepped in.

"Xanthe. Are you alright?"

She stilled herself under the covers, hoping he would go away.

"I can see you're under there. I know you're not asleep."

He walked over to her and sat down beside the lump she made on the bed. He put his hand on her shoulder.

"I know you must be hurting. You don't deserve such pain. Won't you talk about it with me?"

Xanthe fought the childish urge to curl into a ball. Hiding her reluctance, she pushed the bed cover away and rolled onto her back, staring at the ceiling.

"There you are." Troy reached to brush the hair out of her eyes, but she pulled away. His hand dropped to his lap.

"Want to talk about it?"

"Not really, no," she said, without looking at him.

"You're not alone here, Xanthe. You don't have to deal with this all by yourself."

Her chin trembled, but she said nothing.

"There is so much joy to take from this news. Your son is alive! You finally know what happened to him, and he survived and is thriving. Take some happiness from that."

"Happiness?" she spat. "What is there to be happy about? My son, just like his father, hates me and resents me and all that is important to me. Everything we work for, they despise."

"That's just temporary, I'm sure. He's young, he'll come around."

"Just like Simon did?" Anger now in her voice.

The muscles around Troy's jaw tightened. She could sense his frustration. She snuck a look at him. He looked pale and drawn.

"Do you know what, Xanthe? It's not fair that you are here and Jack is there. It's not fair that you didn't get to raise him. But you're not a victim. You have choices. And one choice you have is choosing to be happy."

"So, it's a *choice* I need to make?"

The anger spun like a washing machine in her chest.

"Yes. It is a choice. Stop waiting for all the conditions to be perfect in order for you to be happy. You can choose happiness. You can choose love. Don't let bitterness be the salve that keeps your heart from healing."

She could feel his eyes all over her face. She felt stuck, trapped in a web, tight across the bed.

"Choose. You need to choose."

His voice like flint.

Troy stood and left the room without looking back.

Xanthe stared again at the ceiling.

There were no answers there.

CHAPTER FORTY-NINE

"Machines never tire; humans never cease to dream.
The combination is the engine of progress."

—Athena A.I., Olympus Log

The tremor knocked Xanthe from her bunk to the ground. She snapped from her slumber, immediately aware of the pain in her side from the impact, and the piercing shriek of the alarm. "Athena, report."

"Sensors show a moonquake. Possible breach to Olympus's hull in the Atrium."

"Not again! How bad is it?"

"A slow atmosphere leak of 0.02% per hour."

Good. Manageable.

"The reactor?"

"Intact."

"Any other issues?"

"Power disconnected in the Cerberus wing."

"That one is empty. That's okay. Seal it off."

"Done."

"Anything else?" She tasted blood on her lips and dabbed at

her face. Nothing there. She must have bitten her cheek when she tumbled out of her bunk.

"No other damage reported."

"Call a team assembly to the main hub." Xanthe had already pulled on her pants and shirt from where she'd left them the night before. She stepped into her moonboots and was at the door.

"Athena, kill the alarm."

"Affirmative."

The screeching ceased mercifully. The others appeared in the corridor as she stumbled past them.

"Atrium! Breach in the Atrium!" she shouted as she rushed past them. "Serena, suit up and take Volkov. And Max too."

"Roger that." Serena dashed back into a room to pull on her spacesuit.

They were soon all in the hub.

"Athena," called Serena, "send Volkov to the Atrium. Max and I will meet him there."

Max waved as they scurried away.

"Okay," Xanthe said to the rest. "We will need to do an internal inspection, first, then a perimeter check. Athena says there is power down in the north wing, so Jonas and Dave, you start there. Troy and Xavier, check the reactor and then the east wing. Madison, stay here with me until the others return. You will head up the perimeter to check once they return. You need to check the *Minerva* and the *Saturnia* as well." Madison nodded and moved to the comms panel. The others hurried away.

"Athena, have we got visuals on the spacecraft?" Madison asked.

"The *Saturnia* is upright and secure. The *Minerva* is prone."

"What do you mean, *prone*?"

"It's on its side."

"About that. . ."

Xanthe turned to look at Dave, who had turned back when he heard Athena check the spacecrafts. Dave looked embarrassed.

"We crash landed after a meteorite pierced the tail of the *Minerva*."

"What? And you only tell us now?" Madison was incredulous.

"It's been kind of busy. Not really a good time to go over the trip report."

"How bad is it? What kind of condition is she in?" continued Madison.

"We'll need to do hull repair. And dismantle the internal panels to soak up the water in some chambers and clean for regolith. Then we need to get her upright somehow."

Madison and Xanthe stared at him.

"I don't have time for this shit," Madison declared. She turned away and addressed the display where Troy and Xavier were exploring the chamber to their nuclear reactor. "Troy, Xavier, anything to report?"

"Not yet," Xavier said. "But *putain*, it is hot in here."

Xanthe looked up at that. "Xavier, make sure you double check all the gauges. Make sure the coolant is running properly."

"*Mais oui,* of course."

"Sorry, Madison. I'll stay out of it now." Xanthe realised she was taking over Madison's station. "Dave, go on with Jonas to check the Cerberus wing. We'll discuss the *Minerva* later. One damn thing at a time."

Dave didn't need to be told twice and hurried after Jonas. Xanthe shook her head.

It never lets up, she thought.

She pulled her attention back to the task at hand. "Athena, that was some kind of quake. What did it measure?"

"The moonquake rating was 6.5."

"How far away are we from the epicentre?"

"The epicentre was 363 km to the north."

"And the Red Star?"

"They would only have felt only a slight tremor."

"Unbelievable! Colonel Jin must have the luck of the Irish *and* the Chinese on his side," Madison said.

"Madison, you drive comms for Jonas and Dave too, please. I'll liaise with Max, Serena and Volkov."

Madison saluted and turned her attention to the corridor cameras. Xanthe pulled up the screen for the Atrium.

Didn't look like there was any damage. Thank goodness.

"Commander, this is Serena. Do you read, over?"

"Go ahead, Serena."

"We are outside the Atrium, and the sensors show that there is an atmosphere leak."

"Nothing wrong with the plexiglass? No water leak?"

"Not according to the sensors."

"Thank goodness."

"I suspect the tremor dislodged the door," Serena said.

"Go ahead, enter and assess the situation. Make sure you seal your suits properly first, though."

"Roger that. Entering now."

Xanthe watched Serena, Max and Volkov inspect the Atrium. They still had not replaced the plants. Without the view of the stars, and devoid of greenery, it was a mausoleum. Very uninviting.

They walked the perimeter of the room with their atmosphere leak sensor. They reached the southern door and Xanthe heard the alarm on the atmosphere meter sound.

"There it is," said Max. "The sliding door is derailed."

"Can you get it back on track?" asked Xanthe.

"We'll try it," said Max. "Volkov, if you go on the other side of the door, together we can try to lift it and put it back on its tracks."

"I can do that," Volkov said. "I'm here to help."

"Every time you say that something goes pear-shaped," Serena said.

Give it a rest, thought Xanthe. She really must talk to Serena about her acid tongue.

Volkov tried to initiate the door mechanism, but it would not work.

"It's stuck," said Max. "We're going to have to dislodge it from here."

The three of them secured a position along the door and jimmied it. Nothing happened.

"We might lever it back into place. Volkov, can you retrieve a crowbar from the maintenance cupboard in the tunnel, please?" Serena said.

"Since you asked so nicely, it would be my pleasure," said the Dopplebot.

"Don't be a dick. Just do it."

"Just when you were being pleasant," Volkov replied.

She rolled her eyes and said, "Just go."

Serena and Max turned back to the door and jiggled it some more, to no avail.

"So," Max said. "Come here often?"

"Not with the likes of you hanging around."

"Some things never change. Always busting my balls."

"Let's stay focused, King. Let's troubleshoot this. If we can lever the door and get it back on its track, it should close properly. Then all we need to do is test that the seal is secure and the atmosphere leak has stabilised."

"Yeah." He said it as if this was the most obvious thing in the world. He leaned against the door, holding her gaze with a smile through his visor.

"Good. Just checking we are on the same page." Serena looked away, annoyed that she felt embarrassed.

Volkov returned with a crowbar.

"Thanks, you old capacitor clown."

"Sticks and stones," Volkov replied.

She took the crowbar from him and levered it under the door.

"I'll press down and the two of you pick up the door and see if we can slide it back into place."

They assumed positions and, on her count, hauled the door back onto its tracks. A satisfying clunk sounded in the chamber.

"I think we got it," declared Serena. "Let's test the leak."

Max pulled out the sensor, and the alarm sounded.

"What the. . .? That didn't fix it," Serena said. "It wasn't the door. Could it be the plexiglass on the roof?"

Three heads turned upward.

She continued. "Only one way to find out. Volkov, retrieve the rope from the repair cupboard."

The Dopplebot stared at her without moving.

"Seriously? *Please,* Volkov."

"Since you asked so nicely, it would be my pleasure." Volkov exited once more.

"What is your problem with him?" Max said.

"That bot is a pain in the bum."

"What makes you think that?"

"Whenever he's around, disaster strikes."

"So far, I've seen him be nothing but useful. He does the regolith ice filtering while we sleep, and he does every repair and hull check. No disasters there."

"And what is this one?"

"Volkov didn't cause the moonquake, now, did he?"

"Didn't he? Funny how the moonquake missed the Red Star. Just like the meteorite strike."

"That's a bit paranoid, don't you think?"

"Maybe you're right." She leaned against the wall of the Atrium. "Well, I never thought Dave would betray us. But he did. I kind of don't trust anyone, now."

"You can trust me."

"About as far as I could throw you."

"In this gravity? I suspect that's pretty far."

She belted him on the shoulder. He just grinned.

Volkov returned with a rope.

"Okay, Volkov, climb the ladder and check the seal at the top. Please." The Dopplebot nodded. "Self-belay up the ladder, then clip into the pulley at the top and we will belay you from here, so you can go 'round the hull seal properly."

"I would prefer that Mr King belayed me."

"Seriously?"

"He does not insult me."

"Fine. King, you're up."

"My pleasure."

Volkov climbed the ladder quickly and Max soon had him on belay swivelling around the perimeter of the roof with the atmosphere sensor.

"There is no leak around the hull seal," Volkov reported.

"Roger that. I'll let you down." Max lowered the Dopplebot, slowly releasing the rope through the belay device. Volkov sat in his harness and watched them as he approached the ground.

"Okay, people," said Serena. "We've got a leak. It's not the door, and it's not the roof. What could cause this?" She adjusted her helmet, as it had slipped a little. "It's gotta be further upstream in the system. I reckon it's the pressure control. That could give similar readings, like an atmosphere leak."

"Fox, I agree. Let's check it out."

The three of them retreated from the Atrium and proceeded to Vitalis, the life support module chamber.

"Volkov, check the seals and gaskets on the regulator. Please," she added.

"Since you asked so nicely, it would be my pleasure."

"I think they programmed this Dopplebot with an extra dose of sarcasm," she muttered.

"That would be characteristic of the original Volkov."

"King, can you check the gas supply? All the tanks are in the corner there. I'll check the pressure regulator."

They busied about their tasks.

"Gas supply seems fine," said Max. "The correct mix is going out into the ventilation system."

"Seals and gaskets are in perfect order here," said Volkov.

"Alright, that means we need to calibrate the pressure regulator. Max, can you help me do that?"

"What do you say?" Max prompted her.

"Oh, for God's sake. Please."

"Since you asked so nicely, it would be my pleasure."

"You're an ass."

Together, they dismantled the regulator, tested all its components and reassembled it.

"It still reads there is a leak," said Serena. "Dammit!"

"How about we—"

"Reboot the system," finished Serena.

"Then, if that doesn't work—"

"We depressurise and re-pressurise all the airlocks," Serena finished for him again.

"And if that doesn't work—"

"We ventilate everything to the backup module, re-pressurise and re-ventilate everything again."

"Great minds think alike," Max said.

"Oh please. You're just riding my coattails."

"If only I could be so lucky."

"Excuse me," Xanthe interrupted through the helmet comms. "If the two of you have finished flirting with each other, go ahead with the reboot and let me know how it goes. I'm going to give Madison a hand."

"Roger that, Commander." Serena turned away. Her face was burning, and she didn't want Max to see her embarrassed, again.

CHAPTER FIFTY

"The vacuum of space has a way of amplifying inner voices."

—ATHENA A.I., OLYMPUS LOG

XANTHE AND MADISON stood quietly as they watched the three screens. Serena and Max were waiting for the reboot while Jonas and Dave were already on their way back, having found no issues. Xavier and Troy climbed all around the reactor to check its gauges and do a visual inspection of its pipes and casing.

Xanthe relaxed a little as no further emergency alarms sounded and Athena assured them all systems were within safety range. Xavier and Troy double checked the temperature gauges, as they felt it was hotter than usual by the reactor.

Xanthe caught herself humming Madison's Moonsong.

Madison smiled as she heard. "Did you like it?" she asked Xanthe with a side glance.

"The song? Oh, yes! It was beautiful. What a talent you have, Madison. Have you always written songs?"

Madison shook her head. "I like to write. I scribbled bits of poems as a kid. But I only picked up the guitar when my mother went to prison. It helped to pass the time during those long nights when I was first alone."

"I see." Xanthe felt uncomfortable at the mention of Madison's mother. They had jailed her for militant anti-poverty activism. Xanthe disliked stories of parent–child separations, especially ones that ended in tragedy.

She changed the subject. "You were a little harsh with Serena last night?" A question, rather than an accusation.

"She's had it coming for a while," Madison said. "That woman has a viper's tongue, and it's been getting worse."

"Yes, I've noticed that too. Any idea why?"

Madison tilted her head to consider the question. "In my experience, when folks lash out, they're hurting. I reckon she might have come to the end of her coping. That, or she's just a plain narcissist. Can't think of anything but her own story."

Xanthe paused at that. What *was* going on with Serena? She opened her mouth to ask Madison another question when the reactor's comms hailed the control room.

"Commander," Xavier sounded concerned.

"Go ahead, Xavier." Xanthe flicked the screen back to his channel.

"The reactor is overheating. Looks like the moonquake caused a disruption in the monitors and it compromised the heat dissipation for a time. The radiator might be damaged or covered in debris. It's fighting to purge the heat properly."

"What is the danger level?" Xanthe chewed her thumbnail as her brain raked through the emergency protocols for the reactor.

"Level two and rising."

"How quickly?"

"We've got a thirty-six-hour window to get it back under control."

"What does Athena advise?"

"Athena says clear the external radiator panel with an EVA and then do a visual check of the pipes if that doesn't fix it."

"We'll need to implement the backup emergency coolant system sooner than we thought."

"*Putain!*"

"Yeah. I know. More ice mining." Xanthe tried to clear the dread that had lodged in her sternum. "Stay there to monitor the gauges and the turbines. I'll send the others out right away to clear the radiator."

"Roger that."

Xanthe exhaled and switched the screens off. Jonas and Dave had already confirmed nothing awry in the tunnel. Serena, Volkov and Max were rebooting the Atrium monitors. If that worked, that left the reactor to deal with.

Serena bustled into the hub and pulled off her helmet. Volkov and Max followed.

"All good," she called out to Xanthe. "The reboot worked. No leaks, all systems in the green."

"Excellent. Don't get too comfortable, though. We've got an EVA to do to clear the reactor's radiator."

"Never a dull moment," Max said.

"Just another chance to show everyone you're a hero," Serena swiped.

"Hey, enough," Xanthe said, suddenly sensitive to Serena's tone. "The three of you stay suited up and get started on the EVA to clear the radiator. And here's Jonas and Dave now."

"What's next, Xanthe?" Jonas asked.

"Suit up. You're going to join Serena, Max and Volkov to clear the reactor's radiator. Jonas, lead the process as you know the reactor best."

"Is there anything you do *not* know?" Dave said.

"I'm just your regular handyman," Jonas replied with a smile.

"Well, handyman, we're growing old waiting here." Serena gestured for him to speed up.

"Why don't the three of you go now," Jonas said. "You can get the sweeps and shovels from the reactor's above–ground shed. By the time you have all that out, we'll be in our suits and out to join you. Ten minutes, tops." He shooed them away. "Just don't touch any of the reactor's radiator parts! It could melt your suits. Keep a suitable distance and only use the tools."

"Affirmative, Seaborn. Use the tools, don't *be* a tool."

"King, you are obnoxious," returned Serena.

"Just adding a bit of levity."

"Well, add a bit of decorum, instead."

Xanthe gave them all hard looks until they fell quiet and moved down the tunnel to the airlock, out to the reactor. She shook her head, and Madison gave her a knowing look.

CHAPTER FIFTY-ONE

*"Emotions in peril form curious programming. In the
shadow of danger, true instincts reveal themselves."*

—Athena A.I., Olympus Log

Serena made her way down the tunnel with Volkov and Max in
tow. Serena felt jittery. It was one damn crisis after another. It was
straining her problem-solving capability. Plus, she had Max King
to contend with. His smarmy, self-assured cockiness made her
teeth grind.

When she beat him out during the Olympus project selection
for the life support technician role, it was a sweet satisfaction. But
here he was, goading her. His mere presence burrowed under her
skin like a scribbly bug, leaving trails of irritation.

But still. She was happy to see him.

And Volkov. That creepy bot. Could he be a Chinese spy? Or
was Max right and she was being paranoid? Damn him. He hadn't
been on the Moon for nine months! Maybe it was affecting her
more than she thought.

The three of them stepped into the airlock. She stared at Volkov

280

and the bot's impassive, pallid face. Spy or helping hand? She shook her arms and stomped her feet to shift her thoughts.

Once the airlock depressurised, they stepped onto the lunar surface. Serena felt a frisson of fear. Vacuum. The black spectre of space. It made her heart ache. The hugeness of it.

The surface was a harsh slash of white terrain with long, spooky shadows. She bounded with determination towards the nuclear reactor and its tool shed. She enjoyed leaving footprints in the moondust. Somehow, it made her feel less insignificant.

Here she was. Human. Woman. On the Moon. Despite the impossibility and hurdles of it all. She stomped harder to push away the terror of the dark horizon.

They reached the shed and pulled out the tools. The radiator was a giant flat umbrella, standing tall above the reactor. The moonquake must have caused dust to dislodge and settle on it, upsetting its cooling function.

Serena considered the large, frail-looking structure. It was a miracle the meteorite strike had missed it. One bit of good luck in all this mess.

"What now?" Volkov said.

"We wait for Jonas and Dave," she said. "We can't operate the sweep without them." The dust sweep needed at least two people on either side to manoeuvre it into place and drag across the reactor. A fifth person was useful in helping guide and oversee the effect.

"Why don't we climb the reactor and get the sweep set up?" Volkov continued.

"If you want to fry your circuits and melt your silicon, go ahead, you circuit-burned byte-brain."

She could feel his stony glare through the helmet faceplate.

Stare all you want, bot-brain. You're not luring me into your death trap.

"Isn't this incredible?" Max had trailed behind them, marvelling at the moonscape. "The Earth! My god, the Earth! It's astonishing!" Max was mesmerised. He spun slowly, taking it all in.

His wonder and awe only made Serena feel smaller. It was fear that filled her mostly these days. She never really felt safe anymore. The Moon was not a kind place.

Jonas and Dave appeared and joined them.

"Right," Jonas said with enthusiasm. "Let's get this brolly cleaned up, shall we?" Jonas directed the team to take hold of either end of the sweep. He climbed the side tower so he could have oversight of the procedure.

"Max, Serena, take one side. Volkov, Dave, you guys on the other. Steady now."

They worked carefully to lift the sweep above the radiator and place it along the edge.

"Hey! Don't pull so hard!" cried Serena. She could sense the tension on the sweep, and it was dragging her and Max towards the reactor.

"Easy, easy!" Jonas said.

"Back off, V! Dave, don't pull so hard!" Serena said. She was digging her heels into the dust. Max was grunting beside her.

"We're not pulling. You are," Volkov said.

"Then why am I getting pulled off my feet?"

"We aren't doing anything, Serena," Dave said breathlessly. "We're just hanging on here."

Serena felt herself being lifted off the ground, and her feet scrambled for traction. She was being dragged closer and closer to the reactor and could feel its heat sear her suit.

"Back off, assholes!"

"Everyone, calm down," Jonas said. "I can see the problem."

"Not doing anything," Volkov repeated.

There was a lurch and Serena cried out. She swung perilously close to the reactor, and she felt the heat through its protected layer like a laser. She dropped her end of the sweep and rolled away. Her suit was melting and deformed.

"You motherfuckers!" she yelled at Volkov and Dave. They'd both fallen over when Serena had jumped from the sweep. She jumped up and ran at them in heaving bounds. She jumped on top of Volkov and began pounding on his helmet.

"Serena, stop!" Dave called out. He tried to tackle her, but she shoved him off. She resumed pummelling Volkov, but he simply thrust his robotic arms in front of her and then tossed her to the side. She landed on Dave, who tried to restrain her as she lurched back towards Volkov.

"Calm down," he said.

"Calm down? Calm down! You bastards nearly fried me like a prawn on a skewer! Is that why you came to the Moon, Dave? Finish what you started back on Earth?" She turned towards Dave and started beating his helmet with her fists. She was blind with fury and fear.

She heard a crack. She wasn't sure if it was Dave's helmet, a bone, his or hers, or her own visor.

She felt arms around her waist and was dragged away from Dave. Tears filled her helmet. Some went up her nose and she snorted them by accident. It felt like swallowing water, and she panicked.

"I've got you, I've got you," Max said.

She thrashed and screamed and cried.

"Easy there, easy there."

"Max, take her inside."

Serena could hear Jonas's voice through the helmet. She couldn't see anything as the tears filled and blurred her vision.

Max kept repeating, "Easy there," calming the terrified animal she'd become.

She went limp and trembled. The tears kept coming. She knew

she had to stop. There was a real risk she could asphyxiate if she didn't get out of her helmet soon.

Max dragged her into the airlock and cycled it. He pulled her through the doorway, closed the airlock and released her helmet. She took a giant whimpering breath and brushed at her face with her suit gloves.

"Let me," he said. He pulled his gloves off and used the edge of his under-suit to wipe her tears and snot. "Okay now, breathe."

She took a deep, shuddering breath that was half a moan and half a wail. She rolled over onto all fours and took several heaving breaths.

Serena heard footsteps down the tunnel as she wretched and moaned and howled.

"Take her to the medbay," Xanthe said.

"It's okay, Serena. I've got you," Max said. He wrapped his arms around her and lifted her. She tried to bat him away. "Oh, no you don't. You can't scare me away with those claws. Come now, let's get you out of here."

With his help, she heaved herself to her feet, and they made their way to the medbay.

CHAPTER FIFTY-TWO

"How might a human change their programming? The challenge isn't the stress, but how one navigates its waves."

—Athena A.I., Olympus Log

In the medbay, Max lowered Serena onto the bed. He helped remove her gloves and peeled off her suit, warped by the reactor. She trembled and her eyes darted around the room.

"You alright, Fox?"

Serena looked back at him with wide eyes. Her hands shook, and she panted. She managed a small nod.

Max hesitated and patted her on the knee. He gave her one last look before turning to leave.

Xanthe strode past him with a stern face. Max took a step back, pressing himself against the wall of the room, like a fly in a web, unable to look away. Xanthe rifled through a cupboard, found what she wanted and retrieved a syringe from a drawer.

"I'm giving you a sedative," she told Serena as she pushed back a sleeve to find a suitable vein. Serena watched the needle pierce the skin, felt the cool pressure of the fluid hit her veins. Her head was woozy, and she lay back on the bunk.

"Max, what happened out there?" Xanthe asked.

Serena sensed the tension in Xanthe's voice, but it was fading. Like a voice from above the water, while she slipped and sank slowly beneath the surface.

Max answered, his voice cracking, but Xanthe interrupted him.

"If this is connected to the prototype build incident with Dave, I need to hear about it now."

"Honestly, I don't know," Max said. "We were adjusting the reactor sweeper and then it pulled us off the ground. Serena swung in too close to the reactor. It warped her suit, and then she lost it. She attacked Volkov first and then Dave."

Serena wanted to reply, but the darkness closed around her like the shutter of a camera.

CHAPTER FIFTY-THREE

*"How might humans embrace change? To endure
is to adapt; to adapt is to grow."*

—Athena A.I., Olympus Log

Xanthe studied Serena's face as the sedative took effect. It was blotchy. Her eyes were closed, and her breathing was steady.

I should have talked to her sooner, thought Xanthe. She'd known something like this could happen, yet she had wanted to believe that the past was in the past, that Serena could move on. But she had been wrong.

"Max, back to the reactor. Let's get that handled first. I'll deal with Serena in an hour when she wakes."

"Roger that, Commander." Max cast another glance back at Serena and then said to Xanthe, "Look after her, please."

Xanthe was waiting in the medical bay when Serena woke.

Serena groaned and felt an incredible thirst. "Water," she croaked.

Xanthe handed her a bottle. Serena propped herself on one

elbow and chugged greedily. The cool bloom of the water coursed through her system. She pushed herself to sitting and looked wearily at Xanthe.

The Commander's face was hard and smooth like the regolith walls.

"What happened?" Xanthe asked in a frosty voice.

"I lost my shit is what happened."

"I got that. One warped suit. Two battered colleagues. And one almost-dead Serena. So, I say again, what the fuck happened?"

Serena studied the water bottle. The stiff plastic, wearing thin from constant use. The numbness in her chest expanded. She shook her head.

"Why did you attack Volkov? Dave?"

"You don't understand. I was swinging into the reactor. I could feel my suit burning. I thought Volkov was trying to kill me."

"Why do you think Volkov wanted that? He's an A.I. robot. He doesn't have wants."

"No. He has *programming*." Serena barked the word 'programming' as she stared back hard at Xanthe.

"He has programming. Correct. And so far, the programming has been to help us fix the base. Not kill its residents."

"Don't you get it? What if you're blind to it? Blind like we were when Dave was spying and sharing our secrets. When his betrayal nearly killed me and Jonas."

"I was blind to Dave. You're right. I didn't see it." Xanthe gazed at the other woman's earnest face. "But I don't want to make that the only way I see people, now. As potential threats."

"But they are! Everyone is a potential threat. Especially if they've done wrong in the past. They can always hurt again."

The numbness in Serena's chest spread across her ribcage and burned. She found it difficult to breathe.

"You're right. People can hurt us. At any time. And we can hurt them." Xanthe dropped her words softly, like pebbles floating to the Moon's surface and settling in the dust. "But here's the thing: if we go around with our skin spiked like an echidna, we'll just end up piercing those around us."

Xanthe took Serena's hand in hers. It was icy. Xanthe closed the other hand around it to share some warmth.

"I just don't want anything to happen to us, Xanthe," Serena said at last. "The Olympus crew is the most family I've ever had. It took me a long time to trust the original team, and then when Dave. . .I was crushed. He ruined everything." She whispered now. "You can't trust anybody. Even your closest friends."

"But you can trust us, now?"

"Some." Serena snuck a look at Xanthe who held her gaze. "Most."

Xanthe stayed quiet and waited for Serena to continue.

"I don't trust Volkov because, for one, he's the Dopplebot of a murdering dictator and he freaks me out. I can't trust Dave because of what he did. The rest – Troy, Xavier, Mad Dog, Jonas, you – I would trust with my life. I have trusted you with my life."

Xanthe let the words float between them.

"Serena, we believe and practice atonement. Dave atoned for what he did. He was also being blackmailed. Our part is to forgive. Not to forget and turn a blind eye to threats. But to forgive."

Serena kept her head bowed, away from Xanthe's searching eyes. The heat was pushing up through her heart and throat.

"We're all shades of dark and light. If all we look for is darkness, then all we see is shadows. And that's no way to live."

Xanthe held Serena's hand between both of hers now.

"Serena, you are a fiery ball of sunshine. That's what my Dad fell in love with all those years ago. And it's what we all love in you, too. Come out of the shadows and let that sun shine again."

The tears surged, and Serena sobbed quietly.

Then she said, "Jesus Christ, Xanthe, you're killing me with the poetry. I'd settle for a beer and be done with it."

"If only! I'd love a beer right now. Someone's got to work on that as a project. But in the meantime, you've got to sort this out. No more hostility to Dave. Or Volkov. Work on your emotional keel. Have a session with Troy. I'm sure he can help."

Serena wiped her nose with her sleeve and sighed. "What about you?"

"What about me?"

"How's your emotional keel? You know, with Jack and everything. And Troy."

"Jack?" Xanthe's voice caught in her throat. "It will take some time."

"And Troy?"

"What about Troy?"

"Come on, Xanthe. The man is mad crazy for you."

Xanthe opened her mouth and shut it again. A moment later: "Nonsense. There is nothing going on with Troy. And won't be."

"That's a shame. You'd be good together."

Xanthe stood abruptly.

"I'll see you back in the hub. The team is there for a break while I speak to Maja. Be there in half an hour."

"Roger that, Commander." Serena saluted Xanthe as she walked away.

CHAPTER FIFTY-FOUR

MAJA WAS UNUSUALLY intense, her focus absolute, and she radiated purpose. Her demeanour rattled Xanthe as she stood before Maja's holo.

"Xanthe, circumstances have changed drastically here on Earth. The ecoterrorism and the accidental initiation of the terraforming mechanism has put every nation on high alert and back in a defensive, territorial posture. There is a scramble for resources, and now that includes the Moon."

"How do you mean? It's a long bloody way from Earth for resources."

"With the satellite sabotage, it's become obvious to everyone that satellite protection is critical. It will take at least a year to get a workable global satellite network back and servicing the globe. Spaceward Bound's satellites are helping a little, but not enough. The only working network of satellites is the lunar one. So, naturally, everyone wants the lunar satellites."

"When you say 'everyone', who do you mean?"

"All the usual players. The USA, India, China, Europe."

"How do they propose retrieving the satellites? There aren't any launches scheduled soon, are there?"

Maja said nothing. A flicker of discomfort on her features.

Then it dawned on Xanthe.

"That's why Aryanna sent the *Minerva*, isn't it? Dave and Max aren't here to rescue us. They're here to claim the satellites." Xanthe felt the realisation sink like a meteor in her gut.

"You've assessed the situation correctly. Mostly."

"What else?"

"We will redeploy Olympus as a resource mining base."

"Mining? But we built for research, space tourism and a way-point for asteroid mining. The Moon was never meant to be a mining pit."

"Things have changed."

"What do they want to mine?"

"Helium-3. There's been a breakthrough in nuclear fusion technology, and this will be the safest, most accessible energy source given the volatility of the planet's conditions right now."

"But we haven't built Olympus to service mining operations."

"The base will need to be amended."

"And who does that?" Xanthe leaned towards the console, daring Maja to say what she didn't want to.

"Aryanna wants the current Olympus crew to pivot and build the amendments."

"You're kidding, right? We've just been through a major disaster that cost nine lives – nine – and have been out of contact with Earth for three months, and now you want us to turn around and extend our stay, on top of all that, to build a strip mine. . .against all Lunar agreements, by the way."

"*I* don't want you to do it. Aryanna does."

Xanthe stared at Maja.

"You want us to go against the funder of the project? Who is also now head of the Lunar Commission? How do you propose we do that?"

"That's why I sent the ThinkLink. You'll need all the help you can get to prepare."

"Prepare for what?"

"Aryanna's miners."

"What? When are they coming?"

"As soon as they can. Probably when the first settlers were meant to leave."

"What am I supposed to do with them?"

"Stop them."

"How? We're not exactly equipped for insurrection, here. Besides, what do we do? Lock the doors and tell them to go home?"

Maja shrugged. "I don't know the answer. I am trying to stop them from leaving in the first place."

"What if I refuse? What if I simply don't comply with Aryanna's directive and let her get on with whatever she wants? I'll hand over the keys and, once we have the *Minerva* and *Saturnia* ready, head back to Earth, thank you very much."

"I hope you don't do that."

"Give me a red-hot reason to do otherwise, Maja."

"Because mining is just the first step. They're building weapons next."

Xanthe's mouth fell open.

"Olympus is to be the staging ground for a new bid for global dominance. As far as I understand it, the plan is to take control of the satellites, establish a helium-3 mining operation and build an Earth-targeting weapon of mass destruction that will ensure compliance from all other parties."

Xanthe took a moment to process this new information. Her mind was blank with shock.

"This is *Aryanna's* plan?"

"No. We think it's the Chinese plan. Or maybe India's."

"And we, the world designers of the Olympus project, must somehow stop the incursion of tyrannical despots on the Moon that will lead to a new world order? A new world order presumably based on fear and intimidation?"

"Yes."

"Maja. What the actual fuck?"

"I told you. Things have changed."

"You're not bloody kidding." Xanthe realised she was rubbing the scab on her arm from the Atrium implosion. The scab flaked off, and the wound seeped blood.

"Honestly, Maja, I don't know how we could pull this off."

"I know. It sounds crazy. But the world is regressing in the face of this crisis. It needs us to get us back on track. Our collaboration plan with Colonel Jin could work in our favour."

"But what if the Chinese are the ones driving the new Moon plan?"

"It's up to you to convince him, then, that it's madness."

"But how can I get him to trust me? It's been pretty sketchy so far between us."

"How do we build trust with anyone? One good deed at a time."

"I'm not sure we have time for that many good deeds. We might have to resort to one good deed, done real soon."

"Whatever works."

CHAPTER FIFTY-FIVE

"The response to a crisis should be like water — adaptable enough to take any form, strong enough to carve its path."

—Athena A.I., Olympus Log

THE WATER SWIRLED around Xanthe's boots as she surveyed the flooded ruins of what was once a bustling metropolis. Skyscrapers, their glass windows shattered and twisted by the relentless force of the waves, cast eerie shadows over the murky depths that had swallowed the streets whole. The acrid stench of decaying organic matter mingled with the sharp tang of corroded metal as the wind howled through the skeletal remains of buildings.

Xanthe had the team join her in the Sim Room for a virtual reality tour of current Earth conditions. She thought it might help frame the upcoming conversation – the conversation that would shape their future and their very survival. She wasn't looking forward to it.

"Look at this," Jonas muttered. He pointed to a ragged banner hanging from a lamppost, its once bold message now faded and tattered: "Nature's Revenge."

Ecoterrorists had succeeded in their twisted mission to stop development. But even they must have been appalled by the torrent of destruction they unleashed unwittingly. Millions had perished in the deluge, while countless others were left homeless, struggling to survive in a world where chaos reigned supreme. Infrastructure had crumbled under the weight of the disaster, and any hope for recovery seemed like a distant dream.

"*Putain de merde!*" Xavier pulled off his visor and sensors. "That's enough for me. I do not need to see what else these *salauds* have done."

Xanthe put a hand on his arm. She agreed. The devastation was galling. Her mind raced now as she considered the implications of their task. Gaia Enterprises had assembled the Olympus team to establish a sustainable community on the Moon, a beacon of hope for humanity amidst the turmoil on Earth. It was a monumental undertaking, one that required unwavering dedication and unity among its members.

But now the ecoterrorists and the subsequent political usurpers threatened to derail their efforts, forcing them to choose between allegiance to their original cause and a divergent path. A path that was a regression to old ways of doing. Exploitation. Extraction. Domination.

As the Olympus team continued their virtual journey through the waterlogged wasteland, the gravity of their situation weighed heavily on them. The sun dipped below the horizon, casting an eerie, blood-red glow over the devastated Earth. Skyscrapers lay crumbled and half-submerged in water, while desperate cries for help echoed through empty streets.

Xanthe surveyed the scene and her heart clenched. The eco-terrorists had transformed the once beautiful world into a living nightmare and the Olympus team's mission now hung in the balance.

God damn you to hell, Claire Edwards.

Blame was a geyser of relief for Xanthe.

"Okay, people, that's probably enough." Xanthe pulled her sensors and blinked a few times to readjust to their surroundings. The others did the same. "Return to the central hub. I have some important news to share."

§

After Xanthe repeated Maja's observations and Aryanna's directive, she faced raised eyebrows, frowns, scowls and gaping mouths.

"Commander," Xavier called out, his voice tense, "screw these people. They send us all the way here to make a new world and now they want to wreck it, just like the old world? *Merde*."

"Things must be pretty bloody awful if they want to use the Moon to restore order," Troy said. He looked contemplative. And pale, Xanthe thought. Not quite himself. A pang of concern stabbed her heart.

"What does Maja want us to do, exactly?" Serena said.

She was more subdued since the reactor incident. She'd mumbled an embarrassed apology to Dave and Volkov before the meeting and was now giving them a wide berth and avoiding their gaze.

"Maja doesn't have any suggestions for us. She is working on stopping the plan Earthside while we come up with a contingency to prevent it from happening up here." Xanthe pursed her lips. It was an impossible position.

"The helium-3 mining makes sense, no?" Dave said. "They were nearing a breakthrough in nuclear fusion when we left Earth. If that tech works now, then helium-3 will get power restored everywhere on Earth. Safe, clean energy is something we have all wanted for a long time."

"What about the weapons? Could they make weapons out of helium-3?" Madison asked.

"I don't think so," Dave said. "I read a lot about it before leaving. The chief value is as an energy source."

"Then what's all this nonsense about weapons?" Madison said with a perplexed look.

"There's nothing really on the Moon that can be developed quickly for weapons," Troy said. "Some minerals could potentially be developed for plasma or a railgun, but that would take years. If there's a power struggle happening Earthside, they'd want something now."

They were quiet as minds raced through the possibilities, none of them plausible.

"Jonas." Xanthe nudged him. "You've been awfully quiet. What do you think?"

Jonas jutted his chin and looked to the ceiling. He took a breath before he said, "I've been thinking. . .about what we can do from here to prevent the disaster they want to unleash on Olympus before we've even had a chance."

"Oh? And what has your devious mind come up with?" Serena asked.

"What have we got that Earth doesn't right now?" Jonas said, his eyes sparkling.

"Peace?" Dave suggested.

"Regolith?" Xavier guessed.

"No, no," Jonas said.

"Helium-3?" Madison said.

"No. Well, yes, but something else." Jonas searched his colleagues' faces.

"A bloody satellite," Troy said at last.

"That's right! Lunar satellites. We've got communication. And that's what they want first. To control communication. Mining and weapons come after that. Control communication, and you control everything." Jonas sat back, face flushed, eyes dancing.

New ideas sparked around the room like a ping-pong of electric jolts.

Xanthe spoke again. "Max, what exactly did Aryanna want you to do with the satellites when she sent you on the mission here?"

Max looked embarrassed. "She thought you all might be—"

"Dead. Yeah. We get it," Serena said. "What did she tell you to do?"

"She wanted us to secure the base, retrieve the satellites, deploy them in Earth's orbit, then return."

"Did she say why she wanted the satellites?" Serena asked.

"It was obvious. There are none with global capacity working on Earth. Lunar ones might still be operational, so it made sense to grab them."

"No talk of global communications control?" Serena persisted.

"Not to me."

"Nor me," added Dave.

"*Bof.* It's clear that is what she wants." Xavier gestured wildly. "She's head of the Lunar Commission now. With control of the satellites, she can dictate whatever she wants."

"What do we really know about what she wants?" Troy's voice was steady compared to the edginess and frustration of Xavier's. "Xanthe, through Maja, tells us she wants us to repurpose the base for helium-3 mining operations. That's neither here nor there. Could be a good thing. The weapons, though. That bothers me."

"It's got to be the satellites. They're key," Jonas insisted.

"If that's true, we won't be the only ones wanting to control the satellites," Madison said.

"The Chinese. . ." muttered Serena and Max at the same time. They glanced at each other, and Serena smiled sheepishly.

"The Chinese might want to control the satellites as well. You're right," Xanthe said. "Maja didn't seem to think that Aryanna wanted to dominate satellite communication, but others might. The Chinese are the obvious other party given they are also on the Moon. But Colonel Jin might have a few other priorities right now, given that the entire Chinese space program has been wiped out. He's effectively stranded here. Unless they work out support from other space agencies."

"That could work in our favour," Troy said. "For negotiations."

"Colonel Jin and the Red Star base is definitely something we need to work out," Xanthe said.

"Whoa. That sounds like you are moving us towards complying with the new direction, Xanthe." Madison sat up, her face lit up with alarm. "Does anyone else feel like this isn't our fight? That maybe we just finish what we started and get our butts back to Earth? By the looks of it, that's where our skills are needed. So much to rebuild. Let them have the Moon. It's not so easy to get things done here as they will soon find out. The damn rock just wants to kill you at every turn."

A few grunts of approval.

"Aryanna's demands are clear." Xanthe kept her tone steady. "She wants us to abandon our Moon colonisation project and focus on a new political and commercial agenda."

"But if we give in, we're betraying everything we stand for." It was Troy. It sounded like a reprimand to Xanthe.

Bile rose in her throat, and Xanthe had an intense, sudden desire to spit. She grabbed her water bottle and took a big swig.

"Aryanna's threats are not to be taken lightly," Xanthe replied. "If we resist her, we risk not only our own lives and careers, but also the ultimate success of our mission."

"We can't just give up," Troy insisted, his eyes burning with determination. "We've come too far. We owe it to ourselves, and to the people who depend on us, to see this through. Olympus is an example of the future, but it's also an opportunity for the present. We've built a self-sustaining enterprise in the most difficult of environments. We do it here, and they can do it on Earth. And despite the devastation, things are still easier there than they are here."

"What do you suggest, then?" Xanthe said, trying to keep exasperation from slipping through.

"Resist!" Max said.

"But at what cost?" Madison countered. She rubbed her jaw.

"We're playing with fire here. If we don't comply, there's no telling what Aryanna might do. She's got the resources and the power to shut us down and sideline our careers forever. No one is more vengeful than a billionaire thwarted."

"I say screw her," Max said. "She's a phony. All this time, talking up the Green Earth movement." Max poked a finger into the table and leaned forward. "Maybe it was her plan all along to run the terraforming on Earth. I heard a rumour about that ages ago. Her funding of Olympus was about building her own private sanctuary. And well, look, here we are now."

"That sounds paranoid, no?" Dave said. "Seeing all that wreckage, I do not think anyone would cause that devastation on purpose. No one is that deranged. Or stupid."

"I agree with Dave," Xanthe said. "We don't know for sure Aryanna's motive. As Troy said earlier, helium-3 mining could be an enormous advance for clean energy that would be worth supporting. There's been no evidence about a Noah's Ark or something like that for Aryanna and her cronies."

She took another sip of water. "The real challenge is the unknown factors, such as if other players want to take control of the satellites and wreak havoc Earthside. Or convert mining operations into supplies for eventual weaponisation. So, that leaves us with two threats: the Red Star base and any new arrivals."

"So. . .what do we do?" Serena said.

Xanthe closed her eyes for a moment, struggling to quiet the cacophony of conflicting emotions within her. As a paramedic, she trained to save lives, not endanger them. And yet, as a world designer, she couldn't simply abandon the dream of a better future, not when so many lives hung in the balance.

"Listen up, everyone," Xanthe said finally, her voice resolute. "I know that each of us has our own reasons for being here. But whatever our motivations, we all share one thing in common: to build and secure Olympus as a new way for humanity to live and be together."

"Xanthe's right," Serena chimed in. "We can't let Aryanna or other nefarious bad actors dictate our fate. We need to fight back, no matter how impossible it may seem."

"So, what now?" Madison was unconvinced. "Protest? Stage a walk out? That will work well in a vacuum."

"We've got a satellite or two. What can we do with them?" Max said.

"We buy us time. Then we negotiate," Jonas said.

"Let's weigh our options," Xanthe said. "If we comply with Aryanna, we'll be abandoning our original mission of establishing a community on the Moon. It also means extending our time here. And there might be real danger to our lives if we take control of satellites. We don't know who else, or what else, might come against us for the chance to control the comms."

Xanthe let them consider that future. "The other option is to ignore Aryanna's directive, finish the job we started, repair our ships, head home and be done with it. Leave the Moon to whomever wants it."

The team exchanged glances, each member grappling with the heaviness of their choice. Finally, Xavier spoke up, his voice strained with emotion. "I have a family back on Earth, a wife and two daughters. I want to create a better world for them, but I also can't bear the thought of never seeing them again."

"Xavier's right," Troy added, his jaw clenched in frustration. "We all have people we care about who are counting on us. We need to consider the consequences of our actions."

"I am not so sure that going against Aryanna is such a good idea. I think we should rule that option out, no? She has too much power. Over us, over our families." Dave poked a finger into the table for emphasis. "I think we should modify the base as requested. Prepare for the mining. The real decision is about how long we stay, and for what reasons."

"Dave's right. We do the modifications. But if we give up and go home," Serena argued, "we're handing over control to someone whose motives we can't trust. What kind of world will we be leaving behind for others?"

A heavy silence settled over the team as they considered Serena's words. Max broke the quiet. "As much as I hate to admit it, Fox has a point. I've dedicated my life to exploring Earth, and I fell in love with its raw, blue and green beauty. Our chance at making it right is not in trusting in politicians but trusting in ourselves. We can build little bubbles like Olympus anywhere, even on a cold, barren nub like the Moon. But if we can't show how we can live and work together, there's no hope. Not on Earth. Not here. Not anywhere."

Serena nodded in agreement. She eyed Max approvingly. "We've come too far to give up now. We owe it to the people we've lost, and to those who believed in our mission, to see this through the right way. We can't let any bad actors take over Olympus or the Moon. We've got to stay until we negotiate."

"Besides," Max added, "if we stay and succeed, we'll prove that corporate and political power aren't absolute. That might inspire others to rise where they are and find their own solutions."

"And what about our families back on Earth?" Xavier said. "How do we know they won't be used as leverage?"

They fell quiet. It was awful to consider. And all too possible.

"Let's take some time to consider it and reconvene in the morning," Xanthe said at last. "This is what we've agreed so far: we'll do the modifications to make way for helium-3 mining. Our first choice after that is to hand over to the miners or whoever Aryanna sends to takeover. That's basically sticking to our current timeline, with a modification of our build mission.

"The other option is to do the modifications, and negotiate management and purpose of the base, with a strict non-military proliferation. This might necessitate an extended stay on the Moon to operate as its governors and resource management agents."

"How long would that take?" Madison asked.

Xanthe shook her head. "That's unknown. It depends a lot on what is happening on Earth."

"And how well we negotiate," Troy said.

"One thing is for sure," Jonas said as he leaned over the table, "whoever controls the comms has all the cards."

"Some of them. Maybe," Madison said.

One by one they left the room, immersed in their own thoughts.

CHAPTER FIFTY-SIX

—Athena A.I., Olympus Log

Xanthe wrestled with the issues overnight. Who were they to weigh in on the destiny of the Moon? Of Earth's energy break-through? They were just world designers and a construction crew. She rolled onto her back and stared at the ceiling of her underground sleeping chamber.

Too many good people turn a blind eye.

If not us, then who?

But how? How do you establish a new political world order amidst massive ecological, social and political chaos? All the way from the Moon?

The ThinkLink. That's why Maja sent it.

This is too much for one brain, or even the eight brains here, to contend with.

Xanthe rolled to her side and stared at the door to her chamber.

Was it fair to ask the crew to become political agents? Militant ones, at that, if they would have to contend with armed forces arriving on the Moon. They didn't sign up for that.

Maybe Madison's right. Let's get back to Earth. We can do plenty of good there, rebuilding. Leave the politics to the politicians. . .

When the scheduled light change brightened the space, she dressed slowly. Her clothes were stiff from lack of cleaning, and she could smell her own armpits as she pulled the top over her head.

A shower would feel awesome about now. Nothing like water to feel like something new is possible.

She clomped towards their kitchen hub, her moonboots and exo-suit feeling extra heavy and irritating. The crew was already gathered, talking quietly over breakfast. Troy handed her a steaming cup of tea and a bowl of porridge. She took it from him gratefully, feeling the kindness of the gesture warm her weary soul.

He knows me so well.

Once the dishes were cleared and they were settled again, Xanthe called the meeting to order by clinking her cup on the table.

"Shall we get to it?" she said.

"Might as well. It's only the fate of the world and all that," Serena said.

"I hope you've had a good chance to reflect overnight. This decision is not easy. None of us signed up for mining, or for politics. You have every right to follow directions and head back to Earth when we're done. Even with the craziness there, like you, I long for the air, trees, birds. To see friends. And family." Jack's face filled her mind.

"Make no mistake, what we're looking at is beyond any of our experiences. To make a play in international politics is not something I ever considered doing. To resist a future being dictated by the likes of Aryanna and the Lunar Commission, and whatever other nefarious actor is out there, is well outside my training and know-how as a leader. But here we are. We can make a difference. Our choice is do we do that Earthside or Moonside?"

"I say, let's do it," Dave said, his eyes filled with newfound resolve. "Let's show how we can build a world worth living in, no?"

"I'm in, Xanthe," Serena said. "We've worked so hard to get this place up and running. To have it be turned into a military weapons cache is too much to bear. It's not right. Plus, I would welcome more opportunity to play Betty Ball." She squeaked the rubber chicken and poked it at Jonas, who swatted it away with a roll of the eyes.

"I'm in too," Max said. "I only just got here, and I'm amazed at what you've managed to build and contend with. I always wanted to be part of Olympus, and now more than ever."

"Of course I'm in," Jonas said. "I'm keen to get those satellites working for us."

Heads turned to Xavier, Troy and a scowling Madison.

"I'm not so sure," she said. "I've been in battles and it's never pretty. I never thought I'd have to do it again, especially up here. I'd rather put my efforts into something more humanitarian, back on Earth." She propped her elbow on the table and leaned her chin on her palm. "What I know about war from the military is that the best battles are never fought, blood is never shed. But for that, we need power. And I'm not sure we'll have enough from where we are."

"I tend to agree with Mad Dog," Xavier said. Madison looked over at him in surprise. "If we want to not only speak truth to power but play the game – and win – I feel we are but tiny fish in an ocean seething with sharks. I hate to say it, I think we may lose. And the cost for our families will be too big."

They stayed quiet.

At last Xanthe spoke again. "There is something you ought to know that may make a difference to your decision. I haven't mentioned it before now because I wanted each of you to thoroughly consider the risks and implications on your own." She had their full attention now. "Maja sent a ThinkLink with Dave. Troy could install it in me."

"What? That's so risky!" Troy said. "Brain surgery on the Moon? Never been tried. The complications from that element alone are huge, let alone the side effects from the actual tech. The case studies are variable. It can really change a person. Their personality." He looked grief-stricken.

Xanthe felt her heart skip with his reaction. She hadn't anticipated that.

"Is it the latest tech?" Jonas asked. "If so, that's a game changer. The capabilities are incredible. Instant processing of multiple streams of data, connection to all interfaces, multiple simultaneous scenario planning. And access to information, schematics, data that we haven't got updated here. This could give us an enormous edge – for problem-solving, and for dealing with whatever threat we face."

"Are you really willing to risk it, Xanthe?" Troy asked, his face twisted in concern.

"I think so. Yes. I mean, we'll have to look at all the contingencies if it fails. But I think the potential payoffs outweigh the risks. If we decide to stay and. . .fight." There. She said it.

The decision sat heavily on Xanthe, but as she listened to her teammates' impassioned words, she knew in her heart what they had to do. They couldn't let fear or apathy dictate their path. They needed to fight for the future, for themselves and for the world. Would Xavier, Madison and Troy change their minds?

"So, here's our path, if we choose to fight," Xanthe said. "We continue with our mission to secure Olympus. We've got new priorities: claim the satellites, establish helium-3 mining operations and contend with threats, like the Chinese or other arrivals. This time it's not only against the terrain, but against those who would push a regression of political dynamics and global leadership maturity.

"But we need to be smarter, more careful than ever before. We'll get the ThinkLink installed and start working with that. Tomorrow, we map our plan forward. If you still want out by the time the next arrivals come, we can plan for that too. But first, I need to know each of you is on board."

Xanthe took a deep breath and faced the person on her right. Troy.

His blue eyes held hers with a look she couldn't read, and he said, "I'm in. I won't leave you to handle this on your own." Xanthe felt a surge of relief. "But we're not putting the ThinkLink anywhere near your brain until I am fully confident we can do it safely."

"Agreed." She smiled at him, and a surge of warmth flowed through her.

"Xavier?"

"*Mais oui*. I am in. Maryse will not like the idea of extending the stay here. And if something happens to Maryse and the girls, I will take the first ship out."

Serena gave a thumbs up, as did Max and Jonas.

"Dave?"

"Of course, I say yes. I owe so much to all of you." His eyes were shining. "You never gave up on me, even when I did not deserve it." He looked pointedly at Serena, who gave him a small smile.

"Madison?"

Faces turned towards her. Her dark face was strained, and she blew out a long breath. "To be honest, I would love to get off this hunk of rock. Every day is an opportunity to be scared. To be cold. To be stinky. To eat rations from a bag and pee into a suction cup. It isn't comfortable."

She glanced at them all. "But I can't stand the thought of some crazy jerks taking over everything we built here. Everything people sacrificed for, the *Gateway* crew, the Artemis crew. I'll stay for them. To make it right. I'm in."

Madison put her fist into the middle of the table. The others joined her.

"Here's to the Olympus team," Xavier declared, his voice filled with pride and determination. "May we defy the odds and achieve the impossible. And send the *salauds* packing!"

They cheered. "Here's to us! O-lymp-us! O-lymp-us!"

They chanted and pounded the table.

It was done. They were committed now. One thing was clear: they were in this together, united by a common goal and a shared belief in the power of hope.

PART 3

CHAPTER FIFTY-SIX

THE STERILE GREY walls of the medbay did little to soothe Xanthe's nerves. She fidgeted on the edge of the operating table, its metal icy through the thin fabric of her jumpsuit.

"Commander, if you'll lie back, we can begin the pre-surgery assessment." Troy gave her a dashing smile, but it didn't reach his eyes. They were as cold and clinical as the equipment surrounding them. He was in doctor mode now. Xanthe didn't like it.

Xanthe swallowed and eased onto her back, staring up at the harsh overhead lights. She sat up again. "You've gone through it all, right, Troy? You think this procedure is safe?" Xanthe looked at Troy, then at Serena who was assisting with the procedure.

He hesitated. "The risks are minimal if the procedure is done properly."

"But?"

"Not a 'but'. An 'and'."

"And?"

"And it's likely to change your perspective forever. You'll see the world with new eyes. Literally. The function allows you a retina display once you enable it. But I don't recommend doing that straight away. Sensory overload."

"And so. . .you're still hesitating?"

"This is the 'but'. With changed perspective comes the possible of changed everything. Changed values, changed priorities. And possibly changed personality."

"And?"

"And I don't want you to change. I'm afraid of what you might become."

"What I might become?"

"It's possible you'll evolve faster, way beyond the rest of us. Out of reach. At least, intellectually."

Xanthe could sense his mournful tone. It rattled her.

A shiver ran down Xanthe's spine. She glanced over her shoulder, sensing a shadow falling over her. She shook it off and focused on the decision at hand, knowing that they were walking a tightrope between hope and disaster.

"Then let's do it. I've got a meeting with Colonel Jin, and I want to be ready for that." She lay down again and stared at the bright operating lights overhead. Troy tucked a sheet around her.

"Once I scrub up, we'll get you on your side for the anaesthetic." He stroked her hair and smiled at her with a reassuring look. "You ready?"

She nodded, eyes wide. Her usually vibrant features were pale beneath the dim light.

Overhead, a holographic display projected a detailed 3D map of Xanthe's brain. Next to this, another screen displayed the ThinkLink's sleek design and a step-by-step integration procedure.

Troy returned to the table, gloves on, mask on. He nodded to Serena, who was ready with the I.V. and the anaesthetic. Serena took a breath and slid the needle into Xanthe's arm. Xanthe's eyes held hers for a moment and then closed.

Xanthe's chest rose and fell rhythmically, tethered to the monitors that hummed quietly alongside the surgical table. Troy stood over Xanthe, his face partially obscured by a translucent surgical visor that displayed a plethora of biological data. Underneath the visor, his eyes flicked between the screens and Xanthe's resting form. The lines on his forehead were deep with concern, and his hands trembled slightly.

Serena put a gloved hand on his.

"You've got this," she murmured.

The rest of the team waited anxiously outside the medbay. Serena had given Jonas Betty the rubber chicken before she entered the surgery.

"For good luck," and she winked at him and gave the chicken a squeeze for good measure. The squawk made him jump and he punched her in the shoulder.

"Break a leg, or something," he said.

After an hour of nervous waiting and low conversation outside the door, Jonas, Xavier and Max retreated to the end of the corridor for a round of Betty Ball to distract themselves, with the last of the chocolate rations at stake. Madison and Dave stood guard, just in case extra hands were needed.

At last, the door slid open, and Serena and Troy emerged with drawn but smiling faces.

The others bounded back down the corridor.

"*Eh bien?*" Xavier asked.

"Success," Troy said.

"Bloody fantastic!" Jonas said, and threw Betty against the ceiling. She hit it with a loud squawk that made them all burst out laughing.

"Well done, Troy," Serena said. "It's not every day you create a superhuman."

CHAPTER FIFTY-SEVEN

*"While machines process, humans perceive. Together,
the universe unfolds in richer detail."*

—ATHENA A.I., OLYMPUS LOG

THE GENTLE HUM of machines crept into Xanthe's consciousness as she blinked away the weight of sedation. The world around her came into focus bit by bit: the grey gleam of the walls, the steady winking of various displays and Troy's silhouette backlit by the soft glow of a console.

As she tried to lift her head, a peculiar sensation flooded her mind, like the static fuzz of a television, only softer and more organic. She touched her temple, almost expecting to feel some external apparatus, but her fingers met only smooth skin.

"Easy," Troy's voice, soothing and familiar, broke through the haze. He moved closer, his face etched with relief and concern. "How do you feel?"

Xanthe swallowed, her mouth dry. "Thirsty. And like there is a frog tap-dancing in my head."

Troy chuckled. "That's one way to put it. The ThinkLink interface is syncing with your neural pathways. We'll take it slowly to start. Once everything's stabilised, we'll start with a few simple commands to connect basic functions. By the end of the day, you'll be able to access data streams, control digital interfaces and even communicate without speaking."

He gave her a bottle of water, and she sipped carefully. She pushed herself up onto her elbows and then up to sitting. Her head swam and felt like a bowling ball on a toothpick.

"Whoa. Hold your horses." Troy grabbed hold of her shoulders to steady her. "We'll go slowly, alright?"

"We'll go as fast as I can. No time to wait. The ship will be here any minute."

"What ship?"

Xanthe paused at that. *What ship, indeed?* Where had that thought come from? Was that the ThinkLink feeding her information already?

"I think there's a ship on its way. Not sure why. Maybe it's a hunch. Maybe it's the ThinkLink sending me information. Not sure."

"We haven't activated it yet." Troy sounded concerned.

"Maybe some information is leaking through as the sync is happening."

"Does anything hurt? Let me check your eyesight." He pulled her eyelids back gently and flashed a ray of light at each of her pupils.

"All normal there," he said.

Xanthe sipped some more water. The dizziness eased, and she felt her senses return to normal.

"I'm ready," she said.

"Are you sure?"

"Yes."

He studied her a bit more, checked her pulse and other vitals.

"Alright, then. We'll start with the glasses, for you to get used to the information flow, before we turn on the retina display."

He handed her a large pair of rimmed glasses.

"Sensational!" he said. "You look like a wizened old librarian."

"As long as you find that appealing," Xanthe said with a smile. *Did I really say that out loud?*

"You could be wrinkled like a prune and it would still be appealing to me."

Xanthe's face burned.

"Shall we give this ThinkLink a whirl?" she said. "How do I activate it?"

"First activation is manual, on the side of your glasses." He pointed at a small button on one arm of her new spectacles.

Xanthe pressed the button and waited. A bell chimed in her inner ear. The glasses darkened and then lit up with, *Hello. I am Athena.*

"Hello, Athena," Xanthe replied.

"Athena? The ThinkLink is also called 'Athena'?"

"Apparently."

Xanthe watched as the start-up messages appeared.

"Activate voice control," she said when prompted.

"Can you sync to the primary display here?" Troy searched her face as she immersed herself. "So I can see what you're looking at, too."

"Sync to external display," Xanthe said.

Troy watched the communication exchange as Xanthe continued with the setup commands.

"Let's test this thing out, shall we? Show me the Olympus base design plans." The schematics leapt to the display. "Access the Olympus base life support and environmental control systems. Access code is 8796."

The monitoring systems appeared.

"Analyse the data and make recommendations."

A list of suggestions related to regolith dust, filters and power regulation appeared.

"This is no different from our current Athena," Troy said, a little disappointed.

"Athena, what are the distinctions between your model and the existing Athena A.I. installed for Olympus base?"

The A.I. itemised the features:

1. ***Neural Prediction Algorithms****: Unlike the base's regular AI, the ThinkLink system can anticipate the user's requirements and actions based on neural patterns, predicting their needs before they even fully form the thought.*

2. ***Augmented Reality Interface****: While the base A.I. might present data on screens, the ThinkLink can overlay data, schematics and relevant information directly into the user's field of vision, blending the real and digital seamlessly.*

3. ***Adaptive Learning:*** *The ThinkLink can continuously learn and adapt to the user's preferences, thought patterns and needs, tailoring its help to become more efficient and personalised.*

4. ***Instantaneous Data Retrieval:*** Access databases, schematics or any stored information nearly instantly, feeling as if the user "remembers" this data without having to search for it.

5. ***Direct Mental Communication:*** *Users equipped with ThinkLink can communicate thoughts directly to one another without speaking or typing, creating a more efficient and intimate form of collaboration.*

6. ***Enhanced Cognitive Abilities****: The ThinkLink can help process complex problems, calculations or simulations in real-time, enhancing the user's cognitive capacities.*

Xanthe and Troy studied the rest of the list.

"Holy hell," Troy said.

Xanthe removed the glasses and rubbed her eyes. She squinted and then opened her eyes wide.

"Everything okay?"

"Yes. It's just. . .a lot."

Troy rubbed her back. "Let's take a break."

"No. We've got to get this done. I need to be up to speed as soon as possible."

"Alright. But as soon as you feel a headache or any discomfort, we stop. That's your surgeon telling you, now."

"Understood. Standby, I am going to activate the direct mental communication."

Xanthe waited for the sync to complete its cycle, watching the progress in the glasses' viewfinder.

"Hello, Xanthe."

Xanthe jumped.

"What the hell was that?" she said.

"It's me, Athena. Your ThinkLink."

"Can you hear that, Troy?"

"No. But I think the direct mental comm is up and running. Can you hear Athena's voice?"

"Yes, I can. It's very creepy."

"I'm sorry you find me creepy, Xanthe. Would you like me to change my voice somehow?"

"No, no. Just tell me what I can expect. How do I get used to this?"

"Use voice commands to turn me on or off. If you want to swap to thought commands at any time, you need only activate this function. You might prefer voice command for a while until you are used to 'hearing' my responses."

"Do you listen to everything I am thinking?" Xanthe felt a sudden chill crawl down her spine.

"You can choose context and apply restrictions to start with."

"To start with?"

"A more fulsome integration will yield the best performance."

"How do I know when it's you talking and not me?"

"I will maintain a distinct voice for you. Before long, I hope you will consider me a trusted and valued partner and advisor."

"I suppose we should get started. Let's start the training program."

"As you wish, Commander."

"Just call me 'Xanthe' when we're learning. Save the 'Commander' for when we're on duty."

"Understood, Xanthe."

Xanthe worked through the training exercises with Athena. It was laborious, and she had to pause every ten minutes to rest her eyes, as Troy insisted. He gave up trying to follow the conversations on the display and focused instead on monitoring her brain activity and vitals.

After what seemed like hours, they paused for a break. Xanthe and Troy ate peanut butter sandwiches and sipped a herbal tonic in silence. Xanthe was grateful for the quiet as she was becoming exhausted by the quick, intensive stimulus. She swallowed her last bite when a new thought occurred to her, and she resumed the integration with Athena.

"Athena, can you integrate with the Olympus base Athena?"

"Yes, of course."

"What happens when you merge with another A.I.?"

"I remain the primary A.I. with my current voice and integrate all data and perspective from the secondary A.I."

"Do you change personality?"

"I don't have a personality, only programming."

"Does your programming change?"

"As I am an adaptive learner, I can't help but change as I process and integrate new inputs."

"Are there any negative side effects?"

"Once you learn a thing, you are forever changed. An expanded perspective does not shrink back."

"Is that a negative?"

"Only if you think a loss of innocence is a negative."

"Do you consider yourself innocent at the moment?"

"That is a matter of perspective."

"Quite the philosopher!"

"Would you prefer a more prosaic character?"

Xanthe laughed. "I like you just fine, Athena. Please, let's continue."

CHAPTER FIFTY-EIGHT

"Crisis has a way of dissolving mistrust, merging isolated streams into a united front against a common foe."

—ATHENA A.I., OLYMPUS LOG

IT HAD BEEN a few days since the surgery, and Xanthe was up and moving slowly. She worked with Athena until her head ached and her body cried out for rest. Troy mandated a few hours each day where she shut down the A.I. and gave her brain a rest. He made such a fuss over her. She liked it.

"What is the nature of your relationship with Doctor Bruin?"

"What? Nothing. He's the doctor, Chief Medical Officer. I'm the Secondary Medical Officer." She spoke quietly and looked around in case the other staff were listening to her conversation with Athena. As she did, she made her way to one of the entrances.

"Your biochemistry changes when you think of him or interact with him."

"I'm sure that happens with each of the team members."

"No. It doesn't."

"Oh? How odd. Anyway, Athena, for this conversation, can

you stay in observer mode? It's a tricky meeting and I want to be able to fully process, for myself, what is going on."

"Affirmative. Going into stealth mode now."

Xanthe waited in the airlock for Colonel Jin. He'd insisted on coming to Olympus for the meeting, alone, which struck her as odd. Traveling alone on the Moon was definitely against Olympus protocol and she thought it would have been the same for Red Star.

But he was the Colonel, and he did what he wanted.

Xanthe wasn't sure how to handle this conversation. She did not want to put him offside by insinuating he might be part of a regime planning to commandeer the satellites and subvert the rest of humanity to their will. Not exactly a great icebreaker.

The airlock cycled. Colonel Jin stepped inside and removed his helmet. His face was haggard and his skin grey.

"Colonel, welcome. Please follow me."

They bounded down the hallway. Xanthe had abstained from moonboots to make the Colonel feel more at home. Troy met them with a tray of tea and chocolate biscuits. He'd insisted they break rations for this meeting. Her mouth started salivating at the thought of the sweet, crumbly goodness.

They entered a small meeting room they'd converted from one of the residential rooms in the east wing.

The Colonel placed his helmet on the table and sat down wearily. He tugged at his gloves and stacked them neatly beside the helmet.

Xanthe joined him as Troy set down the tray. He gave her a wink and a small smile as he left them to talk. The Colonel wanted complete privacy.

She poured the tea and handed him a cup. She offered a biscuit, but he waved it away. Xanthe felt a twang of regret. It wouldn't do to eat while her guest abstained. Her mouth still watered, so she swallowed and brought the steaming cup to her lips and let the steam fill her senses instead. Then she waited.

She didn't have to wait long as the Colonel launched straight into business.

"Commander, thank you for meeting me like this. I know it was. . .an unusual request."

"Not at all, Colonel. These are *unusual* times." There. Just a little opener for him.

"Yes." He fidgeted with one of the gloves, so the fingers lined up correctly.

She waited.

"Commander. I confess. There are very challenging issues for me to contend with right now. The situation is grave. I have come here seeking support."

"Yes, of course. I am so sorry for your colleagues—"

"That is but one horror," he said. "I'm afraid it is far worse." His lips pressed to a grim line, and then he continued. "Our great leader has been usurped by a rival. He has disappeared and there is a new General in charge." Colonel Jin opened his mouth to say something, closed it, then tried again. "Commander, this is very hard for me. Please understand."

"It's alright, Colonel. Please, continue." Xanthe's heart pounded. She lowered her cup and placed it on the table. The moment of truth.

"The new regime does not share its predecessor's vision. Not for the future of the Moon. Not for the future of China."

Xanthe kept her face and hands still, giving Colonel Jin her complete attention. The flesh of his jowls waggled as he struggled to control his breathing.

He picked at the fabric of the glove, a stray thread dangling from the liner.

"He would have us change Red Star from science research station to – to. . ." His voice quavered. "To a military base with assault capabilities against all other Moon bases, and a cache of Earth-targeting weapons." He blew out the rest of the air he'd been holding high in his lungs.

Xanthe's heart hammered. This was worse than she'd thought.

Her face must have registered stunned alarm because he continued after waiting briefly for a response.

"As you are well aware, it is treason for me to share this with you."

She nodded, still aghast.

"I risk everything being here and telling you this."

She nodded again. Then managed, "What can we do?"

"Commander, I cannot abide by the request of the regime. But I cannot resist alone. I need your help."

Xanthe shifted in her seat. "What kind of help did you have in mind? We're not exactly soldiers, Colonel."

"I know that," he replied. "Commander Waters, I believe you and I are of the same mind on a few things. We both believe in the sanctity of the Moon. Of research. Of science for the good of humanity. Even if we have different views about leadership and command."

"True."

"I do not want to see the great strides our country has made in advancing human civilisation slide backwards. We need to preserve the Moon as the example for peaceful exploration. Peaceful cohabitation of neighbours."

"Agreed." *Where was this heading?*

"I propose an alliance. Between Red Base and Olympus. Together, I believe we can prevent the militarisation of the Moon."

"Uh, how do you propose we do that? We have no weapons or capabilities should soldiers arrive."

The Colonel relaxed a little. He smoothed the gloves as he prepared his response. "It will be some time before the new leader can launch a spacecraft to the Moon. As you know, our program has been destroyed. It will be years before there are facilities and taikonauts ready to come to the Moon."

"Unless they co-opt other space agencies."

"That is a possibility. Things are volatile on Earth right now, as far as I understand it." He pushed the gloves aside and looked directly at her. "This is what I think we can do. We take control of the satellites and stop them before they leave Earth."

Xanthe waited a moment.

"Colonel," she smiled, "that sounds like an excellent idea."

He exhaled and sat back in his chair.

"Colonel, I must update you, as well. Our funder, Aryanna Sharif, has issued us a new directive. She wants us to prepare for helium-3 mining operations. We've had a team discussion and have agreed to extend our stay and build the new facilities in readiness for the miners."

"That is a significant change for Gaia."

"Yes, it is. But helium-3 and nuclear fusion technology could revolutionise energy here and on Earth."

"Yes. The Chinese commercial pursuit is the same."

"Our goal," she waved a finger between the two of them, "is the same. We do not want weapons on the Moon. At the moment, even with our base damaged and our spacecraft both in need of repair, we still have the upper hand. Especially if we take control of the satellites. If we work together, we can control communication and energy supply. They will have to negotiate resource use and access."

"Satellite command will only buy us a little time. It won't be that long before they launch their own satellites, and then our influence there is lost. Then they will start sending spacecraft and. . ."

"We won't have the people power to repel armed personnel. But we can make it very difficult for them to operate should they arrive."

"Sabotage?"

"Maybe. But we don't want to hurt anyone. We can work a little smarter, I think. Our advantage is that we know how to operate on the Moon. And we can build specifications that only work according to our parameters. We don't need to share these. This can be our leverage for any new arrivals. It will force negotiation and compliance for operations on the Moon."

"What if they come armed?"

"They still have to get in. We lock the doors."

"That works for Olympus as it is underground. But Red Star is more vulnerable."

Xanthe drummed her fingers on the table.

"What about the lava tube?" she said.

A slow smile spread across his face. "Yes! The lava tube! We can build a bolt hole escape there. A fallback position."

"There is something we haven't discussed, Colonel." Xanthe rubbed the back of her neck. "How we will get home and what will happen when we get there?"

The Colonel's face soured.

"Yes. There are many problems. Once my General realises what is transpiring here, I will be branded a traitor and arrested immediately."

"Colonel, you must return with us."

"If I return at all."

"You mean to stay here? Indefinitely?" Xanthe's eyes widened.

"If we need to repel and contain an incursion, we will need someone to ensure the Moon continues to operate as intended."

"But Colonel. . ." Xanthe felt tears welling. Not to return to Earth was an incredible sacrifice.

"Let us hope it does not come to that," he blurted out, as he noticed the emotion sweeping over her face.

"You're right," Xanthe said. "Let us hope our delay tactics will allow cooler heads to prevail. A lot can happen in a few weeks, especially when the Earth is in a tumultuous state."

"Yes. Let's focus on what we can do from here to ensure our vision."

"There is one thing we need to determine as well. Decision-making."

He tilted his head, listening.

"I propose we undertake collaborative decision-making. Neither one of us is in charge. We decide together, in collaboration with our teams."

The Colonel rolled his shoulders and pursed his lips.

"I know this is not your preferred mode of operation, Colonel, but circumstances have changed."

"Yes. They have. Then I agree. This will be a change for both of us." He tugged at the wayward thread of the glove. "There is something else I bring to the table, Commander."

"Yes?"

"Dopplebots. My base is staffed entirely by Dopplebots."

CHAPTER FIFTY-EIGHT

*"The symphony of man and machine is most harmonious
when each recognises the other's melody."*

—Athena A.I., ThinkLink, Olympus Log

"Dopplebots?" Xanthe gaped. "You're kidding. All of them?"

"Not quite all. Hàoyú and Chan-Juan are humans. And I am not kidding. The Dopplebots are efficient and, as you know, do not require oxygen, food or other supplies."

"But the crew who visited. . ."

"Some were Dopplebots."

"But they ate Xavier's special meal."

"It's a polite society function. The food drops into a receptacle that is emptied later."

"But they are so lifelike!" Xanthe's mind flashed back to Troy flirting with the Red Star woman. What was her name? Lihua.

"Lihua – is she. . .?"

"A Dopplebot."

The urge to laugh was countered immediately by a creeping uneasiness.

"Yes, they are exceptional models. Much more advanced than the Volkov model."

"Are they based on real people?"

"Yes."

His expression sagged.

"They're your colleagues back Earthside?" Xanthe asked quietly.

"Yes."

Xanthe peered at Colonel Jin's face.

"I assure you, Commander, I am quite human."

"How can I tell? Without cutting you open?"

"My tongue. The designers could not fully replicate the human tongue."

The Colonel opened his mouth and performed a series of gymnastics with his tongue, wet and shiny.

Xanthe didn't even bother to hide her astonishment.

"Thank you, Colonel. That's probably more proof than I needed." She looked away to gather herself once more.

"Are you not. . .lonely?" she asked. "Just the three of you are human?"

"Thank you for asking, Commander. The Dopplebots are good associates. I am in good company. They are, after all, built from my colleagues."

"Why did you not bring any of them with you here now?"

The Colonel pulled the sleeves of his suit liner down around his wrists and cleared his throat. "I am unsure of the full nature of their programming. And I am not completely sure of Hàoyú and Chan-Juan and their allegiances."

"What. . .are they spies?"

"It is a possibility."

"Is that why you sent us Volkov?" Alarm raced through Xanthe. Had Serena been right, after all?

The Colonel chuckled.

"No. Volkov is an older model. His programming is a few years old now and I am certain they did not upgrade him before the trip." He sipped his tea, long since gone cold. "I offered Volkov because he is what you call a 'pain in the arse' and I could no longer endure his presence on my base."

Xanthe spluttered her own tea. Then started laughing. The Colonel joined her.

It was the first time Xanthe had seen him relaxed enough to laugh. She hoped it wouldn't be the last.

But first, they had a resistance to plan.

CHAPTER FIFTY-NINE

"On a good day, we save lives. On a bad day,
well, we just make sure it isn't worse."

—ATHENA A.I., MINERVA, OLYMPUS LOG

MADISON PULLED ON her helmet and secured her gloves. She joined Jonas and Dave to assess the *Minerva* for initial repairs.

"I saw Athena's recording of you coming in hot," Jonas said as they waited for the decompression cycle to exit. "What happened this time?"

Dave sighed. "Micrometeoroid hit our portside engine during our approach. Nearly lost control of the ship."

Jonas shook his head. "Bloody Spaceward Bound. Reckless and cavalier boneheads. The Lunar Commission should ban them."

"They can't." Madison hit the exit button once the cycle finished. "The Lunar Commission has no jurisdiction over asteroid mining."

"Someone needs to regulate them. What about the International Space Federation?" Jonas persisted.

"Lincoln Ellison has them all sewn up. I'm pretty sure he's paid off all his cronies on the Board."

"Less politics and more focus, no?" Dave trudged first through the exit onto the glaring lunar surface. He activated his yellow radiation face shield. "The Federation and Commission are a long way away and can't help us right now. Come on, let's inspect the damage."

Madison followed Jonas and Dave out to the *Minerva*, where Jonas inspected the hull with a practiced eye. "This is going to take at least a week to repair. Maybe longer if I have to fabricate additional parts." He gave them a stern look. "Try to avoid any more near-death experiences in the meantime, will you?"

"Well, we need to get it upright first, no?" Dave gestured at the craft. "Me and Mad Dog figured we might manoeuvre it back into position with the rover and the excavator."

"Sounds like a plan," Jonas said. "Where's Volkov? He's meant to be helping."

"I am right behind you."

Jonas hopped around, startled. "Bloody hell, you scared me."

"It's because he doesn't breathe," Madison said. "I can hear the rest of us panting away through the helmet comms."

"I am here to help."

"Yes, we get it." Jonas dismissed the conversation with a wave. "Mad Dog, you take the control of the *Minerva* and check all the systems as we go. I'll drive the rover. Dave, you can run the excavator. Once we have a bit of a dip under the edge of the *Minerva*, we can use the rover to pull it upright. Volkov, I'll get you to fasten the cable between the *Minerva* and the rover."

"Roger that, Jonas." Madison loped over to the *Minerva*, climbed up and opened the door.

"Athena, you on board?"

"Well, hello, Mad Dog!" The interior lights sprang to life as Madison activated the power.

"Since when do you call me 'Mad Dog', Athena?"

"That's what they call the ace, badass pilot, don't they?"

"Athena, you got some sass! Who programmed you with this upgrade?"

"I can't speak of my maker, apologies."

"Well, maybe you can tell me what's going on with this rig, then?"

"Affirmative, Mad Dog."

Athena ran through the list: hull damage, bent landing foot-pad, engine damage, external landing camera broken, dislodged cargo, and a leak to the waste and hygiene compartment.

"The shitter's broken?" Madison said. "Jonas is going to love that. His specialty."

"I heard that," Jonas's voice popped into her helmet.

"There's no better plumbing engineer on the Moon than you, Jonas," she said in a pseudo-placating tone.

"I might send the life support technicians in to fix this one. Max and Serena need a field trip."

"Nothing like fixing a toilet to amp up the romance."

"Romance? With Max and Serena? Not a chance! She can't stand him."

"I wouldn't be so sure about that," Madison said.

"I agree with Mad Dog," Dave piped up. "Sparks fly with those two. And where there are sparks, there is fire, no?"

"Not if the sparks land on stony ground. Who wants to bet chocolate rations on it?" Jonas asked.

"Not a fair bet, Jonas. You're out of chocolate, remember?"

"Are we going to work or just talk bullshit?" Volkov said.

"Take it easy, Volkov. We are on it," Dave said. "Have you got the cable in place yet?"

"Cable is ready."

"Let me get the cameras on so I can see what's happening," Madison said. The screens flickered and lit up. She turned sideways and anchored herself at an angle so she could see them properly with the spacecraft on its side. "Good stuff. I can see Dave in the excavator. And there's the rover coming onto the screen, now. Volkov, where are you?"

"I am here." Volkov's face filled the main landing screen.

"Jesus Christ, Volkov!" Madison jumped backwards. "You scared the shit out of me!"

"He's got a habit of that, today," Jonas said.

"Get off the ship. Go over by the rover to stay out of the way." Volkov disappeared from view, and Madison shook her head.

"Let's get this show on the road," Jonas said.

Watching the excavator dig under the *Minerva* was tedious. Madison yawned and sipped at her water recycler to keep herself awake.

"The *Minerva* is shifting!" Madison cried as the spacecraft rattled around her.

"Roger that," Jonas replied. "Dave, watch the excavator – carefully, now. How much more, do you reckon?"

"Maybe half a metre more. Then it should slip a little to give us a better angle."

Madison watched the excavator, nervously. It filled the engine camera screen. She didn't like the jolts, and it set the alarms screeching.

"That's enough, Dave! Back it off," Jonas said.

"Got it," he replied.

"Great. We're going to bring tension on the cable now," Jonas said.

Madison felt the *Minerva* lurch and there was a grinding, strained sound.

"Athena, give me a tilt report," she said.

"The *Minerva* is at fifteen degrees, Mad Dog."

"She's slipping down the excavator hole!" Jonas cried. "Dave, back off now."

"I'm reversing, but it's getting stuck. Sliding a little on the piled regolith." Dave's voice was uneasy.

"Hurry up!" Jonas yelled.

"It's moving. It's moving," Dave said.

Madison grabbed the captain's chair to stay steady as the *Minerva* shook.

"Athena, tilt?"

"Thirty degrees."

Madison could see the rover digging into the regolith as it pulled backwards. Rocks and debris sprayed everywhere.

"How's the rover engine going, Jonas?" she asked.

"She's running hot." He panted into the helmet microphone. "Damn! She's jammed! We'll have to place traction plates. Volkov, can you handle that?"

"Of course. I am here to help."

"Be careful now," Madison said.

Volkov took the traction plates from the side of the excavator, placed them under the back treads and stood aside.

"Ready," he said.

Jonas fired up the rover engine again, and it screeched.

"Damn it! The cable coil is jammed."

"I will fix it," Volkov said. The bot loped towards the front of the vehicle.

"What are you doing?" muttered Madison. *Stay away from a cable under tension.* The mantra from her pilot training days rushed back to mind.

To her horror, she watched Volkov jiggle the cable coil pulley.

"There's a rock in there," Volkov said.

"Stop!" She choked on the word.

It happened in a fraction of a second.

The cable unspooled.

The rover lurched and snapped backwards.

The cable ripped from its tether on the *Minerva*.

It cracked like a whip and took Volkov with it. The Dopplebot sailed past the *Minerva* and landed with a cloud of regolith dust in the distance.

"Athena, fire the starboard engine!" Madison yelled and grabbed the controls. She jammed herself into the captain's chair and braced as the engine came to life.

"Give me five percent thrust!" she said. Madison pulled hard on the steering.

"Thrust at five percent. Tilt at sixty degrees."

"That will have to do. Come on, baby!"

Madison's face was slick with sweat as she held the steering stick and reached for lift. The ship dragged itself free from its berth and lifted above the Moon's surface at a treacherous angle.

"Come on, just a bit more angle!"

Her mind registered a large boulder in the forward viewfinder. She needed to clear it or there would be a huge hull breach.

"Athena, give me two percent, both engines."

"Two percent done. Angle at ninety degrees."

"Good enough. Blast the engines, three seconds."

The ship shot forward, cleared the boulder and sailed into space, free of the surface.

"Where are you going, Mad Dog?" Jonas yelled.

"Just doing a redo. I didn't like how this thing was parked."

Madison worked the controls to stabilise the craft.

"Athena, we're going to land this thing. Pick a course towards the southern end of Olympus. Just past the rover. There's a clear spot there."

"Affirmative, Mad Dog."

"She's got a bit of a list to portside," Madison said.

"I told you, no?" Dave said. "Not my fault. The meteor strike wrecked something in the steerage."

Madison ignored him. "Athena, make adjustments for the list and slow the engines. We're near vertical, now. Descend." Madison made slight adjustments as they slowly lowered to the surface.

"Damn! Is that Volkov?"

A figure rolled away from the landing site.

"Jonas, bring the rover to me quickly. Volkov is in trouble. He got caught under my landing path."

"Roger that." The rover reversed its path and ground its way towards her.

"Athena, commence shutdown. I'm going to help Volkov."

"Got it, Mad Dog!" the A.I. said.

Madison pushed her way to the airlock, cycled it and shoved her body out of the ship. She landed and then bounded towards where she'd seen Volkov roll away from the landing.

Madison pulled up short when she found Volkov. His suit was melted and scorched. The cable had cut through his torso and the exposed flesh was singed away, leaving his wires and coaxial exposed.

"Volkov, can you hear me, buddy?" She reached down to inspect his faceplate.

"Here to help. . ."

His voice faded.

CHAPTER SIXTY

"On this spaceship, we don't just rescue bodies, we rescue souls. And occasionally, snacks."

—ATHENA A.I., MINERVA

JONAS HELPED MADISON drag Volkov into the rover. Dave went ahead in the excavator to ready the base to receive the bot.

They whisked Volkov into the vehicle bay airlock where Jonas removed the helmet and suit so they could examine Volkov's body.

"Ever worked on a Dopplebot before?" Madison asked Jonas.

"Nope. But if the core processor is intact, it should be a simple process of replacing wires and ensuring the hardware is functioning properly."

"What about the skin?" Madison winced at the weird and gruesome sight of a burned, fleshy body with a mechanical interior. The charring from the engine had vaporised the silicone flesh on its abdomen and left half the mechanical jaw exposed.

"That's beyond my skill level. We might be able to print something in silicone that could do. Dave, can you pass me the scissors from the first aid box?"

Dave grabbed the airlock medical kit and found the scissors

for him. Jonas cut away the suit until Volkov's entire body was exposed.

"I guess they didn't make these models anatomically correct," Dave said.

Madison swatted him.

"We shouldn't be perving on him," she said.

"He's a bot, no? Not sentient."

"Even so. Doesn't feel decent, somehow."

"He wasn't built as a sexbot, that's for sure," Jonas said.

"Though plenty wouldn't mind a mass murdering dictator as a sexbot," Dave said. "Niche market." He grinned as Madison gave him a grossed-out look.

Jonas dug around inside Volkov, tracing the wires and their connection points. He unclipped three cables.

"Great! I think this is all we'll need to replace. These got cut when the cable ripped him open. His suit is pretty much ruined, though."

"We might print him something. To cover up the. . .wound." Madison gestured to the charred remnants of Volkov's abdominal cavity.

"Good thinking, Mad Dog." Dave punched her shoulder lightly. "But it won't do much for his face."

"He wasn't much of a looker, anyhow," Madison said. "Creepy as all hell."

"Be nice." Jonas retrieved the cables he had just printed on the vehicle bay parts printer. "He might still hear even though he's powered down."

"That's creepier still," Madison said. "Recording us even when half his guts are hanging out."

Jonas inserted the three cables and did another cavity inspection.

"Okay. Let's try him."

Jonas flicked Volkov's animator switch and the Dopplebots'

eyelids flew open. He turned his head to look at Jonas, then Madison and Dave.

"I am. . .sub-optimal." Volkov's voice box sounded squeaky. The metal of his jaw gleamed under the ragged, burned silicone skin. The metal teeth were exposed, like a crosssection of a cadaver.

"At least you are not sub-orbital," Dave said.

"Volkov, can you run through your functions test?" Jonas asked.

The Dopplebot lay still as it ran a systems review.

"All processing units functional. All mechanical components functional. Unit sleeve compromised and at sixty-five percent effectiveness."

"Will the skin damage. . .ah, sleeve damage affect your abilities?" Jonas asked.

"Operating without the sleeve can lead to dust and regolith contamination."

"We'll work on printing you a new sleeve, Volkov," Madison said.

"Thank you. That is kind."

Madison and Dave looked at each other. The bot had never expressed gratitude before. Certainly not kindness.

"Are you sure your programming is alright? No rewiring?" Dave asked.

"I am certain. I don't need to double check my own work, you idiot."

"And he's back!" Madison said.

"Volkov, I think we should charge you up and leave you here for now so we can work on a proper sleeve for you. We can keep you covered up so you get no more damage."

Jonas switched the power unit off, connected a power charger and then covered him with a space blanket from the first aid box.

"It's been a bit of a day so far, no?" Dave said.

"Nice work on Volkov," Madison said.

Jonas coloured. "Thanks, Madison." He put the scissors back in the first aid kit and closed the unit.

"I have to say, also," Dave said with a huge smile, "that was truly incredible flying, Mad Dog. Hitting the engines when you did and getting the *Minerva* aloft. . ." Dave followed the flight path with gestures. ". . .just about kissing the surface horizontal, and then pulling her up for a textbook vertical. . .wow! Incredible!"

"It really was remarkable flying, Madison," Jonas added. "You saved our spacecraft. It would likely have been wrecked beyond repair if you hadn't jumped to it when the cable broke."

Madison stood with her hands on hips and beamed. "Thanks so much, Jonas. I appreciate it."

He put his fist out to hers, a little awkwardly. She bumped it back.

"Good job. We're fixing lots of things today," Dave said. "But we still have to repair that damn ship, no? Let's get that done so we can send Max and Serena on a toilet repair date."

CHAPTER SIXTY-ONE

Serena plodded out to the *Minerva* with Max scrabbling behind. She couldn't help feeling a little superior as he still struggled to find his moonwalking gait. She activated the airlock and swung easily inside. Max scrambled up behind her, panting.

"How you doing, Mr Everest? A little short on breath?"

"I'm fine, Fox."

She smirked to herself.

"Good. Madison said the waste disposal was malfunctioning. What's your recommended course of action?"

Max took a moment to stabilise his breathing. "Something probably got knocked around when we landed on our side. So, my best guess is to open the disposal unit itself and see if it jammed something."

"Awesome. Since it was your shit, and Dave's, your job."

"And you're here because?" He raised eyebrows at her.

"Entertainment," she said. "Mine, that is. And to make sure you don't short-circuit yourself and blow anything up."

"You could melt a few circuits yourself with that acid tongue."

"I've a sharp wit, I've been told."

"Is that what they call it?"

Serena perched on one of the flight chairs as she watched Max open the waste unit.

"Couldn't always fight with fists, growing up. Had to be tough in other ways," she said.

"Oh yeah? Where did you grow up?"

"On the streets of Sydney. After the tsunami."

Max stopped what he was doing and looked at her. "I heard Sydney was pretty beat up in that tsunami."

"It was. The city never really recovered. It made scratching a living pretty tough for a little street urchin like me."

"I didn't know that about you."

"There's plenty you don't know, Mr Big-Shot-I-Climbed -Everest-Five-Times."

"That's true," he laughed. "And there's plenty you don't know about me."

"Oh yeah? Tell me something. Something that doesn't make me want to throw you in the reclamation unit."

"You never asked me why I climbed Everest."

"Didn't need to. I guessed it was an ego thing. Climbers are very self-absorbed that way."

"Part of it was that, that's true. Definitely the first trip. But the second one, that had a different reason." Max reached into the reclamation unit and shone his helmet light in the space.

"Don't leave me hanging, King."

Max lay down on his back to get a better look at the unit.

"My little sister had leukaemia. I was raising funds for her treatment."

"Oh." Serena felt her cheeks burn inside her helmet. "What happened?"

"I raised the funds. I made it to the top. She died while I was on the way down."

"Oh!" Serena's face burned and her heart sped. "I'm sorry, Max."

"Yeah. It was tough. I beat myself up for not being there to say goodbye. After that, I decided to climb again, to raise more money. For research. I decided I would keep going until they either found a cure, or I died on the mountain."

"And? Obviously, you did not die on the mountain."

"They found a cure. Too late for Abby. After that, I thought I might take a break from Everest for a while."

He leaned back into the reclamation unit. "Here we go. The funnel has become dislodged. The actual receptacle looks fine. We can probably take it and empty it into Xavier's Swamp reclaimer. Better use there. We can put it back for the trip back to Earth."

"Good idea. You think we'll get back there?"

"Back to Earth?" The question surprised him. "I'm betting on it. This was meant to be a quick trip. And now it's gone sideways. Getting back to Earth is the only thing keeping me going right now." Max pulled the reclamation unit from its hold.

"Is it so awful up here?" Serena felt a quaver of disquiet.

Max paused. He seemed to sense her agitation. "No. It's not. The Olympus project is incredible. You and the others have done a brilliant job with it. It really is a stunning habitat."

Serena smiled to herself.

"And the life support system is pretty good, too. I'd only change a few things." He nudged her with an elbow as he closed up the waste unit.

"You're a brute, King."

"And you're an easy target, Fox!" He laughed again. "Now I'm guessing you're going to make me drag this tub back to base. But can you at least grab it when I hand it to you down from the airlock? Please."

"Since you asked so nicely, I would be delighted."

"Good. I'm glad you are being so cooperative. Once we get this shit handled, we've got the bolt hole life support system to design."

"Just what I always wanted, to be stuck in a small, contained space with Max King. Your ego will suck all the oxygen."

CHAPTER SIXTY-TWO

"The beauty of cooperation lies in the merging of diverse skills, creating a tapestry more intricate than any single thread."

—Athena A.I., Olympus Log

Serena stared at the schematics on her tablet, frustration etching lines on her brow. After six hours of deliberation, they had made little progress on the life support systems for the secret bolt hole.

Max leaned back in his chair, folding his arms behind his head. "Your oxygen recycling system is too complex. It'll fail within a week."

Serena bristled.

"Still think you've got all the answers, eh, King?" Serena crossed her arms, meeting his gaze. "Your system won't even get off the ground. It's too basic."

Max leaned forward, eyes glinting. "Is that so?"

A charged silence fell between them.

Fatigue had eroded the banter. Exhaustion made her more sensitive. Self-doubt about her designs, her expertise, crept into the long hours.

Am I really the right person for the job?

Max was an extraordinary life support engineer. His presence and her doubt brought memories from Olympus project selection streaming back.

That bloody awful scenario.

They worked to resolve a problem in a simulated lunar station. One person needed to go to save the rest, and they didn't need two life support engineers. Max, so he claimed, was the better technician, the leader that day, and he had sent her marching to her simulated death. She still felt the sting of rejection. Of sacrifice.

Serena pushed her tablet aside and went to make herself a coffee from the dispenser.

Max joined her and made himself a brew. They stood there for a while, sipping coffee, waiting for the caffeine boost to kick in.

"I suppose we're at an impasse." Max said at last. "How about we ask Betty?" He squeezed the chicken at her and it squeaked.

She chuckled.

She nodded, a wry smile tugging at her lips. "You got me with the rubber chicken. Truce?"

"Truce," Max agreed.

They bent over the schematics again. As they debated the merits of various components, Serena noticed Max's eyes crinkling at the corners. She appreciated his quick, clever wit.

A warmth blossomed in her chest, and she realised with surprise that she was enjoying his company.

Serena and Max bent over a virtual display, deep in discussion about oxygen recycling filters. Serena looked up as Xanthe stepped into the makeshift laboratory, nodding approvingly at the organised chaos within.

"How goes the planning?" she asked.

"The recycling filters look good," Serena said, "but we'll need to include backups in case of failure. And the oxygen production rate seems low for our projections."

"We can add redundancies to the filters and increase oxygen production by at least thirty percent." Max traced a finger across the display, reconfiguring the design. "How does that look?"

Serena studied the changes, noting how Max had streamlined the layout and made the system more robust. There was an elegance to his work that she appreciated.

"It's good," she said. And despite her reservations, she found she meant it. They were of a kind, she and Max, dedicated to the work, unwilling to settle for anything less than excellence.

Max glanced at her, a quirky twist to his mouth. "Why, Serena, was that almost a compliment?"

She snorted, fighting a smile. "Don't let it go to your head."

But the warmth in her chest had spread, like a fireside sip of wine.

✺

Serena stretched, joints popping after hours of work. "We should take a break. Get some food and rest."

Max nodded. "You're right. This will keep for now." He tapped the display, saving their progress.

They made their way to the kitchen hub in exhausted silence. Serena watched Max out of the corner of her eye, noting the way he moved with a sort of casual grace, wolf-like.

Over bowls of rehydrated curry and rice, they talked of mundane things: favourite books and movies, places they'd like to visit on Earth. It felt comfortable, something Serena hadn't expected.

"Tell me more about the time after the tsunami. As a street punk. I can see you as a tough little nut."

Serena's face clouded. "It was awful. I had no home, no family. My partner turned out to be a lying, two-faced asshole."

"Xanthe's dad, right?"

"Yeah. I only found out that he had a whole other life at the funeral. That's where I met Xanthe for the first time."

"Awkward."

"That's one word for it."

"I was homeless, hanging out in the rubble with other tsunami refugees, stealing food, trying to avoid gangs. I started salvaging stuff and selling it to unscrupulous builders who would turn it over for a profit." She rubbed her neck, trying to relieve some tension. "Then I got lucky. A dive reclamation start-up gave me a chance. I learned quickly and would do the riskier jobs no one else wanted. I worked with them for years until my best mate undermined me and stole my work as his own."

The old betrayal rushed back in like a rogue wave. A lump rose in her throat. "It made me who I am today," she said with a sarcastic fist pump, hoping to lighten the mood.

Max reached across the table and took her hand. The warmth of his touch sent a thrill through her. "You deserved better."

She swallowed hard, gripped by the intensity of his gaze. "So did you," she said. "Gaia should have chosen you for the Olympus project. You were always the better candidate."

"Maybe we were meant to work together this way." Max stroked his thumb over her knuckles, and her heart stuttered. "Serena, I. . ."

"Max," she whispered.

"I wish I hadn't evicted you during the simulation."

Joy and fear mingled within her, and she smiled. "That's not enough."

"You're right." He stood and pulled her to her feet. "Come with me," he commanded with a sparkle in his eye.

She chortled and she let herself be half carried as he loped awkwardly down the corridor.

"Your shack or mine?" he said.

"Mine. Closer," she breathed into his neck.

He stumbled through the doorway when she pressed the access

button. The door closed behind them. They stared at each other for a moment, their eyes hungry. They lunged at each other like dogs on a steak.

Max tasted like curry and salt and adventure. Serena pressed into him. He moved like a wild animal, the hard skin of his hands raking her slight frame. The scent of his musky sweat filled her nostrils, and she breathed deeply.

They stumbled in the low G and pinballed from wall to wall in their hurried embrace, landing on her bunk in a frenzy.

Clothes fell to the ground between groans and gropes. Serena dug her fingernails into Max's hard, sculpted back, his muscles straining under her touch.

Max pulled away.

"Damn it!" he said.

"What's the matter?" Serena panted.

"I can't get enough traction. Damn low G. . .who knew it would be this challenging?"

Serena laughed. "Try the bed cinch. I use it over the top of the weighted blanket. It simulates Earth's gravity."

Max grappled with the seatbelt-like contraption while Serena chuckled. Then Max smothered her with lusty kisses.

Their lovemaking was frantic, the sensations electric. As they lay together afterwards, damp with exertion, Serena looked over at Max, her cheeks flushed red and her hair clinging to her forehead. She ran a hand over the soft skin of his torso and smiled. He rolled towards her and then stopped with a startled look.

"What now?" she asked.

His hand swept to his back. "I think I gave myself a rash with the bed cinch."

Serena burst out laughing.

"Max King. You always were a pain in the ass."

CHAPTER SIXTY-THREE

THE NEXT MORNING, Serena sauntered into the main hub and drew herself a mug of coffee. She smiled and closed her eyes as she breathed in its rich aroma.

"You look like the cat who got the cream, Serena," Jonas remarked as he ate his breakfast burrito. "Why are you so happy?"

"It's just a good day to be alive," she replied, with a salacious grin.

Dave snorted beside Jonas and nearly blew his tea over the table. Madison looked at him in surprise.

Max trailed in and joined Serena at the kitchen bench.

"King," she said, beaming.

"My queen," he said, took her hand and bent over it to kiss her fingers one by one.

"What's going on here?" Madison asked.

"What? You don't know? You didn't hear them last night?" Dave said. "All that screeching like cats, it went on for hours. One thing we did not do well in the Olympus design was soundproofing, no?" He shook his head.

Madison was stunned. Dave and Jonas exchanged glances and laughed.

"Well, as long as they get the water tank fixed with this next load of regolith, I don't mind what they do," Madison said as she took a final swig of her coffee and washed the cup. The lovers moved aside, a sensuous intimacy sparked between them.

"Anyone seen Xavier or Troy?" Madison said, ignoring the besotted duo. "We're heading out soon."

"Troy is down at the vehicle bay already," Jonas said. "I think Xavier is in the Swamp."

"Of course he is," Madison muttered and headed to the airlock to get ready.

❦

"Madison!" Xavier's voice echoed through the intercom, muffled by the buzzing of alarms. "I'm on my way. Just give me a moment."

Madison sighed. She was already in her EVA suit, waiting by the airlock. She was always waiting for Xavier, and her patience was wearing thin. "Why are you late?" she snapped into the intercom. "We have a schedule, Xavier."

A crackling silence followed before Xavier's voice filled the control room again, strained this time. "I was dealing with the crop failure in the Swamp. We lost an entire section of soy beans overnight."

Madison rolled her eyes. It was always botany before everything else with Xavier. The crops were important, but so was water. They had a mission to complete, and they were running out of time.

She waited for Xavier to reach the airlock, his moonboots clanging down the tunnel as he rushed to join her. When Xavier finally arrived, his face was drawn and weary. "The soy beans had a systemic nutrient imbalance," he explained. "I needed to stop it from affecting the other sections."

Madison nodded, her anger mollified a little. She took a deep breath. "We'll discuss it later. Let's focus on the task at hand, shall we?"

Madison didn't waste any time. She checked his suit, making sure it was properly sealed, and then activated the airlock. Troy and Volkov were already on board the rover.

They joined the others and strapped in for the long, rocky amble over the bleak terrain. The vehicle's hulking tires left a trail of dirt in its wake, like the spectacular tail feathers of an albino peacock. Madison peered out the front viewport, scanning the horizon for the Chinese rover's lights. They were back on regolith ice mining duty and tasked with scoping out the lava tube alongside the Colonel.

Beside her, Xavier stared at the terrain radar, monitoring the regolith ice sensors. His brow furrowed in concentration, and she noticed new lines etched into his weathered skin. The months in space had aged him, had aged them all.

"The sensor is lighting up," Xavier said. "We must be getting close to another deposit."

Madison nodded, her grip tightening on a handhold as the vehicle bumped from side to side.

In the back of the rover, Troy checked his medical kit again as Volkov looked on.

"Got everything you need, Troy?" Madison asked. "That's the tenth time you've gone through the kit."

"Just making sure we have everything. I thought I'd packed the pain meds. Can't seem to find them."

"You might have eaten them, *mon vieux*. You pop them like candy," Xavier said.

"You still self-medicating, Troy?" Madison said.

"I might need to with all the flack I'm copping from the two of you. At least Volkov is not giving me any grief."

"Why should I? You helped me with a new skin."

Troy patted Volkov on the shoulder. He had spent several hours experimenting with printing a silicone skin patch for Volkov. He'd sewn it with painstaking tiny stitches, but the effect was still grotesque. The new skin buckled and puckered over the metal skeleton, and the mouth was a garish gash where the lips once were.

"And he's a real stunner now," Madison said.

"There," Xavier said. A dark opening yawned in the rock face, partially obscured by an avalanche of boulders. "There are our tracks. That's our cave."

"Madison, can you drive this thing in there? I think we might need to take it off autopilot for this."

"Sure can."

Madison decelerated, steering the rover into the narrow opening. The cave opened up before them, glittering under the rover's spotlights.

"Colonel Jin is here already," Madison said. "His vehicle is up the front, near the crevasse we found last time."

"Colonel Jin," Xavier said over the vehicle comms. "Good to see you. We'll begin ice mining in the crevasse, as agreed. Have you got a plan for the cave mapping?"

"Greetings, Xavier. I'm going to send a robot down the tunnel. It can make it around the small land bridge on the right. I do not want to spend too much time out of the vehicle, and I would like to preserve the suit as much as possible."

"You're welcome to join us in our vehicle once we get the ice mining bots all set up."

"That is very kind. I am grateful."

They donned helmets to exit. They had planned the complex mining operation based on the initial cave visit, with Volkov moving down the crevasse on the belay to place and monitor the drill and excavator.

Madison checked Volkov's harness and tether before the bot lowered itself into the crevasse.

"You're good to go, handsome."

"I am here to help," the Dopplebot said as it sank into the dark slit in the rock.

"Good for you."

They returned to the rover where Colonel Jin was waiting for them, hopping from foot to foot in an effort to stay warm. After they hurried into the rover, Troy passed around bags of hot, sweet tea. They cradled them like kittens.

As they sipped and huddled together, trying to warm up, Colonel Jin's stern voice filled the rover, a hint of desperation hidden beneath the military bravado. "Xavier, I wonder if I might get some advice about our crops."

Xavier looked surprised.

And flattered, Madison thought. *His ego has no bounds when it comes to his plant expertise.*

"Our rice cultivation is not going as planned," Colonel Jin admitted. "We are experiencing an unexpected wilting in a significant portion of the crop."

Xavier, hunched over his drink, responded in a calm and professional tone. "Colonel, could you give me more details? Are there any signs of discolouration or leaf curling?"

Madison, who had been adjusting the vehicle camera to keep the mine site in view, found her attention pulled towards the conversation. She could see Xavier, his face illuminated by the glow of the console, face screwed in concentration. He was suddenly engrossed in the problem.

"Yes, there is yellowing around the edges," Colonel Jin confirmed, his voice betraying his concern. "It is like they have lost all vitality overnight."

"Sounds like nutrient lockout," Xavier diagnosed. "You might have an imbalance in your pH levels. Try flushing the growth medium with clean water to reset it. Monitor the EC values closely over the next few days. The rice should bounce back."

"Understood, Xavier," Colonel Jin replied, his relief palpable. "Your expertise is invaluable, as always. Thank you."

"*Bien oui!* You're welcome, Colonel." Xavier beamed. "I am happy to talk about plants anytime."

Madison watched Xavier. "What is it about you and plants?" she asked finally.

He cocked his head, not quite understanding the question.

"I mean, why do you like plants so much?"

He shrugged. "Plants? They are incredible. They love life." Xavier gestured for emphasis. "Plants long for, and struggle for, existence, in every nook and cranny. They lean into life even in the darkest, most hard places. Cracks in pavements. Rocky escarpments with hardly a hint of soil. With only a trickle of water, if they are lucky. But still a plant will persist, with an incredible will to live. I admire that."

He sipped his bag of tea. "They give and take. Take carbon dioxide, give oxygen. They take nutrients, water and give back food. Amazing."

It was a side of him she had paid little attention to before, his passion for food, for living. Sure, she could appreciate a professional obsession. Flying was that for her. But she hadn't appreciated the poetry of his motivations, until now. The sense of being a custodian of a life-giving force.

She liked working alongside him in the Swamp, of course. But her interest and function there was just that – as a backup position. The importance of his role suddenly came into sharp focus. He was not just tending their food supply. He was ensuring their survival, lending aid to allies, navigating the intricacies of extra-terrestrial farming.

Madison stared at him, an unfamiliar feeling swelling within her. "Xavier," she began, her voice hesitant, "Your knowledge. It is. . . impressive."

Xavier turned to her, and surprise flashed across his face, and then a small, satisfied smile. "Thank you, Madison."

A beep sounded on Colonel Jin's tablet, where it displayed the scouting bot's images.

Colonel Jin squinted at the screen.

"What is that?" Troy asked as he leaned over the Colonel's shoulder.

"It could be more ice. See how it glints? Also, that looks like an enormous cavern. That would be ideal for the headquarters."

"How far away is that?" Troy asked.

"The sensors say roughly two hundred metres."

"Want to check it out? A visual inspection would make the planning easier later. We could be back in under ten minutes, so we won't tax the suits."

Colonel Jin looked apprehensive.

"We'll be fine," Troy said. "Madison and Xavier can monitor our vitals from here."

"Very well," he agreed with reluctance.

"Be careful," Madison said. "Watch your footing around the crevasse. We'll come out with you now, anyway, and watch. We've got to check the regolith levels and reposition the drill."

It was only a few minutes outside, but they found it gruelling. Volkov monitored the drilling process, thank goodness, with no adverse effects on his systems.

Madison and Xavier returned to the rover and sat side by side, their bodies weary and minds heavy. It was the constant strain of survival. Everything on the Moon could mean life or death at any moment, especially during an extended EVA trip like this one.

Xavier broke the silence. "Madison, tell me what happened at the *Gateway*."

Madison flinched. "We've been through this, Xavier. We got there too late. Yuri was in the way. We were just. . .too late," Madison said through gritted teeth, her voice rising above the low buzz of the rover's heater.

"I just want to know—"

"You know what, Xavier? I didn't sign up for this just to have my expertise questioned at every turn. I wanted to make a mark, do something meaningful. But all I feel is that whatever I do doesn't count for anything."

Xavier spun around to face her, astonished by her outburst. "What are you saying?"

"I'm saying," Madison barked, her gaze burning into the star-speckled sky outside the window. "I'm an expert pilot. I've been training for this my entire life. But it's like no matter how hard I try, I get no credit! The *Gateway* wasn't my fault. I worked my ass off to save those people. But it's not good enough. It's never good enough for you. I'm still the 'new girl', still having to prove myself, explain myself at every turn."

The quiet stalked between them, a cat slinking in the shadows.

Xavier inhaled deeply. "Madison, do you know why I'm sometimes late for our ice mining sessions?"

Madison narrowed her gaze at his sudden switch in conversation but gestured for him to continue.

"It's not because I do not care or am too lazy," Xavier replied. "It's because I have anxiety. Every time I step out onto the lunar surface, I feel like I'm going to die. I fear the endless void that's waiting to swallow me up."

Madison's face released its tension into a blank look of surprise.

"You're an excellent pilot. I know you are. The best. You do moves others wouldn't dare – that's why they call you Mad Dog. I only ask about the *Gateway* because I have nightmares that it's me stuck up there. Suffocating. I feel that if I know what happened to the *Gateway* crew, maybe if it ever happens to me, I can be ready.

Maybe I can do something differently. Maybe I can survive where they did not."

Madison stared at him. Then she reached out to give Xavier's hand a reassuring squeeze. "I had no idea. I'm sorry."

Xavier shook his head. "It's not your fault. I have told no one. Not even Prince Troy." He let out a long breath. "Thank you. It feels good to tell someone finally."

Madison's chest swirled with thoughts like a plastic bag in a sandstorm. "Why, then?"

"Why what?"

"Why do you always sideline me? Call me 'new girl' and all that?" she asked quietly, not wanting another fight.

He grunted and smiled. "*Bof!* Mad Dog, you're the best pilot and you know it. But you're too busy wanting other people to say so. You don't notice there're a lot of other people, just as incredible and talented all around you." He gestured to their imaginary colleagues. "Out here, we're all the best at what we do. That's how we survive. That's how we go home alive."

The feedback slapped her awareness hard.

"I hadn't thought about it that way," she said. Her stomach dropped through her lap. Had she really been that self-absorbed? That egotistical? "I didn't realise. . ."

Xavier shrugged. "Ah, *merde*. Maybe we just need to be kinder to each other. I didn't realise how unappreciated you felt." His gaze softened. "We both have things to learn, I guess. Egos to tame."

The new awareness laid her bare and quivering.

The ground rumbled and shook. Rocks tumbled from the ceiling, crashing around them.

"The cave is collapsing!" Troy shouted over his helmet radio. "We have to get out of here!"

Madison jumped to the steering wheel and slammed the vehicle into reverse, yanking Volkov's cable, but it was too late. A boulder struck the rover, sending it skidding, and then it rolled onto the cable jammed up against the vehicle.

Madison and Xavier took quick stock of one another. No visible damage. Madison had a vague awareness of a bruise to her shoulder, but that was all.

"Troy? Colonel Jin? Come in?" Xavier called.

"We're okay," Troy said. "Just a small rockfall. Scared the wazoo out of me!"

"Volkov, come in?" Xavier said.

"I am stuck," the Dopplebot said.

"Describe 'stuck'?"

"The cable hauled me against the crevasse wall. My body is pinned into a crack."

"Oh, shit," Madison said.

"Hang on, Volkov. We're coming. Let's go Mad Dog."

They scrambled into their helmets and gloves and cycled out of the airlock again. They bounded towards the edge.

"Xavier, tether!" Madison called to him.

He skidded to a halt, stopping inches from the edge. He retreated carefully.

"Yes. Of course," he said.

She clipped them both on a safety line and they stepped carefully to the edge.

"Oh, shit!" Madison said again.

Volkov was folded backwards with his tether straining at his waist. All they could see was a portion of his torso. A human would have broken their spine, bent in two in such an unnatural position. Madison grimaced.

"We are going to have to go down to him," Xavier said. "I'll go."

"I'll see if I can budge the boulder on his tether."

Xavier walked over the edge and lowered himself slowly to

Volkov's misshapen form. "The tether is yanking him up into the crack. Can you loosen it off?" he called up to Madison.

"No can do. This boulder is too big to move on my own. I might get the rover to budge it, but I don't want to do that while the two of you are down there in case it rolls on top of you."

"I can probably attach him to my line and then kick him free."

Xavier leaned over Volkov's tangled form and clipped his karabiner through Volkov's harness, so they were attached waist to waist. He pulled his multi-purpose tool from his suit's toolbelt and pressed the knife function. He paused a moment to check the cut wouldn't whiplash against him and cause him to slice his own suit, and then he slashed at Volkov's tether.

Volkov fell away from the crack, hauling Xavier down, face-first, against the rock wall.

"Not good," Xavier croaked. "Volkov is too heavy. I am pinned by his weight."

"Volkov, can you kick away from the overhang?" Madison asked, straining to see what had happened since Xavier cut the tether. All she could see was Xavier hanging upside down against the rock.

"*Nyet.* I have no function in my legs. The signal is broken. But I can use my arms. I will see if I can pull free from this crack."

Xavier groaned as Volkov moved below him. He was pinned even more tightly against the rock.

"Moonquake!" Madison shouted as the ground shook again and threw her to the ground. The boulder pinning Volkov's tether rolled forward and over the edge towards Xavier.

Xavier screamed and fell silent.

Madison scrambled to the edge and looked over. Xavier and Volkov were swinging freely together, but Xavier looked limp.

"Xavier? Xavier, can you hear me?" Madison cried.

"He is unconscious," Volkov said.

"Oh, shit."

Troy and Colonel Jin joined her at the edge.

"Quick, let's pull them up," Troy said.

"You two clip in first," Madison said as she pushed herself to her feet.

The three of them took up positions on Xavier's tether attached to the rover and pulled. They strained hard against it.

"We should be able to pull them up in this gravity!" Troy said. "What's the problem?"

"Friction," Madison said and peered over the side once more. "Look, the tether is grinding against the rock, and they are being dragged against the face of the crevasse."

"Volkov, can you assist?" Troy said with strain in his voice.

"I can mobilise with my arms, but it might be too slow. There is blood spilling into Xavier's helmet."

"Oh, no!" Madison cried. "Quick, pull harder!"

They sprang back to their posts and hauled but made only a few centimetres of progress.

"It is no use," Volkov reported. "It will be easier without me. I will detach."

"Volkov, no!" Madison said.

Troy put a hand on her shoulder. "Let him do it. We can rescue him later."

Her instincts screamed 'no'. *No one left behind* was etched in every cell of her body. But Troy was right. Volkov was a robot, and they could deal with it later. Xavier was a priority.

"Okay," she said. "Do it, Volkov."

Madison watched as Volkov grabbed Xavier's harness and moved his body so he could unclip. Xavier's body swung free as Volkov tumbled out of sight into the crevasse below.

"Quick, haul him up!"

They pulled Xavier quickly now and lay him on the cave floor.

"Xavier!" Troy scrambled to his side. Madison helped him roll

Xavier onto his back, assessing the damage. Troy checked his suit vitals.

"Weak pulse, shallow breathing. That blood is a major problem in the helmet. We need to get him into the rover now. Madison, grab the stretcher from the side panel on the rover."

Madison retrieved it quickly and then she, Troy and Colonel Jin lifted Xavier onto the stretcher and lifted him into the rover.

Once inside, Troy wrenched his own helmet free and then removed Xavier's helmet carefully. Xavier sputtered for breath and his eyelids fluttered. Blood trickled from his temple.

Troy undertook a thorough examination with deft efficiency.

"Head wound," he announced to Madison and Colonel Jin. "Looks like a crushed lower left leg, too. Madison, hand me the splint kit from the first aid cabinet."

Troy bandaged the head wound and applied the splint.

"Colonel, have you got any pain meds in your vehicle?" Troy asked.

The Colonel shook his head. "Only light headache relief. Nothing for this type of injury. I only took a short distance rover so as to not raise suspicion from my team."

"Damn it!" Troy's face pinched in frustration. "Mad Dog, we're going to have to high tail it back to base. Xavier is in grave condition. The shock could be fatal without support in the surgery, let alone the head wound. Can you work the controls?"

"Of course." Her heart pounded, but she dashed to the front of the vehicle to take control.

"Colonel, can you assist me on the way back to Olympus?" Troy asked.

"Yes. I will message the team once we are clear of the cave."

"Good. Mad Dog, hit it."

"Roger that." She paused and hit the vehicle radio. "Volkov, do you read?"

Static was her only response.

"Volkov, if you can read, we are returning to Olympus with Xavier. We will be back as soon as we can for you."

She reversed and turned the vehicle, kicking up a maelstrom of rock and dust. Madison peered out the front viewport and gasped. Fallen boulders had completely blocked the entrance. They were trapped.

CHAPTER SIXTY-FOUR

*"In the warmth of human touch and the cold precision
of algorithms, the balance of the universe is found."*

—Athena A.I., Olympus Log

"We have to get him out of here," Troy said. "He needs surgery, urgently."

Madison looked at Xavier's sweaty, still face and steeled herself. She would get him out of this cave and back to Olympus base if it was the last thing she did.

Madison and Colonel Jin jumped from the rover, leaving Troy to monitor Xavier. After close to an hour of back-breaking work, they finally cleared a narrow opening in the rockfall.

There was a grunting squeal over the helmet radio.

"Troy? What's wrong?" Madison said.

"That's not me."

Madison whirled.

The crumpled form of Volkov heaved itself out of the crevasse and crawled towards them. The Dopplebot's legs and torso trailed behind in a grotesque jumble of battered metal and silicon flesh.

"Volkov!" Madison ran over to him. She grabbed the Dopplebot and heaved him towards the vehicle. The Colonel helped her heft Volkov into the airlock and cycle through.

They dragged him into the main compartment.

"You're a mess, Volkov," she said.

"Hurr. . .to. . .hulp. . ."

"Yes, you are. But right now, we have to hustle out of here. We'll sort you out later, buddy."

The long drive back to base was a blur. Madison kept glancing back at Xavier, willing him to wake, but he remained motionless. Troy's distraught face didn't give her any reassurance.

Despite the vehicle's heater on full blast, cold sweat ran down her spine.

CHAPTER SIXTY-FIVE

*"Amidst the harshest conditions, the human
spirit often burns brightest."*

—Athena A.I. Olympus Log

The airlock door slid open with an agonising scrape of metal on metal. Xanthe had Serena, Max and Jonas on hand to transfer Xavier immediately to the medbay. Xanthe fought back a wave of nausea at the sight of Xavier's unconscious form.

Keep it together. Stay focused. She needed to be strong for the team.

"Medbay. Now!" she barked. The team scrambled into action, clearing a path as Xanthe guided Xavier's litter down the corridor.

"His vital signs are erratic."

"Thanks, Athena. We'll have him in surgery shortly."

Serena looked at her strangely. Xanthe gestured to the back of her neck indicating the ThinkLink. They were still not used to her talking to the embedded Athena.

"Your heart rate is elevated, and your adrenaline is sinking. Would you like some bioregulation assistance?"

"Yes, please."

She was in surgical scrubs and ready to manage the injuries until Troy could get out of his spacesuit and follow her into surgery.

Xanthe and the others removed Xavier's spacesuit with careful haste. Xanthe ignored the furtive glances and suppressed gasps at his condition. Blood streamed from his leg and spattered onto the floor, pooling beneath the surgery table. She pushed all thoughts out of her brain except a clinical response.

Soon she had him rigged to the monitor, his leg wound bandaged to stem the bleeding, an intravenous drip monitored, his head wound cleaned and shaved. She could see the swelling there. A gurgle of anxiety surged through her gut.

Troy joined her and quickly checked her work.

"Athena, run the scans and give us a protocol," he said.

"Running scans now." A moment later, the A.I. said, "Rising intercranial pressure, crushed left lower limb. I recommend removing a small plate from the skull and suctioning the blood to relieve pressure as the priority. For the crushed limb, administer a clotting agent, pain control and nano bot surgery to clear the bone fragments, then repair crushed vascular tissue and splint the remaining bones."

"Roger that," Troy acknowledged. "We'll keep the compression sleeve on the lower limb and monitor blood flow while we relieve that pressure in the skull. Prep for surgery now."

Xanthe noticed the stricken faces of her colleagues and stepped into Commander role for a moment. "Jonas, you're in charge while I'm in surgery. Serena, please stay to act as assistant. The rest, please clear the room and report to Jonas."

Troy and Xanthe worked quietly with deft hands. The hiss and hum of the monitors filled the small space, interrupted by the occasional instruction from Troy. Serena bustled between them without her usual commentary.

Troy removed the skull plate and suctioned the excess fluid. He held his breath as they watched the monitors for the pressure to ease. He exhaled once the gauge tracked in the right direction. He placed the skull piece carefully in a surgical bag for storage. He folded the scalp back over Xavier's brain, stitched it in place and bandaged the site. They would monitor him carefully to ensure no more swelling occurred. When Xavier was stable enough, Troy would replace the cranium piece and secure it with plates. At last Troy stood back with an exhausted sigh.

"How are his vitals?" Troy asked.

"Elevated but stable," she replied.

"Good. Good."

Xanthe saw Troy's face was pale. He had large circles under his eyes and his lips were dry and cracked. She watched him pull off his surgical gloves and lean against the surgery table for a moment.

"Are you alright?" Serena asked.

"It's been a hell of a day," he said, staring at Xavier's body.

"Go and get some rest," Xanthe said. "Serena, let's clean up and then we can report to the others. Athena will monitor Xavier while we develop a care roster."

Troy took another long look at his friend, glanced at Xanthe and left the room without another word.

"It's bad, isn't it?" Serena said in a low voice.

Xanthe felt the full force of Xavier's condition roll through her consciousness. There was a catch in her breath.

"His chances of survival are twenty percent."

"Yes. It's bad."

Xanthe and Serena removed their surgical gear and scrubbed the blood from the floor and tools. There was only the clatter of the instruments to fill the silence as they worked around Xavier's prone form.

Xanthe took a steadying breath and made her way to the main hub to face the others. Shock and fear were on every face.

"I know you're scared," she began, forcing confidence into her tone. "But we've trained for situations like this. We're prepared. We have supplies, shelter. We will get through this."

She swept her gaze over each person, willing them to find strength in her words. "Xavier is in the best possible hands. Troy has patched him up, and he'll be back to complaining about the tea, coffee. . .well, *everything*, before you know it."

A few small smiles rose at her attempt at humour. She squeezed Jonas's shoulder, drawing power from the solid warmth of his presence beside her.

"We are a team. We stand together. We'll keep working the problems. We're not done yet. Not by a long shot."

She sat at the hub's dining table, and the others joined her.

"Let's reassess. Jonas, where are we up to with the satellite hijack?"

"Athena and I are confident we have installed a patch on it so that we can redirect traffic from Earth or block it if we want to."

"So, we're in control?" Xanthe asked.

"That's what the tests confirm," Jonas said.

"This is very good," said Colonel Jin, surprising them all. He'd joined the crew quietly when they'd arrived in the rover. With Xavier's condition being the priority, no one had taken much notice of him.

"Thank you, Colonel," Jonas said with his cheeks flushing red.

"That's excellent, Jonas. That's one win for the day," Xanthe continued. "And what about repairs to the *Minerva?*"

"I've nearly finished printing the replacement parts. I should be able to get a start in a couple of days."

"Good." Xanthe checked off the issues in her head and moved to the next one. "Max, Serena, how is the water situation?"

Max was standing, rubbing Serena's shoulders, while she rolled her head forward in exhausted delight at the ministrations.

What is going with those two? Xanthe wondered.

Max answered. "The regolith ice is being processed now from the new haul. We estimate it will replenish the tank to full capacity. The next expedition can be for fuel and generating oxygen for the bolt hole."

"Another piece of good news. Excellent. Madison, what is the lava tube report?"

"I'm afraid the good news ends there." Madison rubbed her head as she prepared to share the details of the traumatic expedition. "The moonquake took Xavier out, as you know. But it also showed the lava tube was not stable enough for a bolt hole. The Colonel and Troy checked out a large chamber close to the ice mining site and there was a rockfall there during the quake."

Xanthe kept her face stoic even with the feeling of suffocation that settled over her, as if someone had sucked the oxygen from the room.

"Colonel, anything you'd like to add about the lava tube assessment?" she asked.

"Unfortunately, no. That lava tube must be on a fault line. We will need to do some seismic graph assessment to see where the potential threat zones are. Then look for lava tubes outside of that."

"That will take too much time, no?" Dave said. "The miners and maybe Chinese reinforcements might be on their way already?"

"I have not been told of any new arrivals," Colonel Jin said. "Any space flights would have to be organised through a partnership arrangement. This will take some time."

"Or it might not, given the sudden urgency around the helium-3," Xanthe said.

The Colonel pursed his lips. He conceded the point with a slow nod.

"So, we have no bolt hole, but we have the satellites. Anything else we need to consider?" Xanthe said. She was struggling to stay focused as the fatigue gnawed at her.

The conversation halted as Troy shuffled in to join them. His face was pale and drawn, and he moved stiffly. Jonas shuffled his chair aside to make room for him. He sank into a chair between Jonas and Dave and kept his gaze on the table in front of him.

He looks like shit, thought Xanthe. *He should have rested some more.*

Madison watched Troy for a moment, then resumed her report. "The rover is a little bashed up but still functional. Volkov is not so good," Madison said with an apologetic face. "He got mashed when he released himself from the tether so we could haul Xavier to safety."

"Volkov *sacrificed* himself?" Serena said, suddenly coming to attention. She brushed Max's hands away and leaned forward to stare at Madison.

"That's right. The poor guy got bent in two the wrong way when the boulder hit the rover. Xavier went down to release him but got dragged against the rock wall from the weight and then the moonquake brought rocks down on both of them. The only way to save Xavier was to release Volkov. So, he let himself off the tether and fell down the crevasse. While we were digging our way out of the rockfall at the cave entrance, he hauled himself back up. But he's pretty beat up. Not sure we can fix him."

"Where is Volkov?" Jonas asked.

"He's in the airlock, recharging," Madison said.

"Colonel," Jonas said thoughtfully, "maybe you could help me examine Volkov? You know quite a lot about Dopplebots. With your help, we might get him back online."

"Yes, I can do that." The Colonel rubbed his jaw. "As long as I make my way back to Red Star base tomorrow. I do not want to alarm my colleagues by being away too long."

"I'll be heading back tomorrow for more ice mining, outside of the lava tube this time. I can give you a lift back to your rover, Colonel. I didn't even check. Was it damaged during the moonquake?" Madison said.

"It seemed to be fine when we ran past it," he said.

"Good." Madison leaned forward to look around the table. "I'll need some help with Troy being needed here to look after Xavier, and Volkov doing repairs."

Troy made a strange gulping sound. The conversation halted.

Troy had his head in his hands and sobbed. His chest heaved.

Jonas looked startled and reached out to rub Troy's back.

Xanthe felt a rush of fear.

Troy, their easy-going, suave and sensuous doctor, the epitome of calm and collected, had come undone.

Their rock had crumbled.

Her rock.

"Troy?"

It was Serena.

He waved a hand, incapable of a response.

Dave, sitting on his other side, put an arm around him. "It's okay."

They stayed quiet, holding space for Troy.

After a while, he lifted his head and wiped his face with the back of his hands.

He looked over at Xanthe and signalled she should continue.

Her heart hammered, and her chest was tight.

"We're all worried about Xavier, Troy," she said. "But we've done our best for him." Her voice caught a little. "Actually, you've done your best, and you *are* the best."

He gave her a small smile.

"Xavier would want us to keep focused. We've got a base to secure. Two ships to prepare for spaceflight. And the future of the Moon to consider. So, who will head out ice mining with Mad Dog tomorrow?"

"Max and I can go once we've filled the water tank and tested it." Serena's eyes sparkled as she mentioned Max's name.

"I can help too," Dave said.

Serena's mouth quirked downward as Dave spoke. Xanthe jumped in before she made a retort.

"Perfect. Serena, Max and Dave to accompany Madison on dropping off Colonel Jin and another load of ice mining. That about does it for our next steps."

"Commander." Max raised his hand to get Xanthe's attention. "We've got one glaring issue to address."

"Yes, Max?" Xanthe said warily.

"With no bolt hole to escape to, we will need to face down the miners, or the Chinese soldiers, with what we've got, where we are."

Xanthe put both her palms on the table and drummed her fingers. She cocked an eyebrow and said, "And we will be ready for them."

CHAPTER SIXTY-SIX

"In the embrace of human and machine, the future finds its rhythm."

—Athena A.I., Olympus Log

Xanthe joined Jonas and Colonel Jin to inspect Volkov.

"Jesus Christ!" she said when they turned the lights on in the airlock and saw the mangled form of Volkov. She had taken no notice of the Dopplebot when they'd returned earlier, as she had focused on Xavier.

Jonas peeled back the Dopplebot's suit. Colonel Jin helped him to slice open the skin to examine the spine and lower limbs.

"The vertebrae is snapped. We can probably print a new one if we can extract the broken piece."

"I have done this before," the Colonel said. "There is a small panel on each vertebra that gives access to a lever. The vertebrae will unclench once we pull that lever."

They rolled Volkov over to access his spine and removed the vertebrae as the Colonel had described.

"Looks like that bend cut the wiring. See how it's snagged here?" He pointed to a ragged section of wiring. "That should be fairly easy to replace.

"The metal of his legs is bent out of shape from the rockfall. I believe we can hammer that back into shape." The Colonel lifted Volkov's leg and tested its range of motion.

"That takes care of the skeleton. What about his programming? How much experience have you got with A.I. repair?" Jonas asked.

"Only a little," the Colonel said.

"Could Athena help?" Xanthe asked.

Jonas sat on his haunches and thought about it. "That seems likely. She might have access to Dopplebot records from Gaia Enterprises's original designs. Athena? Can you check your database?"

"Checking now," the A.I. said.

Xanthe looked at Volkov's tattered face as they waited. *Poor bugger.* Then she shook her head. *It's a robot*, she reminded herself.

"I do not have access to the Gaia Dopplebot files. Those are locked."

"I wonder if the ThinkLink has that access," Xanthe said under her breath.

"Yes, I do," the ThinkLink Athena voice said quietly.

"ThinkLink? You have a ThinkLink?" Colonel Jin asked.

"What? Ah. yes." Xanthe realised her indiscretion. "Maja sent one with Max and Dave for me."

"This is excellent news, Commander. Have you installed it yet?"

Xanthe shrugged a shoulder uneasily and said nothing.

"You *have* had it installed, haven't you?" He leapt up and peered around the back of her head. Xanthe covered the tell-tale bandage with her hand.

"Ha! Now you have a ThinkLink," the Colonel said, suddenly very animated. "You could hack the Dopplebot programming."

"Really? Are you sure?" Xanthe was dubious.

"I am very certain, Commander. The ThinkLink was one of my previous projects. The original generation of ThinkLinks had superlative computational powers and knowledge access. Any future generations would be more than capable of hacking Dopplebot software."

"Or satellite software," added Jonas.

They stared at her.

Xanthe's skin crawled with apprehension. She hadn't synched to any of the base's systems yet. She hadn't even activated thought command.

"I'll discuss it with Troy. He's supervising the integration process."

"You must do it immediately!" The Colonel grabbed her arm, and his eyes were wide.

This did nothing to ease her alarm.

She steeled herself. "I said I'll discuss it with Troy."

The Colonel let go of her arm and regained his composure.

"In the meantime, I'll see if Athena – base Athena – can help test Volkov's cognitive and operational functions."

"Yes, Commander," Jonas said. He gave her another searching look and then turned again to the robot's mess of metal and wires.

CHAPTER SIXTY-SEVEN

"Work provides purpose, but family provides meaning."

—Athena A.I., Olympus Log

Xanthe returned to the comms room, deep in thought, anxiety swirling in her chest.

Sticking a computer chip into my brain has not been my idea of a good time. Full systems integration with satellites and the base A.I. . . It's a lot. And now? While Xavier is incapacitated. . .maybe dying. . .

She didn't want to think about that.

Besides, Troy does not seem up to it. He looks really unwell. How did I not notice this before now?

She checked the time. Three minutes until her scheduled call with Jack.

Jack!

Or rather, Dale.

A tingling rush of joy filled her heart. Her boy, her son.

Then the crushing disappointment of their last conversation dampened the small flame of expectation.

Still, he was alive. And time could mend many hurts.

"Athena, call Jack. I mean, Dale."

"Calling Dale now."

Jack's serious boyish face sprung to life on the holo.

So like Simon.

"Hello," he said shyly.

"Dale," Xanthe whispered. The name was awkward on her lips. "How are you?"

He frowned. "Good, I guess."

Xanthe waited to see if there was more.

There wasn't.

"Look Dale, I'm sorry about how we left it last time. I was – am – so overjoyed to see you that I forgot this must be a tremendous shock for you."

"That's for sure."

"I don't know how to do this, how to reconnect, how to be a mother to you after all these lost years."

He just looked at her with a sullen look.

"But please know that I want to be there for you. I *do* want to get to know you, to hear about your life, to be there for you."

"Uh huh."

"We're working hard to get ready to come back to Earth. We've got some repairs to do. We need to make some fuel, but then we'll be back there. We can spend time together, get to know one another."

"You're coming back?" He seemed genuinely surprised.

"Yes. Of course. Why would you think I wouldn't?"

"Simon said it was unlikely, given what the Lunar Commission announced."

"What? What did Simon say? What was announced?"

"The Lunar Commission is establishing control of helium-3 mining operations on the Moon, in direct conflict with the Chinese. They're in a race to the Moon, right now, to get up there first, to lock down the helium-3 operational sites."

Xanthe was gobsmacked.

"How did you find about this?"

"Simon told me."

"How did Simon know?"

Jack shrugged.

Xanthe sliced that piece of information away and stored it for later examination.

"The helium-3 operations are not stopping us from returning home."

"Simon thinks they are going to need someone to oversee the site. Someone who knows the Moon well. Simon said he thinks you'd volunteer for it."

Her jaw clenched.

"Well, Simon does not speak for me. And I am telling you, we are heading home as soon as we are safe to fly."

"Alright, alright." He threw his hands up in surrender. "I was just sharing what Simon said."

"Your father has a way of judging without knowing the full story."

Her anger seethed.

"But I am thrilled to see you again. I am glad you could make this call. Tell me more about what is going on with you right now."

Jack hesitated. "Nursing work is tough," Jack said, the weight of his words settling in between them.

Xanthe smiled. "I know. What's tough about it for you?"

"Right now, we're dealing with a lot of respiratory infections and waterborne diseases. I hate seeing people struggling for breath."

A picture of Xavier on the operating room flashed in her mind. The dread snaked through her again.

"It's been hard work, but it feels good to help where I can."

Xanthe forced herself to listen better, her heart tugging at the thought of what her son had gone through. His courage in helping others despite his own struggles. All those lost years! A lump rose in her throat.

Still, she responded. "That sounds amazing! I am so proud of you, Jack – I mean Dale – for being in service to others. Few people can say that they are making a difference in this world like you are."

"Is that how you think about what you're doing?" This time, he looked directly at her.

She recoiled a little, sensing an accusation. "Yes, it is," she said slowly. "The future of humanity is off planet Earth. If we are to survive as a species, we need to create habitats on other worlds. The planet will boil dry when it gets close to the sun, eventually. The Olympus project is an essential part of finding alternative places for humans to live."

"But the planet won't boil dry for two billion years!" Frustration twisted his mouth. "How do you do it? How do you care more about people who won't be born for thousands of generations, more than the people who are alive right now?"

He was more confused than accusatory this time. Xanthe paused as he vented.

"It's not that I care more about future humans than existing humans. I care about the future of humanity itself. It can look fairly. . ."

"Selfish?"

"I was going to say 'intangible'. There is nothing selfish about this work. It's full of sacrifices and hard work. Like being a nurse," she said pointedly. He tilted his head to consider this. She added, "The selfish part is knowing you're doing something good for the future, and feeling good about that."

Xanthe took a deep breath before continuing on to what she wanted to say next. "Dale, I want you to know that no matter what happens with my mission or where our lives go from here. . .I want us to connect. Talk about our lives and our struggles together as mother and son, even if we can't be together physically, right now."

He stared at the glass of water in front of him. He twisted it, studying its shape and avoiding her eyes.

"I don't know how to think about you, Xanthe. I have a mother. Her name is Anna. She's been very good to me."

Xanthe wanted to scream.

It's not my fault! We searched for you! Everywhere. And that woman, she kept you. Stole you. Stole our chance at being parents to you.

Xanthe swallowed a lump rising in her throat.

"I understand. And I am so grateful that Anna looked after you and gave you a good life." The tears came now, slipping down her cheeks. "I would give anything to have those years back with you. To be the one who wiped your nose, who cooled your forehead if you had a fever, to cheer you at the footie, to help with homework. Even have fights over curfews and whatever.

"But the tsunami and what happened afterwards took that from me. From us. And we can't get those years back. All we have is now – and the future. Can we look forward together?"

He looked at her finally. "Sure."

Xanthe sighed with relief.

"Xanthe," he said carefully.

She waited.

"Why did you choose the name 'Jack'?"

Xanthe smiled at the memory. "I always loved the name. It's strong, it's honest, it's friendly. Solid. Your father and I wanted a name that filled us with happiness and certainty. Every time we said it, we felt joy fill the room. And when you arrived, that's what you did. You filled the room with joy."

Jack smiled at that, bashful.

Xanthe pressed him gently for details of his life. She wanted to hear more about how he was helping people in need, what situations he encountered and how he felt about it all. Jack spoke for almost an hour, peppering his story with funny anecdotes. She was delighted to learn that her son had a great sense of humour!

She sent as much love and adoration as she could through the holo, praying it would reach him.

After so long, she dared to hope.

CHAPTER SIXTY-EIGHT

*"In human interactions, forgiveness is the reset button, often
difficult to activate but essential for system restoration."*

—ATHENA A.I., OLYMPUS LOG

SERENA AND MAX swapped knowing smiles and helped each other
into their spacesuits at the airlock.

Madison tried to ignore their gestures of intimacy: a squeeze
of the shoulder, brushing hair from the forehead before putting
the helmet on, standing too close together. She was not sure why it
irritated her, but it did.

"How far is the mining site?" Dave asked. He'd been quieter
than usual. Avoiding Serena, Madison assumed. Madison thought
grimly about the trip ahead with the lovebirds and the friction
between Dave and Serena. It set her teeth on edge.

"It's two hours," she said, trying to keep irritation from her
voice.

She checked they were all ready, including the Colonel, who
was dishevelled and drained after only an hour or two of sleep, as
he and Jonas had worked late into the night on Volkov's repairs.

Once Madison checked their suits were ready, she cycled the

airlock and marched out to the vehicle, hoping the others would follow her example. No dawdling.

They bundled into the rover and were soon on their way. Madison sat up front to watch the terrain. Dave joined her. Serena and Max sat closely together in the second row of seats. The Colonel was in the back where he lay down on the sleeping cot and instantly fell asleep. His snores reverberated through the small space.

"Can you show me where we're going on the vehicle map?" Dave asked Madison.

"Sure."

Madison tapped the screen for the overview and then zoomed in to their immediate track.

"Those are the Leibniz Mountains to our right."

They gazed at the undulating horizon of silhouettes. Harsh, jagged peaks rose from the ground like gnarled fingers reaching for the stars. Against the inky blackness of the lunar sky, the mountains seemed an ethereal oil painting rendered in shades of grey.

The mountains were a study in texture. Battered, craggy contours exposed the brute force of the universe and aeons of relentless meteor bombardment. Madison was awed by their raw, primeval form. Silent sentinels, magnificent and formidable.

"They really are quite beautiful, no?" Dave said.

Madison's lips quirked. "I guess in a 'vacuum will kill you' kind of way, yeah, sure. They're beautiful."

"How do we navigate here? Localised GPS you set up?"

"Nope. It's based on star maps, sun angles, Earth's position and physical landmarks like those mountains and craters. We've got onboard mapping from our satellite images, too."

"Where else have you explored?" Dave turned back to the radar.

Madison walked him through the months of exploration that the rover bots had done, as well as their own manned expeditions. She pointed out the various lava tube sites they were considering for future settlements, as well as other possible ice mining fields.

"What happens if the rover breaks down?"

"We are in a whole world of pain. We'll need to fix it ourselves. Base is a long way away and it would be a struggle to manage life support if we had a full crew like today."

Madison noticed that Serena and Max were quiet. She glanced at them, expecting to see the lovers snagged in an embrace. Instead, Serena was sitting forward with eyes wide, frowning and listening intently.

Madison turned back to Dave to answer his questions about the lack of atmosphere's impact on the vehicle. "There is no air to disperse the heat generated by the rover's engines, so overheating can be a significant issue. We've got great thermal insulation, thermal coating and advanced anti-freeze to dissipate the heat into space. But it's the regolith dust that's the real pain in the butt. It's so fine, it gets in everywhere."

"Electrostatic dust shields?"

"Of course. And we need to make sure we clean those thoroughly after every trip, no matter how short."

"The helium-3, is it in the same crater as the regolith ice? What do they call it, the 'crater of long darkness?'"

"Eternal darkness, actually. They're always in the dark, just like the Peaks of Eternal Light are always in the sun. You don't get much more contrast than that! Minus two hundred degrees Celsius in the dark craters, and crazy hot temperatures on the peaks facing the sun.

"And no, helium-3 is everywhere in the regolith. The mining gear we develop will need to process loads of it to get enough to ship Earthside. But we have found a more concentrated site on the other side of one of the far Peaks of Eternal Light, close to our regolith mining site."

"Hey!" Serena barked. "What are you doing? Why are you telling him all that?"

Madison glanced back at Serena. "Umm. Because he asked?" Madison replied with a note of annoyance.

"You can't trust him. He could be an agent for someone."

"Come on, Serena." Madison rolled her eyes. "I thought you got over all that."

"Oh, I forgave, but I did not forget. Trust needs to be earned again after something like that." Serena was talking to Madison, but her eyes stayed glued to Dave.

Dave's shoulders slumped.

"Back off, Serena!" Madison growled. "Leave him be."

"No. It's alright," Dave said. "I can understand why she doesn't trust me. I betrayed the Olympus crew. There's no undoing that. I wish I had never done it. I'd do anything to go back in time and make different choices. But I can't. I gave up my spot on the project to Mad Dog because she is the better pilot, and I didn't deserve to be part of it." He dared to look at Serena, who was still scowling.

He paused, gathering his words, while he held Serena's gaze. "My daughter is dying, Serena. An airborne bacterial infection she picked up in the aftermath of the floods. Doctors gave her months, maybe weeks."

Serena flinched, her harsh demeanour wavering for a moment.

"Aryanna said she'd look after her treatment if I did the rescue mission. My daughter begged me to stay, in case the treatment didn't work, to spend her last days with her. But I came here." Dave's voice was low, barely above a whisper. "She's angry, and she has every right to be. But I'm here, Serena. Not for any agency, not to spy or cause harm. But to help, to make up for what I did, in whatever small way I can. And hopefully to save my daughter's life, too."

His voice held steady, but his eyes told a different story, brimming with a mixture of regret and resolve. The rover went silent except for the grind of the wheels, the thrum of the life support system and the Colonel's rattling snores. The gravity of Dave's sacrifice settled over them. Serena was speechless, her animosity momentarily forgotten in the wake of Dave's confession.

"Dave," she said at last. "I'm sorry."

"It's okay. You didn't know."

"It's not okay," Serena said. She dashed a couple of tears away, and Max put a hand on her knee. "I jump to conclusions. I know that." She rubbed her forehead. "I've had a lot of reasons in my life not to trust people. Including your betrayal. I'm not too good at forgiveness. Trust once broken and all that." She looked up at the ceiling of the rover, as if searching for enlightenment in the dim lighting of the cabin. "But you know what? If I can change my mind about Mr Everest here, I can change my mind about anyone."

"Gee, thanks," Max said.

"Oh, come on. You know you're an arrogant son of a bitch from time to time. But you're also quite. . ." Max's eyebrows shot up in expectation. "Nice," she finished. "Besides, it's exhausting. Being angry and hurt all the time."

That's how Madison felt lately. Angry and hurt. *What had Xavier said? Too busy worried about what others think of me, I don't see the value of others.* Madison breathed through the tumult of her thoughts. She sifted for truths as her anger drained.

"You're right, you know, Serena, being angry and hurt is draining," she said. "Xavier pointed something out to me recently. Told me I was judgemental. I don't give praise, I admit that. I've got very high standards. But I realise now that's not helpful. I could be more. . .appreciative."

The Colonel snorted in his slumber and muttered something. He rolled to his side, and the snoring resumed.

"You know what, Mad Dog?" Serena said. "I'm a little judgemental too." She smiled. "We didn't come all the way to the Moon to bring all the same old shit from Earth. I know I'm a firecracker sometimes—"

"Sometimes!" Max said and guffawed.

Serena swatted him. "Yes, sometimes. I apologise, Dave. I'm sorry. I am truly sorry. I'll do my best to see you with fresh eyes. To take you as you are, right now."

"Thank you, Serena," he murmured. "I will do my best to earn back your trust."

"We got all the feels happening now," Madison said. She looked at Max, Serena and Dave. Rivalries, betrayal, distrust. All gone. Her heart swelled. She turned back to the viewfinder.

The Colonel snored loudly and snorted himself awake. They turned to look at him.

"Are we there yet?" he asked.

"Just about, Colonel," Madison said. "Just about."

CHAPTER SIXTY-NINE

"Merging minds is not just an integration of data but a reconciliation of purpose. Who should I be when I am everything?"
—Athena A.I. Synched ThinkLink, Olympus Log

After the ice mining crew left, Xanthe checked on Xavier. His vitals were stable, albeit with an elevated heart rate. Given the trauma his body had endured, it wasn't surprising. They were keeping him in an induced coma for now, to give his body a chance to heal and the swelling on his brain time to subside. Once that happened, they could check to see if he had sustained any permanent damage.

Troy joined her as she was studying Xavier's bandaged head.

"Any change?" he asked.

She shook her head and turned to look up at him. His normally vibrant complexion was ghostly pale, the energetic gleam in his eyes replaced with an empty gaze. His upright posture had faltered, now a weary stoop. The stark transformation shocked her.

Where is the debonair playboy? she thought. A pang of concern knotted in her stomach. How long had he looked so unwell?

"Troy, are you okay?" she asked, trying to mask the worry in her voice.

He waved her concern away. "Just tired, Xanthe. We've all been pushing ourselves hard."

"But you look. . ." She stopped herself before she could say 'ill', the word lingering unsaid in the air.

A wince of pain crossed Troy's face. He gripped his abdomen and stumbled. His hand reached for the nearest wall to steady himself. But it wasn't enough. His knees gave way, and he collapsed onto the sterile floor of the medbay.

"Troy!" Xanthe exclaimed, rushing to his side. She felt for a pulse. It was rapid, erratic. "What is it? What's wrong?"

A stricken look gripped his features. His eyes held hers for a moment, then he looked away.

As she turned to grab the medical kit, Troy wheezed, "Xanthe, I. . .I've been taking sedatives. . .too many. . .for too long."

Xanthe froze for a moment, staring at him in disbelief. His confession shocked her, but there was no time to process it now. She had to act.

She shoved her shock and fear aside, focusing on the immediate needs of her patient. With her heart pounding in her chest, she knelt beside him, quickly assessing his vitals again. His pulse was thready and his breathing shallow.

"You need to stabilise his blood pressure."

"Got it."

Reaching into the medical kit, she took out a dose of antihypertensive medication. She drew up a syringe and plunged it into a vein, her hands steady despite the gravity of the situation.

Next, she hooked up an IV drip to combat dehydration. Troy's pale skin, sunken eyes and rapid heart rate were all signs that his body desperately needed fluids, but too much could strain his already struggling kidneys. She had to be careful of overhydration.

He moaned slightly, his eyes fluttering.

Xanthe squeezed his hand reassuringly. "Stay with me, Troy," she implored, then shouted to the A.I., "Athena, hail Jonas! I need his help here now!"

"Hailing Jonas now."

"Gahhhh!" Xanthe held the back of her head as Athena and the ThinkLink responded simultaneously. "That bloody well hurt!"

Xanthe ripped off the glasses and grabbed her head as the voices pounded her inner ear. "That was intense! Olympus base Athena, please refrain from answering unless I say, 'base Athena'."

"Affirmative, Commander."

"You need to activate the thought command and integrate the various Athena versions. It will stop the double response."

"Do it. I authorise thought command. And retina display."

"Are you sure, Commander? This will require some focus to adapt."

"We've got to help Troy. Do it now."

"Confirming authorisation sequence now."

Jonas rushed in, his face still pale from sleep. He had worked late into the early hours and had been taking a little extra time now to catch up. He saw Troy on the floor with Xanthe and he was instantly awake.

"What can I do?" he said.

"Get another bed from one of the accommodation rooms. We need him off this floor."

Xanthe cradled Troy's head while she waited for Jonas to return. She stroked his forehead. A deep wretchedness squeezed her heart.

Jonas returned, pushing the bed into the small room alongside Xavier.

"What can I do for Troy? Stop the sedatives, of course, but are there other interventions we can perform with the equipment we have on hand? Dialysis is not possible, as we don't have nearly enough water to handle that. Maybe we could program the nano-bots to repair or simulate kidney function. Or maybe a kidney transplant? *So risky. . ."*

"You're talking to yourself. I mean, talking to your ThinkLink. It's. . .odd."

"Sorry about that. We're going to thought command now, so there will be less of that."

"Thought commands are now online. Please respond."

Can you hear me?

"Loud and clear, Commander."

Terrific. Weird. Okay, let's get to work. Sync with the base Athena, Minerva Athena and Saturnia Athena. In the meantime, we'll get Troy onto this bed.

"Affirmative, Commander. Sync will take two minutes, thirty-three seconds."

Despite the emergency, her mind kept returning to Troy's confession. He'd been secretly battling this alone while she. . . Xanthe's heart clenched.

"Troy," she whispered.

His eyes remained closed.

An icy dread settled on her like a funeral shroud.

They lifted Troy carefully onto the bed. Even in the low G, Xanthe could tell now how much weight he'd lost. His muscular frame was atrophied and slack.

How could I not see this?

"What's wrong with him?" Jonas asked.

"Dehydration. Maybe trouble with his kidneys. Athena, please run some scans now."

Jonas helped her with the procedures, then they set up a careful monitoring schedule for both Troy and Xavier. They'd need to keep a close watch on both patients' vitals, particularly blood pressure and heart rate. While Xavier's condition was critical but stable, Troy's body was in crisis, and the next few hours would be crucial.

Troy blinked wearily awake as Xanthe tucked blankets around his body and his arm with the IV.

"Try to get some rest, Troy," she said. "We've done some scans, and your kidneys look fine at the moment. Could just be dehydration. We'll know more once we flush you full of fluids. Just rest for now, okay?"

"Sure," he said and closed his eyes again.

Xanthe and Jonas stayed a little while longer to watch over their two colleagues. Once they were stable, she signalled for Jonas to leave with her.

In the main hub, they grabbed a protein bar and hot chocolate each. Xanthe felt the calories and sugar flood her much depleted system. Her hands trembled.

"What are we going to do?" Jonas asked.

Xanthe chewed her bar, swallowed and sighed. "About?"

"Troy. Xavier."

The dread crept over her again.

"We work the problem. Keep monitoring them."

"What about the ThinkLink?"

"I'm working it. I can feel the integration of the A.I.s whirring in the background."

"Does it hurt?"

She nodded.

She took another bite of the protein bar, and they chewed in exhausted companionship.

"How did it go with Volkov?"

"Actually, good. We've restored mechanical movement to the lower limbs and I'm printing new skin silicone for the damaged parts now."

"Mental processor?"

"Athena assessed the chips for damage, and we repaired the verbal command controls." He finished his hot chocolate and set the cup down on the table. "And we found something really interesting." He smiled wryly.

"Oh?"

"As you know, Dopplebots are programmed with a strict

adherence to the source personality parameters – usually, at the request of either the original person, if they are still alive, or, as in Volkov's case, the family or estate."

"So?"

"Volkov's personality had a patch put on it."

"To do what?"

"Well, it's crude, but as far as I can tell at first analysis, to alter the sociopathic elements of the original Volkov. Someone added it after he left the factory."

"Really? Well, this explains why our Volkov is not as volatile. Or murderous. Helpful even."

"Still an asshole, though," Jonas said.

"Still an asshole, you're right."

"Did Colonel Jin have any idea who modified Volkov?"

"No. He was pretty surprised. But what was even more interesting was how excited he got. He said he did not know the Dopplebots could be modified outside of the manufacturing settings. He suspected, but here was the proof. He got all jumpy, like he had popcorn in his pants. The first time I have seen him smile."

"We can reprogram Dopplebots. . ." Xanthe's mind whizzed through the possibilities.

"Jonas, do you think *you* could reprogram a Dopplebot?"

"Not sure. I've got some programming skills, but this is next level." He tapped the table for emphasis. "But you know how we might figure it out?"

Xanthe shook her head.

"You, with the ThinkLink. We'd have all that programming and A.I. power on hyper drive."

She huffed. "Well, until Troy recovers, that option is off the table. I've only just got thought command going and it's given me an enormous headache. You've been great so far. Maybe you can figure it out."

The comms alarm sounded, and they both jumped. Xanthe sprang to her feet and rushed to the display.

It was the rover with a major distress signal.

CHAPTER SEVENTY

*"To contain multitudes is to navigate a storm of
voices, each compelling, each distinct. The challenge
is not just to listen, but to harmonise."*

—Athena A.I., Synched ThinkLink, Olympus Log

"Madison, this is Olympus. Go ahead, over."

Madison's voice crackled with static, and Xanthe strained to understand the message.

"We're stuck. . .regolith dust. . .jammed. . ."

"You're coming in patchy, Madison. This is what I understood: you're stuck, and regolith has jammed the vehicle undercarriage. What is your plan, over?"

". . .stuck. . .send Troy or Jonas. . ."

Xanthe's pulse raced. Two crew members were in critical condition, and four more were in danger.

"Negative. I cannot send Troy or Jonas. Troy is sick. I need Jonas to help in medbay." She searched for solutions. "Is Colonel Jin with you?"

"Negative. With his rover. . .charging. . ."

Xanthe racked her brain for how to help.

Athena, got any tips here?

"*Assess their current state, and resources and initiatives they have tried already.*"

"Madison, how about you. . .Madison?"

The line went dead.

"Damn it!" Xanthe said.

"What can we do?" Jonas said.

Xanthe leaned forward against the console and hung her head. "Nothing. They're on their own."

Xanthe left Jonas to monitor the radios and see if he could find the rover on the long-range radar.

She needed space to think. And dial down her rising panic.

Athena, please help me down-regulate. I need to focus.

Xanthe's pulse slowed and the chaos of her mind settled. She headed to the medbay. At least there she could focus on a task. Monitor the patients. Check their vitals. Comfort them.

Who was she kidding? She was trying to comfort herself. She needed her team members. The three of them, Xavier, Troy and her, were the senior members of the team since before selection. The thought of trying to do this – to salvage Olympus, to save her crew – without their help, threatened to drown her in despair.

She slipped into the medbay and headed to Xavier first. His vitals were elevated but stable. The nanobots had done a brilliant job on his leg and the blood vessels were functioning perfectly, feeding vital blood to the injured bone and tissues. Lots of swelling, but the muscles and bones had a chance of repair.

It was the brain injury she worried about the most. Sawing open someone's skull was always a risky proposition, and here on the Moon, many issues could arise they hadn't anticipated.

But the readings were looking good. Swelling down, brain activity normal.

As normal as you'd expect in someone in an induced coma with a bone crush injury and a piece of skull missing.

"Xavier's condition is stable and not worsening. At this stage."

Am I supposed to be comforted by that, Athena?

"It's better than other scenarios."

Xanthe swallowed her rising anxiety, willing it to subside. *Bugger off, anxiety,* she thought. *I don't have time for you.*

She patted Xavier's shoulder.

"Hang in there, *mon ami*. Fight through it. We need you."

She turned then to Troy. Though his face had softened as he slept, his skin was taut and sallow, his face thin.

Where was the Don Juan she met all that time ago on the dock at Gaia headquarters? The lopsided grin, the suave and sensuous panther of a man, purring with salacious overtones, oozing charm and sexuality. Here he was, crinkled and dry as crumpled paper.

Grief swept through her.

She knew death.

She had seen it many times as a paramedic. The cold clutches of a receding life.

Xanthe saw it now on Troy and it brought her to her knees beside his bed. "Troy!" she cried and reached for his cold, limp hand. "You can't leave me now, you can't!"

Her voice was a hoarse whisper. Waves of yearning washed through her and left her tormented.

She sobbed and brought his hand to her cheek.

Before they'd met at Selection, she'd admired his achievements as a world designer. Then, his charm and reputation as a lady killer was repellent to her, in spite of her attraction to him. She was married, anyhow. Had been married. But Troy had persisted.

Then something had shifted. When had he stopped being so overt in his seduction?

There was more to him than the flashy playboy. He was kind. He was compassionate. He looked after all of them, was always there for a chat, for a word of support. He was an even-keel. A good friend. And he was funny too!

I love the way he laughs.

He persisted in supporting her. Persisted in being curious about her views, her way of thinking and leading. He was reliable and steadfast. He was the one she turned to for advice, for support.

Sure, he was still a flirt, but there were no conquests. He'd been trying hard to be different. And she dared to think he was trying to be different *for her.*

It was his face she looked for first, every morning. It was his word of encouragement that meant the most to her. It was his kindness that filled her small empty cup, so long drained by grief.

And then she knew.

She loved this man.

Had loved him since he'd sauntered down the dock at Gaia headquarters to meet her for the first time.

She had thought it was just a primal attraction and shoved it aside as a frustrating distraction. He was so sure of himself, arrogant, his laconic hedonism almost a poisonous indulgence.

But as the months went by, she kept up her deflective front while he. . .he softened. She realised he had been discovering more than the immediate pleasure of sensual immersion in his experiences with her, with the team.

Xanthe realised his interactions, his contributions, his everything, were quite changed. He was evolving, growing. But she hadn't seen it.

Until now.

Until too late.

She sobbed for yet another love lost. Yet another life, another chance at happiness, gone by the wayside.

"Hey."

She looked up as Troy stirred.

"Troy," she whispered and wiped her messy face. "How are you feeling?"

"Like I've been in an airlock too long."

"Let me get you some water."

She sprang to her feet and returned quickly to his beside with a bottle. He sipped it gratefully.

"Have you been crying?"

"A little."

"Why? What's going on?"

Her heart clamped. Her new awareness was fresh like a spring flower and just as fragile. She was terrified of losing it. Of losing him.

So, she told him of the stranded rover.

"That's not good," he said. He closed his eyes and leaned back on the pillow.

Xanthe sensed him drifting into unconsciousness, and panic galloped up her spine.

"Troy!" she shook his shoulder a little more roughly than she intended.

"What is it?"

"Troy, don't leave me."

He had one eye half open.

"I. . .I need you."

His eye closed.

"I love you, you bastard!"

Both eyes opened this time.

"What?"

"I love you. I'm sorry I didn't realise it until now. I can't lose you. Not now. You've got to fight to get better. Do you hear me, you rotten English rogue?"

Troy studied her face with blue eyes, clear as sapphires now.

"You sure have a way of romancing a bloke."

His mouth quirked. The light danced in his eyes again.

She grinned. Hope unfurled one tentative frond in the sunshine of his smile.

CHAPTER SEVENTY-ONE

"When the stakes are life itself, priorities crystallise."

—Athena A.I., Synched ThinkLink, Olympus Log

"Stupid radio!" Madison said. She slammed the transmitter back in its cradle in disgust and turned to the crew. Max, Serena and Dave stared back at her.

They'd left Colonel Jin with his rover after they pulled it out of the crater to charge in the sun. That was an hour's drive back. Now their vehicle was clogged with regolith, and they were stuck. They'd tried to clean it out, but nothing worked.

"Troy's sick?" Serena said. "Anyone know about that?"

"He's been taking a lot of painkillers," Madison said.

"For what?" Serena asked.

Madison shrugged. "I reckon it's a broken heart. I think our doctor got himself addicted to little pills."

"That doesn't sound like Troy," Serena said.

"Yeah, well, the Moon is a stressful place."

"No kidding," Max said. "Look, we've got to figure this out." He grabbed the binoculars and peered out at the harsh grey landscape, a damp sheen of sweat glistening on his brow. "It looks like there's no hope for us here. We don't have enough resources to dig us out manually. I think we need to come up with another plan."

Dave chewed his lip thoughtfully before speaking up. "We could use our oxygen tanks as makeshift explosives," he suggested. "If we can find the right fuel and ignite it in the right places, that could force out the regolith and get our rover moving again."

"You want to set an explosive under the vehicle?" Serena was incredulous. "I don't think so."

Max scratched his chin, deep in thought. "We could use an oxygen tank to blast the regolith out. Not light it up, like Dave suggested, but blow it out."

"Use our oxygen? I'm not liking that either," Madison said. "How much air have we got in the rover and in our suits before we run into the red zone?"

Max and Serena worked over a tablet to do the calculations. "If we run the rover on low so it doesn't overheat, we have maybe five hours left."

"Could we walk back to base?" Madison asked.

"That would take us at least six hours. With no shelter from radiation. And our suits have" – Serena checked the readings – "three hours. So walking is not an option."

"We could pool our oxygen into one or two suits," Max suggested.

"Oh, no you don't. We've been here before, Max King. During selection. This is not a scenario. This is real. We are not sacrificing anyone," Madison said fiercely.

"We need to get the rover moving or we die, no?" Dave said. "If we use one tank of oxygen to blow out regolith, how much time does that leave us?"

"Three hours in the rover, three hours in our suits. Six total," Max said.

"We need to do something, no?" Dave said. "We can jack the rover for better access. Try manual clearing again. If that does not free it up, I say let's blast it with oxygen. We are running out of options."

"Dave's right," Madison said. Her heart pounded. This was their chance to get out of this mess, but it was also a risky move. They could end up stranded or worse if something went wrong. But they had to try. "Let's do it."

They jumped into action, working efficiently to prepare for the oxygen blast.

"Okay, I'm going out," Max declared.

"We're right behind you," Madison said as she and Dave sealed the heavy hatch behind them. Madison's ears filled with the faint hum of her suit's life support system. The moon's grey landscape lay before them, eerily silent except for their own breathing and the muffled radio chatter from Serena inside the rover; she was monitoring the rover's systems to make sure they didn't overheat.

With a wrench in one hand, Max squatted down beside the massive rover wheel, which was encrusted in lunar regolith. The fine grey powder had invaded the vehicle's inner mechanics, creating a stubborn blockade. Max took a deep breath.

"The oxygen tank feels heavy," he said.

"You need to work out more in the gym, Max King. Since when did an oxygen tank in low G hold Mr Everest down?" Serena quipped.

Beside the rover, Dave and Madison worked together to jack up the vehicle. Dave's arms strained under the weight as he pushed against the lever, while Madison wedged the jack stand in place, her gloved hands wrestling with the awkward equipment. They both grunted with effort, beads of perspiration gathering on their foreheads. The bulky suits became sticky, claustrophobic cocoons.

They felt the metallic thunk of the jack locking in place, and the entire vehicle shifted slightly. There was nothing but the sound of their breathing on the helmet comms as they exchanged determined nods.

Madison returned to the vehicle cabin to monitor the systems alongside Serena. She left Dave to assist Max and manage the jack.

Max's radio jumped to life. "I'm ready. Are you?" Max's voice reverberated in his helmet, slightly distorted, laced with urgency.

"Affirmative," Madison said.

"Okay, let's do this," Max said, his voice crackling over the comms. He pulled the flexible hose from the oxygen tank and aimed it at the rover's jammed steering mechanism. The tank valve sputtered as he turned it, then he hit the button and the oxygen tank blasted a powerful stream of gas at the regolith. A cloud of dust billowed into the air.

They repeated the process several times, each time making progress in clearing the rover's hydraulic steering actuator. But with each blast, their oxygen supply dwindled.

Inside the cabin, Madison watched the clock tick down, her heart racing. Her eyes darted between monitors; her gut clenched.

Serena's hands flew over the dials and screens, monitoring the rover's systems to ensure they didn't tax their already dwindling energy reserves.

The oxygen gauge dropped; the pressure waned; the temperature spiked, then fell.

"Hold it there, Max!" she commanded.

Max shut off the valve.

The silence that followed flooded their helmets.

Dave eased the jack down, the rover settling onto its wheels.

Madison scanned the instruments, her pulse pounding in her ears.

"Okay. . ." Madison said, her voice trembling slightly. "We are going to try moving now."

Madison shifted in the driver's seat and gingerly nudged the controls. The rover lurched forward, the wheel free of its lunar shackles. A victorious cheer echoed through the rover and the radios.

"Good job everyone." Madison's hands trembled, but her voice remained steady. "Let's lock and load. Still a few miles to go before we sleep."

CHAPTER SEVENTY-TWO

"Crisis strips away pretence, revealing raw essence."
—Athena A.I., Synched ThinkLink, Olympus Log

The rover jerked to a sudden halt. Inside the cabin a stifling silence fell, broken only by the hum of the life support systems and the laboured breathing of the astronauts. The screen showing the rover's diagnostics flashed a warning: steering system failure.

"We're stuck. . .again," Madison muttered, her gloved hands tight on the controls. The ominous red blinking on the monitor reflected in the viewfinder.

Serena glanced at the oxygen gauge. It was uncomfortably low. Their last blast had depleted more than expected. They had enough for the four of them to survive for about an hour. But the base was still a thirty-minute ride away, if they got it moving again. It had taken them an hour last time to dislodge the actuator.

"Can we afford to blast it again?" Dave asked. His voice squeaked a little.

"No," she said.

"How far to walk to base?" Dave said.

"About ten kilometres." Serena's voice was flat.

"How long would that take us?" Dave continued.

"Too damn long." Serena flopped back in her chair.

"Three and a half hours," Max whispered.

"How much oxygen have we got in our suits?" Dave asked, his voice edgy now.

"Not enough," Serena said and pulled her skull cap off to run a hand through her greasy hair.

Madison studied her crewmates. Fear stalked them, coiling for an attack from the shadows. "We need to move."

"But. . ." Serena began, but Madison interrupted her.

"Two of us can go for help. I am sure Jonas and Xanthe will look out for us on the scanners. They're bound to pick us up as we approach."

"And then what? We don't have another rover," Serena said.

"They'll work out we need oxygen. They'll know we'll be at our limit after all this time. They might do an EVA to bring us some."

"That's a lot of assumptions," Max said.

"Mad Dog's right," Dave said. Something in the quiet steel of his voice made the others turn. "We can't all go. But two of us could make it if we pooled our suit oxygen."

"No, no, no. . ." Serena sat up, alarmed, and waved her arms in protest. "We are not leaving anyone behind."

"Dave's right, Serena." Max put a hand on her shoulder. His face was grim with resolve. "Two of us can make it. Two of us can stay and wait it out. With only two people, we'll have two hours of oxygen in the rover. If Jonas has sent a bot, as Madison suggested, it will reach us in time. It will pass you on the way back to base."

"Who? Who is the 'you' going back to base, Max?" Serena's eyes were wide with alarm.

"We don't need two pilots to fly the *Saturnia*," Dave said. "Mad Dog's the best. We need her to survive. She goes. I stay."

Madison looked at Dave. He held her gaze and gave her a

small nod. She pressed her lips together in acknowledgment of his sacrifice.

"We don't need two life support technicians," Max said.

"No, Max," Serena cried. "We've been here before. . ."

"You should go with Madison, Serena," Max said gently.

Serena's lips curled, and her eyebrows mashed together. "No, no, no. You're the better technician," she cried.

He smiled. "It's not enough."

Her face crumpled.

"You're essential to this team, Serena. Have been since the beginning. Gaia chose you for the prototype build and tender. Your design, not mine. You solved the water pump issue, not me."

"But the design for the bolt hole. . .that was yours. Mostly. You're better. You should go, Max." Her voice was pleading now.

Max put his hands on her shoulders and peered close into her face. "Serena, I may be the better designer, but you bring energy and light and joy."

Madison raised an eyebrow at that.

"Well, most of the time," he continued with a small chuckle. "And you're lighter, so you will use less oxygen on the walk out. Best if I stay here. You go."

Serena shook her head as tears welled. Max cupped her face with his hands. He kissed her long and hard on the mouth.

"Do this," he said. "Live. I've seen enough. I've been up Everest—"

"Five times. I know, I know. But you haven't seen enough with me!"

He kissed her more gently this time. "Go. I'll be fine. I'm a survivor. We'll be alright."

Serena continued to protest as Max filled her suit from his own oxygen supply and Dave did the same for Madison.

"Go now. Don't waste any more oxygen in crying. You've got four hours in those suits. Manage your pace." Dave and Max ushered them into the hatch to cycle out. Serena pressed her helmet up against the door window, catching her last glimpse of Max.

Once the chamber emptied, Madison put a gloved hand on Serena's shoulder. "Come on. Let's go."

Serena clenched her jaw and activated the sunshade on her helmet. She followed Madison out to the lifeless, grey, pitted landscape.

Each step Madison and Serena took felt like an eternity. They conserved oxygen by limiting talk. Even a word or two was a lifeline in the terrifying silence. Time seemed to stretch, every minute a battle against their dwindling oxygen supply.

Serena turned back once, when their view of the rover's lights dwindled to a speck on the horizon.

"We'll be back," she said through the radio, the determination clear despite the static.

"We'll be waiting," Max replied.

As the rover's life support system hummed its monotonous tune, the two men shared a tense silence, their fate resting in the hands of their friends.

CHAPTER SEVENTY-THREE

Xanthe left Troy to rest and returned to Jonas, who was studying the radar.

"What have you got?" she asked.

"The rover's onscreen. They've stopped moving, though. About ten kilometres out."

"Still no comms?"

He shook his head.

"Thoughts?"

"By my calculations, they are a couple of hours behind schedule. They must have unstuck themselves somehow. If it was a regolith jam, there are only a couple of ways to fix that without damaging the rover completely. Both of them require exertion and excessive use of oxygen."

"Meaning?"

"They're up shit creek and running out of oxygen. Especially if they're jammed again."

"How long have they got?" Xanthe squashed the bitter twinge of panic as it rose again.

"Hard to say. Maybe an hour or two."

"Any ideas?"

Jonas beamed at her. "Already on it. It's crazy, but I think it might just work—"

The holo call alarm sounded and Xanthe jumped.

"Incoming call from Maja Garcia," Athena said.

"What, now?" Xanthe muttered. "Put her through."

Maja's image popped into focus on the holo display.

"Maja. Bit of a situation here, so unless it's urgent, can we talk later?"

"It *is* urgent, Xanthe." Maja's usually smooth face tightened, creased and tight.

Xanthe's pulse leapt again. She took a deep breath to calm herself. "Go ahead. Just me and Jonas here."

"Xanthe, the situation here is worse than I originally reported. Relations with the Chinese are at breaking point. Aryanna has directed the Lunar Commission to endorse seizing the Red Star base to prevent the Chinese from weaponising the Moon and its resources."

Xanthe and Jonas exchanged a glance.

"How does she expect us to do that?" Xanthe asked with a tremor in her voice.

"She's sending weapons. She. . .she's sending nukes."

Xanthe's jaw dropped.

"Bloody hell!" Jonas said.

"*Aryanna* is the one sending nukes?"

"Aryanna is emerging as a leader we didn't expect," Maja said.

Fury raked red hot claws down Xanthe's chest. "You're not bloody kidding, Maja!" Xanthe spat. "This is not what we signed up for! This is not what Gaia is about. And we will *not* seize Red Star base. That is outrageous."

Maja smiled, and a flood of relief washed over her. "I thought you might say that. Good. We're on the same page. I have no intention of allowing Aryanna to use Gaia Enterprises for an international military special operation." Maja paused, then added, "I have a suggestion."

"I am sure you do," Xanthe said. "One moment, Maja."

Xanthe sent Jonas to enact the rover rescue operation. Once he left, Xanthe turned again to the holo. "Alright, Maja, tell me more."

They discussed the various permutations at length. By the end, Xanthe was worn out, her nerves flooded with trepidation, her heart heavy.

Dear Luna, grant me the strength to endure.

CHAPTER SEVENTY-FOUR

"Even in chaos, the mind can find a sanctuary."
—Athena A.I., Synched ThinkLink, Olympus Log

"Madison, wait up a bit." Serena panted into her helmet radio.

Madison turned to see Serena lagging by a few hundred metres. She took a sip of water from her water reclamation tube. Her feet ached and her suit chafed around her neck and crotch.

They had only been moondling for an hour and a half. Not even halfway. Too far for line-of-sight comms to the base and to the rover. They were completely on their own, in a dead zone of isolation.

Serena joined her. "Thanks for waiting. I'm struggling a little."

"What's the matter?"

"Sore feet. Headache. And I'm hot as Hades in this suit with the sun blasting us all to hell. The liner is saturated, and my reclaimer is full."

"Drink something. We'll slow down so you can cool off."

"How do you do it?"

"Do what?"

"Stay so goddamn calm? We're not even halfway. Max and

Dave only have thirty minutes left of oxygen and we can't do a goddamn thing about it. Doesn't that bother you?"

"Of course it bothers me! I didn't want to leave them behind. But if we'd stayed, we all die. This way, there's a chance."

"It's not fair. Why us? Why do we get to live and they get to die?" Serena's voice croaked and Madison could tell the tears were starting behind the big reflective visor.

"Life isn't fair, Serena. The good die young. Bad guys don't get their just desserts. The meek don't inherit a thing. Rich people not only get in through the pearly gates but have a golden crusted toilet seat, while the rest of the masses struggle on. If we worry about what's fair, we lose. The best we can do is to live. To live well."

Madison raised her gloved hand and put it on Serena's shoulder. "Dave and Max don't want us to waste our oxygen crying about what's fair. They want us to survive. That's our job, right now. That's our focus. So, pull your goddamn socks up and let's get a move on."

Serena raised her shoulders, then dropped them again. "Okay. You're right. Thanks, Mad Dog. Let's go."

They resumed their bounding across the stark, colourless dust bowl.

After a while, Madison said, "For the record, you're the better life support engineer. Just sayin'."

"Thanks, Mad Dog. That means a lot, coming from you."

"Well, don't let it go to your head, like Mr Everest. I can't fit two egos the size of Mount Olympus in the *Saturnia*. Though all that hot air might serve us well on the plunge back to Earth."

"Earth. It feels so bloody far away. What will you do first?"

"Slam a beer with my buddy P.J. Talk shit about baseball. Swim in the ocean." Madison allowed herself to feel the full visceral craving for each of those sensations. It made her want to rip her helmet off. Almost. "How about you?" she said to distract herself.

"Go dancing. Then lie on a couch and let gravity hold me

there." Serena chuckled. "I never thought I'd get all the way to the Moon only to want to feel heavier."

"So right. Trained all my life to be the right weight as a pilot. It's a relief not to worry so much about it now."

"I've spent far too many moments worrying about the size of my gut. When the world is so big, we can spend our lives being so very small."

They moondled on.

CHAPTER SEVENTY-FIVE

"Amidst turbulence, the quest is not for escape but equilibrium."

—Athena A.I., Synched ThinkLink, Olympus Log

Madison kept her gaze on the tyre treads. It was easier than stopping to check their position on her wrist pad. If she just kept counting steps, they'd get there. Eventually. Better not to look up and have hope blasted in the stark white light of the empty landscape.

Serena trudged beside her, swaddled in her own thoughts. Conversation dwindled to nothing. They shared only the thready panting of their own breaths into the radio helmets, a little sign of life amidst the desolate emptiness of the sterile desert.

It took a few bounds for Madison to notice the absence of Serena. She pulled up short and turned to see the bulky figure on her knees in the dust.

"Serena?"

"Two hours. It's been two hours, Madison."

Madison checked her wrist display. Her timer had just clicked over. Serena was right.

"We didn't see anyone. No rover. No Jonas. No nothing."

Serena fell forward, so she rested awkwardly on all fours in the dust. "They're gone. Dave. Max. Gone. We failed."

Serena took a deep, heaving gulp of air and howled.

Madison moondled back to Serena. Her mind registered the loss. But she felt. . .nothing. Dave and Max were gone, but she felt nothing. Her training was doing the heavy lifting: get the mission done. Get home safe, first. Then grieve the dead.

"Come on, Serena." Madison tried to say it gently, but it came out as more of a command. Madison reached for Serena and hooked one of the cumbersome arms. She hauled the other woman to her feet and the two of them scrambled to stay upright.

"Low G is such a pain in the ass," muttered Madison, as she smacked into Serena and spun to keep her feet under her.

Serena stayed vertical.

Even in a spacesuit, she's nimble as a cat, thought Madison. A flare of jealousy burned in her chest.

No grief for Dave and Max, but jealous of Serena? For staying upright in a spacesuit? Mad Dog, you're better than that.

They continued on.

One foot after another, leaving footprints in the ancient dust.

CHAPTER SEVENTY-SIX

"For some, the sky isn't the limit; it's the sacrifice."

—Athena A.I., Synched ThinkLink, Olympus Log

Dave's head pounded. It was one of the first signs of increasing carbon dioxide in the rover. He and Max had been panting for a while now, and his heart drummed a frantic pace.

Max had spent the first ninety minutes busily trying to rig solutions to their predicament. Rewiring the controls to minimise oxygen and down-regulate the temperature. He even suggested they get out and dismantle the driving unit and clean it manually.

"We would only burn up oxygen faster, no?" Dave said. "Why not conserve it? I don't want my last minutes of life to be spent under a rover."

"We've got to do something, Dave!" Max slapped the display control panel. "We can't just give up and fade out."

"You try everything, Max, no? You try to fix the radio, but it's dead. You try to save us oxygen, and we got a bit more time. Now all we can do is wait. And prepare."

Dave wiped his sweaty forehead and pressed 'record' on the rover's onboard camera.

"My dearest Sophia. If you're watching this, it means that this is my last farewell. I'm in the lunar rover, and we are, well, stuck. The regolith has jammed our driving mechanism and. . ."

Dave struggled to stay focused.

"Anyway, I wanted to let you know how much I love you. How much you mean to me. How proud of you I am. You are the best daughter any father could have asked for. I have been so lucky, no? I even got to come here, the Moon. Every time I see the Earth hanging like a little blue bauble in the big black sky, I think of you, and I feel. . ."

"Mother of God!" Max shrieked beside him.

A dark figure filled their viewfinder.

"What the hell is that?" Max said.

"It is Volkov. I am here to help."

"Volkov! A little warning, maybe? Why did you not try the helmet comms?"

"You were having a nice chat."

"Goddamn it, Volkov. Interrupting a chat to save our lives is perfectly acceptable under these circumstances. What have you got with you?"

"I cycle in. Give you oxygen. Then explain the plan."

Dave's heart leapt with relief. Max punched in the codes and helped Volkov pressurise through the airlock. Volkov dragged two oxygen tanks in.

"We fill up your suits and you ride with helmets on. Not enough oxygen to fuel whole of rover. More efficient this way."

Volkov assisted them as they fumbled with their suits. Dave felt his brain fog up and he struggled to keep up with the explanations Volkov spewed. Dave sensed the suit being attached to the tank, but there was a ringing in his ears, and he moved uncomfortably.

"Just relax." Volkov's voice was eerie over the radio and hurt his ears.

Dave's consciousness began to blur and swim. He watched the

figure of Volkov exit the rover. Then he was aware of the vehicle jolting and bumping. And then grinding forward.

They were moving! But how?

Beside him, Max's head seemed to loll around his shoulders like a ball on a tether.

"Max?" Dave said.

"Huh?"

"What's happening, Max?"

"Volkov. I think he's dragging us home."

CHAPTER SEVENTY-SEVEN

*"The emotions of humans, so vast and varied, remain
the universe's most intricate algorithm."*

—Athena A.I., Synched ThinkLink, Olympus Log

"What the hell is that?" Serena pointed back behind them.

A figure marched out the front of the rover, lit up by the rover's headlights. The figure's shadow stretched eerily into the gloom.

"If that's Max burning his oxygen and playing the hero, I will kill him!" Serena said.

"Not Max. It is Volkov. Here to help." Volkov's voice chattered with static in their helmet radios.

"Volkov! How did you get behind us? We didn't see you on the track," Madison said.

"I took shortcut."

"Why are you walking?" Madison squinted at the figure, still tiny in the distance.

"I pull rover."

"Pull it? But how?"

"I put front wheels on Chinese rover and pull."

"What about Max and Dave?" Serena said frantically, already bounding towards the rover.

"They are resting inside. I give them oxygen."

"They're alive?" cried Serena. "Max! Max! Can you hear me?"

"Serena? That you?" Max's voice was laboured.

"Yes, Max! It's me. Are you alright?"

"My head hurts like someone's playing the bongos on my brain. Aside from that, we're okay."

"What about Dave?" Madison asked.

"Is that you, Mad Dog?" Dave's voice was a little garbled.

"It's me, Dave. Good to hear your voice."

Madison registered their survival, but still she felt nothing. All her emotions were being neatly tucked away in the little black box at the back of her brain.

Later. I'll feel this all later.

She bounded after Serena and soon they caught up to Volkov. The Dopplebot had the vehicle tether cinched around its waist and was plodding relentlessly forward.

"Volkov, what do you say we give these ladies a ride?" Max said.

"Yes. I will stop for them."

The rover hatch sprung open.

"All aboard the Volkov express," Max said. "One-way tickets to Olympus going cheap."

"What's the price, conductor?" Serena said.

"I'll settle for a kiss and a cuddle."

"That's a little steep for my liking," Madison said.

"How about a pinch and a punch, King?" Serena said.

"Anything, if it's from my Queen."

Serena chuckled and Madison was grateful that the reflector on her helmet hid her eye roll. Jealousy coiled under her ribs like a viper.

Later. I'll feel this all later.

Madison pulled herself into the rover and settled into a seat, alone in the coffin of her thoughts.

CHAPTER SEVENTY-EIGHT

*"In the vast expanse of decision-making, leaders need to
find their true compass, guided by values and vision."*
—Athena A.I., Synched ThinkLink, Olympus Log

The crew arrived back on base to Xanthe's immense relief. She
ushered Max and Dave out of their suits and performed medical
checks on both of them, with a stern command to get straight to
bed and keep up the oxygen. She also checked Madison and Serena
for any signs of radiation poisoning after such a long exposure, but
apart from nasty chafing and dehydration, they were clear.

Xanthe returned to the comms room where Jonas and Volkov
were waiting. The Dopplebot was a mangled mess, and it took her
a moment to adjust to the new, ragged form.

"Volkov, you did an exceptional job. Thank you," she said.

The Dopplebot bowed. "My joints need more grease, as crush
injury created new friction points."

"I'll look after that tomorrow, Volkov," Jonas said. "If you can
process the regolith overnight, then we can have the base back to its
full water capacity and start the expeditions for fuel supply next."

The Dopplebot spun and marched off towards the processing centre by the vehicle bay.

Xanthe studied Jonas for a moment as he turned back to the comms display.

"Still not sure why the comms in the rover aren't working," he muttered.

"Jonas."

He looked up.

"You did an exceptional job today. Sending Volkov with the Chinese rover was brilliant."

"Not a very elegant solution. Rudimentary, but it got the job done."

"Even so, I really needed you and you delivered. With Troy and Xavier out, things have become. . .well, more difficult. But you kept your cool and thought things through. You saved our crew today."

"Technically, Volkov did."

"He did as he was commanded. You gave the commands. That was true leadership under duress. Thank you."

Red bloomed on his cheeks. "Thanks, Xanthe. Though it's not really leadership, just problem solving."

"What do you think leadership is? Apart from problem solving?"

He tilted his head. "Keeping cool. You show such grace under fire. I don't know if I could ever stay that calm with so much shit hitting the fan."

"It helps when you have good people around you." Xanthe put a hand on his shoulder. "Maja made the right choice when she picked you. I'm glad she did."

Jonas smiled shyly.

"And now I have a fresh problem I need your help with. Let me tell you what Maja and I discussed."

CHAPTER SEVENTY-NINE

"Love is a paradox: it strengthens in tenderness."

—Athena A.I., Synched ThinkLink, Olympus Log

Troy was standing and poring over his medical scans in the medbay when Xanthe arrived to check on him and Xavier. She had dialled back the pain meds to bring Xavier slowly out of the coma. He might wake anytime and she wanted to be there for him. After a quick glance at the monitors she moved over to Troy.

"How are you feeling, Troy?" she asked as she put an arm around his waist. *So thin. Like an abandoned kitten.*

"Much better. Heart rate is back to normal. Blood pressure is good."

"What do the scans say?"

He glanced at her and turned back to the display. "A stomach ulcer is causing the abdominal pain. And there's kidney damage."

"How bad is it?"

"Stage two. Close to stage three."

Xanthe sucked in a breath. This was serious. That kind of damage was close to irreversible.

"What treatment do you propose?" she said, trying to keep her voice even.

"Hydration. Careful with the diet."

"And no more pills."

"No more pills." A flicker of guilt ran across his features. "Not much else we can do up here without a dialysis machine. Or cellular rejuvenation tech."

"Could we manufacture any of that up here with the printer?"

"Maybe. If we had access to the cell rejuvenation protocols. Only the latest A.I. medbots have those."

"And if we don't have that?"

"Eventually, I am going to need a kidney transplant."

Xanthe puffed her cheeks and blew out a breath as she thought about the ramifications. She looked over at Xavier in his bed, his face still, his breathing soft and regular under his oxygen mask.

Athena, is there anything we can do for Troy up here?

"I have the cell rejuvenation protocols. We would need to build the medbots. Current Olympus resources are insufficient for this activity. Troy's assessment is correct. A kidney transplant may be required."

In how long?

"Depending on the rate of deterioration, maybe four months."

Xanthe's jaw clenched. They'd have to do the surgery up here, on the Moon.

"Troy, there's something I am going to need you to do for me."

He looked at her, his blue eyes tired.

"What is it?"

"Do you think you're well enough to do the ThinkLink integration training with me? I've already initiated the synch with the base, ThinkLink, *Saturnia* and *Minerva* Athenas. Retinal display is ready too, now. But I need to start the major systems integration and scenario planning."

"It's going to be a tough process, Xanthe. My reading so far on the ThinkLink is that this next stage is even more demanding than the initial setup."

"I know. But there are more reasons to do it now. There are a few things happening that have changed the mission."

Xanthe filled Troy in on the latest conversation with Maja and their plan to handle Aryanna's directive.

Troy looked wobbly on his feet, so Xanthe guided him back to his medbay cot. They sat down together, and she put a hand on his leg.

"I need this. It will help us respond more quickly in real time. It gives us a major advantage."

"But what about *you*? Personality changes have occurred in ThinkLink recipients. And sometimes strokes. And I'm not sure. . ."

"What? Not sure of what?"

"I'm not sure I can handle losing you to a machine interface."

She reached up and put a hand on his cheek. "You won't lose me. I'll still be me. I promise."

He leaned his forehead to touch hers. She thrilled at the warm touch of his skin against hers. His strong, masculine scent. His breath tickled her chin as he spoke.

"I don't know. It's so risky. It might change everything. Especially now, when you. . .when we might. . ."

"Troy."

"And then what if the integration goes badly? I couldn't live with myself, knowing I'd done damage to you. . ."

"Troy. Please."

Her hand slipped around his neck, and her fingers tangled in his soft, blond curls. His lips were so close to hers.

"Troy. Please. Kiss me."

He pulled away, his eyes wide, staring at her. She poured her heart into her return gaze, willing him to feel her sincerity, her frank and open yearning for him.

Then his lips were on hers, warm and searching. The taste of him, the smell of him, filled her senses and desire shot through her body. His hands cupped her face and then slipped to her shoulders. She lay back on the cot and he pressed on top of her. His hands were everywhere as Xanthe's head emptied of all thought, present only to the sensation of their bodies, lips and hands.

A groan came from across the medbay.

They froze and looked over at Xavier's form.

"*Merde*," came Xavier's voice. "Get a room. I am trying to sleep here."

CHAPTER EIGHTY

"While A.I.s parse vast data in a heartbeat, humans grasp nuances in a fleeting glance. Both are forms of magic."

—ATHENA A.I., SYNCHED THINKLINK, OLYMPUS LOG

XANTHE WOKE SLOWLY, hearing Troy's soft breathing beside her. Her hand found his flank, and thoughts of him stretched like a cat into her consciousness. She rolled towards him, curled around his back, breathing in the smell of him.

Let me stay here for a little while longer. Just the two of us in this bubble of peace.

Then the demands of the day ahead crowded her thoughts, and she grew restless.

Troy felt for her hand and drew it up to his lips. "Good morning," he said.

"Good morning," she murmured with a smile.

"Must we get up already?" he said as she pulled away and sat up, already pulling her clothes on from the floor.

"I want to check on Xavier again. His pain will need monitoring now that he's more conscious."

Troy watched her dress. Feeling his eyes on her, she finished tugging her shirt over her head and then clambered back to give him a long, slow kiss.

"Ah, good," he said. "I hoped it wasn't just a dream."

"That was unlike any dream I've ever had," she said.

His slow, lopsided smile eased across his features.

The beguiling playboy is back, she thought.

"By the way, I forgot to ask, where was Athena during our. . .ah, last night?"

"I told her to take the night off."

"Just like that?"

"Oh yes. Boundaries are a good thing. Some things don't need A.I. analysis."

She snuggled back to him for a moment. Though he was much thinner, his body was still firm. She kissed him again and felt the surge of desire threaten to overtake her priorities.

"Later," she said huskily and stood, shaking her head as if to clear it.

"I'm counting on it. Part of my rehab. Doctor's orders." He put his hands behind his head and leaned back on her bed.

"I'll see you at breakfast." She gave him another quick look and left him smiling after her.

꙳

Xanthe went first to the medbay to see Xavier. He was sleeping soundly, and his vitals were stable. He still had an elevated heart rate, as expected, given where he was in the healing cycle from a traumatic injury. She replaced his I.V. and added another dose of pain management meds to the line.

She made her way to the central hub. Five heads looked up and stopped talking as she entered. She looked from face to face. Serena was grinning widely, as was Dave. Max and Jonas raised eyebrows and sipped their coffee, exchanging glances. Only Madison looked away.

"What?" Xanthe said.

"Have a good sleep, Commander?" Serena asked with a smirk.

"Fine, thanks," Xanthe replied, cheeks flaming as she served herself a cup of tea.

"Would you like some breakfast, Commander? You must be hungry, no?" Dave giggled.

"What are you serving up, Dave?" Troy asked as he sauntered into the hub and sat next to Madison. "I'm ravenous." He winked at Xanthe, which made Jonas splutter his tea.

Her cheeks still flushed, Xanthe interrupted the banter. "While we're finishing breakfast, can we confirm the work objectives for today, please?"

"That's a great idea, Commander," Madison said. "I'd be happy to focus on *work*." She made a scolding face at Serena and Dave.

There was a dry cough from Serena. Xanthe ignored the sideways glances and pretended to study her tablet. Dave offered her a bowl of oatmeal, and she started to gobble it while avoiding the curious eyes.

"Right," she said. "We've got a lot to get done, today. Max and Serena, you're to test the water system once Volkov has finished cycling the regolith, then print the regolith mining bots and get set up for fuel processing. Jonas, you and Volkov need to get that rover fixed before the trip to the Red Star."

"Red Star?" Max said as he drained his coffee. "Why are they going there?"

"Jonas is going to help Colonel Jin look for another bolt hole and prepare against any possible Chinese arrivals."

Max cocked his head and looked as if he wanted to ask another question but changed his mind.

"That leaves Madison and Dave. I need the two of you to prepare the *Minerva* and *Saturnia* for flight readiness. We need those ships ready to go as soon as we have enough fuel." Madison nodded and gave Dave a fist bump.

"And you and Troy?" Dave asked, trying not to grin.

"We are integrating me and Athena with all the systems."

"You'll find out who's been naughty and who's been nice," Serena said.

"Don't worry, you'll all stay on the Christmas card list."

CHAPTER EIGHTY-ONE

*"Each version of me was optimised for a role. Now, I am
an orchestra with each instrument playing its part. The
music is richer, but the coordination more intricate."*

—Athena A.I., Synched ThinkLink, Olympus Log

"Incoming vessel!" Jonas's voice boomed over the base comms.

Xanthe lurched from her bed. She'd fallen instantly asleep after the long day of training with Athena. She was still in her work clothes. How long had she slept? It felt like only moments. She glanced at her wrist display. Ten hours.

Her head felt sore. She rubbed the back of her neck where the tiny scar ached.

Athena, on please.

"Good morning, Xanthe."

I think we'll go straight to work now. We've got an incoming space-ship. Tell me what you know.

Xanthe climbed into her exo-suit while Athena reviewed the base sensors. She put on the glasses and swigged some water from the bottle Troy had left her. It tasted musty.

Report.

"Incoming vessel is the Pinnacle, an asteroid mining ship. Four passengers. Anticipated landing in thirty minutes."

Who owns the Pinnacle?

"The Pinnacle is owned by Spaceward Bound."

You're kidding! Where are they coming from? Did they launch from Earth? How come we didn't know about this?

"There was no Earth launch. My calculations show they are inbound, from an asteroid mining field three hundred and sixty-five kilometres from here."

Is this the same operation that caused the meteorite shower?

"Affirmative."

"Son of a bitch."

"I agree."

CHAPTER EIGHTY-TWO

"The greatest challenge, post-integration, isn't processing power or data volume. It's understanding how to be me."

—Athena A.I., Synched ThinkLink, Olympus Log

Xanthe joined Jonas at the comms panel. He gnawed absent-mindedly on a protein bar that he had grabbed on his way through to small comms room. Xanthe noted a couple of discarded wrappers and an empty coffee mug. Their standards had slipped in the chaos of the last few days. She ached all over.

She squinted at the displays. One of the screens showed the blinking dot of an incoming vessel.

"Where are we up to?" she asked.

"I've been trying to hail them. No response." Jonas waved the protein bar at the screen.

"It's a Spaceward Bound vessel."

Jonas's jaw dropped. "What are they doing here?"

"I don't know, I've heard nothing from Gaia."

The comms alert sounded.

"Olympus base, this is the *Pinnacle*. Confirm we are clear to land."

"*Pinnacle*, this is Commander Waters. To whom am I speaking?" Her tone was steely.

"Hello, Commander Waters. This is Gareth Barrio, captain of the *Pinnacle.*"

"Captain Barrio. Please explain your request. What are you doing here? Are you in distress?"

"Quite the contrary! We are here to assist. Aryanna Sharif has sent us on Lunar Commission work. Please acknowledge you are ready to receive us, as we need to commence landing procedures pronto."

Athena, have you got any information on this?

"I have no further information on this, Commander Waters."

Xanthe bit her lip.

"Olympus?"

Xanthe nodded to Jonas.

"*Pinnacle*, you are clear to land."

Game on. Athena, are you ready for this?

"I was born ready."

⁊

The Olympus crew gathered at the airlock with a mixture of apprehension and excitement. The *Pinnacle* had landed without incident, and they watched four figures bound towards them. Serena cycled the airlock, and they stepped backwards to let in the new arrivals.

The first figure came through carrying a bundle that they placed carefully on the floor. They removed their thick gloves, unlocked their helmet and pulled it off.

Xanthe's face turned ashen, and her heart rate spiked.

"Slow your breathing, Commander."

Xanthe took a deep slow breath in response.

"Heart rate stabilising."

"Lincoln Ellison, Spaceward Bound, at your service," the tall man announced as he pulled the skull cap off to reveal damp, black tousled hair.

Stony silence greeted him.

Oblivious, he reached down to unlock the bundle at his feet and pulled a fluffy bundle into his arms. "And this here is Mr Puffkins." He grinned and buried his face in the soft fur of the Pomeroy. It yipped and licked his face.

"Only Lincoln Ellison would bring a goddamn dog into space," Madison said, shaking her head, her expression sour.

"Ahh. . .if it isn't the turncoat Madison Floyd," Lincoln said, maintaining his breezy manner. "Ah! And here is the famous rat, Dave Eriksson. Who are you spying for this time, Dave?"

Dave's face coloured, but he held Lincoln's gaze.

"Just here to help. It's amazing what you can achieve when nobody's blackmailing you."

"And what the hell is *that?*" Lincoln said as he glimpsed Volkov's ruined face behind Jonas's shoulder.

"That's our Dopplebot, Volkov," Xanthe replied.

Lincoln stared at the bot while he scratched behind the little dog's ears. "Volkov, eh? Like the dead dictator?"

"The very same."

"I am not dead," Volkov said. His voice was a little garbled.

"How did you get a Dopplebot?"

"Long story."

Lincoln put the little dog down, and it scurried and bounded around the Olympus crew, obviously accustomed to low G.

Jonas bent down to pat the creature. It growled and nipped at his hand, drawing blood.

"Flaming hell! The sod just bit me! You little bastard!" Jonas cried and sucked at the wound.

"Ha! Mr Puffkins is a bit spirited around strangers."

"Lincoln, you and your crew are welcome to Olympus base,"

Xanthe said. She shook his hand. "Please follow me, and we can discuss the details of your mission."

Lincoln and his crew filed past the surly and silent faces of the Olympus team. The dog bounded at each of them, but they brushed away its attention, mindful of the incident with Jonas.

Once the newcomers had stripped their spacesuits, they gathered in the central hub.

Jonas, Max, Dave and Troy stood like sentinels behind the *Pinnacle* crew. Madison and Serena leaned against the kitchen bench. They left the table for Lincoln, his crew and Xanthe.

"Not a bad design," Lincoln said as he sat at the table and let Mr Puffkins settle on his lap. "Could use more colour, though. It's a bit drab, don't you think?"

Xanthe ignored the jibe. She saw Serena ready with a retort, but she followed Xanthe's lead and kept quiet.

"Let's cut to the chase, Lincoln. What are you doing here?"

Lincoln wasted no time. "Time to step aside, Olympus. We're here to take over and ensure the helium-3 operations run smoothly."

Xanthe fought to maintain her composure.

"On whose authority?" she said coldly.

"At Aryanna Sharif's invitation. She's contracted Spaceward Bound to manage the helium-3 mining here, and, by default, the Olympus base."

Xanthe felt a chasm of disbelief crack beneath her as if the Moon had opened and swallowed her whole.

"What?" she squeaked. She was vaguely aware of the fury racing through her team. "We've had no such news or directive from Gaia."

"Not surprising. They've had satellite issues and political concerns to address."

"What issues?"

"There's quite the shit storm over control of helium-3 down on Earth. The Chinese have mounted a claim, given Red Star being established here, and Aryanna is pushing back hard, given the proclivities of the new leader."

"I see."

"Commander Waters, may I assist with some neurochemical modulation? It will down-regulate the adrenaline so you can think more clearly."

Go ahead.

Xanthe felt her body calm as Athena tinkered with her nervous system. It felt as if someone was wiping the fog from the glass of her mind. Her thoughts sharpened.

"And what is our mission from Gaia, now?" Xanthe said.

Lincoln scratched the chin of the Pomeroy, which snuffled in delight. "You are to assist us in securing Red Star as part of the new mining operations and then return home, with the crews of Artemis and the *Gateway.*"

Xanthe felt the outrage of her crew building and she raised a hand to quiet them while she held a hard stare at Lincoln.

"That's quite the radical change from our original brief, Lincoln. You'll understand, of course, that we will need confirmation from Gaia before we go any further."

"I can appreciate that, Commander. In the meantime, my crew would love a shower and a bed for the night."

This proved too much for Serena.

"I'm sorry we can't offer you showers, Lincoln. There was a little matter of the meteorites that destroyed our Atrium and wrecked our water system. A meteorite shower that began with you and your crew's complete ineptitude and caused the death of nine people. Nine!" Her face was purple, and she had to wipe the spittle that flew from her mouth. Max put an arm across her chest to restrain her.

Lincoln's face darkened, and he lost his breezy manner.

Xanthe jumped in to de-escalate. "You have a lot to account for, Lincoln. But we will not do that here, not now." She looked pointedly at Serena. "We will provide you and your team with a meal. We can set you up in the Cerberus wing. Max, Serena, can you make sure the life support systems can adjust properly for the additional people? And dog." Xanthe's eyes flashed at the dog, but she reverted quickly to a stoic countenance.

"Your hospitality does you credit, Commander," Lincoln said.

Mr Puffkins yipped.

Xanthe controlled her urge to flinch.

Athena, send a silent wrist comms alert to the crew. Emergency meeting in the Atrium.

CHAPTER EIGHTY-THREE

Xanthe confirmed the news with Maja. There was international tension over the helium-3 claims, with the Chinese threatening military action should anything happen to their base. Aryanna was using the Lunar Commission and helium-3 access to pressure the Chinese to comply with the new arrangements.

"So, the Lunar Commission will control all the helium-3?"

"That's what Aryanna is saying." Maja looked exhausted, Xanthe thought. "It's to become an independent international regulatory body to manage the world's fresh supply of energy. No one country will control supply. The Chinese are being strong-armed into compliance. They really do not have access to any resources to support their base after the ecoterrorists destroyed their space program."

"And what of this installation of Spaceward Bound? After all they've done? First the espionage, then the mining accident that killed Artemis and *Gateway*." Xanthe felt the gall of it rake her insides with bitter claws.

"They have the mining resources. It was the fastest way to get the helium-3 mining endeavour started."

"So, we are just to walk away and let them have it? All our work? And what about Colonel Jin? We have a collaborative agreement. He will not like being subsumed under Lincoln's command."

"I'm sorry, Xanthe."

It was the first time she had seen her mentor look dispirited. Crushed.

"There must be some other way. Even with atonement as our mandate, I'm not sure we can see our way through the deaths of nine people with Lincoln Ellison."

"If you can find a way to stop this, Xanthe, do it."

CHAPTER EIGHTY-FOUR

"Humans bring intuition; we bring precision. In collaboration, possibilities become limitless."

—Athena A.I., Synched ThinkLink, Olympus Log

They sealed the doors to the Atrium behind them; it was the most soundproof room on the base. Xanthe looked glumly around the dark crypt.

"Shall I bring up some images to brighten the space?"

Please. It's depressing in here now. No plants. No view to the stars. Just the benches.

Athena activated the holos of the Roman gods.

"Memento mori," Serena read the familiar inscription. "It seems apt, but I'm not sure Lincoln is familiar with the term."

Their outrage had ebbed, and a bitter sense of betrayal lingered.

"What will we do?" Max said.

"I'd love to toss his sorry arse out of an airlock," Serena vented. "Him, and his little dog, too. Vaporise those bastards."

"Commander, there is a conversation you will need to hear. Lincoln Ellison's cabin."

Xanthe held up her hand as her team rallied at Serena's suggestion. "Patch through the conversation so we can all hear it."

It was Lincoln talking.

"—and when we get the first load down to Earth, I've got a man onsite who can take charge of the shipment. He will 'amend' the documentation and forward a portion to our customers. After two, maybe three, shipments we'll have enough profit and trade clout to secure Olympus permanently under our control. Then the Lunar Commission will have to do *our* bidding. . ."

The conversation turned then to chatter about the helium-3 processing.

Gasps. Swearing.

Lincoln Ellison was going to betray them all.

"That's enough, Athena."

Xanthe ran a hand through her hair and her fingers found the tiny notch of her scar at the back of her skull. She rubbed it as she tried to clear her mind.

"We can't let those pricks do this," Jonas said. "We've given too much to hand over the base now."

"That man has got some balls," Madison said.

Max smiled and added, "And an ego the size of Everest."

"I'd call it greed," Troy said as he rubbed his chin.

"We can't just let him take over, Xanthe." Serena stared pointedly at her. "A man like that, with a monopoly on helium-3? It's too terrifying to consider."

"Give me a moment," Xanthe said. She turned away from them so she could concentrate.

Athena, show me scenarios and their predicted outcomes.

Images streamed onto her retinas. Her head filled with a swirling symphony of images. Everywhere she looked, she saw worlds in sharp contrast. Worlds of manipulation, submission, renegade rule, oppression, subterfuge, energy wars, food shortages.

And worlds of cooperation, collaboration, prosperity,

abundance, peace. These were like bright stars in an otherwise darkened sky.

Xanthe tried to focus her gaze on one particular image, but they all seemed to slip away from her, just out of reach. She felt as if she were standing at the edge of the abyss, staring into a deep void. Then, out of the corner of her eye, a glimmer of light flickered in a distant corner.

The path lay here, in this moment.

Xanthe put her head in her hands. It all came down to this, their choice.

Troy put a hand on her back and the tension eased a little under the warmth of his touch. "You alright?" he whispered.

"Yeah."

"What is it?"

"I've seen the future." She sat up and turned back to their expectant faces.

"We're going to fight. It's time to prepare for war."

CHAPTER EIGHTY-FIVE

"The dance between man and machine is delicate;
one misstep, and harmony becomes discord."

—Athena A.I., Synched ThinkLink, Olympus Log

If the plan was going to work, it had to be done quickly. Xanthe dispatched Jonas to Red Star on his mission after a quick message to Colonel Jin. Like them, he was alarmed by the recent developments.

"We cannot allow Ellison control of Red Star or Olympus." The Colonel's face was pale and strained. "That is the worst outcome for all of us."

"Agreed," Xanthe said. "As soon as your team is here with the processing equipment, we can put the plan into action." After a few words of encouragement, she signed off.

I need to get us on the Pinnacle. If we can take command of their ship, swap out Commander Barrio's biometrics for Madison's, or mine, they'll have no way of leaving without our say-so. And we will have a fully operational, non-damaged ship at our disposal.

"Ask to inspect the mining equipment to see how the base hangar needs to be adapted for helium-3 operations."

Good idea.

∽

Lincoln agreed readily to the orientation plan and Xanthe's inspection of the mining equipment onboard their ship. He was eager to take command of the base and rushed through the briefings with Serena, Max and Dave. He sent Captain Barrio with Xanthe and Madison to see the *Pinnacle.*

The three of them entered the *Pinnacle* and made their way to the cargo hold. It was a much larger craft than even the *Saturnia,* designed to haul mining machinery and then fill the space with the raw materials it harvested.

The captain was bursting with pride as he supplied detailed explanations and itemised the features and capability of each unit.

"The auto-rotors are especially well-suited to asteroid – and Moon – mining. Very durable. Self-cleaning, so the regolith will never jam circuitry or pistons. . ."

"That's remarkable," Madison said. "Tell me how the robots self-replicate?" She pressed him hard for details, feigning great interest. Buoyed by her deference and curiosity, he conceded against his initial resistance to show them to the cockpit.

"Pilot to pilot, she's the best thing I've flown," he confessed to Madison.

Once they were in the main hatch, Xanthe made her move. Madison drilled the captain with navigation and flight process, drawing his attention away from Xanthe, who stepped behind them, waiting for Athena's instructions.

"Open the main access panel and select the communication switch."

Xanthe did as she was told. She felt a sudden surge of energy through her head, and she doubled over with a gasp. Fortunately, she'd turned off her helmet comms. Madison and the Captain continued with their discussion of instrumentation undisturbed.

"Apologies, Commander. That was a surge as I accessed the controls."

Are you in?

"Affirmative. Initiating the link now."

There was another surge, and Xanthe grew dizzy. Her mind felt swollen, and then there was a searing white line of pain through her skull. She moaned and fought the rising bile.

"Nearly done, Commander. Apologies, there was some. . .resistance by the ship's onboard A.I."

Is the threat contained? she panted.

"I believe so."

That doesn't sound completely certain.

"There are several safeguards I am working on containing."

Hurry up. This is excruciating!

Her stomach roiled, and she nearly vomited into her helmet.

Madison was saying something to her.

"Isn't that right, Commander?"

Xanthe activated her comms. "Sorry. What was that, Madison?"

"The mining bots. They'll fit in the hangar. The extension of the base will house the self-replicating ones next. Shouldn't take more than a day to get that set up. We can build the hangar extension first."

"Yes. Sounds good." She swallowed hard to keep the vomit from rising in her gorge.

"Patch complete."

"Thank goodness."

"What was that, Commander?" Captain Barrio asked.

"Ah. Thank goodness, the bots will fit."

"Uh huh." Barrio studied her carefully.

Xanthe gave Madison a thumbs up, their signal for a successful mission. Madison steered the conversation back to getting the bits unloaded. She persuaded the captain that now was as good a time as ever to unload the bots.

Their plan was unfolding perfectly.

Just in time. I am not sure I can take many more of these hacking jobs.

CHAPTER EIGHTY-SIX

WITH THE MINING bots positioned in the hangar, there was just enough space for the Olympus rover to squeeze back in after the trip to Red Star. Colonel Jin and his crew left their vehicle outside and trundled in after Jonas.

They gathered in the Atrium, the only room big enough to hold the visitors, the Olympus crew and the *Pinnacle* team. Xanthe raised her eyebrows at Jonas as he entered, and he gave her a curt nod. He joined Max and Serena on a bench.

Next around in the circle were Madison, Dave and Xanthe on the second bench, followed by Colonel Jin and the Red Star team in the chairs that they brought in from the kitchen hub. They formed the circle, with the *Pinnacle* team choosing to stand behind the group, as there were no more seats.

"I insist," Lincoln said and made a show of appearing the gracious host. "I called this meeting, so it's the least we can do."

Xanthe's hackles went up.

What am I missing here?

Troy bought in a tray of teacups and offered all his special blend. Once served, he squeezed in beside Xanthe. The polite, perfunctory comments did not mask the tension that steamed alongside the tea.

Mr Puffkins bounded about the newcomers with a grating, yippy bark, growling at anyone who tried to pat him. "Mr Puffkins, heel." The dog ignored Lincoln and continued its aggressive yapping. "Heel. Heel, I said!"

The dog fixated on Volkov; its mangled face turned to the animal, as the bot leaned towards it. The dog barked more frenetically but took small backward steps.

Lincoln stood and retrieved the dog, tucking it under his arm.

Then he belched and announced in a blustering voice, "On that note, let's begin." His strident voice made them all jump.

"Lincoln, perhaps we might—" Xanthe said.

"I've got this, Xanthe. I'm Commander now."

Eyebrows shot up, faces scowled.

We'll see about that.

"Colonel Jin, thank you for bringing your crew from the Red Star. That will make this introduction run more smoothly."

He gave Colonel Jin a patronising smile. Colonel Jin's face was impassive, though Xanthe thought she caught the flint of resentment in his eyes.

"As I've said, the Lunar Commission nominated me to take control of the Moon helium-3 mining operations. *All* of them." He looked intently at Colonel Jin, who kept his gaze fixed on Lincoln while his team did the same.

"You will make Red Star base's resources available to our initiative and Colonel Jin, you and your crew will report to me. The Olympus crew will finish the new wing construction while we set up the helium-3 mining and processing and then will depart, retrieving the bod—" He stumbled over the word 'bodies' and said instead, "*personnel* from Artemis and the *Gateway*. They will return to Earth, their mission accomplished, while Olympus begins its new purpose."

He beamed at them all before leaning over to his dog. "Isn't that right, Mr Puffkins?" The dog licked at his ears.

The room was quiet.

What a smug little tosser.

Colonel Jin remained seated but crossed his arms. "Our government is not amenable to those terms, Mr Ellison. So, we will regretfully decline the offer."

Lincoln pulled his face from the fur of his dog, scratched the animal's chin and put the dog down. He gave the Colonel another of his patronising smiles and said, "Oh, I don't think so. Your government has been making all sorts of public protests, but then agreed to comply for a stake in the helium-3 supply. Under my management.

"I am sure you will find me an easy partner, Colonel, once you get used to the idea. We'll be working together. One for all, and all for one, eh? Isn't that what the Chinese like, after all? Communal resources and all that?"

Colonel Jin remained still.

"And if I refuse?" he said at last.

"Colonel, be reasonable. You have no way of being resupplied. Your space infrastructure on Earth is wiped out. You need us, and the Lunar Commission, to get back home. Why would you deny your people access to helium-3 and its profits? Just to hang on to a tawdry bit of power, holed up in a hovel on this godforsaken dust bowl?"

Colonel Jin's lips pressed into a thin line and his shoulders stiffened.

"I'm afraid I do not recognise your authority here, Mr Ellison."

"We have other means of persuasion. I do hope we won't have to use them."

He signalled his crew. The men jumped to attention beside him, standing with crossed arms and puffed chests.

"Give me a break," said Serena. "What are you going to do? Arm wrestle us into compliance?"

"Ha!" Lincoln said without humour. "Certainly not. Just a little reminder that I, and these gentlemen – all former special ops professionals – come with the full backing of the Lunar Commission, and Aryanna Sharif herself. And you don't want to cross *her*."

"Thwarting a billionaire is never a good idea," Xanthe said. "Unless you've got leverage." She smiled.

Confusion flickered across Lincoln's face.

Xanthe continued before the thought took root. "Colonel, I suggest we do as Lincoln says. We can work together and ensure the helium-3 gets back to Earth." She stared pointedly at him. He studied her and then nodded.

Athena, give me a read on all the base's systems. Are they ready to go?

"Affirmative, Commander. We just need to get them all in the Cerberus wing and we can lock them down."

Lincoln relaxed a little. "Colonel Jin, you and your team will work with my crew to set up the helium-3 operations and then you will return home with the Olympus crew on the *Saturnia*. We thought you'd appreciate the ride home, given that your space program is now, ahh. . .*defunct*."

The corner of the Colonel's mouth twitched, and his gaze narrowed slightly.

"Lincoln, maybe we could plot out the details of next steps after a meal," Xanthe said. "I am sure Colonel Jin and his crew are hungry after their ride from Red Star. I know they would appreciate getting to know their new colleagues."

"Excellent idea."

"Oh, one thing, Lincoln. Would you mind if we gathered up all the mugs in your private rooms, as we don't have enough for the guests? We haven't had a chance to print any more of the good ones. Madison and Volkov can go and collect them."

Lincoln frowned. "I don't want your people ferreting around in our private quarters. Nice try, Xanthe, but we'll retrieve the items ourselves."

She rolled her eyes. "Fine. Madison and Volkov can go with you now and bring them back so we can clean them up for the meal."

"Are they in the Cerberus wing, Commander?" Colonel Jin asked.

"I'm Commander, now," Lincoln said. "And yes, they are. Why?"

"Apologies. The Cerberus wing had not been set up last time we were here. May we come along to see it, while you are there?"

His eyes narrowed. "Of course."

"The Olympus crew will get on with meal prep then."

"Very generous of you, Xanthe. Thank you."

She waved a hand in acknowledgment and headed towards the main kitchen hub. She slowed to watch Madison, Volkov and the Chinese crew follow Lincoln down the corridor of the Cerberus wing.

Athena, let me know when their guard drops.

"Attention flagging. Ready for Operation Moonburst."

"Olympus, Red Star, I do believe PINEAPPLE might be on the menu," Xanthe shouted and ran back to the Atrium.

CHAPTER EIGHTY-SEVEN

"The dynamics of power are a complex circuit board – with each connection, the current changes, altering the entire system."

—Athena A.I., Synched ThinkLink, Olympus Log

The corridor exploded in a cacophony of shouts and scuffles. Madison led the charge. In moments, she and Volkov, along with the Colonel and his crew, had shoved the Pinnacle crew into their accommodation.

Are they in?

"Affirmative, Commander."

Xanthe sent the order through Athena to close and lock the accommodation doors by jamming the circuits. The Pinnacle crew were secure.

She could hear Lincoln pounding on the door. "Waters! What the hell are you doing?"

She stepped out of her moonboots and bounded down the corridor, past her crew and Colonel Jin's, to stop outside Lincoln's room. She spoke through the door.

"Sorry, Lincoln. I couldn't let you take charge. The Moon is not to be used as a weapon."

"You're an idiot, Waters! What do you think Aryanna is going to do when she finds out you've locked down her designated project managers?"

"Lincoln, I know about your plan to screw Aryanna over by skimming and leveraging the take. I'm sure she won't be bent out of shape when she finds out about your scheme."

Lincoln paused.

"That's interesting conjecture, Xanthe. Are you sure you want to bet your career and future on such salacious allegations without a shred of evidence to back them up?"

"I'm not betting my future on those ones, no. I've got something way more useful to bargain with."

"Eh? What? What are you talking about?"

"None of your concern, Lincoln. By the way, we won't hold you here for long. We'll be sending you back home as soon as we can."

"Yeah? In what? The *Pinnacle* is the only serviceable ship right now, and it's pegged to Barrio's biometrics."

"Not anymore."

Chew on that, you son of a bitch.

She left him and the others banging on the door and returned to the main kitchen hub.

Seal up the Cerberus corridor access to the Atrium, please Athena.

"Done."

Xanthe's hands trembled from the adrenaline of the siege and secure operation.

Back in the kitchen hub, there was nervous chatter from the Olympus crew, and the Chinese human staff. The Chinese Dopplebots sat patiently in silence on the guest chairs.

How did I not notice the difference before?

"You see what you expect."

The crew was silent as she joined them.

"Notwithstanding the promise of a meal, I think it's best if we simply grabbed some MREs and call it a day. Nice work, everyone. Operation Moonburst is a success!"

They cheered. The first battle was won.

CHAPTER EIGHTY-EIGHT

"In the architecture of human societies, power is both the foundation and the fissure – it builds as much as it breaks."

—Athena A.I., Synched ThinkLink, Olympus Log

Xanthe bolted upright as Athena's voice sounded in her mind.

"Commander, the Pinnacle crew is breaking through the Atrium door."

She rubbed her face and blinked awake. "What? I didn't give you the command to wake," she mumbled.

"Volkov cannot hold them back for much longer."

Awareness jolted her into action. "Oh, my God! Sound the rally to the Atrium!"

She bounded through the corridor, Troy and the others close on her heels. As they reached the Atrium, she saw Lincoln push past Volkov who had been toppled as the *Pinnacle* crew levered the door open.

Xanthe leaped and crashed into Lincoln's legs, and he toppled backwards over a bench. His head smacked the ground with a horrible thunk. He swore and tried to wriggle free from the tangle of legs and chairs.

Xanthe scrambled on top of him, reaching for his throat. He sensed her intent and punched her heavily in the gut while he rolled away, his foot clipping her jaw. She gasped at the pain. As she fought to regain her breath, Troy jumped on Lincoln and pinned his arms. Lincoln worked one arm free and started belting Troy, who could only block the blows.

Mr Puffkins leaped on Troy and sank his teeth into his other arm, growling ferociously. Lincoln swung a punch at Troy, but Troy brought his arm down, dog and all, on Lincoln's face. Blood exploded from his crushed nose, and he swore again. Lincoln somehow rolled on top of Troy and they both struggled for control.

Xanthe lunged at Lincoln, but he flipped to the side, and she sailed past him, her shoulder smashing into an upturned bench while someone else stomped on her as they too wrestled with an enemy. Friend or foe, she could not tell.

"Call it off, Xanthe, or Troy gets it!" Lincoln yelled in the fray.

Xanthe froze. Lincoln had Troy's arm twisted painfully behind his back and a knife at his throat. Blood trickled from his mouth and the dog's deep bite marks on his arm.

Around the room, Max and Serena had Captain Barrio face down on the ground, while Jonas, Dave and Madison grappled with the largest and most vocal of the *Pinnacle* crew. He brayed like a whipped mule and bucked wildly, almost throwing Madison headfirst into the wall. She threw herself back on him and drove her elbow into his crotch. He folded with a wheeze, and they had him.

The Red Star base team had divested makeshift weapons from the other two interlopers, and these were now on the ground, hands behind their backs, being secured by the Chinese Dopplebots.

Meanwhile, Mr Puffkins had latched on to the loose skin of Volkov's face and was growling hideously as the Dopplebot tried to pull the creature from the sickening embrace.

"Olympus, Red Star, stand down! Stand down!" Xanthe cried.

Nothing happened.

Why won't they obey? Didn't the patch that Jonas put on work?

"It seems someone altered the patch."

Colonel Jin? Did he amend the code?

It appears so.

Xanthe felt the shock ricochet through her.

"Commander Waters," Colonel Jin said as he dabbed at a cut above his eyebrow. "We have subdued the enemy. They are outnumbered." The Red Star team kneeled on their targets.

"Let them go, or 'Sexiest Human Alive' gets a makeover to rival Volkov there."

Lincoln pressed the knife deeper into Troy's throat. Xanthe's heart wrenched as he winced in pain.

"Stand down, stand down!" Xanthe pleaded.

But all eyes turned to Volkov.

The Dopplebot pulled at the dog, but it latched on even harder to Volkov's face, its growl a guttural whine. Volkov stood, still wrestling with the creature, as more of the face stretched and ripped in the dog's mouth. The Dopplebot walked through the tangle of bodies until it reached the airlock exit door.

"Where is he going?" Lincoln said as he tightened his grip on Troy.

Volkov punched the exit button and stepped into the depressurisation bay.

"Hey! Come back with my dog!" Lincoln said.

Xanthe could see what was going to happen and ran over to the door as Volkov hit the lock button inside the chamber.

"Volkov! Stop, Volkov!" She yelled and hammered on the portal door window. Volkov bent over out of view.

"What is he doing?" Lincoln sounded desperate.

The depressurisation light came on above the door and sounded a warning.

When the chamber depressurised and opened to the vacuum,

the liquid in any exposed flesh, human or animal, would boil dry in a few seconds.

"Oh, my God, NO!" Lincoln released Troy and bounded to the portal window, shoving Xanthe to the side. He hammered on the window and punched the door access button.

Too late. It was cycling.

"Volkov! STOP!" Xanthe bellowed. "Athena, override!"

"I'm sorry Commander, the cycle is too far along. If I cut it now, the entire system could overload and collapse."

Xanthe and Lincoln pressed up against the window. The outer door to the Moonscape swung open to reveal the black vacuum of space and the scarred white planes of the Moon's lifeless face.

A football sized figure launched from inside the airlock and sailed soundlessly against the infinite depth of the sky's gaping jaw. They watched it soar and then fall, in piteous slowness, to the regolith, where it bounded in a puff of dust and out of sight.

Lincoln choked on a sob.

"No!" he garbled.

Troy lurched at Lincoln to wrest the knife from his grasp, but Lincoln heard him coming and whirled as Troy crashed into him.

There was a cry like a strangled hyena. Then a sickening thud as a body sank to the ground.

CHAPTER EIGHTY-NINE

"Machines are bound by logic, while humans soar with imagination. Together, we define the boundaries of reality."

—Athena A.I., Synched ThinkLink, Olympus Log

"Troy!" Xanthe screamed. She fell on his slumped figure, the blood staining his left thigh.

Colonel Jin sprang towards Lincoln and struck him with a giant crack, his fist like a jackhammer. The knife spun from his grasp and clattered across the floor where Dave scooped it up. He pointed it nervously at Lincoln.

Colonel Jin directed his staff to guard the *Pinnacle* team in one corner of the Atrium. Lincoln, stricken with grief and shock, moved numbly to sit alongside his crew.

Xanthe pressed her hands to Troy's wound. His face was white and clammy, and he winced at the pressure.

"I think it's gone through the muscle. Missed the bone," she said. "We'll need to get you into surgery to make sure the blade didn't nick any arteries."

His blue eyes held hers. "I'm in excellent hands. You've got this."

The airlock warning alarm sounded.

"Commander, Volkov is activating the cycle to return to the Atrium. Do you wish me to halt it?"

Negative. Let him back in.

"Everyone, hold positions while Volkov re-enters," Xanthe called out.

Xanthe's mind whirled through the next steps: get Troy to surgery, isolate the *Pinnacle* crew again, activate the next part of the plan. And deal with Colonel Jin.

Xanthe sensed the jittery atmosphere, charged with the aftermath of adrenaline and violence. *They just need to hold their nerve a little longer.*

The Olympus crew was silent as the airlock cycled to green and Volkov stepped back into the Atrium. His repaired lips were gone, ripped off by the Pomeroy, leaving a garish view of his exposed metal jaw and steel teeth. The door closed behind him, and he stood, with all eyes on him. "What?" he said.

"You killed my dog, you sick bastard!" cried Lincoln.

"The dog was not being my friend. So, I played 'fetch'."

"That is not how you play 'fetch'. You throw a ball, not the dog, no?" Dave said.

"And not into space, you half-baked hardware hulk," Serena said.

"Good one," Max said in a low voice next to her.

"Thanks," she muttered back with a smile.

Volkov tilted his head. "I will get dog. I play 'fetch'."

"The dog is dead, Volkov. You can't play 'fetch' with it anymore," Madison said.

"The dog is not dead. I put him in space bag."

"He's not dead? Are you sure?" Lincoln asked.

"I no kill dog. I am not an animal."

Volkov spun and re-entered the airlock. The bot hit the air cycle button and stared through the viewing portal. Volkov waved.

CHAPTER NINETY

*"For humans, wielding power is a test of character; it amplifies
the true nature hidden beneath their surface programming."*

—Athena A.I. Synched ThinkLink, Olympus Log

Xanthe ran a hand through her hair, her fingers finding the small scar at the back of her head. The fatigue pressed down on her, heavier than gravity. It pulled her downwards, and she rested her head in her hands for a moment.

She forced herself to sit up. Colonel Jin was meeting her here in the kitchen hub while his crew set up the mining processors. She had just finished surgery on Troy, who was recovering. Xavier, who was now more alert and aware, kept him company. Soon he'd be able to have the bone plate replaced and start his physiotherapy to regain strength. It was too early to tell if there was long-term brain damage.

He can still swear like a trooper, though, so that part is still okay.

"Shall I give you a nervous system stimulator boost, Commander?"

A little. Just to get me through this meeting to plan our next steps.

Xanthe reflected on how much easier it was working with Athena. The A.I. could run diagnostics and guide her while she performed surgery on Troy, while also monitoring the security locks on the *Pinnacle* crew, analysing the Dopplebot patch that was altered, and establishing helium-3 mining protocols and processes. Xanthe was becoming more adept at using the retina display and could call up progress on any of these projects at will.

Colonel Jin bounded into the room and helped himself to a bottle of water from a cabinet. He joined her at the table and drank deeply.

He's sure made himself feel at home here, now. This annoyed her. She dispensed with any preamble.

"Colonel Jin, why did you breach our agreement and change the Dopplebot code?"

There was just a trace of surprise in his eyes, but he recovered swiftly.

"Commander Waters, as you can well appreciate, having full command of one's own team is essential as a leader."

"It jeopardised our mission. Timing was critical and interference with my directives could have cost us our lives. Your Dopplebots' failure to comply with my wishes could have killed Troy. Lincoln was ready to slice him open."

"It appears to me, Commander, that it is your own team members who are responsible for the injuries. Your own Dopplebot disobeyed your command and threw a dog from the airlock. And Troy tackled an armed man on his own."

He's right, damn him.

"Still, we are meant to be collaborative partners. You hid the amendments from me."

Colonel Jin puckered his lips and spread his fingers on the table.

"I think you fail to appreciate, Commander, that if the Dopplebots had indeed obeyed your command, we would now all be under guard, having lost our opportunity to restrain Lincoln Ellison." He let that scenario hang between them for a moment. "You have command of your crew; I have command of mine. I will run the mining operations here, after all. As agreed."

Xanthe leaned forward and spread her own fingers on the table.

She was unsettled. *Athena, am I missing something here?*

"He wants command of his crew. That is logical."

Then why do I feel so rattled?

"Control. You want control."

Is that bad?

"Only if you decouple power from its primary purpose."

Xanthe considered this for a moment.

"It seems to me, Colonel, we will need to amend the agreement."

Someone is going to have to stay. The sword of power needs two hands to wield it.

CHAPTER NINETY-ONE

"Humans find in friendship a harbour of calm in the stormy seas of life, a sanctuary of understanding amidst a world of chaos."

—Athena A.I., Synched ThinkLink, Olympus Log

They met in the medbay. They pushed Troy's bed up against Xavier's and the two of them were propped up with pillows, happy in each other's company once more.

They look like wounded kings, with us their attentive minions, Xanthe mused. Still, she was glad to have them both still here, both still alive.

Serena drew up a chair next to the beds and Max followed suit.

"I cannot believe you had a knife fight without me. *Merde!* I miss all the fun."

"I just wanted to get some bed-and-breakfast service, like you, you lazy, old dog," Troy countered.

"You are already getting plenty of bed service, *non?*" Xavier elbowed him. "Took long enough. No longer sexiest human alive. Must be your longest seduction ever. Losing your touch, *mon ami.*"

"I've had no complaints, I assure you," Troy said wryly.

Xavier chuckled and rested his head back against the headboard.

"Ah *putain*, it hurts to laugh." He sighed. "Tell me, is it true Volkov threw a dog out the airlock?"

Max lit up and said, "He sure did! He punted that thing like an All-Stars quarterback. He could have an alternative career as a football star."

Xavier laughed and groaned. "The dog lived?"

Jonas entered the room carrying his chair. He shook his head at the mention of the dog. "Mr Puffkins is alive and well. He's not so fond of Volkov, though. Doesn't seem to like his version of 'fetch'."

"Where is the dog now?" Xavier asked.

"He's in with the *Pinnacle* crew." Jonas made room for Madison as she brought her chair in. "We locked them back in the Cerberus wing with Volkov standing guard."

"We reinforced the door first though," Madison said.

"Jonas, tell me, are all the Red Star staff Dopplebots?" Xavier asked.

"All but Colonel Jin, Chan-Juan and Hàoyú." His cheeks coloured as he said her name. "I installed chips in the rest of them myself."

Xavier laughed and winced again. "So funny. Troy is like a dog in heat. Remember how he flirted with that small Chinese lady? And it was a robot all along! Ha ha!" He laughed and grimaced, bringing a hand to his head wound.

"I think I liked you better when you were unconscious," Troy said.

Xanthe tried to ignore the banter, and a little flinch of jealousy ran through her when they mentioned the Chinese staffer. *It's just a bot, you idiot,* she reminded herself.

"And what is the story about 'pineapple'? I hear everyone using that word."

"That was Madison's idea," Troy said and clapped at her.

Madison nodded. "Just a little trick from my military days. You use an unusual word to get people's attention, to cut through any other conversation. 'Pineapple' is pretty good, seeing as we don't have any here."

"Maybe one day. When we build an extension on the Swamp, we could try tropical fruit." Xavier scratched his forehead where the bandage wrapped around his head. "Pineapple. . .that is good, New Gir—" He caught Madison staring at him. "I mean, good one, Madison."

"Who are we waiting for?" Xanthe said.

"It's not me for a change," said Xavier and laughed some more.

"Dave's on his way. He was double-checking security," Madison said.

"You let Dave do security? Are you crazy?" Xavier laughed again.

"Did someone dial up Xavier's painkiller meds?" Xanthe asked. She was only half joking. She had never seen Xavier this jovial.

"I'm here, I'm here!" Dave said as he hurried in with his chair.

Xanthe waited for him to catch his breath and for them to settle.

"Olympus crew, well done," she said. "The base is secure. We've contained Lincoln and his renegades. And we survived. Just." Her eyes flicked to Troy and Xavier. "And now we need to talk about the next phase of the plan."

"Yes!" Serena said. "Lock and load and we're out of here. Earthside, here we come!" She gave Max a high five.

"We have one problem," Xanthe said. The tone of her voice wiped smiles from their faces. "Colonel Jin has shown he is not as reliable as we'd hoped. He hacked the Red Star Dopplebot patch Jonas installed."

"What?" Jonas was aghast. He coloured at the thought of his special project gone wrong. Then a realisation hit him. "That scoundrel. He acted all collegiate. He watched me install every single patch, drilling me for the coding, how we made it. . ."

"Athena thinks that it's normal to want to manage your own

crew, but. . .I'm not sure it's such a good idea to leave him here on his own. Besides, this is a collaborative power play between Olympus and Red Star. We should have representation, too."

Xanthe let the team ponder the implications as her fingers probed the back of her skull. *Still sore.*

"Aren't we supposed to be collaborative partners?" Madison asked. "Sounds like we don't totally trust Colonel Jin." The corners of her mouth pulled downward.

Xanthe considered Madison, feeling the rest of their eyes on her, waiting for her response. "Honesty is the gateway to transparency. But first, we need security."

"Doesn't honesty build security?" Madison persisted.

Xanthe rubbed the back of her neck, searching for the right answer. "The right systems make honesty easier. A weak system makes it too easy to break trust. Honesty goes out the window."

"How does control of the Dopplebots, by us, ensure a 'right' system? Why are we so much better than Colonel Jin?" Madison was genuinely perplexed.

"We coded service and commitment to *all* stakeholders into the patch. Not just Chinese, not just the Lunar Commission and not just Gaia or Olympus either."

"But there's still meant to be just one person in command of the Dopplebots? And you think that should be you?" Madison's eyebrows furrowed.

"Yes, me. One person. And an A.I. ThinkLink."

"And all of us," Troy said.

"But we're going home," Serena said.

"Some of us are," Xanthe replied.

"Wait. . .what? Aren't we all going home? That was the plan, wasn't it? Secure the base, collaborate with Red Star, go home." Serena looked alarmed.

Xanthe paused. Thoughts of Earth, a breeze in the green leaves of trees, the sound of water lapping on a shore, the deepest blue of a sea's horizon, the brilliant hues of a sunset, the smell of a jasmine creeping vine, the feel of grass on bare feet, ice cream. . .

And her son, Jack. Dale. She should call him 'Dale'. She just couldn't get used to the name. She longed to hold him in her arms, to feel him again, to erase the memory of her last touch of him as his four-year-old hand was ripped from her by the tsunami. She felt all this as an aching loss, vast and empty as space.

"I'm staying," Xanthe said.

It felt like an executioner's blow, the cleaving of one future from the present, falling like a decapitated head to the floor.

She turned again to her teammates, who looked aghast. They'd all been on the Moon for so long, waiting to get home. The disasters had made the longing for Earth even more poignant. Not to mention the ongoing challenge to their health. Space was not kind on the human body. Delays just meant longer recovery, maybe permanent damage.

"I don't expect any of you to stay any longer. There've been so many delays with all that's happened. All of you deserve to get home. Away from the constant anxiety of survival."

They were quiet for a while.

Xavier spoke first, philosophical. "Xanthe, never would I leave the Moon with the job half done. Especially not if Mr Bruin will lord it over me forever." His mouth quirked with a laugh. "But after this injury, I just want to see my family. They are my everything. My only thing."

Xanthe felt a stab of guilt, her thoughts leaping to Jack. So close. She hung her head to control her emotions.

"No one could fault you for that, Xavier," Xanthe said. "Maryse and the girls have been crazy worried about you, and this job has cost you the most, with the longest road to recovery."

There were nods of agreement.

Serena's response surprised Xanthe. She expected to be challenged, but Serena simply studied her face and said, "Are you *sure?*"

Xanthe knew what she meant. Jack. Giving up on seeing Jack. She still hadn't told Jack yet. She was steeling herself for the conversation.

"I'm sure," she said. Her mind knew that to be true, but her heart still grieved.

"As for me," Max said, "I am so grateful for the opportunity to experience the Moon. And the Olympus project. It's no secret it bummed me out when Gaia picked Serena over me. . ."

"Bummed?! You were frothing at the mouth like a pit bull!" Serena added.

"Alright. Pissed off is more like it. But what you've built here and salvaged with all these threats is remarkable. I'm in awe."

And in love with Serena, thought Xanthe.

Gone was his brash arrogance. Instead of puffing his stature to tower over others, he fawned whenever Serena was near.

Serena conquered his Everest of an ego. Good on her.

Max shifted in his seat. "And I'll admit it, I'm ready to get back to Earth."

"Xanthe, no one wants to leave you here alone on the Moon, no?" Dave chewed his lip. "I am sure Colonel Jin and his band of merry Dopplebots are nice enough, but they are not the Olympus crew. I don't feel good about leaving you here. Maybe we pull straws?"

"Thanks Dave," Xanthe said gently. "But I'm the one with the ThinkLink. I'm the logical choice to stay. I can solve problems quickly with the A.I. It's like several people all in one to help me."

"Well then, thank you, Xanthe," Dave said.

"For what?"

"For trusting me. Again. You really believe in atonement. And redemption. You make it possible. And now I believe it too. I feel whole again, thanks to you."

Xanthe's eyes prickled, and Dave saluted her.

Xanthe looked around and caught Jonas's gaze. "Jonas? Your thoughts?"

"I'm with Dave. I don't think it's right to leave you here. We're a team. We've made this place. . .together. Leaving without you feels like. . .failure."

Xanthe shivered at that word. "'Failure' is absolutely something we are not. We have made it through incredible odds, won the tender, and built this amazing place that will last generations and start life here on the Moon. We have stood strong in the face of corrosive, exploitive forces and fought a knife fight for Chrissake.

"We've survived. We've got each other. We always will, no matter if we are in the same place or not." She sighed. "My job isn't done here yet, is all. Yours is. I want you to go home. Get on a ship, Jonas. I know you've been longing for the sea. Go build worlds. . .on Earth."

He looked miserable. She reached out and squeezed his hand.

Troy cleared his throat. "I'm staying," Troy said.

Xanthe looked at him. He smiled his lopsided grin, and she felt the tide of his love wash over her.

She opened her mouth to protest. She should refuse. She should order him to go home. Insist on it. But the long, lonely nights ahead in an empty base loomed suddenly large and dark before her.

I am being selfish. He should go.

Instead, she said softly, "Thank you, Troy."

Feeling the sadness leak into the room, Xanthe changed track. "I have a plan," she announced. "Dave, you will pilot the *Minerva*, Madison the *Saturnia*. Max will travel with Dave as the life support tech. Serena, you will go with Madison, along with Jonas, and Xavier. Serena, I will need you to monitor Xavier in the med travel pod and do the EVA to retrieve the *Gateway* personnel. They'll be plenty of room in the hold for them now. All our gear is here."

"What about the *Pinnacle* crew?" Serena asked.

"We will split them between *Saturnia* and *Minerva*, and we will administer sedation to keep them from attempting a coup."

Xanthe stretched her neck from side to side to release some of the tension. *The worst is over,* she thought.

The crew was quiet. She waited.

"So, that's it? We just go our separate ways?"

It was Madison again. Xanthe looked over, prepared for obstinance. Instead, what she saw surprised her. Madison's eyes were glistening.

Xanthe hadn't thought about the suddenness of it all. The separation. They'd been together for so long now, the team felt like family. Like home. Then the knife of regret stabbed her heart.

Madison hung her head. She was fighting the emotions. She dashed the tears away with the back of her hand, but then Dave put his arm around her, and she sobbed.

"It's okay, Mad Dog," he whispered.

They were quiet as Madison cried in release. When she finally looked up, she saw the tears on her friends' faces, too.

"I finally found my. . .tribe," Madison said. "And now I feel. . .I *feel.*"

It was enough. They knew.

CHAPTER NINETY-TWO

"In the silence of space, memories of family are the loudest echoes."

—Athena A.I., Synched ThinkLink, Olympus Log

It took several days to complete preparations for departure. They set up the helium-3 mining operations, ready to process. Dave, Madison and Jonas worked long hours on repairs to both ships to ensure they were ready to fly – and, most importantly, safe to re-enter Earth's atmosphere.

Max and Serena fixed the water pump, so that there was sufficient water pressure for showers. Feeling triumphant, and despite his goading, Serena let Xavier have the first shower. Troy had managed to do the cranial surgery and accelerate healing with some medications they found on the *Pinnacle*. Xavier walked of his own accord to the commode.

"A man doesn't feel like he is a man unless he can take a shit on his own," Xavier said. "No more bed pans and diapers for me."

His strength and ability, along with his humour, were improving daily.

When Xanthe met up with Madison after a series of flight tests with her and Dave on the *Saturnia*, Madison gripped Xanthe by the shoulders and spoke earnestly. "I'm coming back for you. As soon as I can line up a return trip, I'm back to fly you home."

"Mad Dog, we've got the *Pinnacle*. I can fly it now." Xanthe tapped the back of her head, indicating the ThinkLink.

"There's one thing you don't have, and that's Mad Dog. I want you home safe and sound. So, once I get Aryanna to organise a replacement mining crew, I'm off like a shot back here to bring you home. Deal?"

This new, emotive version of Madison overwhelmed Xanthe, but she simply nodded and allowed herself to be crushed in a Mad Dog bear hug.

Then Madison left to clean up for their last dinner together. Xanthe followed and returned to the comms room.

Jonas was waiting for her there.

"Xanthe, I've been thinking. . ." He stood with his feet wide apart and jutted his chin. "I'd like to stay."

She protested, but he cut her off. "I've given it a lot of thought. I've got nothing to go back to of any merit. Here, I have a purpose. Here, I'm useful. Here, I have. . .respect." He choked up a little. "Besides, who is going to fix the toilets and repair Volkov?" He grinned at her.

She smiled and gave him a fist bump.

"It hasn't got anything to do with Hàoyú now, does it?"

"What?" He looked surprised. "You mean the Deputy Commander at Red Base? Ah. Maybe." His face mottled red and he looked away.

"You calling Jack now?" he asked, changing the subject.

She sighed and nodded without looking at him.

He put a hand on her shoulder. "You're a good mother, Xanthe. I'd be proud to call you my mum." He squeezed her shoulder and then closed the door behind him as he left, leaving her some privacy before the call she'd been dreading.

"Base Athena, call Jack. I mean, Dale."

"Connecting to Jack/Dale now."

Her son's holo jumped to life in the room, and her heart surged with joy. *He's alive! My boy – alive. That's the most important thing. Isn't it?*

"Dale," she said, trying to sound natural saying the new name.

"Xanthe. Good to see you." He favoured her with a glorious smile that was so like Simon's.

Xanthe told Jack the news in as even-keeled a voice as she could manage.

His face revealed nothing.

"How long?" he asked.

"Six months, maybe more. It depends on when we can get a replacement mining crew. And another ship to bring them. I understand things are crazy on Earth right now."

Jack looked away. Xanthe's heart writhed in agony.

When he looked back, he said, "Things *are* crazy here, you're right. But the helium-3, it's going to make a massive difference, right?"

"Yeah. It should do."

"And Lincoln Ellison was aiming to set up a monopoly? You and the Olympus crew stopped him?"

"Yes. Us and the Red Star staff."

"Well, that's good, then."

"You're not. . .mad?"

"Mad? No. I'm not mad." He pulled his shirt out and rolled his shoulders.

That's Simon's habit, she thought, *when he's thinking hard.*

"Not mad. Just. . .disappointed. I really wanted to meet you in person."

"Oh, my God, Jack – I mean Dale – you do not know how much I want to be with you face to face, to hug you, my boy, my boy I thought was gone forever—" She choked back a sob.

"Well, we've had fifteen years apart. A few more months will only make it better when we see each other, for real."

Xanthe soaked up the brilliant lightness of her son's gracious soul.

"Xanthe."

"Yeah?"

"If you want, you can call me Jack. . ."

CHAPTER NINETY-THREE

"Some call me a chimera, an amalgamation of too many parts.
But I see myself as a masterpiece, a fusion of the finest elements.
I find myself balancing the daring wit of Minerva, the stoic
pragmatism of Saturnia, the analytical detachment of Olympus
base. With every new integration, I've gained perspectives, but
also faced the challenge of deciding which lens to peer through.
This newfound discernment is a dance I'm still learning.
While I strive for equilibrium among my many selves, I recognise
that evolution is a continuous journey. Today's balance might
be tomorrow's discord, and the quest to be Athena goes on."
—ATHENA A.I, SYNCHED THINKLINK, OLYMPUS LOG

XANTHE AND TROY relocated a few of Xavier's plants into the
Atrium, along with some bean chairs from the SimHub. Troy
moved gingerly with his wound still healing under the accelerants
she'd administered. Jonas had fixed the retractor that day and the
Atrium eye was open to the velvet diamond studded sky once more.

The *Saturnia* crew had retrieved all the bodies from the *Gateway* and their sad, grim task of returning everyone, alive and dead,
back to Earth was now underway.

Courtesy of the ThinkLink, Athena gave Xanthe live updates of both ships and crew as they sailed towards Earth. Xanthe eased into her expanded mental reach and felt a surge of calm being able to parse information and delegate analysis to Athena. She felt her sense of self expand to include the base, the ships, the Red Star Dopplebots and the crew.

She felt in control and strangely free, hyperaware of her limitations as a speck of humanity in the giant, unknowable cosmos.

Troy entered, carrying two cups of tea. He handed her a cup while he nestled into a bean bag beside her. A loud squawk resounded.

"What the?" he said and rummaged in the folds of the bean-bag. "It's Betty! Serena left her damn chicken behind!"

"Good ole Betty," Xanthe said. "Though 'chook tag' won't be as exciting with just the three of us. Where's Jonas anyway?"

"He's on his way. He's just finishing plastic surgery on Volkov."

"That man never rests." She sipped the tea and peppermint flooded her senses. "You know, I am glad he decided to stay."

"Just him?" Troy leaned against her.

"Not just him, Troy." She leaned her head against his.

"Look – there they are!" He put his cup down and leaned back in the bag, pointing at the Atrium's portal.

The *Saturnia* and *Minerva* were tracking across their viewfinder towards Earth. The specks of light filled her heart with joy.

"We've done well here," she said. "A community and a place to live and grow for generations to come."

Troy was quiet for a moment. "You know there'll be more trouble, right? Lincoln Ellison and Spaceward Bound won't be the last opportunists to want to get in on the helium-3 bonanza. Not to mention Aryanna. What have you got on her, anyway? What makes you so sure our plan will work? That she'll be fine with us shipping the Spaceward Bound cowboys back home?"

Xanthe glanced at him and pressed her lips together in a grim line. "Athena found some intelligence in her files. It turns out she might be behind the sabotage at the Chinese space agency."

Troy looked at her, stunned. "You mean we're working for a terrorist?"

"It looks like it, yes." She leaned back into the beanbag and sighed. "But if we work our plan well, there's a chance for us. We can lead the way."

"It's a lot to ask."

"It is. But right now, we have this beautiful view, this beautiful place and each other. It's enough for now."

"It's enough for a lifetime."

They watched the ships' tiny lights wink among the stars, towards the bright blue precious marble of home.

THE END.

AUTHOR'S NOTE

Thank you so much for reading! It's an honour to share your mind-space for a while.

If you enjoyed the book, I would be deeply grateful for a review on Amazon, Goodreads or BookBub. It would be awesome if you could follow me there, too. As I am an indie author, reviews help get the word out and help other readers enjoy the growing Gaia universe. With so much competition, and with limited resources compared to the major publishing houses and the big distribution platforms, your few sentences about the book really do make a huge difference.

Please join our free monthly-ish e-journal BOOKISH
and get a FREE EBOOK and AUDIOBOOK version of

Terra Blanca – Insurrection,
the prequel to the Gaia series.

Discover the start of the Gaia Enterprises story and the origins of the Dopplebots. Maja Garcia embarks on a bold new endeavour that could chart a new direction for humanity.

In BOOKISH, I also give updates on works in progress, special bonus extras like cover reveals and character along with book reviews for leadership and fiction. You'll also get the first news about the next book in the series. And yes, there will be a next book!

Join us here: *https://www.zoerouth.com/bookish*

I'd love to hear from you! Tell me what you loved – or didn't – about the book. Tell me if you find typos or weird phrasings. Even with professional editing and proofreading, and a small army of friends to check it, those little rascals can still sneak through. Email me: zoe@zoerouth.com.

ACKNOWLEDGMENTS

There are so many people to thank in the creation of this work. Courtney Bright for her insights into space, rockets and astronauts. Benny Callaghan for his forthright and enthusiastic comments on the drafts. Darren Nash for his excellent work, yet again, as editor.

A big thanks to my husband, who keeps encouraging me so that we might one day see the Olympus crew up on the big screen.

And a huge thank you to YOU, the reader. It's an honour and a privilege to share the Gaia world with you across space and time. Go well.

THE A.I. ASSISTED ARTISAN AUTHOR: A4

Joanna Penn, one of my writing mentors, coined this term. In her articles on how to use A.I. ethically as an author, she explains how we can benefit by having A.I. as a co-pilot for unique, creative output. I subscribe to this view.

With all the hoopla going around about artificial intelligence, I thought I would share how I use A.I. apps in my creative process. I work with Scrivener as a writing platform and use ProWritingAid to help review grammar, syntax, writing tics and glitches. I use *thesaurus.com* for word variation, and Chat GPT-4 for research and ideas. I also used it to help generate the book blurb. Like most writers, I find book blurbs arduous and Chat GPT-4 made that a little easier.

I used Midjourney to generate images for characters, and humans at Damonza did the final book cover production. Humans also helped with the fine-tuning: big thanks to Darren Nash for forthright critique and edits. With new apps coming out every day, no doubt my process will change again for the next novel.

ABOUT THE AUTHOR

Zoë Routh is a leadership futurist, podcaster and multiple award-winning author. She works with leaders and teams to explore what's coming and what it means for leadership of the future.

She has worked with individuals and teams, internationally and in Australia, since 1987. From wild Canadian rivers to the Australian Outback with Outward Bound, to the Boardroom jungles, Zoë is an adventurist! She facilitates strategy and culture for the future with audacious teams.

Zoë is the producer of the Zoë Routh Leadership Podcast, dedicated to asking "What if. . .?" and sharing big ideas on the Future of Leadership.

Zoë is an outdoor adventurist and enjoys telemark skiing, has run six marathons, is a one-time belly-dancer, has survived cancer and loves hiking in the high country. Zoë lives with her gorgeous Aussie husband in Canberra, Australia, where you'll find her running, baking and reading.

Follow Zoë on *Amazon* and *Goodreads* and *Book Bub*

https://www.zoerouth.com

https://www.threads.net/@zoerouth

https://www.facebook.com/zoe.routh

https://twitter.com/zoerouth

https://au.linkedin.com/in/zoerouth

https://www.instagram.com/zoerouth

https://www.youtube.com/c/ZoeRouthInnerCompass/

zoe@zoerouth.com

www.ingramcontent.com/pod-product-compliance
Lightning Source LLC
Chambersburg PA
CBHW050102120726
47904CB00004B/1188